Julie Anne Lindsey is an obsessive reader who was once torn between the love of her two favourite genres: toe-curling romance and chew-your-nails suspense. Now she gets to write both for Mills & Boon. When she's not creating new worlds, Julie can be found carpooling her three kids around northeastern Ohio and plotting with her shamelessly enabling friends. Winner of the Daphne du Maurier Award for Excellence in Mystery/Suspense, Julie is a member of International Thriller Writers, Romance Writers of America and Sisters in Crime. Learn more about Julie and her books at julieannelindsey.com

Elle James, a *New York Times* bestselling author, started writing when her sister challenged her to write a romance novel. She has managed a full-time job and raised three wonderful children, and she and her husband even tried ranching exotic birds (ostriches, emus and rheas). Ask her, and she'll tell you what it's like to go toe-to-toe with an angry 350-pound bird! Elle loves to hear from fans at ellejames@earthlink.net or ellejames.com

Discover more at millsandboon.co.uk

IMPACT ZONE

JULIE ANNE LINDSEY

HOMICIDE AT WHISKEY GULCH

ELLE JAMES

MILLS & BOON

First Published in Great Britain 2020
by Mills & Boon, an imprint of HarperCollins*Publishers*
1 London Bridge Street, London, SE1 9GF

Impact Zone © 2020 Harlequin Books S.A.
Homicide at Whiskey Gulch © 2020 Mary Jernigan

Special thanks and acknowledgement are given to Julie Anne Lindsey for her contribution to the *Tactical Crime Division: Traverse City* series.

ISBN: 978-0-263-28316-7

0121

Printed and bound in Spain
by CPI, Barcelona

IMPACT ZONE

JULIE ANNE LINDSEY

Prologue

"We're coming to you live from the scene of our city's second bombing in just three days," the tenacious female reporter declared. "I'm standing across the street from what remains of Burger Mania. As you can see, this popular twenty-four-hour fast-food restaurant was all but completely destroyed in the explosion early this morning. Police and bomb-squad officials are combing the wreckage now for clues as to who might've done this, and whether or not the culprit was also responsible for the bombing of a Grand Rapids real-estate office earlier this week."

The bomber coughed into his fist, covering a smile as the reporter rambled on. Law-enforcement officials wouldn't find a single clue about who'd made that bomb or the previous one. He'd taken great care to be certain of that. Officials would still waste their time looking, of course. They had to. But there was nothing to find.

From his place on the sidelines, he could see the big picture. The reporter couldn't. She could only see the loss of a building and a few lives. Same for her hapless viewers and the gaggle of lookie-loos gathering at his sides. They didn't understand the planning and precision that went into something like this. The sheer skill involved in what he'd done. They only saw the aftermath. The wreckage. They missed what truly mattered. The revenge.

Winter in Michigan is starting to heat up, he thought, chuckling internally at the joke.

The reporter twisted at her waist, wide brown eyes jerking between the camera in front of her and the rampant chaos behind. Her deep brown skin flushed slightly as the coroner's van trundled into position, joining the collection of emergency and first responders in the Burger Mania lot.

So there had been casualties. Just as he'd planned. Pride puffed his chest and satisfaction warmed his gut. He'd created the chaos and the carnage that made the pretty reporter shake in her high-heeled boots. If that wasn't power, then what was?

A gust of icy wind blew sleek black tendrils across her cheeks and against her glossy red lips. The scents of burning grease, hair and flesh seemed to fan her fear. "Five customers have been escorted from the building so far. Each was taken to a waiting ambulance, and most have already been rushed to local hospitals. Sources on scene are reporting three casualties, all Burger Mania night-shift employees," she said, her expression comically sad, as if she'd ever met any of those people. As if she'd ever graced a grease-mill like Burger Mania with her upscale, picture-perfect presence. "There's no word yet as to whether or not this week's two explosions are related," she said, "but you can count on us to keep you informed with up-to-the-minute details as they are released." She held her canned smile a few seconds longer, until the bright light on the camera dimmed, and the cameraman removed the device from his shoulder.

The microphone shook in her trembling grip as she passed it to him. She was right to be afraid. They all were.

The bomber lingered another moment, reveling in the panicked whispers around him. They had no idea how powerful he was. That he alone was responsible for the bombs destroying their comfortable little worlds. He smirked at the flimsy line of yellow plastic fluttering before him, nearly as pathetic as the ones who'd strung it. As if they could keep him back if he wanted to go. As if they could stop him from doing anything he wanted to do.

So far, he'd executed two perfect plans in three short days. He'd even taken a day in between to enjoy the news coverage and watch local police chase their tails.

He hoped his next victims were watching. He hoped they were afraid, too. Afraid to go to work. Afraid to leave their homes. Afraid because he could reach them anywhere. He was just that good.

The bomber watched a few more minutes, until the satisfaction began to slowly fade, and the grip of seething hatred returned. Then he walked away. Fresh churning and burning in his core. Renewed anger begging for release.

Two down, he thought. *And two to go.*

Time to get back to work.

Chapter One

Tactical Crime Division director Alana Suzuki strode confidently from the elevator onto the seventh floor of the Traverse City, Michigan, FBI building. Her high heels clicked across the hard tile floor, her determination growing with each new step. The TCD would leave on assignment again today, and she never took their deployment lightly. The specialized unit of experts on everything from combat to poisons and hostage negotiation was infinitely capable and collectively unstoppable. But more than that, they were family.

"Good morning," Alana called, crossing into the oversize boardroom and making her way to the front.

The team was already in place around the massive table, tired eyes instantly on her. She didn't have to check her watch to know it was barely 5:00 a.m.

"Thank you all for coming in so early and on such little notice." Alana dragged her gaze over the fatigued faces before her, then rested it briefly on the giant FBI logo clinging to one wall. A sense of pride rolled up her spine. Pride for the Bureau. Pride for the thirty years she'd spent there. And pride for this team. "If you've seen the news, you can probably guess why you're here. There was a second bombing in Grand Rapids early this morning, and their local law enforcement could use our help."

The group exchanged silent glances, then turned their attention on Max.

Special Agent Max McRay had taken a seat at the front. Brows furrowed and hands folded on the table, he'd likely been there for a while. It was Max who'd woken Alana at half past two this morning, requesting she consider this assignment for their team, or send him alone if necessary. Max was an explosives expert, and there was a bomber in Grand Rapids. A city just two hours away by car and home to Max's ex-wife and toddler son.

"Grand Rapids detectives suspect a serial bomber," Alana continued, drawing the team's focus back to her. "After a long talk with their chief of police, I've agreed to send the TCD to their aid." She nodded to Opaline Lopez, the curvy, bleached-blonde tech guru seated at the back of the room.

Opaline lifted a small remote, and a big screen lowered from the ceiling behind Alana, images already appearing on the white backdrop.

"Thank you."

Opaline smiled, her brightly colored clothing and hair accessories never a match for her impossibly upbeat personality. She was a much-needed source of light on many dark days in their office, and one more thing Alana appreciated deeply.

"There have been two bombs detonated in three days," Alana said as photos of the carnage flipped across the screen. "Five people are dead in total. More are injured. The first bomb went off inside a small stand-alone real-estate office three days ago, at seven eighteen a.m. Two of the office's twelve employees were killed in the blast.

A female office manager and a male real-estate agent. No one else was in the building. Official hours are nine to five."

Alana paused while the slide changed, then went on. "The second blast occurred at approximately two o'clock this morning. This time the target was Burger Mania, and the building was all but destroyed. Three were killed. Two employees in the kitchen and one behind the counter. A night manager and two staff members."

Selena Lopez lifted the pen from her mouth. "Similarities or connections among the casualties?" she asked. Selena was Opaline's younger sister and a K-9 handler. As the team's specialist in surveillance, tracking and suspect apprehension, she rarely missed a beat.

"None that we're aware of at this time. Two men and one woman at this location. All in their twenties," Alana answered.

Opaline changed the slide on-screen to one with candids of the deceased from both bombings.

Selena made a note on the paper before her. "Thank you."

Alana nodded. "Right now, local detectives and bomb-squad members have no leads, and the bombs are the only connections they've been able to make between the two attacks."

Max shifted, catching Alana's eye. "What links the bombs?"

The slide changed again, and Alana stepped aside, making sure everyone had a good view of the screen. Images of the aftermaths glowed in the dim room. The charred metal remains of the devices were showcased beside snapshots of the damage done in the immediate areas. A list of bomb contents according to a local lab formed a column beside the photos.

Alana folded her hands in front of her, giving her team time to take in the visuals before answering Max's question verbally. "Both bombs were homemade. Both used pressure cookers and materials available at local stores or online. Both were set off with a cell-phone detonator. The explosive in both was Tannerite."

Max's head bobbed slowly, knowingly. He swiveled in his chair to face his teammates. "Tannerite is a material designed for use in long-distance target practice. It creates a small explosion when the target is hit, sending up a puff of white smoke. The result saves the shooter a long walk to see if they landed the shot. If they're successful, there's smoke. Used incorrectly, as seen too often on You-Tube—" he grimaced "—people lose limbs and lives."

Alana's gaze slid unbidden to Max's black dress pants. It was nearly impossible to tell, but Max had lost a leg, below the knee, to a similar device eight years ago in Afghanistan. Pressure-cooker bombs were widely used by rebel forces and militant groups there. Max's position in the bomb squad had put him in close proximity to dozens of such devices over the years. She'd recruited him for the TCD a year after the amputation, pulling him straight from the gym at Walter Reed National Military Medical Center before he could sign papers to reenlist. An army superior in her circle had given Max an unparalleled recommendation, and Alana wasn't in the business of letting opportunity pass her by. Max had intended to return to combat full-time, but she'd persuaded him to accept her challenge instead. Many civilian lives had been saved because of that decision. And he'd never let the loss of his limb or the prosthesis in its place slow him down.

"Tannerite is packed into a pressure cooker," Max continued. "It's surrounded with small metal objects meant to become projectiles and shrapnel. Nails and ball bearings, nuts, bolts and BBs are popular choices. A cell phone typically detonates the explosive. The pressure in the cooker amplifies the blast. These are rudimentary bombs with detailed instructions available online. Materials are inexpensive and easy to acquire. No skill is necessary for a successful build."

Axel Morrow leaned in across the table, anchoring his elbows. "So we're dealing with devices like the ones used in the Boston Marathon." Short blond hair and sharp green eyes gave Axel the stereotypical "boy next door" look. His easy smile spoke of mild manners and a wholesome upbringing, but looks were deceiving. At thirty-four, Axel was the team's supervisory agent, a fierce friend and formidable opponent.

"Exactly." Max nodded.

"And there was nothing unique left behind at the bombing sites?" Axel asked, swinging his attention back to Alana. As the team's criminal profiler, Axel was in his wheelhouse looking for patterns and clues in the details. "No calling card or other source of pride?"

"None," Alana answered.

"Is he targeting a specific neighborhood?" Axel asked. "Could these be locations of convenience? Maybe random sites near his home?"

"Possibly," Alana conceded, turning to examine the screen as Opaline changed the image once more. "The businesses aren't in close proximity to one another, but it's possible the bomber frequented the locations, making them familiar and emotionally comfortable."

A map of the city showed the bomb sites circled in red. Clearly several miles apart.

Opaline danced her fingers over her laptop's keyboard. "I'm sending you all everything I have so far. Photos, police reports, initial findings, witness accounts..."

Phones buzzed and chimed collectively before she'd finished speaking.

"Local law-enforcement officials weren't able to make any connections between the victims," she said. "The detonation days and times were different. The casualties had no obvious commonalities in appearance. A basic surface review revealed nothing useful. I, on the other hand, hope to have plenty of leads for you by the time you reach your temporary headquarters in Grand Rapids later today."

"Which will be at the local police department." A familiar voice sprang through the open door a moment before Rihanna Clark entered. The former special agent and current TCD liaison for local PDs, press and the public smiled widely at the team. Her sleek black hair fell over her shoulders and her onyx eyes sparkled as she set a pair of stacked cup carriers on the table. "I thought you could all use a little help waking up. So I made a stop on my way in, while I worked out some details by phone with Grand Rapids PD."

The team went for the coffees, thanking Rihanna as they made their selections and returned to their seats. Dr. Carly Welsh, the TCD toxins expert, abstained, having brought her own large cup, as usual.

"TCD has access to a large conference room at the Grand Rapids PD for as long as we need it," Rihanna continued. "I've been assured the space is ours alone. We won't have to share or move for any reason, and we have access to anything within the department we might need. Personnel included. Their force is aware of what's going on, and they're highly motivated to protect their city and its citizens. As always, I'll be there to make any other arrangements you need. Just ask." She nodded at Alana, then took a seat near Opaline.

Alana nearly chuckled at the notion of anyone having to ask Rihanna for anything. She was a troubleshooting genius who anticipated the needs of her team with uncanny skill, then met those needs with precision and efficiency.

"Grand Rapids PD is expecting you this morning," Alana told her team. "Go home, make arrangements, then meet back here for departure. You know how to reach me if you need anything more."

Satisfied, and with a scheduled conference call in only a few moments, Alana excused herself from the room, confident the men and women of her TCD would get the job done.

MAX FLIPPED THROUGH the details Opaline had sent to his phone, grimacing at the senseless carnage. This wasn't the work of kids, drunks or idiots screwing around. Those kinds of people blew up old washing machines, microwaves or vehicles. This was someone who wanted to kill. Someone who intended to get the job done. Max pressed a palm to his knee, soothing the phantom pain several inches below the joint, where a prosthetic limb had long replaced his own calf and foot.

His insides tightened and ached at the memories. He'd thought for sure he'd die on that dirt road, a world away from home. And worse, he'd thought he'd gotten his team killed, as well. In reality, they'd all lived that day, though they hadn't all come home.

"Hey." Axel slid onto the seat beside him, delivering a cup of coffee Max hadn't been motivated to collect himself. He'd nearly finished a pot on his own before driving in today.

"You okay?" Axel asked, leaving the question open-ended. Allowing Max to decide what and how much to share.

"I've been better. I'm glad we've got the case, but I wish I could've talked Allie into leaving the city for a few days."

Axel pursed his lips. "No go, huh?"

"Not even close."

He bobbed his head in understanding. Axel had been around for the whirlwind romance Max had shared with Allie. And for the divorce that had followed less than two years later. He tapped his thumbs against the table. "Alana wants you to take the lead on this. Are you okay with that?"

Max dipped his chin. "No problem."

The rest of the team moved in closer, filling the space around Max's end of the giant table.

"Have you spoken to Allie?" Opaline asked, her voice thick with genuine concern.

The question earned her a hard, slashing glare from her sister Selena's eyes.

"I did," Max said, defusing the sibling tension as simply as he could. "She's aware of the bombings, but given there's no reason to suspect she's a target, she plans to go on with business as usual." Taking their son, Max Jr., along with her. All over town. To any number of places where a bomber could be setting up to kill another enemy.

Worse, she'd barely spoken with him when he'd called. Max Jr. had been up, crying, teething, according to Allie, and she was in no mood for a directive from her ex-husband. So he planned to talk to her in person as soon as he got to Grand Rapids this morning. Hopefully, he'd have a better chance of changing her mind by light of day.

He rubbed his chest where a dull ached formed at the thought of his family as collateral damage. Max had already screwed up once, putting his job continually before them. Letting his desire to protect others take precedence over his duty to be present with his wife and son. He'd ignored Allie's warnings, and she wasn't one to wait long on someone else to make her happy. She'd left him and moved to Grand Rapids, where she could be with her parents and sister. They'd been there for her as she built her small company and raised their son. All while Max was off saving lives and preserving other families instead of his own.

The gonging silence turned his attention back to the team, now staring. Their expressions ranged from supportive and understanding to compassionate and clearly laced with pity.

"What do you make of what we have so far?" Aria Calletti asked, breaking the silence. Aria was the rookie on the team, a narcotics expert and an agent who'd earned his respect on her first TCD mission not long ago. She was young, beautiful and petite, not the package bad guys expected to find disguising a powerhouse. Folks underestimated her, and she knew it. She used that to her advantage often and well.

"I think this is about revenge," Max said. "The bomber's not blowing up old appliances to see if he can. He's blowing up people at work. He's not going for crowded marketplaces. He's not detonating at the busiest times of day. He isn't killing to kill. His goal isn't mass destruction. It's pointed. He wanted someone dead at each of these two locations and at those specific times. Times when the target would be one of the few people around."

Carly nodded at that, sipping gingerly from her home-brewed coffee. The tall blonde had been with TCD for three years and specialized in biochemical terrorism. Her honey hair and willowy stature reminded him of Allie, but Carly was guarded. His teammates all had a ghost or two in their pasts, something that kept them quiet at times, even mildly haunted. "Revenge," she said. "It's a powerful motive. And certain unstable individuals view bombings as loud and clear ways to assert their strength after feeling small or weak for too long."

Aria straightened, eyebrows high. "Well, all right. Let's go to Grand Rapids."

The team agreed and headed for the door. Pulling their lives together on the fly, well enough that they could leave for an indefinite amount of time, meant a serious hustle. Most were used to it. Max kept a well-equipped go bag that would carry him up to a week without having to call for laundry service.

He stretched out of his chair, eager to get on the road. He'd requested this assignment, and even offered to take vacation time and go alone if Alana didn't think the situation required the entire TCD. He'd planned to show up at the Grand Rapids Police Department and beg them to let him consult. Thankfully, Alana had worked it out. Max was good on his own, but better with his team.

Axel sauntered along at Max's side. "You know, Allie and Max Jr. are going to be fine," he said. "We'll be there soon, and shut this bomber down before he ever sees us coming."

Max dared a look in his buddy's direction, wishing like hell he could will those words to be true. "You can't know that," he said. There were too many variables. Too many unknowns.

"Sure I can." Axel clapped Max on the back as they made their way to the elevator, smiling that trademark smile. "I know it's true because we've got you."

Chapter Two

Allie McRay motored through the crowded downtown parking lot in search of a decent space. Nothing too far from the mall doors or a lamppost. Winters in Michigan were frigid, and though it was daylight now, it would be dark before dinner this time of year. Allie needed to be prepared. She could blame her mother, the media or growing up as a woman for her intense fear of walking alone at night, but the real credit went to her ex-husband, Max, and all his horrific true stories of real women never seen again.

She shivered at the thought, then pressed the gas pedal a little harder. A minivan in the next aisle was exiting a prime spot below a security light. Allie's car slid in response to the acceleration, fishtailing slightly on a patch of ice as she made her way around the corner. Her knuckles ached as she gripped the steering wheel more tightly and cursed the freezing temperatures.

She trundled into the spot beneath the light, then shut down the engine and centered herself. Retail work in January was always a wild ride. Shoppers came out in droves to return ill-fitting and unwanted Christmas gifts. Many were less than pleasant about the exchanges, but that was the price of doing business. Thankfully, most people were thrilled with their Baby Threads purchases, and an upside to the January madness was the number of shoppers with newly acquired holiday cash ready to give her products a try.

Baby Threads was Allie's passion project, a small but mighty company she'd started at home so she could spend more time with her son, Max Jr. Now her custom-designed infant-and-toddler clothing business had its own kiosk at the mall.

She climbed out and hooked a series of bags over her shoulder. Her purse. Her laptop. A tote with more stock. Then she hurried inside, careful not to slip on any ice in the process.

The mall was warm and bustling as she made her way to the escalator. Scents of everything delicious wafted from the cafés and restaurants around the food court, making her wish she wasn't still committed to her New Year's resolution of making healthier choices. In other words, no more loading up on caffeine and sugar to keep her awake and peppy. This year she would rely on nutrition and exercise to help with those things. And only the occasional cinnamon roll, she reasoned. Because she wasn't Superwoman.

Allie made her way to the Baby Threads kiosk and opened it with a smile, thankful for the coveted space, if a little nervous about the bomber on the loose. She could thank her ex-husband for that fear, too.

He'd called her at three o'clock in the morning, upset about footage of a local bombing he'd seen on the news. She'd answered, barely able to hear his words over their screaming, teething son, whose poor little gums had kept him in misery for the past few days. She'd gotten the gist of Max's problem and request. He knew there was a bomber in her city, and Max wanted her to leave town until the man was apprehended. Not a wild idea, and certainly one she'd thought of many times this morning while she prepared Max Jr. for a day with her parents and herself for work. One bombing had been awful, two had been worrisome, and what she hadn't thought to tell Max last night was that she'd seen the most recent explosion. She'd run out for infant pain reliever when Max Jr.'s temperature had risen enough to make her fret. So she'd packed him into the car and headed to the local drugstore. He'd gotten a few blessed moments of sleep in his car seat, until the blast had woken him, and the emergency responders' sirens had kept him up. By the time Max had called, she was home and in survival mode. She could barely concentrate on anything other than her baby's cries, and she'd rushed Max off the phone.

In her sleep-deprived mommy mode last night, the whole experience had felt like a desperate blur, but as she'd gone through her morning routine, that had changed. She still wouldn't leave town. Being a single parent and the sole proprietor of a growing business meant she carried the bulk of responsibility for her little family's financial future. But she wanted to talk to Max again. Let him know she might've been a witness.

She rubbed chills from her arms as she set up her laptop and logged in to her inventory software. Memories of the blast and her ex-husband's pleas weighted her thoughts, but she couldn't let Max get into her head right now. Max Jr. was safe with her parents, and so far, the Grand Rapids bomber hadn't blown anything up during regular business hours. So there was nothing to worry about. She hoped.

Allie opened her tote bag and liberated the pile of new

stock she'd brought from home. She put several items on display, then arranged older items on pegs and across the narrow countertop.

Today would be a good day, she decided. Usually, that was all it took. The right mindset and a positive attitude.

A couple with a stroller stopped to look at the tiny faux fur vests Allie had hung above the counter.

She smiled, then let them take their time perusing the displays while their baby slept at their side.

"Five are already dead and a bunch more were injured," the man said, staring at his phone and speaking to the woman. "Two bombs in three days. Both at public locations. Businesses. Like this one," he said, raising his hands to motion around them. "It doesn't make any sense to be here today. Especially not with Chloe. She shouldn't have to be in harm's way because you got a little time off work."

The woman rolled her eyes and continued flipping through hangers. "No one is bombing the mall. Pull it together already. If someone was going to bomb the mall, they would have closed it."

"If it worked like that, they would've closed the real-estate office and Burger Mania." He pushed the stroller behind her, clearly distressed as she rounded the kiosk's corner.

Allie worked up a warm smile when the couple looked her way. Max had said the same thing last night. He'd wanted her to stay home today, but how could she? The bills wouldn't pay themselves. And bomber or no bomber, Allie wanted to see Baby Threads succeed. She wanted to make it on her own. Without needing Max's help to get by.

The man laughed at something the woman said, then

dropped a kiss on her forehead. "Humor me," he said. "Let's do what you came here to do and leave. We can spend the rest of the day at home. You can rest. I'll make lunch and watch after Chloe."

The woman froze. Her gaze flicked to Allie, then back to the man. "Deal." She stacked the items from her hand onto the counter in front of Allie. "We'll take these. I have the sudden urge to go home." She pulled the man's mouth to hers and pressed a kiss against it while Allie tallied up the total.

She smiled at the couple as they walked away, ignoring the pinch of regret in her gut. She and Max had had days like that once, and she missed those times terribly.

Truthfully, she missed *him* terribly. Even when he called at three in the morning demanding she leave town. It was kind of nice to know he still worried about her.

Allie yawned. Desperately in need of sleep.

Her ex-husband was clearly still in her head, because she swore she saw him approaching through the crowd. She strained for a clearer look at the fierce expression on an absurdly handsome face. Could it be? The resemblance was uncanny, right down to that towering presence that had always made him feel so much larger than life.

She narrowed her eyes as she took him in. Specifically the distinct gait in his walk, the result of a pretty high-tech artificial limb. She'd know that walk anywhere. He used to call the prosthesis his bionic leg to make her laugh. He wasn't wrong. The piece came complete with a battery-powered ankle that functioned a lot like a real one. Her favorite part about it had always been the man who got up every day, put it on and got to work. Because nothing stopped Max from protecting people. Not even losing part of himself, and nearly his life, to the cause.

Butterflies flew wildly in her stomach at the realization, and heat flushed instantly over every part of her. It
was completely unfair that even now, after eight months
of divorce, he had the same impact on her as the day
they'd first met.

She tugged the ends of her too-curly hair and wished
she'd taken more time with it this morning. *Dumb*, she
complained internally. Why did she have to spend precious time on her unruly locks to feel attractive when
Max woke up looking like that?

He smiled as he crossed the final few feet to her kiosk,
the same devilish and dangerous smile that had pulled
her in three years ago. One she'd yet to develop an im-
munity to, it seemed. "Allie."

"Max." She squared her shoulders and smiled politely
back, willing her traitorous body not to go in for a hug.

"You look good," he said, taking a moment to drag
his gaze over her.

"Thank you." She bit her tongue against the urge to
tell him he looked good, too. This wasn't a casual visit
between friends. This was an ambush. He'd asked her by
phone not to come to work, and she'd ignored him. So he
had come in person to press his point.

She crossed her arms and waited, trying not to get
hung up on the way his rich brown skin and tawny eyes
had always seemed straight off a billboard, or the way
the added stubble on his cheeks begged for her touch.

"About our talk last night," he said, casting a careful
look at the shoppers around her kiosk.

"I guess Director Suzuki agreed with your request."
Allie wasn't surprised. He'd told her about his plan to
contact the TCD director and ask to get the team involved

in the local bombing case. He'd wanted to come to Grand Rapids. And Max always got his way.

Except when he'd told her to stay home today, so here he was, working on that.

"Doing a little after-Christmas shopping before you get to work?" she asked.

He frowned, and her gut twisted as another possibility rushed into mind. Could he be there because he was right? Was there a bomb in the mall? Her gaze swept over the masses around them. Friends and families. Young and old. Her stomach dropped and the chill of fear raised gooseflesh on her arms.

"I just wanted to see you," he said, stopping her erratic train of thought before it completely derailed. He leaned an elbow on the narrow counter beside her and flashed an irresistible grin. "Remind you that I have a pretty great condo in Traverse City that you and Max Jr. would really enjoy."

The shoppers moved around him, comparing items and prices from her kiosk while obviously eavesdropping.

Allie smiled sweetly back. "That's very nice of you, but like I said before, I can't. I have to work. These Baby Threads don't make themselves." She cast a congenial look at the shoppers.

When she turned her attention back to Max, her heart gave a heavy thud. There was pain in his fathomless brown eyes and frustration in the set of his jaw. "You should reconsider," he said, moving into her personal space. "You deserve a few days away. I'm sure that's all it will take."

"No."

Max pressed his lips tight, and she imagined kissing them open. He smelled like heat and spice and man.

She gave herself a few hearty internal kicks. "But I'm glad you're here. I was hoping to talk to you about something."

The remaining kiosk shoppers headed for the escalator, leaving her alone with her greatest, most infuriating temptation.

Max watched them go, then flicked his eyes back to her. "I know you think I'm trying to tell you what to do," he said softly, leaning in close to keep their conversation private. "I'm trying to protect you."

Allie shivered at the intensity of his voice, overcome with memories of other emotion-packed moments shared between them. Of promises made and vows exchanged. Her heart ached at once for all they'd lost. Her. Max. And their son.

"Both targets have been public locations," Max continued, dragging her mind back to reality. "Just like the mall. I'd feel better if you were home with Max. More so if you both left the city until I find this guy and haul him in."

She sighed. "I'm staying right here, and Max and I aren't leaving town. But I thought of something this morning I wanted to run by you. It's probably nothing, but I know you think everything is something, and you're usually right."

He smiled.

She shook her head, feeling a senseless heat rise in her cheeks. How she'd missed that smile.

Allie relayed her story about the late-night trip to the drugstore and apologized for her inability to talk or think straight when he'd called. Then she got to the detail that had been haunting her all morning.

"I was stopped at the light on Burns and Hughes when the bomb went off at Burger Mania. I had a clear view of the building, but I was too far away to make out anything specific or useful. The blast woke Max Jr." She sighed, exhaustion tugging at her once more. "It was scary and more than a little surreal. I just sat there when the light changed. I was the only car on the street, and it took a minute to pull my addled thoughts together. At first, I couldn't make sense of what I was seeing. Then I remembered the news story about the realty office, and I realized someone had set off a bomb. I tried to quiet Max Jr. I shushed and sang. I pulled ahead when I noticed the light was green. Then I saw this man on the sidewalk. He just stared at me as I drove past. There was something in his expression. I thought it was shock. Maybe he was a witness, like me." She bit her lip, wondering if her constant internal desire to be useful was planting ideas where there were no grounds.

Max shifted, crossing his arms and rubbing his chin with long, steady fingers. "You think he could've been the bomber."

She pressed her lips together and shrugged. "Maybe."

"You got a good look at him?"

Allie nodded. She'd seen the man's face constantly in her mind since she woke this morning.

"You can describe him?"

Another nod. "Even if he was just a witness, he was closer to the building than I was when the blast happened. He was outside instead of in a car, and he wasn't distracted by a miserable little boy. He could have vital information either way."

Max worked his jaw, clenching and releasing the muscles. "I'll tell the team and local PD. You should meet with a sketch artist as soon as possible. Until then, what can you tell me about him? I can pass that on, as well."

Allie brought the stranger's image easily back to mind. "He was about five foot ten. Late thirties. Unkempt hair, too long for the cut. He had a beard, maybe two weeks' worth. And he wore one of those shapeless, hip-length coats." She touched her hips as a visual. "It was black with big rectangular pockets on each side of the zipper in front. And I could see the wool or fleece lining around the collar and inside the hood. Pale gray or dirty white. I don't know."

"That's good. All of that helps. A sketch artist will bring it to life, but this will get us started," Max said. "I'm going to head over to the station. I'll pass this information on when I meet with the team. Think about that condo in Traverse City."

She crossed her arms over her chest, fighting the sensation of infinite loss. "Go on," she said as warmly as possible and forcing a smile. "Get out of here and catch this guy. Then neither of us will have to worry anymore."

Without thinking, she rose onto her toes and pressed a kiss to his stubble-covered cheek. Her hand rested briefly on his sculpted chest, and his heart beat steadily against her palm.

Max's hand covered hers as she rocked back onto her heels, capturing her fingers against his shirt. The intensity in his gaze was enough to double her heart rate and buckle her knees. The heat in his touch, the contrast of his large hand holding her smaller one. She shivered.

"Can I come over tonight?" he asked, his voice deep and low.

Allie's jaw sank open. She wanted to say, *Yes!* And *No!* And *Yippee!* But only a little squeak sound came out.

"I'd like to see Max Jr.," he clarified. "If that's okay with you."

Her hearty exhalation turned to soft laughter. "Of course." He wanted to see their son. Like a good father would. And Max was an excellent father, even with the distance she'd put between them when she'd moved closer to her parents.

She wiggled her hand free from his grip, then stuffed her tingling fingers into her pocket. "You're welcome anytime, Max."

He nodded, a fresh smile blooming on his ridiculously attractive face. "All right. I guess I'll see you tonight."

And she hoped, naively, that this time he might really show up.

Chapter Three

Max left the mall with hope and a headache. Hope, because Allie's unexpected information might lead to a quick arrest and save the city from further bombings. A headache, because he still wanted her to take Max Jr. and leave town until the bomber was under arrest. Max had known better than to think he could change Allie's mind on the spot, but he'd had to try. That was one of their fundamental differences. He always erred on the side of caution, and she always assumed he was overreacting. Which he wasn't.

Allie thought she was the levelheaded one. She never rushed to take shelter from storms or hurried to merge with traffic when her lane ended in a mile. Why? She still had a mile. She wasn't hasty or rash, and she loved telling him to relax. She always thought there was more time. Ironically, Max had thought there was still time to save their marriage, and he'd been wrong.

He checked the clock on his dashboard as he made his way across town to the Grand Rapids Police Department. He should've stayed at the mall a little longer, pushed harder for her to take his advice. He should have insisted. Or begged. Whatever it took, because now he was running late and heavily distracted.

It hadn't helped that she'd looked so damn good. Her fuzzy sweater clung in all the right places and so had her nicely fitting jeans. She'd looked soft and smelled like all his best memories. The deep green of her top had made her hazel eyes glow, and he'd imagined running his fingers through the soft blond curls tumbling over her shoulders. The fantasies had gotten more specific the closer he got to her, making it impossible to argue properly. He'd been lost in her stare, wanting to say everything he'd never been able to say before and wondering what she thought of him now. Did she still see him as the broken and emotionally unavailable fool who'd let her and Max Jr. down?

And what had caused the fantastic blush that had spread across her cheeks before he left? He'd asked to stop by and see Max Jr., but she'd clearly been thinking of something else. Did it have anything to do with him?

He could count that as one more thing guaranteed to circle his brain until he saw her again. Allie might've divorced him eight months ago, but she'd surely still be the death of him. He was lucky he hadn't crashed his SUV just thinking about her in that damn sweater.

Max hit his turn signal with a groan, then slid into an open space at the GRPD lot.

The Grand Rapids Police Department was located in a squat but sprawling one-story facility on the edge of town. It was nondescript, without bells or whistles. Just a big sign and a whole lot of traditional black-and-white cruisers out front. He entered through the main doors and introduced himself at the desk inside. The female officer gave him an appreciative once-over as she pointed him in the right direction.

"Thank you." He made his way through the mix of

uniformed officers and others in suits or plain clothes. The familiar white noise was a comfort, and he felt his muscles begin to unwind. Another reason Allie had left him. Sometimes work felt more like home than his home. How could anyone blame him? He'd been serving nearly half the years he'd been alive. First with the military, then with the TCD. Somewhere along the line he'd forgotten how to be present in an off-the-clock moment, and it had cost him.

He spotted Axel and Carly outside an open doorway and knew he'd found the right place. He'd passed all his team members' vehicles on his way in and could only hope they weren't waiting for him to begin.

"Hey," Axel said, lifting a logoed disposable cup in greeting. "You made it."

Max nodded at his buddy, then at Carly, the team's biological warfare specialist with her personalized travel mug. "Hope I'm not holding things up."

"No," Carly assured him, a warm smile on her face. "We're waiting for Rihanna and the local law-enforcement representatives. I'm loitering out here to avoid sitting again after that drive."

"Same," Axel said, watching Max with trained eyes. "No luck with Allie, I guess?"

"Not in the way I'd hoped, but she had some interesting information I think we should look into a little further." He relayed the details of the man on the street outside Burger Mania just after the blast.

Axel jotted the information down, then excused himself and headed for the closed door at the end of the hallway, marked Chief Drees.

Max slipped into the conference room, ready to get the investigation started. It was time to get his head in the game. Find the bomber. Haul him in. Then it wouldn't matter if Allie and Max Jr. wanted to live full-time at the mall or any other public place.

He slowed his steps to examine the unfamiliar space and seating options. The area was roughly half the size and thirty times the age of the team's sleek high-tech boardroom back in Traverse City. The conference table and chairs were easily older than Max, and in lieu of a giant SMART board, an old-fashioned projector screen had been pulled down from a roll overhead and secured to a marker tray by a string.

Max took the open seat across from Aria and Selena, both of whom were engrossed with their phones, likely reviewing the materials Opaline had provided earlier. Max had already committed the pertinent details to memory. There wasn't much so far, and he was waiting for her to work her magic and send more information soon.

Axel and Carly entered a moment later with the TCD liaison, Rihanna Clark, and a trio of local lawmen on their heels.

"Good morning. Again," Rihanna said with a grin. "I'm glad to see everyone made it safely. I'm going to jump right in with introductions so you can get to work." She outstretched a palm toward the men who'd filed in beside her. "These are the faces you'll want to look for if you need anything while you're here. Grand Rapids police chief Martin Drees, Detective Isaac Fohl and Sergeant Jim Sims, bomb squad."

Each man nodded and forced a smile at the sound of his name.

Rihanna then turned to the table. "And here we have the FBI's Traverse City Tactical Crime Division. Our supervisory agent is Axel Morrow." She lifted a palm in

Axel's direction. "Going around the table from there we have Special Agent Aria Calletti, Special Agent Dr. Carly Welsh, Special Agent Selena Lopez and Special Agent Max McRay. Max is our explosives expert, and he'll be taking point on this case."

"Thank you," the police chief said, spending a moment to look each of the TCD members in the eyes. His white hair and face full of wrinkles suggested he was somewhere near Max's dad's age. The tightness around his eyes and mouth spoke of stress, fatigue and determination. He was a man who cared about people, his city and his job. "We appreciate you coming here and getting involved like this. We've never faced a serial bomber, and our citizens are on edge. The phones haven't stopped ringing since we announced the second explosion this morning. A number of school districts have reported record low attendance. Parents don't want to send their kids in case this nut goes for one of our schools next. I need to give the people of Grand Rapids some assurance of safety. And soon, or we'll have widespread panic on our hands."

Axel leaned forward, hands clasped on the table before him. "We understand, Chief Drees, and we'll do all we can to wrap this up quickly. Our goal is to bring the bomber in without any further incidents. Do you have any new leads or information available?"

"No." The chief shook his head, visibly deflated. "Aside from what you told me a few moments ago, none."

Axel turned to the team and shared the details Allie had given Max.

Chief Drees nodded along. "I've put in a call to our best sketch artist. I hope to have the image in all of your hands by this time tomorrow, if not before."

"That's good," Axel said. "Until then, we've got our best tech working hard on this case, as well, and I'm certain she'll have more for us to go on soon." His smile spread to the other team members at the mention of Opaline. He was right to praise her. Opaline was the queen of finding needles in haystacks, and when she was looking for someone, they couldn't hide.

The chief gave an appreciative nod, then turned to the doorway, where a uniformed officer had arrived with a clipboard and expectant expression.

The chief lifted a hand to the room, nodded, then took his leave, exiting the room with the waiting officer.

Detective Fohl pulled out a chair and had a seat at the table.

Sergeant Sims, the local bomb-squad leader, folded his arms but remained standing, his expression grim. "Good morning." Sergeant Sims was young and visibly exhausted. From the looks of him, Max would guess he probably hadn't slept more than a few hours since the first bomb blast.

The team returned the greeting in near unison.

Sims pushed a handful of shaggy brown hair off his forehead, and it sprang immediately back. His clothes were rumpled and his posture slack. "There's nothing new to report on the bomb front. We haven't been able to identify anything significant about the devices. Standard pressure-cooker style. Nothing unique or telling. No special signature to set the bomber's works apart. Nothing to trace back to the maker." He rubbed his eyes hard with one hand, then turned to his counterpart. "Detective Fohl has a little more for you."

The detective opened a manila folder and passed a stack of papers around. "This is a compilation of all the victims' names so far. Casualties first, then the injured. They're sorted further by the blast location." He removed a second stack of papers and circulated them around, as well. "These are the lists of all current employees for both businesses, as well as the names of people who were fired from either in the last six months."

Axel took one of each paper, then handed them along. "We'll want to push that back to a year for good measure." He raised his eyes to Rihanna, who nodded.

"I'll reach out to the businesses," she said, tapping her thumbs against her phone screen. "I'll get an updated list to you within the hour."

"Thanks," Axel said, before returning his attention to the detective. "Is there anyone with a grudge against one or more of the victims?"

The older man narrowed his eyes. "Nothing for certain, but I've spoken to both businesses about the employees who've left or been let go." He inclined his head to indicate the papers in Axel's grip. "There's been a greater amount of turnover at Burger Mania than at the real-estate office, as you can imagine. So we started looking into employees who left the real-estate office first. There were only three. Two were fired. One of those is currently in the hospital, recovering from a surgery. The other moved south and began a new career in landscaping. The last guy left of his own volition, but he did it with a stink, made a big scene. And as far as we can tell, he doesn't appear to have taken another job since."

Aria cocked her head. "Two solid alibis and one wild card," she said, voicing Max's thoughts.

Selena sighed dramatically, her smile widening. "We love a wild card." She slid her fingertip over the page before her, presumably down the short list of former employee names. "Which one is unaccounted for?"

The detective shifted forward, gaze intense. "Fritz O'Lear, and we haven't been able to reach him by phone for comment."

"What do we know about him so far?" Max asked, his mind already running over the most well-known American bombers. *Kaczynski, McVeigh, Helder, Rudolph, Metesky.* All average. All white males. Varied ages.

"Not much," the detective admitted. "Caucasian. Male. Midthirties. Unmarried. No kids. No previous record. And apparently, currently unemployed."

Max stood, drawing the group's attention. He was ready to get out there and get started, and he knew exactly where to go. "Got an address on Mr. O'Lear?"

Chapter Four

Max climbed into the passenger side of Axel's official, TCD-issued SUV, the heat of fresh purpose burning away January's bitter cold. The sooner this bomber was stopped, the sooner Max's family and this town would be safe, and he had a gut feeling about this lead.

He hadn't been surprised to see Axel on his feet in the conference room a bare heartbeat after himself. He and Axel had always been connected that way, always on the same wavelength, and more often than not, they shared the same instinctive responses.

Axel typed O'Lear's address into the dashboard GPS, then pumped up the heat and adjusted the vents. "First thoughts on this guy?" he asked, shifting smoothly into Reverse and heading away from the police department.

Max released a heavy breath and a plume of white fog blew into the air before him. He rubbed a palm against his thigh. "A recently disgruntled guy, who left his job in a huff and hasn't found new work after months of unemployment? I don't like it. And I really don't like that he's been unreachable so far. Could be irrelevant, but—"

"It doesn't feel that way," Axel said, completing his thought.

"Yeah." Max nodded. "As for the fast-food joint being

across town and presumably unrelated to the real-estate office, we won't know until we ask some more questions. Could be that this guy is the link between the two. Any number of things could've taken him to that place, or maybe he's never been there and that bombing was a decoy to throw us off. That wouldn't mean he didn't have a problem with one of the employees who were targeted, or even a regular customer."

Axel took the next right, increasing his speed as local limits permitted and likely working out a dozen possible bomber-motivation scenarios in his mind.

Max's attention, however, was divided. "Allie shot me down this morning," he complained. "Straight off. As if I was ridiculous to even suggest a bomber in her city could impact her. Apparently, it's a big city, and she doesn't know the guy, so she's fine. Max Jr. is also fine." He gritted his teeth against a building rant. *The bomber hasn't been identified.* That was the problem. He could work in the kiosk beside hers, for all she knew.

Max rubbed his forehead and bit his tongue. Axel didn't need to sit through another rail-against-Allie. Though he would, Max knew, without question or complaint. Axel had listened to many similar tirades during and immediately after the divorce. Not before, because Max had never seen it coming. He was too engrossed in his work to acknowledge his home life was falling apart. And the consequence of that was divorce. He cringed internally at the awful little word. Max had thought divorce was some magical, powerful, permanent change to everything. The end of all things as he knew them. He was wrong.

Max's divorce from Allie had only changed a few things, and all for the worse. She and Max Jr. were no longer at home when he got there. He'd lost the companionship of his best friend, his lover and life partner. He'd lost the only woman he'd ever imagined in any of those roles and the sixteen-month-old son whose every breath he cherished. Now Max was on his own, and loathing the bachelorhood he'd once stupidly worried he might miss after marriage. But despite the things divorce had changed, everything else was exactly the same. The sun still rose and set. Max still filled the bulk of his waking hours with work, and he still loved Allie as fiercely as ever. He felt protective of her, thrilled by the sight of her and frustrated as hell by her earlier dismissal. Max wasn't a jealous man, wasn't overbearing or unreasonable. And bombs were his life's work. So when he suggested she take Max Jr. and get out of town for a few days, he'd hoped she would listen.

"Well, maybe we'll get lucky," Axel said. "O'Lear will be our man. He'll confess everything at the sight of us. We'll haul him in, and Allie, Max Jr. and the rest of this city will be safe before lunch."

Max snorted. "If only." He stared through his window at the fittingly bleak, gray day. "I'm not usually that lucky." A phantom limb pain pinched and ached in his missing calf, as if on cue. He'd learned years ago not to reach for it, not to try to soothe it. The pain wasn't real. The limb wasn't there. And he wasn't sure if his subconscious was agreeing or disagreeing with his lack of luck by reminding him of the bombing that had nearly ended his life. He'd lost part of his leg in the blast, but he'd lived, and that made him luckier than too many others.

Max's thoughts cleared, and his vision pulled tight on his reflection in the glass. Not only had he survived, but he'd gone on to meet and fall in love with Allie. They'd married and had a son he adored. Had Max died, he wouldn't be in Grand Rapids now, willing to do whatever it took to protect his family and to keep this bomber from taking a single additional life.

The bomber, he realized, was the unlucky one.

Axel slid the SUV against the curb in a low-income neighborhood a few minutes later. "Not the most impressive residence for a recent Realtor," he said, drawing Max back to the moment.

They stared at the bland yellow-brick building, across a sea of filthy snow and a poorly shoveled walkway. Everything about the property was in need of repair.

Max expanded his scan of the area, moving from the stout three-story building, to neighboring homes and apartments, the street, parked and moving vehicles as well as the sporadic and partially frozen pedestrians hurrying in every direction. "I thought Realtors made a good living."

"Only if they make enough commissions. O'Lear must not have sold enough homes to afford a better place or keep his job. Which suggests he's not a people person. You have to possess a certain set of skills to part people from their money. The fact that the agency let him go is a red flag. Most Realtors are like freelancers, not salaried, and as long as they bring in money for the agency, I'd think staff would overlook some rough-around-the-edges behavior."

Max stepped onto the sidewalk and bundled his coat tighter as Axel joined him. They strode quickly, purposefully, to the tenement. Axel rang the buzzer for O'Lear's apartment. When no one answered, he pressed the button again. Then repeatedly, until a young woman in running shoes and earbuds, her hood up and eyes down, emerged from the locked door and began a jog down the broken sidewalk.

Max's arm snapped out, catching the door before it closed behind her.

"See? Luck," Axel said, stepping into the building's narrow first-floor foyer.

The space was cluttered. A bank of mailboxes lined one wall and a scattering of abandoned fast-food bags, a deflated playground ball and a pair of children's sneakers littered the floor. It wasn't much warmer inside than outside.

Max and Axel climbed the stairs to the third floor, breathing stale, sour air. The scents of garbage, grease and something like marijuana burned through Max's nose and down his throat. He could only imagine the stench during warmer months.

Axel reached O'Lear's door first and knocked. Chin up and shoulders back, the thirty-four-year-old looked like someone not to be trifled with, and it suited him. At six foot two, Axel was taller than the average criminal, fit to a fault and trained in hand-to-hand combat. His wool dress coat, shiny shoes and easy smile left some room for confusion in dumber bad guys. Their tendencies to underestimate him always resulted in Axel's upper hand.

Max could count the number of dress pants and shiny shoes in his closet on one hand, and he rarely wore either to work, never into the field. He was just as tall as Axel, broader and rarely underestimated. He scanned the hall as Axel knocked again, more loudly this time.

Torn and stained carpeting ran underfoot, frayed along broken baseboards and cut off at doorjambs by dented metallic strips. Televisions blared from nearby apartments, accented by warbling voices, a muffled baby's cry and a barking dog.

Only silence filtered through O'Lear's door.

Max tried again, knocking louder and announcing "Delivery! Package for Mr. O'Lear." Still nothing.

Axel stepped back, lips drawn briefly to one side. "Nobody's home. Try again in a few hours?"

"Yep." Max turned back to the stairs with a sigh. He knew their luck had a limit.

The ride to the station passed quickly. There was less traffic and no underlying anticipation. No possibility that they were about to face off with a serial bomber on his turf.

The station was busy, and the cops stared, curiosity plain in their collective gaze. Any officers who hadn't been on duty when the TCD arrived were probably just hearing about the team from Traverse City who'd commandeered their conference room until further notice. Max was sure it must be strange for hosting officers. He nodded and greeted as many as possible. Since they were seen as interlopers, stealing a case the locals could've handled themselves wouldn't bode well when the TCD needed assistance navigating local customs, laws or culture.

A familiar woman's voice spilled through the open conference-room doorway as Rihanna appeared. She smiled at the sight of Max and Axel. "You're just in time. Opaline's on a conference call, and I was about to close the door."

The men ducked inside, neither willing to miss a single word of Opaline's report.

Her warm smile centered a large screen, thanks to a laptop connected to the precinct's projector.

Max smiled, despite himself, in return.

Opaline's head and shoulders were larger than life, the tips of her bleached-blond bangs flamed blue. A perfect match for her eye makeup and glittery top. Hot-pink lips glowed against her light skin. The woman knew how to turn heads, and words like *low-key* and *nondescript* were lost in her presence.

Max had always appreciated Opaline's silver-lining attitude, especially on days he could only see the storm. Divorced, like Max, Opaline knew what it meant to lose someone to the demands of the TCD. Unlike him, however, Opaline dated. Frequently and with great hope. Max didn't see the point. Not when he knew there was only one woman for him, and he'd already wrecked things with her.

The buzzing room quieted as Max and Axel took their seats. Rihanna dimmed the lights, and Opaline became impossibly brighter in the drab, somewhat cramped confines of the Grand Rapids PD conference room.

The entire team was present. Good news for time and efficiency. Everyone would be able to respond and weigh in, then build off one another's opinions, views and suggestions. Launching the investigation in the best possible way. Max nodded to himself. Maybe his luck wasn't all bad. If O'Lear had been home, Max and Axel would've been tied up with him and possibly missed something paramount.

"Hello." Opaline waved on the screen. "I just wanted to touch base and see if you have anything new for me since this morning, and also to let you know what I've got going over here on my end. I'm currently running background checks on all employees for both businesses from the past year. I'm looking into employee records, school records, past jobs, local family and friends, favorite restaurants, hobbies, gyms or anything else I can use to make a connection between the two businesses. I don't have anything yet, but something will turn up, if I have to trace every one of their lives back to preschool."

Max's knee bobbed, unbidden, as adrenaline pooled, desperate for an outlet. Opaline didn't have anything yet. His gaze darted around the room as she continued her update. He found some solace in the fact every team member wore the same expression, looking a lot like he felt. Frustrated. Anxious. Eager and determined to stop the bomber.

"So you reached out to let us know you don't know anything?" Selena, Opaline's sister, asked, her tone unnecessarily harsh and thick with sarcasm.

"I'm working on it," Opaline said, her smile bright but tight. "I always check in frequently in situations like these because everything can change in an instant. You know that."

Max had no idea what the beef was between the Lopez siblings, but today wasn't the day to sort it out. "Do you have lists of the victims' local family and friends?" Max asked.

Opaline took a beat to compose herself and return to the task at hand. Her fingers flew across her keyboard in the silence. "Absolutely. I'm emailing those to you now."

Phones buzzed and vibrated across the conference room.

Max swiped his cell phone to life, quickly accessing the new information. "Let's split up and interview as many of these people as possible. We'll regroup afterward and see if any names come up on both sides of this.

We're looking for someone with a connection to one or more of the victims in each blast."

His teammates raised their phones, too, accessing the lists and talking rapidly among themselves.

"Opaline," Max continued. "I think the times of the blast were significant, as well. The bomber didn't choose one time for both attacks, so I'm guessing the times had more to do with the locations or intended victims than the bomber's schedule. Why two a.m. at the burger joint and seven eighteen a.m. at the real-estate office? Can we find out who was typically present at those specific times and possibly work from there to find a common denominator?"

Carly tapped her pink nails against the table, thin brows furrowed. "Vengeance killings."

Max dipped his chin in agreement, as did the other agents seated at the table. "I think so. Someone with an ax to grind and multiple possible offenders."

Tension pulled Carly's expression tight. "Unlimited offenders," she corrected him. "A guy this unstable likely has a lot of perceived enemies, real or imagined, and unless he had a problem with all the people he hurt at Burger Mania, we can assume he doesn't care if bystanders are hurt, or worse, in the process. If he goes after someone working at a large or busy venue, the collateral damage could be hundreds. We have to hope his next target isn't employed by a concert hall or sports arena."

Or a mall, Max thought, his stomach dropping to the floor.

Rihanna cleared her throat and peeled herself away from the door, where she'd taken up residence. As the team liaison, she often stayed on her feet during meetings. Continually on alert and prepared to deal with local law enforcement, press or the public as needed. Her diligence made it possible for the team to work with limited interruptions. "I thought you might say that." She grinned at Carly as she slid a stack of papers onto the conference table. "I've set up meetings with real-estate office employees and the victims' families."

Opaline beamed. "Excellent. You guys work on that. I'll keep pushing my way through this. And we'll chat again soon." She reached for the screen, then vanished.

The team passed Rihanna's pages around, pairing up and hovering over the text.

Selena muttered something under her breath, presumably about her sister, as she scanned the paper. Beside her, Aria locked her attention on Max. "Selena and I can talk with the real-estate office employees, if you want."

Max nodded, pulling his gaze back to Axel. "Why don't we visit the victims' family members?"

Axel stood as Selena and Aria pushed away from the table. "Call between interviews," he instructed. "Even if it's just to say the conversation was a bust. As you know, communication is paramount in these early hours."

Max pulled up the rear as the group headed for the parking lot, eager to start making progress on the case.

Chapter Five

Aria slid behind the wheel of her SUV and waited as Selena got comfortable in the passenger seat. Ramsey Realty was across town from the police station, and in a situation like this one, time wasn't on the TCD's side. Every moment the bomber went unchecked was another minute he had to plan—or worse, to execute—his next attack.

Aria motored along the snow-lined streets, following GPS directions and hoping to make significant progress with the interviews.

Selena looked over her shoulder every few minutes, into the empty back seat, then frowned again.

"Missing Blanca?" Aria asked.

Blanca, the white German shepherd and K-9 officer, was Selena's partner, and the bond between the two was immeasurable. Being away from her for this case had left Selena visibly on edge, like a mother away from a newborn. Though Blanca was about as helpless as a baby honey badger. Aria knew the feeling, already missing her fiancé, Grayson, and their precious infant, Danny.

"It's weird without her," Selena admitted, facing forward once more. "I keep forgetting she's not there, and it feels like I'm missing an appendage."

Blanca was back in Traverse City, cashing in on some well-deserved time off. Much as Selena had hated to leave her, it hadn't made sense to bring Blanca on this case. She wasn't trained to locate bombs or identify accelerants, so she'd have spent all her time in the freezing cold vehicle, or in a pen at an unfamiliar station.

Aria parked in the Ramsey Realty lot, outside the partially ruined single-story brick building. Yellow crime-scene tape circled the structure, and several signs warned the public to stay back. A corporate trailer had been set up a few yards from the building's front door. A vinyl banner along the side proclaimed, Yes! We're Open! And a Ramsey Realty sign had been attached to the handrail of a small retractable set of steps. "I guess this is the place."

Aria and Selena made their way across the freshly plowed lot, then let themselves into the trailer. The stale air was tinged with cinnamon, and muffled voices carried through a paper-thin interior wall.

"Hello?" Aria called, moving toward the nearest empty desk. The nameplate said Susan Myer. Steam lifted from a mug near a stack of papers, and the computer was powered on. "Susan?"

Quick footfalls tapped along the tile floor in their direction. "Coming!" a bright voice returned. "Sorry," she said, rounding the corner toward her desk with a wide smile. "I didn't hear you come in. The coffee maker is a little persnickety back there, and I did my best to help, though only time will tell."

She paused to assess the agents, and her smile fell. Susan had likely seen enough law officials in the past few days to know a pair when they appeared before her. She pulled in a deep breath. "How can I help you?"

"We're Special Agents Calletti and Lopez," Aria explained. "We'd like to ask you some questions about the bombing."

Susan fell gracelessly into the seat at her desk. "Of course." She lifted her mug with slightly trembling hands. She was too polished for the trailer. From her one-piece black jumpsuit and heels, to her high-end haircut and professionally manicured nails, everything about her clashed with the underwhelming surroundings. "What would you like to know?"

Selena motioned toward the rumble of voices. "Who else is here?"

"Bailey and Frank," Susan answered. "They're hoping for coffee."

Selena nodded, then headed silently in the direction from which Susan had come.

"I'm sorry for your loss," Aria said, her attention focused on the woman at her desk. "I know what it feels like to lose coworkers. We see our teammates more hours a day than our families." Her heart ached at the thought. For Aria, this sort of loss was inevitable, if she stayed on the job long enough. Death was one of those things all first responders accepted long before taking the oath or earning the badge. But not Realtors. Not Susan or the Burger Mania workers. These folks had signed on to sell homes and provide cheap, fast food. They'd never imagined this day could come. And Aria couldn't imagine that kind of blow.

Selena returned with a middle-aged man wearing a logoed polo shirt and khaki pants, and a woman in a gray sweater dress. "Frank Thomas, Bailey White, this is Special Agent Calletti."

Aria nodded in greeting. "Nice to meet you both. Agent Lopez has probably already told you we're here to follow up on the bombing at your office. Would you like to sit while we talk?"

The Realtors moved silently to a pair of desks beyond Susan's, catching their coworker's eyes as they passed.

Frank's fingers curled at his sides. "Tell me you have a lead on the maniac who did this."

"We're working on it." Aria scanned each face carefully, waiting for signs someone knew more than they'd want to announce in a group. The sting of cinnamon air freshener intensified as the trailer's heater kicked on, blowing loudly over them. "Our team is here to pursue the matter full-time until the culprit is apprehended."

Selena moved to Aria's side. "Any idea who'd do something like this?"

The trio of employees shook their heads.

Selena waited before speaking again. A practice Aria used often. When no one blurted anything under the pressure of silence, she continued. "Anyone have a problem with your company, the office manager or Realtor who was caught in the blast?"

Susan frowned. "Maybe Fritz. He didn't come to mind right away, because he hasn't been here in months, but he wasn't happy when he left." She cast her gaze to her fellow real-estate workers.

"Maybe," Frank mumbled. "I don't know. Was he smart enough to do something like this? Isn't building bombs hard?"

Selena's gaze flicked briefly to Aria.

Aria's instincts went on alert. Fritz wasn't a common name, and it had come up earlier in the team meeting. Not a coincidence.

Selena lifted her chin. "Tell me about Fritz."

Susan straightened her posture, apparently accepting

the role of spokesperson. "Fritz O'Lear was an agent here, briefly. We hired him in a pinch and regretted it almost immediately. He interviewed well, if a little flat on personality. But it takes all kinds to sell homes. Some of the fussier buyers don't like Realtors with too much show and pizzazz—they complain we're just trying to sell them something."

Selena's eyebrows quirked slightly. "Aren't you? You're trying to sell houses."

"Sure, but that's not all we do." Susan bristled. "We're matchmakers on the front end, trying to find exactly what each customer wants for a price they can afford. On the back end we're investigators. Number crunchers. And liaisons. We work with area businesses and homeowners to prep and stage their homes for a quick sale while estimating fair market values and jumping through hoops for buyers. Fritz was good at the research and numbers."

"But?" Selena prompted when Susan didn't go on.

Frank leaned across his desk, hands folded. "No one liked him. People didn't want to work with him, and instead of asking for one of us to handle their search or sell, they'd just go with another realty firm. He was terrible for business."

Aria moved in Frank's direction, seeing the weak link among the three. "You didn't like him."

Frank shrugged. His chin jutted. "No. Not particularly. If he disagreed with you, he'd get insulting. And he couldn't take a joke, would always respond in a nasty way. Had a real chip on his shoulder. Would carry a grudge. It was clear he was that way around our clients, too, from feedback we got. So we told him maybe he'd be more comfortable at another firm, maybe a bigger one.

You know, where he could do a lot of office and online stuff and not interact with the public as much."

"You think Fritz is capable of blowing up buildings?" she asked. "Assuming he could figure it out?" She narrowed her eyes, throwing back his earlier accusation that bomb-building was hard, and perhaps Fritz was stupid. "Is he capable of murder?"

"Maybe," Frank said, doing his best to seem indifferent when his posture and the flush of his skin betrayed him. "He was cussing everyone when he left. Throwing blame around like it was someone else's fault he couldn't sell homes."

"He was mad because you guys taunted him," Bailey said, suddenly finding her voice. Her cheeks pinkened and her gaze jerked to Aria. "Frank and Gary made fun of Fritz for his lack of sales. Even when Fritz had a good week, it was never enough. Never close to the number Gary sold, and they never let him forget it."

Frank gaped, then scowled. "You think this is my fault? I teased some guy a little, and his response is a killing spree?"

Bailey backed down, and Aria resisted the urge to dump Frank from his chair.

"Gary and our office manager were lost in the bombing," Susan said, gently rubbing her forehead.

Aria turned, thankful for a place to redirect her attention.

Selena's eyes flashed at the platinum blonde. "Gary was a Realtor who taunted Fritz, and I'm guessing the office manager is the one he faced off with when he turned in his notice?"

Susan nodded.

"Got a picture of Fritz?" Selena asked. "An old ad or mailer or something?"

Susan pursed her lips. "I'm afraid not. We handle our own promotions, and the company's print directory and materials were damaged in the explosion. But his photo was online with his listings. He's been gone a few months, but the internet is forever, right?"

Aria's thumbs were in action as Susan spoke, already digging up images of Fritz O'Lear outside homes with the Ramsey Realty sign. A clean-cut, fox-faced man in his thirties looked back at the camera, inauthentic smile in place. His light brown hair was laced with gray, and his small brown eyes were narrowly set against a long, broad nose. "This him?" she asked, turning the screen to face Susan, then sweeping it slowly in the direction of Bailey and Frank.

"Yes." The trio agreed.

Selena left her business card with Susan.

Aria gave one of her cards to Frank and one to Bailey. "Please keep this information to yourself. It's early in the case, and we don't want to tip off a potential bomber. Also, if you see Fritz O'Lear, do not approach. Call us. We're hoping to talk with him. Maybe rule him out."

Back in the cold, the agents moved quickly to the SUV. Selena's gaze swept to the rear window, where Blanca normally awaited her return.

Both of them knew of Max and Axel's assignment to locate O'Lear. That effort would have to intensify. But they had another location to visit.

"Burger Mania?" Aria asked, thankful for the lead and hoping for more good luck at stop number two.

"Burger Mania," Selena agreed.

Chapter Six

Max pulled Rihanna's notes from the glove box as Axel piloted the SUV into traffic. "We're two for two," he said, feeling more defeated than he liked this early in the game.

Of the families they'd visited so far, both had lost a loved one to the Burger Mania blast. Both families were wrecked, as expected, their conversations soaked in tears, anger and frustration. But no one had any idea who might've done such a thing. None of them seemed to remember a Fritz O'Lear or someone who looked like him.

"Where to next?" Axel asked, motoring toward the nearest main road.

"Sherman Oaks Parkway." Max tapped the address into the dashboard GPS, then settled back in his seat. "We're meeting with Jordyn Knightly's family. If they don't have anything to offer, we'll be out of leads."

Axel glanced at the GPS, then took the next turn. "What do we know about Jordyn?"

"Twenty-three, blond hair, brown eyes." Max flipped the notes around in his hands, reading the limited details. "She worked the night shift at Burger Mania and attended classes at the community college during the day. Looks like she was born and raised in the area. Has immediate and extended family here in Grand Rapids. She shared an apartment with her best friend, Kia."

"Do we have Kia's address?" Axel asked.

"Yeah. It's with the details Opaline put together on Jordyn. We can try there next." At least that added one more thread of hope for the day. If Jordyn's family didn't have anything new to offer, maybe the young woman had confided something to her roommate that would help.

Axel slipped the SUV into Park several minutes later, beside a driveway with multiple cars.

The cottage-style home was covered in gray shake and lined in clean white trim.

Max unfastened his seat belt. "Well, we can eliminate the possibility that the attacks were based on socioeconomic reasons." The first victim's parents had both been physicians, and the second victim's family had lived in a housing project. This was a solid middle-class, blue-collar neighborhood.

"Agreed," Axel said.

Their phones buzzed with incoming texts. A message from Aria with a photograph of Fritz O'Lear in his Ramsey Realty jacket.

Max surveyed the photo. Allie hadn't recalled the hair or eye color of the man she'd seen outside Burger Mania, but it was hard to reconcile the description she'd given with the image before him. Maybe the unidentified man had been a witness after all.

"Looks like Aria and Selena are making more progress than we are," Axel said. "If we don't break this streak, we're going back empty-handed."

Max smiled. "Then we'd better get to work."

The agents met on the sidewalk and made their way

up a snow-lined walkway to the small front porch. A cherry-red wreath hung on a cheery blue door.

"Maybe the third interview is the charm," Axel suggested, then began to knock.

A puffy-faced woman in rectangular glasses and a messy ponytail answered. "Yes?"

Max made the introductions, and the woman invited them inside.

A small collection of adults covered the couch and love seat beyond the door. They'd clearly overheard the exchange so far and had fallen silent in response.

"I'm Jocelyn," the puffy-faced woman said, closing the door behind them. "Jordyn was my beautiful little girl." A powerful sob racked her small frame as she spoke, then doubled her over at the couch's edge.

A man stood to collect her, guiding her to his vacated seat. "Sit, honey. Rest."

A younger woman with curly red hair rose from the love seat and pointed to the woman still seated there. "We're Sage and Grace. Jordyn's cousins. That's our mom, Alicia," she said, pointing to a woman who'd entered the room when Jocelyn had begun to cry, then froze at the sight of the agents. "On the couch is our dad, David, our brother Jim, and Kia, Jordyn's best friend. That's our uncle Brad, Jordyn's dad." She pointed to the man helping Jocelyn get settled.

Max nodded in greeting, thankful to see so many of Jordyn's loved ones in one place, especially Kia, the roommate. "We're very sorry for your loss." He let the words sit between them a moment, hoping to convey the fact he truly meant them. Max knew loss intimately. He'd lost more than his share to senseless acts of violence in the service. All were far too young, and each absence had left a mark on his heart. "We won't take up too much of your time. We just wanted to introduce ourselves and let you know our team is here now, working in conjunction with the local police department to identify and apprehend the person responsible for these bombings. We won't leave until we have justice for you and the others who've lost loved ones." He gave them another minute to process, then added, "We're very good at what we do."

Axel shifted, folding his hands in front of him. "Your local police haven't stopped following up, but it's easy for a force to spread themselves too thin in times like these. Our team, on the other hand, will devote one hundred percent of our time to this investigation, until we've seen it through. You have our complete attention."

Jocelyn wept loudly again, folding forward in her seat on the couch. Her husband crouched before her, stroking her face and whispering words of encouragement.

"We're visiting everyone on the Burger Mania staff," Max said. "Looking for ideas about who could've done this. We'll follow every lead and suggestion to its end, and we never disclose how we came upon a name in conjunction to a crime. Is there anyone you can think of who might've had a problem with one of the victims? Maybe another employee or customer? An ex-spouse or significant other. Anything Jordyn might've told you that seemed extreme or worrisome?"

The group members looked at one another, eager and curious. Then their heads began to shake. No.

"Have you ever heard the name Fritz O'Lear?" Max asked. It was a long shot, but the only one they had at the moment, and worth tossing out there. Though the name hadn't registered to anyone at the last two homes he and Axel had visited.

Kia frowned, as if trying to recall, but didn't comment.

Jocelyn sat taller, her sobs quieted. "Is that the man who did this?" Her voice grew firm and angry. "Is he the monster who took my baby girl?"

Axel unfolded his hands and lifted his palms hip-high, then relaxed them at his sides as she calmed. "He worked at the realty office that was also bombed. We don't know if he's a victim, too. We're hoping to find links between the two targeted businesses. Did any of you have recent interactions with someone from Ramsey Realty? Did Jordyn?"

Max brought up the photo of O'Lear on his phone. "This is Fritz O'Lear." He passed the device to the women on the love seat and watched as they took turns looking, then passing it on.

When the phone reached Kia, her curious expression turned to confusion. "This is Fritz O'Lear?" She fished a phone from her purse and set Max's aside. A moment later, she turned her screen to him. "Could this be the same guy?"

Axel moved in closer as Kia handed Max both phones.

The agents compared a covertly captured image of a man leaving Burger Mania. His hair was longer than in the realty photo, and he had a bit of beard growth, but it was him, and in this more recent photo, Fritz was exactly as Allie had described. Right down to the black hip-length jacket with visible wool at the collar and large rectangular pockets on the chest.

"Jordyn sent me that," Kia said. "He came in a few times and was really nice at first. Typical for an older guy. Jordyn's beautiful, smart, kind. *Was*," she corrected herself, eyes filling with tears.

"Take your time," Max encouraged.

Jocelyn passed a box of tissues in Kia's direction.

The room was silent around them, all eyes on the girl with information everyone wanted.

Kia pressed a tissue to her nose and settled her breaths. "She took his order once, and they talked while the kitchen prepped whatever it was that he paid for. He kept coming back after that, but instead of sitting at the tables or stepping aside, he lingered, always wanting her time and attention. She started taking her breaks to avoid him, but he'd stick around, drinking coffee and waiting until she had to go back to the register. Then he'd approach her. Eventually, he asked her out. It was like he couldn't see she was ghosting him. She turned him down politely, but it didn't stop him. He kept coming in, hanging around, watching her. Then he asked her out again a couple weeks ago. She'd had it with all the nights of feeling uncomfortable because of him. She said it was like she was being punished for ever having that first conversation."

"She said no again?" Max guessed.

Kia nodded. "Yeah. He really creeped her out."

"Wait a minute," Jocelyn said. She scooted to the edge of the couch, tears dried and her husband's handkerchief clutched in her hands. "I remember this. A couple weeks ago, Jordyn told me about an older man who asked her out at work. I told her to report him for making her uncomfortable, and to tell him to shove off!" Jocelyn turned wide eyes on the agents. "He was pushy the second time. Didn't want to take no for an answer. He told her, 'C'mon, give me a chance.'" Jocelyn covered her mouth, tears spilling freely again. "She was firm, like I told her. She told him to pay attention. Her answer was no, and it wouldn't change. When he kept going, she asked if his brain was on the fritz. Like his name."

Her husband pulled her back, his expression crumbling now. Strength gone.

Max thanked them, told them they'd been helpful, but warned them that this Fritz guy might just be a witness and not involved. He didn't want any of them going for vigilante justice, after all.

Max passed his business card to Kia. Then he and Axel let themselves out.

They'd identified a prime suspect. Now they just had to find him.

Chapter Seven

Allie added a second swipe of mascara to her lashes and drove the lip-gloss wand around her red lips once more. She'd changed into her most flattering pair of jeans and chosen a fitted red turtleneck to accent the work she'd been doing at the gym. Max had caught her off guard at the mall, but not tonight. Tonight, she was determined to give him the same thrill he'd given her at the sight of him. Even after all these months apart, one look at Max sent her back to the moments of their early days together. Butterflies in the stomach. Heat in her chest and cheeks. And damn it all, he knew her secret. He was trained to see the subtle changes that broke like fireworks against her fair, freckled skin.

Her heart hammered at the memory of his nearness. His strong, authoritative voice. His broad, sexy chest. Muscular arms and hands that knew exactly what she liked. She'd imagined kissing his lips a thousand times since he'd walked away from her at the mall. Heard his sweet whispers against her ear. Felt the warmth of his embrace. As if he was still hers.

As if he'd ever *really* been hers.

But today, like every day before, he'd left to go to work. Max was who he was, and he was unwavering in his quest to save the world, one case at a time. She and Max Jr. were just two people in a country of millions, and her ex-husband had been purposed with protecting the masses.

Allie had realized, too late, that she'd been selfish to expect more from him. He'd made it clear when they met that his life wasn't his own. His time and attention weren't his to give freely. He had a gift and a calling. And they weren't to her.

She forced away the hollow feeling that always accompanied those thoughts, and tidied the house with increased fervor. Most of the decor at her new place had once been at their shared home in Traverse City, but she'd taken everything when she'd left. Max had insisted on it. While it'd hurt her to think he didn't want anything from their life together, Max had been convinced the move would be easier on their son this way. He'd thought Max Jr. should be surrounded by as many familiar things as possible.

That was one more thing about her ex-husband. He wasn't greedy. Wasn't cruel or jealous, inconsiderate or needy. Max was honorable and compassionate, fair and unwavering. He was everything she'd ever wanted in a partner and more, but he was also something she couldn't have anticipated and wasn't ready to accept. Max was already spoken for. Already wholly committed to the US government and general population.

The oven dinged, turning her toward the kitchen. Max Jr. would be up from his nap soon, and Allie had plenty to do before kissing his precious cherub face again.

She'd prepared Max's favorite meal in anticipation of his arrival, and she'd enjoyed every minute of it. Allie loved to cook, but she hadn't had cause to prepare anything more significant than a variety of soups, sandwiches and salads since moving to Grand Rapids. Cooking for one was borderline depressing, so she'd eaten at her parents' house more often than not. Once Max Jr. had a few more teeth, she planned to revisit some of her old favorites in the kitchen.

For now, she concentrated on the baked ziti assembled in her favorite glass baking dish. She'd already boiled the pasta and browned the ground beef, then layered them with tomato sauce, Parmesan and shredded mozzarella cheese. She slid the dish into the oven to warm up and melt the cheese and set the timer, then sliced a loaf of bread from the local bakery and loaded it with butter and garlic. The bread would go in after the ziti came out.

Allie took a long breath and centered herself. Max had never come for dinner at her new home, but he was coming tonight.

The doorbell rang, and her heart leaped. "He's here," she whispered. "Be cool."

She peeked outside before opening the door, a habit Max had instilled in her when they were dating and insisted upon until it had become second nature.

He caught her gazing through the window and smiled.

"Come in," she said, pulling the door wide and hurrying him inside. "It's freezing out there. How are you? I'm glad you're here." She bit her lip to keep from rambling. "Good day?"

Max watched her for a long beat, humor twisting his lips and something more intense flashing in his eyes. "I'm doing better now. Thanks for the invitation."

She nodded. "Dinner's in the oven. Can I get you something to drink while it bakes?" She frowned. "I didn't think to ask if you have to go out again tonight.

I could've had everything ready when you got here." It wasn't uncommon for Max to be called away at any moment, but it was also highly unusual for him to be on time. "Are you on a dinner break?"

"Unless there's a major change in the case, or another bombing—" he grimaced "—I don't have to leave until morning." He grinned. "You know what I mean."

Allie felt her smile rise. "Make yourself comfortable. I'll pour some coffee." She knew Max liked a good cup more than a cocktail or wine, and she'd bought a specialty blend earlier just for his visit.

She kept an eye on him as he made a loop through the living room. The adjoining kitchen was separated by only a small island, allowing her to watch and evaluate his reaction to her home. Each time they'd gotten together for his visitation with Max Jr., Allie had met him somewhere between the two homes, to save him the added travel time.

She filled a pair of mugs with coffee while Max admired new photos of their son, then paused before a wall of framed images. Including many of himself.

Allie had created a gallery collection along the far wall. Max in his military dress uniform. Max in fatigues. Max kissing her at their wedding ceremony. Max holding their newborn at the hospital. And Max with the TCD. She'd included plenty of framed selfies from their little family's early days, and images of Max Jr. as he grew. "I thought it was important for Max Jr. to see you every day," she said, heading back to the living room with a mug of coffee in each hand. "And to see we were happy once. A subtle reminder that he was made with love."

Max accepted the mug, brows furrowed, scrutinizing.

His specialty. "I didn't realize you still had these photos of me in the military. Or of me and the TCD."

"We're proud of you," she said. "Of who you are and what you do. Whatever else happens in your life or ours, Max Jr. and I are always proud. Keeping the pictures on display is like having a piece of you here, even when the rest of you can't be." Kind of like Max's suggestion she keep all of their things in the divorce. "Consistency is key."

Max watched her, probably seeing through the forced nonchalance. Probably sensing her desire to reach for him. To tell him she loved him despite everything, and that she always would. Hopefully, not reading her more private thoughts about some of the things she missed the most.

"I'm sorry," he said suddenly, his eyes searching hers. "I realized a while ago that I never said that, and I should have."

Allie's breath caught. Her heart thundered. "Yeah?"

He dipped his chin infinitesimally. "I let you down. You and I were a team, and I dropped the ball when it counted. You deserved more. I'm sorry."

She opened her mouth to tell him it was okay, everything worked out, or something equally encouraging, but that wasn't true. And she and Max never lied to one another. "Thank you."

His deep brown eyes crinkled at the sides in warmth and acceptance. "That was easy."

She shrugged. "It means a lot to hear you say, and I appreciate it."

His dead-sexy smile spread, and she felt her bones begin to melt.

A small coo rose through the speaker of the baby mon-

itor on the coffee table, breaking the mood and sending
Allie back a step.

"May I?" Max asked, already moving toward the hallway to the bedrooms. He paused at the edge of the room,
awaiting her permission.

She nodded. "Sure. First door on the left. Thanks."

Allie escaped to the kitchen and traded her coffee for
a glass of iced water, then moved the baked ziti to the
countertop before sliding the bread into the oven.

"There's my little man," Max said. His voice echoed
through the monitor on the coffee table.

Max Jr. babbled and laughed. "Dada."

Allie froze. Her heart swelled, and her eyes stung unexpectedly. She shut the oven door and inched toward
the monitor. Max Jr. had been calling her and both her
parents Dada for days, but it was the first time Max had
heard it.

"Dada," their toddler repeated. "Dada. Dada."

"That's right," Max said, his voice full of awe and
gravel. "I'm your daddy, and I've missed you so much."

Allie drifted to the living room, eyes glued on the little
monitor, its lights dancing with every sound in the nursery. Grainy images of Max and their son filled the tiny
screen. She lifted the device and pressed it to her chest,
savoring the moment.

"I hope you've been taking good care of your mama,"
Max said. "She's tough, but that doesn't mean she can't
use some help from time to time. Like, maybe, after your
naps, you can clean up around here. Do your laundry or
grab the car keys and bring home the groceries."

Allie smiled, and a tear slid over her cheek as Max
changed Max Jr.'s diaper, narrating the process in a silly
voice. The idea her little boy would ever be old enough

to borrow the car was both surreal and bittersweet. The idea Max wouldn't be at her side to worry until their baby got back safely was just sad.

The sound of Max's footfalls echoed in the short hall, and she set the monitor aside. She returned to the kitchen, then filled her son's lidded cup with milk. Hopefully he liked ziti as much as his father; otherwise, it would be peanut butter and jelly for Max Jr. tonight. Probably with vanilla yogurt and sliced strawberries on the side.

Max appeared as she ferried the glass baking dish to the trivet on the table. "Something smells like heaven."

"Garlic bread," she said, turning back to the oven. "And baked ziti." She stole a look over her shoulder, watching as Max strapped their son into his high chair, then dropped a kiss on his head.

Max Jr. grabbed the sippy cup she'd placed on his tray and began to drink immediately while Max stroked their son's generous curls. Their baby was perfect and beautiful, an image of Allie and Max combined. Light brown skin and hazel eyes, the sweetest loose brown curls, and a smile to light up any room.

Allie fought the urge to cry tears of contentment and joy. If only this could be her reality every night.

Chapter Eight

Max collected the plates stacked beside the sink, then set the table while Allie tossed a salad and cut some ziti into small pieces for Max Jr. It was nice moving around the kitchen with her like old times. They'd always had such an effortless flow together, and he'd missed it more than he'd realized. He tried not to read into the fact she'd made his favorite meal, but it was nice that she remembered. Or maybe she made baked ziti every night these days. He couldn't be sure.

Still, what if she'd looked forward to this all day, too? He'd practically run to the hotel to wash up and change before coming over. Axel, always his roommate on trips like these, had taunted him mercilessly for his nerves. Then Max had circled the block twice, killing time so he wouldn't arrive too early or rush her.

Now that he was here, with her and Max Jr., he wasn't sure how he'd be able to leave. He didn't expect to go to work tonight, so the visit wouldn't have to be rushed, but no amount of time would be enough to make the good-bye any easier. Max Jr. had grown so much since he'd last seen him. His little face had changed, filled out and matured. He was no longer a baby. Max Jr. was a toddler, and he could say *dada*. Max's heart gave a heavy thump at the memory. Thankfully, his son hadn't forgotten him. But how long would it be before he did?

"Everything okay?" Allie asked, taking a seat at the head of the table and dropping a napkin onto her lap.

"Perfect," he said. "Thank you for inviting me and for cooking. I'd reciprocate if I could."

She nodded. "Anytime, Max."

If only he really could reciprocate. But that time had passed. He'd blown his chance with Allie, and the devastation returned to him full force. It'd taken months of burying himself in his work to get past it the first time. To convince himself not to call her when he'd had a hard day or heard their wedding song on the radio.

"So how's it going?" she asked. "With the case. A productive first day?"

Max cleared his throat and lowered into the seat to her right. "Actually, yes," he said, trying not to stare too long or hard at her soft curls, full lips or flushed skin. "I'm not one hundred percent certain, but my gut says we've identified the bomber. And I think he's the man you described seeing on the night of the Burger Mania explosion." He shifted to slide his phone from the pocket of his jeans, then accessed the image provided by Jordyn's roommate. "Does he look familiar?"

Allie took the phone and examined the image. "I think that's him." Her hazel eyes widened as she pulled her gaze from the phone to Max, then back. "Same coat. The hair looks right. The beard. I didn't get a great look at his face last night, but the posture and everything else feels like the guy I saw."

Max set the phone on the table. "He's our prime suspect. We haven't been able to find him for questioning, but I think you should see that sketch artist as soon as possible."

"I met with a sketch artist this afternoon. The image was being finalized when I headed home to make dinner," she said, eyebrows rising. "I was glad to help, but your gut is rarely wrong." Allie had always said his instincts were the reason she didn't worry as much as someone else in her position might have. She trusted him and respected what he did. "Who is he?"

"Fritz O'Lear. He was a real-estate agent at the Ramsey Realty office for a while, then left a few months back, frustrated over his poor performance and taunted by a fellow Realtor for low sales numbers. He was rejected twice by a young Burger Mania employee he made uncomfortable, then asked out on a date. The girl and the Realtor who'd given him the hardest time were both casualties."

"Sounds like your guy," Allie said. "Have you found any other possible suspects?"

"Not yet, but Opaline vowed to dig back to preschool if needed." He smiled unintentionally.

Allie joined him. "Opaline isn't to be trifled with. She'll probably come back with his elementary school report cards and Little League photos."

Max laughed, both proud of his coworker and incredibly thankful she didn't have reason to dig into him.

"How is Opaline?" Allie asked. "I always liked her. She's so positive and congenial."

"She hasn't changed, still all sunshine until her sister speaks." That little mystery had been a topic of more than one conversation between Max and Allie. An unsolved mystery he was glad to leave alone since the women were both his teammates, and it wasn't wise to know more than any of them wanted.

"I hope they get that worked out soon."

Max Jr. shoved bits of pasta into his mouth with both fists, his spoon already tossed aside.

Allie wiped his sauce-covered cheeks and fingers with her napkin and gave him an adoring smile. "Do you think this Fritz O'Lear is on the run or plotting another attack?"

Max forked another bite of homemade heaven, inhaling the tangy scent of tomato sauce and the rich, salty aroma of melted cheese. "I've been asking myself the same question all day."

She seemed to consider his answer. "The man I saw was completely unfazed by the fire, the screams, the plume of ghastly smoke." Allie wet her lips and glanced at Max Jr., then leaned in Max's direction. "I think he liked what he saw."

Max stilled. He'd always appreciated Allie's interest in his cases. She was incredibly insightful, and sometimes riffing theories with her was more productive than the work he did with his team. Something about a change of setting, maybe. But he suspected it was Allie's ability to ask the right questions and ferret out the thoughts he sometimes lost in the deluge of information.

Allie had once dreamed of being an investigative reporter, but she'd given that up long before he'd met her. And as much as Allie clearly still enjoyed working the puzzle pieces of an investigation into one neatly defined picture, he knew she'd never take any unnecessary risk now. Not with Max Jr. relying on her, and Max respected that.

"I'm afraid you're right," Max admitted. "He fits the profile of someone who's been rejected and pushed around long enough to have a lengthy list of perceived offenders. And clearly he's snapped. He might plan on punishing a lot more people."

"You always say bombers are in it for the power and control."

"Something they've usually never had," he said.

Allie frowned. "Power is intoxicating, especially to an underdog."

Max nodded. She was absolutely right. And when the underdog came unhinged, their power became incredibly dangerous.

"What's on the agenda for tomorrow?" Allie asked. "Anything I can do to help?"

"No. Meeting with the sketch artist was great. Now I just need you and Max Jr. to lie low and stay safe. The TCD is waiting for more information from Opaline. Until then, we'll keep working any leads we can get. No one we've spoken to had a personal connection to O'Lear, so we're running blind. We've been to his home and both crime scenes, so we've lost the element of surprise."

Allie cringed. "If he thinks you're closing in on him, he'll work faster or retaliate. They always go full bananas when they feel cornered."

He set his fork beside the freshly emptied plate and wiped his mouth with a napkin, utterly content. "Right again." Inwardly, he smiled, warmed by the idea that Allie was acting as if she were part of the team, trying to help out.

"Any idea who the next target could be? Maybe your team can offer them protection while you hunt the bomber."

Max grinned.

"What?" Allie's cheeks reddened.

"You've got a big heart, and you would've made a hell of a reporter."

She pushed a bite of pasta into her mouth and dragged her attention back to their son. "Thanks."

The evening passed in a blur. Hours were gone in minutes, and Max carried his sleeping son to bed at ten, limp and drooling in his arms. He stroked Max Jr.'s piles of sweet-scented curls and wished for more nights like tonight. Then he returned to Allie in the living room.

Max hadn't fought her when she'd served the divorce papers, because he'd known she was right. She and Max Jr. deserved more than a part-time husband and father. They'd argued about it—a lot—leading up to her giving him an ultimatum. His job or his family. He'd put off that decision so long that she filled in the blank herself. He chose the job. It hadn't felt like a conscious choice at the time. He'd known he was needed at the FBI and by the TCD. His happiness had been a necessary sacrifice for the number of lives he'd saved since then.

Funny how he'd once thought losing his leg was the worst thing he'd ever go through.

She leaned against the doorway, watching as he returned. "I'm glad you came tonight."

"Me, too." He smiled.

"Good." She cast a pointed gaze at the clock. "I'm guessing you have an early day tomorrow."

"I do." And he knew that raising Max Jr. on her own meant that she would have to rise early, too. "I should probably get going." He threaded his arms into the sleeves of a well-worn leather bomber and tugged a knit cap over his head. "Can I see you tomorrow?"

Allie's mouth opened, then shut. A smile spread, and she nodded. "We'd like that."

"Then I'll be here. I'll call if anything comes up, or if I'm running late." He reached for the door when she didn't move to let him out.

"Wait." She wet her lips and searched his eyes. "Stay," she said softly. Her shoulders tensed, and a measure of worry clouded her eyes. "Don't go."

"What?" He felt his brows furrow as confusion and hope battled in his heart. "You want me to stay. Here?"

"It makes sense," she said, pursing her pretty red lips and crossing her arms. "Why go to a hotel when you can stay here? You'll get extra time with Max Jr. before you have to leave town. The food is definitely better than whatever they're serving at the hotel café, and the company's not bad. I can make up the couch for you. I know you have a go bag in your truck with at least two days' worth of work clothes."

Max's eyes never left hers as he stripped out of his coat and pulled off his hat, then set the pair gently on the arm of the nearby couch. A strange tension formed in his core.

Allie stepped forward slowly, only breaking their locked gaze when she wrapped her arms around his torso and pressed her cheek to his chest.

He curved protective arms around her, exactly where they belonged, and he breathed in the scent of her skin, perfume and hair. He savored her warmth and the rhythm of her heartbeat against his core. "How about I make breakfast for us tomorrow? A thank-you for the delicious dinner and use of your couch."

She laughed. "Deal. Max Jr. loves scrambled eggs. Lots of cheese. I prefer veggies."

"Done."

Her eyes were glossed with unshed tears as she released him. "I'll get some blankets and pillows for the couch."

She hurried away, and Max stared after her.

The tension he'd noted in his core suddenly began to feel a lot like hope. For what, he wasn't sure, but it'd been a long time since he'd had any hope, and he planned to hold on to it as long as he could.

Chapter Nine

Allie woke to the sound of her alarm for the first time in two years. She hadn't slept especially well during her pregnancy or any night since, and the sensation of waking without Max Jr.'s help was slightly disconcerting. She stopped the alarm, waiting for her son to call out, but there was a distinct silence in her home, save for some shuffling from the living room.

The previous day rushed back with an adrenaline slap. Max was in town. In her home. Right down the hall.

She jerked upright, then darted out of bed and raced for the shower. Thirty harried minutes later, she was as fresh and calm as possible, given the fact she was about to see Max again.

Allie padded barefoot toward the kitchen, following the delightful sounds of her baby's laughter and inhaling the rich, cheesy scent of scrambled eggs and her blessed morning coffee. Max came slowly into view around the corner, their son on one hip as he danced and sang to "Purple Rain" by Prince. His strong, protective arms held him tight as they dipped and turned. Black pants accentuated Max's fit physique. His gray sweater clung to the toned curves of his chest and biceps.

His phone was plugged into her dock on the counter, a

familiar playlist lifting from its speaker. The baby monitor was dark, powered off, beside the dock.

Max Jr. laughed and smacked his daddy's chest with chubby, gleeful palms.

Max caught hers a moment later, not at all surprised by her presence. "Good morning." His gaze traveled slowly over her, steadily raising her temperature. "This guy gets up almost as early as his daddy."

She shuffled forward, making a memory of the scene before her, not realizing how many similar moments she'd too easily forgotten. "Don't pretend you slept."

"What?" Max asked. "Just because I'm at least a foot longer than that couch?"

She crossed her arms and leaned a hip against the counter. "Because you don't sleep. We haven't been apart so long that I've forgotten how you are while on a case." Allie peeked over her shoulder, into the living area behind her.

Max had folded up the blankets and stacked his pillow neatly on top, but a coffee mug, two empty water bottles and a stack of papers cluttered the coffee table beside his open laptop. He must've brought that in from his SUV after she went to bed, along with the change of clothes he was wearing and his toiletries. There was no denying he'd had a shower, or that he'd used his favorite soaps and cologne. Both scents were far more delicious-smelling than anything on the stovetop.

Max carried their son to his high chair and strapped him securely in, then went to plate the eggs he'd scrambled. "I stayed in touch with the team in case of new developments."

"Trying to locate Fritz O'Lear and determine his next target?" she guessed, moving into the kitchen.

"That's about it." Max smiled.

Allie kissed Max Jr.'s chubby cheeks and stroked his soft curls. Then she poured a mug of coffee from the fresh pot. "Any luck?"

"No, but I'm more familiar with the case now. A very good thing," Max said.

Allie agreed. "Everything smells amazing," she said. "Thank you for this. Max Jr. and I usually just have fruit and cereal."

Max ferried their plates to the table, setting his and Allie's across from one another, with Max Jr.'s in between.

Allie watched her ex-husband closely, missing him and mornings like these more than she'd realized. "How are you holding up with this case?" she asked. "You don't get a lot of bombers. And I mean you personally, not the team—how are you really doing?"

Max's gaze flicked to her. He sat straighter, forearms on the table. "You're the only one who's asked that."

"Everyone else is wondering," she said. "They don't want to be rude or overstep."

"Not you," he said, expression blank but searching.

"No. Not me." Allie softened her tone, not wanting to push Max, but needing him to understand he mattered. Not just his physical safety, but his feelings, too. His mental and emotional health were important and valuable. Max was more than a conduit or tool to reach an objective. He was human. And he'd once been her human. "I'm more concerned about how you're doing than my manners. You're dealing with memories your team members aren't, and you're carrying a burden they don't understand. I want to know you're okay."

"I'm okay."

She smiled. "Just like that?" she asked. "It's not a sign of weakness to admit this is hard for you, Max."

His jaw set. "It's my job to carry on without letting my feelings get in the way."

She would've laughed if it wasn't so heartbreaking. He'd been on a case when she'd served him with divorce papers. She hadn't planned that, but the TCD went where it was needed, when it was needed. Max included. He'd stayed the course. Caught the bad guy, then moved out after he'd come home. "No, I guess you don't."

"That's not what I meant."

"I know," she said. "It's okay." She lifted her fork and ate every bite of her eggs without another word. Determined to keep her tongue busy before she said something she'd regret.

She and Max were lucky to have an amicable divorce. Most people only dreamed of a relationship as civil as theirs eight months out. "I just want you to be happy, healthy and cared for," she said, the minute her breakfast was gone. "You spend all your time caring for others. Someone has to make sure you're also taking care of you."

His sour expression loosened. "I'm okay, Allie." He reached for her hand across the table, then curled his fingers around hers. "This is my job, and I'm good at it. I'm probably feeling all the ways you think I am, but I don't want to talk about it."

One more thing that hadn't changed. Max had always told her his pain kept him vigilant.

His phone buzzed, and he released her to retrieve it from his pocket.

Allie recognized Axel's face as Max swiped the screen to life. "Go on. Take the call. I'll clean up."

Max ducked into the living room, tidying the coffee table as he spoke with his friend and supervisor.

Allie cleared the breakfast table, then refilled her coffee while she waited.

When Max returned, his expression was one of regret and anticipation. "I have to go."

She unfastened Max Jr. from the high chair and passed him to Max for a kiss, then hugged him against her hip when Max returned him. "We'll walk you to the door."

Max donned his coat and hat, then paused to look at Allie and Max Jr.

The familiar tug of hope and fear churned in her core. "Be safe."

"Always." He leaned in to kiss their son once more, then stroked Allie's cheek. "Please stay home from the mall today. We don't know who else could be on this guy's hit list, and there are a lot of people working where you do. Any one of them could be a target, which would put you in danger. I can't live with that."

Allie pressed her lips tight, aching to heed his warning, without behaving too rashly. Grand Rapids was a big town, and there was no reason to assume the mall would ever become a target, let alone the specific area near her kiosk. "I can work on custom orders and invoicing from home, but when that's all caught up, I have to make new sales if I'm going to stay afloat. I can't stay here indefinitely."

"Give me seventy-two hours," he said. "Or as much time as you can. That's all I'm asking."

"I'll try."

A slow smile of satisfaction spread across his face. "See you again tonight."

She smiled. "I'll cook. All you have to do is show up,

preferably uninjured." She set a palm against his strong jaw and rose onto her toes, then pressed a kiss to his cheek.

Max lifted her hand from his cheek and pressed a kiss against her fingertips. "See you tonight."

MAX'S HEART BEAT hard and fast as he drove away from Allie's house, heading back to the TCD's temporary headquarters at the Grand Rapids Police Department. Axel had called the team together for a morning meeting, and Max didn't want to miss anything. He clutched the wheel and concentrated on the roads as he pressed the gas pedal with more purpose, images of his perfect little boy and beautiful ex-wife flashing warmly in his mind. He needed to locate and apprehend Fritz O'Lear before he hurt anyone else. *Before he injures or kills someone else's child or loved one.*

The woman at the police department desk buzzed Max through the locked security door before he had a chance to stop and raise his badge.

Most of the team was already in place as he entered the conference room. Anticipation was palpable in the air.

Axel met Max at the front of the long table, dressed in a gray suit and holding a massive disposable cup of coffee. "How was breakfast?"

"Excellent. I made it." Max fought a smile. He'd told Axel he was staying at Allie's last night when Axel texted, wanting to meet him at the hotel bar. The confession had resulted in a long, slow whistle from Axel.

Axel waited for additional information. He raised the giant cup to his lips when the details didn't come. "So you'll be back at the hotel tonight?"

Max's traitorous lips twitched. "No."

He stepped around Axel, then took a seat.

Axel narrowed his eyes. "Interesting." He lowered into the chair across from Max, keeping close watch on his friend.

Max frowned at Axel's summarization. "It's definitely that."

There had been moments this morning when he'd felt certain there was something more still there between Allie and him, but he couldn't be sure or allow himself to dwell. Not now. Not when there was a bomber on the loose, and Max needed his head in the game.

The remaining members of their team filtered in, filling the last few chairs around the table.

Rihanna pulled the door shut behind them. "Good morning. Glad to see everyone's here." She lifted a remote and pointed it at the large projector screen. "Let's go ahead and get started."

The screen lit, and Opaline appeared. She waved and smiled. Her hot-pink lips parted, exposing a wide set of perfect white teeth. "Hello! Good morning," she said. "I hope some of you managed to get a little sleep last night. I didn't." She laughed, then lifted a bowl-sized coffee mug into view. "How about we recap before moving forward? You guys first."

The team members took turns sharing theories and tidbits they'd unearthed about the victims' lives.

Selena took the initiative to sum up the offerings. "So I think we were on the right track yesterday, by assuming this is a vengeance mission. He's targeting people he thinks did him wrong."

Carly tapped her pen against her chin, nodding as Selena spoke. She turned her attention to the team when Selena finished. "I've seen this pattern of behavior a lot.

It's a top motivator in cases involving poison. On the surface, poisonings and bombings seem incredibly different, but their perpetrators are often very similar. In both types of crimes, the killer often sees him-or herself as an underdog. They make a deadly power play from a distance that keeps them safe."

"Agreed," Opaline said, pointing a lime-green fingernail at the camera. "Good. I love it when we're single-minded." She clicked her mouse a few times, then looked back at the camera. "I was able to dig up some details on Fritz O'Lear."

The team shifted, collectively, eager for whatever she'd unearthed. According to their shared thoughts and input, none of them had had any more luck than Max last night.

Opaline smiled, and the team's phones began to buzz. "I just sent you everything I have. It's not a lot, but it's more than we had last night, and I'm confident there will be more to come as this day moves forward. These details have been brought to you by a steady stream of energy drinks and the legendary Lopez tenacity."

Max opened the message and read the brief bullet-point list. Distant family members. Hobbies, including bowling and billiards. "This is a good start, Opaline."

He stood to address the table, unable to be still any longer. "Let's break this list down, split up and move out. We need photos of O'Lear posted at every local pool hall and bowling alley. We'll reach out to the distant family members and try to come away with more leads from each stop. Someone knows where this guy is, and we need to find him. Today."

Chapter Ten

Max followed Axel up the cracked walkway to Fritz O'Lear's building once more. Again the neighborhood was quiet, everyone likely kept inside by the cold. "If he doesn't answer this time, let's knock on some other doors. See what the neighbors think of him." And maybe enlist the local PD in surveilling the man's home until he showed up.

Axel stopped on the small stoop and waved to a man, visible through the cruddy double-paned security window. "Agreed."

Hopefully, the residents would talk. Convincing neighbors, family or friends to share information with law enforcement wasn't always as easy as it should be, and even when people opened up, there was the matter of confirming their tales. Some people were honest and helpful, but others held back for a variety of reasons. Fear of retaliation by the criminal in question or of being flagged as a narc were common holdups, as well as an unfortunate and misguided distrust of officials.

Feelings of allegiance to the suspect were the toughest to get past. It was sometimes hard to convince a friend or family member that their loved one could've been involved in any illegal activity. And on the flip side, there were folks who knew absolutely nothing about the person or problem at hand but intentionally tied up the investigation with all sorts of unfounded stories and blatant lies. Some of those folks were bored, lonely and desperate for the attention. Others were simply troublemakers.

The old man inside the building inched closer to the window, peering back at the agents. Confusion crumbled his bushy salt-and-pepper brows. "Who are you? What do you want?" he asked through the door.

Axel raised his badge. "FBI."

The man squinted at the badge, then swung his attention from Axel to Max. He seemed to weigh his options before deciding to do the right thing.

The door clicked open, and the man cocked his head. "Is that thing real?"

"Yes." Axel stepped forward, pushing his way inside.

The man fumbled to get out of the way, eyes wide. "What's going on?" His hands were full of envelopes and flyers. One of the doors in the bank of mailboxes was open. He hurried around to close and lock it.

Max did his best to look authoritative without intimidating the older gentleman. "Thanks for letting us in. It's getting cold out there."

"What's this about?" the man asked. "What happened?"

"We're Special Agents Morrow and McRay," Axel explained, tapping his chest, then pointing to Max. "Have you lived here long?"

The man furrowed his bushy brows. "Seven years in September."

"Do you know many of the people in this building?" Max asked.

"Most." He fixed his appraising gaze on Max. "Almost

everyone by face, if not by name." He clutched his mail protectively against a baggy Mr. Rogers–style cardigan. Khaki pants hung askew on his slight frame, and Max wondered if the man had lost weight or been given the too-large clothes. He hated the thought of his father or grandfather living in a run-down building like this one.

"I'm Max." He offered the man a hand. "You live here with your family?"

"No. They're all gone now. My Ellie passed in February '03. Kids are grown, living all around the country. No one's in Michigan. Everyone's busy. I'm Henry."

Max smiled. "Nice to meet you, Henry."

He pushed heavy-framed glasses up his narrow nose, magnifying milky blue eyes. "Is someone here in trouble? Or are they on the run?"

"Maybe neither," Max said.

Henry made a derisive sound. "The government doesn't send two big hulks like you out to look for someone who's not in trouble or on the run."

Max grinned despite himself. Neither he nor Axel was considered especially large in their circle, but compared to the man before them, reaching for five-eight, Henry's assessment was one he couldn't argue with. "Do you know the man in apartment 325?"

"O'Lear," Henry said, looking proud.

"That's right. You know Mr. O'Lear?" Max asked, pulling his phone from an interior coat pocket.

"No." Henry pointed to the mailboxes, each with a different last name.

Axel smiled.

Max brought up the photo of O'Lear from the real-estate ad. "Is this him?"

Henry squinted and stared. "Maybe, but he doesn't look like that now, if it's the guy I'm thinking of."

Max flipped to the grainier, more distant shot of O'Lear leaving Burger Mania. "How about him?"

"That's the guy," Henry said, raising his eyes to meet Max's. "He looks like that now. I never saw him looking the other way, like a shiny penny. Like you two. I'd remember."

Max laughed. He'd been called a lot of things, never shiny or a penny.

Axel craned his head for a pointed look up the staircase. "Is Mr. O'Lear home now? Any chance you've seen him today?"

"No. Come to think about it, I haven't seen him since he had that argument with the super." Henry rubbed his chin and jawline. "That's been a day or two. I can't be sure. Sometimes I get fuzzy when it comes to time."

The sound of an old-fashioned telephone interrupted, and Henry pulled a large flip phone from his pocket. He frowned at the number on the screen. "Speaking of losing time. This is my doctor's office. If I miss another appointment, they're going to charge me for not canceling." He raised the phone to his ear and wrinkled his nose.

"Thanks, Henry." Axel moved toward the stairs. "I'm going to take a look. Maybe you missed him."

"Hello?" Henry answered the call.

Max handed Henry a business card. "Thank you for your time," he said quietly. "If you need anything else, or think of something you want to tell us, call."

Max followed Axel to apartment 325 and waited while he knocked. As predicted, no answer.

They parted ways from there. Axel moved to the next door. Max went to the second floor. More than an hour later, they were back at the first-floor mailboxes, with Henry in tow. Max had unintentionally brought him out again by knocking on his apartment door. From there, Henry made introductions. He started with his name and apartment number, then introduced Max. The residents were chattier and visibly more at ease with Henry's company than when Max had knocked alone, so he kept him on the case.

"Anything?" Axel asked, already waiting for Max.

"Not really." Max rested his hands on his hips. "Of the people who answered, and admitted to recognizing O'Lear's name or photo, all I learned was that he was quiet. Kept to himself."

Axel nodded. "Same here. Most folks didn't want to talk, but the ones who did all said he seemed like a nice guy."

Henry stood taller. "You should've had me come along on all the interviews. Folks liked talking to me, and you know, that's what they say about the serial killers. They all seemed like nice guys."

Axel dragged his gaze from Henry to Max. "You took him on the interviews?"

Max smiled.

"Is he a serial killer?" Henry pressed. "I hope not. That guy had a temper."

Max took a beat to process the information. "He was arguing with your building superintendent the last time you saw him?"

Henry nodded. "Yeah. Right out here by the mailboxes."

"What were they fighting about?"

Henry rubbed a soft wrinkled finger against his brow. "Rent, I think. He was late on payment for the month, and the super doesn't have a grace period. He's a real pain. He doesn't want to fix anything around here, but he threatens to kick us out if we're a little short or a couple days late."

"O'Lear's been out of work," Axel said, catching Max's attention over Henry's head. "Probably running through his savings, assuming he had any."

Henry left his eyebrow alone and snapped his finger. "He said he should get a break on rent because his thermostat is broken. I remember now. There aren't any breaks on rent, and I haven't seen him moving, so I figured he's staying somewhere else 'cause it's so darn cold."

Snow had begun to fall in fat, steady flakes outside the filthy security window. Wind whipped through barren limbs and bent saplings in a park across the street. It wasn't a good time for a broken thermostat.

"How long has O'Lear lived here?" Axel asked, drawing Max's attention back inside.

Henry shrugged. "Six, eight months? You sure he's not a serial killer? You guys only come out for serious stuff. Is he a fugitive? Is that your shtick?"

"No. That's the US Marshals," Axel said, sliding his eyes to Max, lips twitching with suppressed humor.

"Well, it's not as if this guy is wanted for robbing a bank," Henry said. "Anyone with money wouldn't stay here. So what is it?" He scowled and pressed a palm to his chest. "Is he a pedophile? We've got kids in this building. That isn't it, is it? He's a pedophile?"

"Not that we know of," Max said. "We think he might know something about the bombs that have detonated in Grand Rapids this week."

Henry cringed. "That's better than a pedophile. But if you're right, I'd hate to be our super." He turned his eyes to the door at the end of the hall marked 101 and also Staff.

The only door neither Max nor Axel had knocked on yet.

"Is that your superintendent's office?" Axel asked.

"Yeah, and it's his apartment, too. He has an office inside the door. Then his apartment is through another door in the office. We take our rent to him in there. He owns the building, so don't let that sign fool you. We don't have any staff."

Max strode in the door's direction, instinct propelling him across the threadbare carpets. He pounded on the door.

"He's not there," Henry said. "I saw him go out after you guys headed upstairs. He goes out every day around now, and he's gone until noon. He comes back with takeout. Then he spends the rest of his day avoiding unhappy tenants."

Axel swore under his breath. He dragged a hand through his hair, then locked gazes with Max. "I'm going to call this in. Reach out to the team. We'll stake out the building."

"Henry?" Max asked. "Will you call me when the superintendent gets back?"

"Sure." Henry patted the chest pocket of his sweater, where the top of Max's business card poked out. "I'll call you if I see the other guy, too. O'Lear. Apartment 325."

"Don't approach him," Max said. "Just let us know he's home."

Henry nodded, the color and bravado bleeding from his face. "Will do."

Max and Axel headed back to the SUV, heads down against the biting wind. Inside, and engine running, Axel adjusted the heaters, and the men sent texts with their new information to the team.

Axel's phone rang a moment later, Aria's face centering the screen. "Morrow," he said, answering the call on speaker and holding the phone in Max's direction. "I'm here with Max. What do you have?"

"I'm thinking about timing," Selena said, forgoing small talk and customary greetings. She was using Aria's phone. "Ramsey Realty was hit four days ago. Burger Mania two days ago. One day in between each. To recover. Recuperate. Gather additional materials," she rattled, "maybe just to gloat and enjoy the press coverage."

Aria's voice echoed from the background. "Bomb day. Off day. Bomb day. Off day. You know what that makes today?"

"A bomb day." The women's voices arrived in near unison.

Max's muscles tightened, and tension coiled uncomfortably in his core. "O'Lear hasn't been back here since he argued with the superintendent."

"Could he be planning to bomb the building?" Selena asked.

Max stared through the icy winter day outside his window. He'd hoped O'Lear had chosen the previous bombing times to limit collateral damage. Just after 7:00 a.m. at the realty office. After 2:00 a.m. at Burger Mania. But what if he was wrong? What if O'Lear's only consideration had been the assurance he would get his target? If he wasn't concerned about the number of additional casualties, then the entire apartment building could be in danger. "The superintendent isn't there right now," he said, turning back to Axel and the phone in his partner's hand. Determination powered his words, and a plan formed in his head. "That buys us some time, but we're going to have to move."

"I'll rally the team," Aria said. "Selena's reaching out to Carly and Rihanna now. We can be there in fifteen."

Max brought up the dial pad on his phone. "I'll get local PD out here along with the bomb squad. Contact Fire and Rescue."

"You've got it," Aria said.

"I'll sweep the building with Sergeant Sims and hope we're wrong."

"And not too late," Axel said. "It's already after ten, and according to Henry, the super gets back predictably at noon. A prime time for detonation."

AN HOUR LATER, the Grand Rapids police had located the building superintendent, William Teske, and moved him to a safe location while Max, the TCD team, first responders and the bomb squad set up outside the building in preparation for the worst.

Residents had been moved to an off-site location with plenty of heat and donated meals from a nearby café while they waited to hear if their homes blew up. Pets were caged and would be sheltered by the local animal protection organization until the building was deemed safe for everyone's return.

Overall, Max was impressed with the cooperation and efficiency of so many local agencies toward a common goal.

He was less impressed, though not at all surprised, however, by the local media's massive response. Once they'd gotten wind of the evacuation, they'd shown up in droves. News vans from all around the county had begun to arrive as residents and pets were relocated, and the reporters continually encroached on the perimeter Max had set.

Now onlookers lined streets and corners, drawn from their homes by Breaking News announcements on their televisions, radios and web browsers. Officers worked to keep everyone back, but there wasn't enough crime-scene tape in Michigan to rope off a radius as large as Max would've preferred.

Snow continued to fall, coating roads, grass and walkways as Max worked out his game plan. Flakes piled on his teammates' hats and the shoulders of their coats, no longer melting immediately from their body heat. Their cheeks were pink from the biting wind, their gloved hands shoved deep into pockets or wrapped around fast-cooling cups of tea or coffee.

The city's engineering department had provided digital blueprints of the tenement building, giving the TCD an insider's look at the bones of the structure. There were only one or two places a bomb the size of those used in the Ramsey Realty and Burger Mania attacks could be placed to maximize damage to Teske's apartment, so those would be checked first. From there, Max would widen the search range for due diligence, viewing every location where O'Lear could have planned to reach his target.

He donned his protective gear on autopilot, fighting memories of the last time he'd geared up as a US soldier, searching for a potential bomb. The EOD—Explosive Ordnance Disposal—suit was heavy, at least sixty pounds, and unbearably hot, worse in a desert region already burning at well over one hundred degrees. Images of that day returned, and his heart rate rose. Heat licked up his neck and across his cheeks despite the current icy winds.

"How you doing?" Axel asked, breaking away from the team to check on Max. The hem of his wool coat flapped in the breeze. "Need any help?"

"Nah," Max said, fastening the final strips of Velcro at his wrists and willing the panic to recede. "I'm good."

"You look flushed," Axel said. "Can I get you anything? Water?"

Max nodded. "Thanks."

Axel went in search of water, and Max pressed his eyes shut. *Pull it together, McRay*, he demanded internally. *You're in Michigan. Not Afghanistan. Now, tighten up.*

He concentrated on his breaths and brought images of Allie and Max Jr. into mind. This was his job, and he was good at it. Once he finished here, he could shower up and be with his family again, something he hadn't gotten to do twice in a row for far too long.

"Hey." Axel returned with a bottle of water and handed it to Max. "Anything else you need?"

"No." Adrenaline coursed through Max's veins as he sipped the cool liquid and scanned the scene around them once more.

This wasn't the desert. His leg was already gone. That mission was over. This one was still ahead.

"You're going to have one hell of a story for Allie tonight," Axel said, taking the nearly empty bottle when Max passed it back.

He forced a tight smile. A bead of sweat rolled over his temple. "No doubt."

Max had so much he needed to make right with Allie. He hadn't lived up to his vows or been what she deserved.

He knew that now. He'd known then, too, but he'd been too proud and stubborn to acknowledge it. The minute he'd pledged his allegiance to Allie, her needs should have come first. Above his, and before the TCD. She'd only wanted him to let her in. To include her in his decisions and travel plans. She'd wanted him to talk to her about his work, but he'd been so busy trying to keep his job and home life separate that he'd ended up being forced to choose between them. When he hadn't, she'd made the decision for him.

Max stared at the building. A possible bomb inside, waiting to explode.

And all he could think about was Allie.

A sharp whistle broke his reverie, and Sergeant Sims came into view. The local bomb-squad leader circled a finger in the air. Time to roll out.

Chapter Eleven

Sweat beaded on Max's forehead and temples as he moved onto the property, followed by two members of the Grand Rapids bomb squad in EOD suits. Mounting anxiety and the uncomfortably heavy gear worked in tandem to slow his every step. He pulled in long, steady breaths, moving through the mental techniques he'd once relied upon to get through each day. Deep inhalations through the nose, slow releases through the mouth. *Concentrate on one thing at a time*, he reminded himself. *Don't become waylaid by the big picture.*

He batted his eyes against a stinging drop of sweat, fallen from his forehead. The helmet that was part of his gear made it impractical to clear the drop properly, but Max would get by.

The crowd fell deadly silent as they watched the trio make their way up the walkway. An earlier sweep of the exterior perimeter had revealed nothing more than mounding snow and debris from local litterbugs along the building's edge.

Now it was time to move inside. He waved two gloved fingers toward the open door. With the eyes of an entire county or more on them, thanks to the abundance of news crews, cell-phone cameras and the internet, Max gave a nod, then led the men inside.

He could only hope the bomber hadn't taken notice of the hoopla yet. If he had, and he'd planted a remotely detonated device, he could end the small squad's life at will.

He and the others split up at the mailboxes. One of the men moved onto the second floor, assigned to search the zone above the superintendent's small office space and apartment. The other man descended a secondary staircase to the basement, searching the area below.

Max stopped at the door marked as 101 and Staff. Henry hadn't seen O'Lear since he'd witnessed him fighting with the superintendent, but according to Teske, O'Lear had returned early this morning, ignoring the office hours Teske said he kept but none of the other tenants seemed to know of.

O'Lear delivered the rent as Teske had demanded, which thrilled the super, but he'd had to leave O'Lear alone in the office for a few minutes. Since Teske hadn't been expecting him, he'd had to return to his adjoining apartment for his glasses and to quiet his small dog.

If there was a bomb hidden in the building, Max suspected he would find it here.

He maneuvered the small key into the lock, then twisted until he felt the tumbler roll. His breath caught and silent prayers went up as the resulting click echoed through his body. The lock had released. Max hadn't blown up. He took a quick, steadying moment, then turned the knob and slipped cautiously inside.

Foreboding churned in Max's gut as he surveyed the surroundings. A large clock on the far wall indicated the time was eleven thirty. If Max's guess on O'Lear's plan was right, Max had thirty minutes to discover and disarm a ticking bomb.

ALLIE CREPT OUT of Max Jr.'s nursery, rubbing the aching muscles in her neck and rolling her head from side to side. She'd stayed home from the mall today as promised, but had gotten very little work accomplished. Instead, she'd carried, rocked and bounced her toddler for nearly two hours while he fought his fatigue and struggled with incoming teeth.

Now that it was finally quiet, she could only hope he would rest and she could focus.

She pressed her hands against the small of her back as she headed to the kitchen, stretching the bunched muscles along her spine.

She flipped on the television, then filled a glass with water and took a seat on the couch to unwind. A news bulletin swept across the screen before her first sip, and she felt her already tense muscles go into lockdown. "Please don't be another bomb," she said, pumping the volume a little higher with her remote. "Do not let Max be in danger."

A familiar reporter appeared on-screen, an expression of undeniable concern on her face. "The apartment building at Hayes and Vine has been completely evacuated by an FBI group known as the Tactical Crime Division, or TCD."

Allie's heart rate spiked. She climbed off the couch and ghosted to the television, leaving her water on the coffee table behind her.

"Even family pets have been removed from this southside tenement, while a team of explosives experts search for Grand Rapids' third bomb."

Allie shook her head at the images before her, willing them not to be true. Crowds lined the streets outside an old yellow-brick building in a neighborhood she recognized near downtown. The door to the building gaped open.

"Sources say the FBI's TCD mobilized yesterday, deployed from the Traverse City headquarters, to investigate the two fatal bombings in Grand Rapids earlier this week. Less than twenty-four hours later, they've identified this man, Fritz O'Lear, as their prime suspect. O'Lear is believed to have had a personal connection to at least one fatally injured victim in each bombing, and records show him as a resident of the building being searched right now."

Allie's gaze fixed on the worried faces of Max's colleagues, and her heart nearly seized. Max's team was unflappable. If they were worried, she was terrified.

Allie jerked the cell phone from her back pocket and dialed her parents' number while she searched for her coat, purse and keys. "Mom?" she asked, the moment the call connected.

"I see it, baby," her mom said. "Your dad and I were just watching while we made lunch."

"I have to go," Allie said, a lump rising in her throat. "I need to be there. He's in there."

A soft knock sounded on her front door, and Allie raced to pull it open.

Her mom smiled, phone in one hand, emotion in her pale blue eyes. "Go. I'll stay with Max Jr. Your dad will bring lunch to me when it's ready."

Allie threw her arms around her mother, jammed her feet into boots, then made a run for her car, threading her arms into her coat sleeves as she hurried out.

Snow fell at an alarming rate as she barreled along city streets, racing toward the area where the news team had broadcasted. The roads were clear of ice and snow, but traffic was thick so close to lunchtime.

Allie worked to swallow and clear her head, but her heart ached with the idea she could be too late. She could lose Max, *really* lose him. And it hit her, for the first time, that she hadn't truly accepted their divorce as the end. She'd hoped that one day he'd get his head on straight and come back to her. His job was important, but so was she, so was their son, and though Max didn't seem to believe it, so was he. He could save the world and still have a family; he wasn't some tragic superhero out of a comic book.

Allie took every shortcut she could think of, scanning the radio for coverage of the situation. Instead of new information, she only received the same update on repeat. The FBI had named a bombing suspect, and they were sweeping a building right now.

Her stomach rolled as haunting images from the news returned to her. The concern on the reporter's brow. The fear in Max's teammates' eyes.

"I can't lose him," she muttered, taking another quick turn into an alleyway and darting down the pitted, unmaintained street.

When she reached the wooden barricades and shivering crowds, she parked along the curb and began to jog. "Axel!" She waved an arm overhead and yelled for her old friend as she drew near. "Axel!"

He turned, scanning the area until their eyes met. Then he began to move in her direction.

He swept the crime-scene tape high, waving off the approaching officer as Allie ducked beneath.

"Is he okay?" she asked. "What's happening?"

Axel set his hand against her back and ushered her

into the little circle of TCD members at the end of the building's walkway.

The women pulled her into a series of hugs. The comfort and ease with which they accepted her back into the fold stung her eyes and nose, and threatened to tip her over the emotional edge. She'd worried they might hate her for leaving Max, but that didn't seem to be true.

"He's doing okay," Carly assured her, keeping Allie against her side with one arm. "If anything had gone wrong, he would've contacted us."

Allie nodded. "Okay." She stared at the building, hoping Carly's words were true and willing her ex-husband to appear.

Axel shifted, turning back to the building. Selena and Aria stood with him, each statue-still. Their jaws were tight. Their backs rigid.

Allie pulled back from Carly, intuition lighting. "There's more," she accused. "There's something else. What don't I know?"

Carly didn't answer.

The others glanced her way, then went back to staring.

"Tell me," Allie demanded. "Please!" She covered her mouth, instantly horrified by the outburst.

Carly rubbed her palm up and down Allie's sleeve before stepping away to face her. "We think the bomber might've planned to detonate the device when his superintendent returned from lunch. At noon."

"Noon?" Allie raised her watch, then said a desperate prayer. It was already ten minutes till.

THE OFFICE SPACE was small and cramped. Max left the door open as he stepped inside. A battered metal desk stood on his immediate left, a rug in the center, and two plastic chairs with metal legs pressed against the opposite wall. Tall beige filing cabinets formed a row between an interior door to Teske's apartment and piles of ancient dust-covered boxes. An evacuation map of the building hung above the cabinets, mostly blocked by a massive pair of faux ferns in cracked plastic pots. A century's worth of cigarette smoke had permeated everything. The air, the walls, the rugs.

Max examined the space, imagining O'Lear coming in to deliver the rent early this morning. He extended the retractable arm on his small tactical mirror and positioned it beneath the desk. No bomb. He opened the file cabinet drawers one by one. Then checked the desk drawers, as well.

He turned in a small circle, searching, thinking. Evaluating each object.

He had eight minutes to find and disarm a bomb or die.

Instinct pulled him to the stacks of ancient boxes. The thick layer of dust on one had been disturbed, as if the box on top of it had been moved.

Max unstacked the pile quickly, removing each lid as he went, then peeking inside for good measure. When he reached the box he'd been aiming for, his gut clenched in warning.

He lifted the cardboard top gently and froze at the sight of a pressure cooker.

The cheap digital watch attached to the lid had less than four minutes before it reached zero. When that happened, Max knew, the Tannerite, undoubtedly packed into the pot, along with every manner of metal projectile, would ignite.

The airtight container would stop the blast for a fraction of a second, creating unfathomable pressure, before exploding and blowing away everything in its path. The resulting fireball would be twenty feet across, blasting thousands of nuts and bolts, nails and BBs, along with bits of the destroyed pot, through the air, like shrapnel. Through everything in sight. And for more than a hundred yards. The red-hot, impossibly sharp bits would move at up to two thousand feet per second, faster than the speed of sound, and anyone in their range would be injured before they even heard the explosion. The shock wave would be felt up to a quarter mile away.

Footfalls on the stairs echoed through the otherwise silent building, and Max backed up until he could be seen through the door. He held one hand out before him like a crossing guard stopping traffic. The pair of local bomb-squad men froze. "I found it," Max said. "There's less than three minutes on the timer." He steeled himself, then forced every bit of authority he could muster into his words. "Go. I've got this." And if he didn't, there was no reason to lose three lives instead of one.

They hesitated, looking from the door, to one another, then back to Max.

"That's an order!" he shouted, imitating the drill sergeant he'd loathed as a new soldier, then admired as a seasoned veteran. "Now!"

The men shuffled quickly away.

Max turned back to the bomb, now at under two minutes, said a silent prayer and went to work.

The watch needed to come off first. He couldn't allow the alarm to activate while still attached to the cooker. Or the Tannerite. He stripped off the bulky safety gloves, his trained and nimble fingers suddenly shaking and unsure. With only one minute and four seconds left on the clock, he gripped the watch with sweat-slicked hands, counted mentally to three, then pulled. The watch separated cleanly from the pot, instantly stopping the timer.

ALLIE WRUNG HER frozen hands and paced. It was nearly noon, and every second felt like an eternity to her panicked, aching heart. The apartment building could go up in smoke at any minute, taking Max's life with it, and she didn't think she could live through that.

She pressed a gloved hand to her mouth to stave off the nausea, and batted away tears. She had to pull herself together. No matter what happened today or any day, Max Jr. needed her, and she needed to get tough for him.

A man in a dark suit broke away from the group of uniformed officers and headed for Axel.

Allie stopped pacing to watch.

The man's grim expression sent a bead of sweat over her brow despite the ferocious cold. "Special Agent Morrow." He handed Axel his phone. "I think you should see this."

Axel accepted the device, looked it over and paled.

"What is that?" Allie asked, unable to hold her tongue. "What's going on?" Her every instinct said whatever was happening had to do with Max, and it wasn't good.

Axel returned the man's phone, then shot Allie a remorseful look.

She could see the message in his eyes, practically hear the words running through his mind, but he was too polite to say them aloud. The specifics of the operation were classified, and she was an outsider. Never a member of the TCD, and no longer Max's wife.

The truth hit like a punch to her heart.

"Look!" Carly raised a pointed finger to the building as a figure appeared in the doorway.

Allie jumped forward, then slowed as two men in protective gear rushed down the walkway toward the sidewalk. Neither man was Max.

Tears blurred her vision and spilled across her cheeks. "Where is he?" she cried. "Where!"

Carly grabbed Allie's waist and held her tight as the men arrived.

"He found the bomb," the first man reported, struggling to remove his helmet and gloves. "There was less than three minutes. He sent us out."

Allie checked her watch, fear ratcheting in her heart. It was noon.

"Stand back," a uniformed officer hollered through a bullhorn. "Move back now."

People scattered, rushing away from the yellow tape.

Axel cursed and moved forward.

Carly caught him by his arm.

Allie wanted to scream. She wanted to collapse. Why wasn't Max coming out? Why wasn't anyone going after him? What was happening?

"There he is!" Carly called. "Max!"

Allie's gaze snapped up, seeking the building and finding Max.

He strode confidently forward, the EOD helmet tucked securely under one arm, his gaze locked on hers.

She pushed her way through the group in a burst of joy, relief and awe.

He dropped his helmet and opened his arms as she launched herself at him.

Allie collided with his chest, nearly leaping into his arms, and he responded by holding her close.

He pressed his lips against her head and whispered, "I'm okay. It's okay."

She fought tears as the team filed in around them, along with at least a dozen local officials she'd never seen before and would never recognize in the future. All that mattered in that moment was that Max was all right, and they still had time to figure things out.

He held on to her as he debriefed the group on what had happened inside the building. Then she watched as Axel offered Max his cell phone.

"Local PD received this text message about four minutes ago," Axel explained.

Max accepted the device, and they looked at the screen together.

Three down, one to go. You won't be so lucky next time.
Kaboom.

"WHAT?" ALLIE LOOKED from Max to Axel, then back. "What does it mean?"

Max tightened his arm around her, pressing his fingers against her waist. "It means he isn't finished."

Chapter Twelve

Adrenaline coursed through Max's veins and lightened his head as he passed the cell phone back to Axel. Coming down from a moment like he'd just experienced inside always left him feeling slightly disoriented. He pulled Allie close once more, immeasurably thankful for her unexpected presence.

She fell easily against him, fear, relief and something deeper pooling in her eyes. She pressed her cheek to his chest, and his breaths began to settle. His heart rate started to slow. Small as she was, and fragile as she felt in his arms, Allie had always been his anchor. And the intense emotional connection flowing between them now was a drug he couldn't get enough of.

He spoke briefly with the bomb-squad captain, relaying the pressure cooker's location and pertinent details. The local team would take over from here, documenting the scene and arranging for removal and disassembly of the device. A bomb often told its maker's secrets, and Max could only hope that this one would give a hint to O'Lear's location, as well.

Max's teammates retreated, gathering near their SUVs while Max briefed the fire marshal and other officials with his findings and assessment. When he finished, his team gave him the space to say goodbye to Allie. He wanted to linger but had to hurry. He needed to get back to work before O'Lear retaliated. Max had ruined the bomber's planned attack, essentially stealing O'Lear's thunder, possibly humiliating him and making him feel exactly the same way he had when he concocted the deadly plan in the first place.

"I should go," Allie said, accurately interpreting the moment and stepping slowly away. She'd never been to a scene like this with Max before, and while her surprise presence had been momentarily comforting, he realized with a slap that it was time she got as far away from him as possible.

"Okay. Be safe," he said, glancing toward his team. "I'd better get back to work."

"Right," she said, sounding suddenly unsure. "Of course." She took a fumbling step back, hurt gathering in her eyes. "Maybe call if you won't be able to make it for dinner?"

"Of course." He nodded, scanning the crowd for signs of O'Lear and hoping that if the bomber stumbled on-site at this moment, he wouldn't understand how much Allie meant to him.

He hurried to his team with long, hungry strides, refusing to let himself look back.

Aria cringed as he approached. Selena shook her head. Axel's attention was somewhere else completely, his gaze trailing something in the distance. Max knew without asking that Axel was watching Allie. He'd keep tabs on her as long as possible, stepping in for Max when he couldn't keep her safe.

When Max turned to check his assumption, there was only a heavy crowd and line of reporters.

Allie was already gone.

The realization that his connection to her had suddenly become her biggest danger was enough to buckle his knees. How could he protect her if he couldn't get near her? And how could he make her understand his behavior today was meant to keep her safe when she'd surely see the exchange as a repeat of so many others during their married life? Of him dismissing her because work called. He could send a quick text, but what would he say? Would she see it as an excuse?

"Max?" Axel asked, prompting a response to a question Max hadn't heard.

"Yeah." Max forced himself back to the crisis at hand. "Let me pack up this suit, and I'll be ready to go."

He sloughed off his cumbersome EOD suit and freed the cell phone from his pocket to send Allie a text.

Sorry I had to run. I will be there tonight. Nothing can keep me away.

But he would be staying at the hotel moving forward. Allie's safety, and the safety of Max Jr., was top priority in Max's world. Everything else could get in line.

CARLY'S HEART WENT out to Allie as she watched her hurry away, then to Max as he rubbed the back of his neck, visibly struggling to get his head in the game. Carly understood the confliction. She'd been the agent taking lead on a case at Christmas, and she'd fallen in love in the process. Those two worlds, love and job, should never collide because it was terrifying. She'd worried for Noah as the case grew trickier, afraid something awful could happen to him because of his involvement and proximity to her. Now the tides had turned, and Noah was the one constantly worried about her every time she was called out on a case. Relationships were tricky for everyone, but for a TCD agent in love with a civilian, relationships were downright complicated.

Max lifted his eyes to hers, catching her staring.

She smiled, and he nodded, a silent exchange that told her she wasn't off base with her deductions. He'd just single-handedly located and disarmed a bomb, at the last second, then found his ex-wife waiting for him on the sidewalk. He'd likely also realized that the bomber was watching. Which had potentially put a target on her back.

"Let's take this meeting inside, shall we?" Carly asked, speaking up while Max pulled himself together.

She tipped her head toward the row of reporters and cameras, all angling for a look at them and the bomb-squad robot being deployed. The robot was fascinating. She could admit that it was fascinating, and not something most people saw every day. The robot would collect the device and seal it inside a container to take to the lab for deconstruction. But unlike the crowd, the TCD had work to do.

The team broke up, climbing into their SUVs for a rendezvous at their temporary headquarters. They'd take notes and text updates to Rihanna from the meeting, and she would do the same in return, sending details from the scene.

Carly raised her hand to Rihanna as the SUVs pulled away from the curb. Rihanna had hit the ground running as liaison the moment she'd arrived on-site, heading into the mix of reporters and before a buzzing crowd of local residents, determined to soothe nerves and deliver accurate information before rumors led to panic.

Traffic was light through town as Carly followed the SUVs in front of her. Axel driving Max, and Aria driving Selena, who was so turned around without Blanca in tow that she'd left the hotel this morning with dog treats in her pockets. The women had laughed about it at the time, but Carly could see Selena was as eager to get home as any of them.

The Grand Rapids Police Department was a flurry of activity when Carly and the team arrived. Officers rushed in and out of the main entrance and through the secured inner lobby. Phones rang off the hook at every desk, and the white noise of walkie-talkies filled the air.

"It's like someone kicked a hornet's nest in here," Carly said, making her way down the narrow hall to the conference room.

Aria smiled, looking a bit nostalgic for her days in blue. She'd been a Traverse City cop while earning her criminal justice degree. Neither was an easy feat. Succeeding at both at once was some other-level stuff. And Aria had definitely succeeded. The rookie had taken down a drug kingpin before Director Suzuki picked her up for the TCD team. "Once this bomb hit the news, these guys were probably instantly underwater," Aria said. "Anonymous tippers, witnesses hoping to help break the case, nuts wanting attention, people afraid their building will be next."

Carly smiled. Aria was right. Chaos always came quickly after something this big went public. The Grand Rapids PD would have their hands full calming a fearful population and stopping criminals determined to take advantage of the department's increase in calls and distractions.

Rihanna would do what she could, but ultimately the

local media would make the difference in how things went from here. Unfortunately, sensationalism sold papers and gained viewers, so things typically got worse before the case was closed.

All the more reason to wrap this up ASAP. Panicky people were a danger all their own.

The team circled the conference-room table and took their seats. Axel powered up the projector and connected his laptop.

Opaline's face appeared on the screen. "Hello," she said instantly, glancing up while typing wildly on her keyboard. "Thank you for keeping me in the loop. I've got all your local news stations on my other monitors. And Rihanna is updating, as well. How are you all doing?"

The team gave a sober round of "Okays," "All rights" and "Fines."

Opaline's bright smile faltered. "Hmm." She leaned closer to the camera, stilling the room along with her. "Max," she said softly. "Can we just…?" She eased back, smile growing, and lifted her hands into view for a slow clap.

Carly smiled as Max shook his head and waved her off. Then she joined Opaline in the steady, appreciative rhythm. As did the rest of their team.

"Okay," Max said. He pushed up to stand, and the applause climbed to a crescendo before eventually coming to a stop. "Thank you," he continued. "Without all of your help, the fast action of this team and the local bomb squad, things could have gone a lot worse today." He blew out a shaky breath. "We were fortunate to get the result we did. Timing is everything right now, so we need to get back down to business or we could be a lot less lucky very soon."

Carly felt a tug of emotion in her chest as she took in his tone, expression and words. Max had done the real work today, putting the safety of others above himself. He'd overcome fear and likely some raging PTSD in the name of duty. Everyone on the team had been through tough things, but losing an appendage to a bomb, then making a career out of disarming the devices, was something completely beyond her ability to reason. She'd often thought that decision either spoke of true insanity or utter heroism. And she'd known Max long enough to say it wasn't the former. Yet he stood there, dividing the success of what he'd done among his teammates and others on scene.

Max smiled, and his dark brown eyes flickered with pride. He pressed his palms to the table and swung his attention to Opaline's bright expression on the screen. "Selena and Aria were smart to point out the pattern on these bombs. One bomb every other day with a rest day in between. It was only a hunch when she commented on it, but this bomb was set to detonate at noon. Three incidents make a pattern. Chances are O'Lear will wait another day, regroup and adjust his plan. Then we'll see the fourth attempt in forty to forty-eight hours, but there's also the chance he'll push his next move up to stay on schedule. We can't take any chances, especially after he sent that text message. We've ticked him off, and that's not good. So let's figure out who his next target will be and beat him to the location. Better yet, maybe even locate him before he makes his move."

"What do we know so far?" Carly asked, redirecting attention so Max could breathe.

He took his seat and waited for someone else to answer.

"We know he's watching," Selena said. "He sent the text. So he knows we're here."

"And working against him," Aria added. "We know he's not worried about collateral damage, and that he has at least one more hit on his list, based on his text. If he doesn't take another crack at the superintendent later."

Selena tapped her pointer finger against the desk, thinking. "What do we know about the number that text was sent from?" She turned to her sister, Opaline, on the screen.

The eyes of the TCD turned with her.

Opaline nodded. "I'm working on that. I've been able to confirm the number belongs to a burner phone, which is turned off. So I can't trace where the device is at the moment. But every phone has a serial number, and I'm running through a database of those numbers now, trying to get the serial number matching the phone number and phone used for that text. With that, I can determine which store the phone was shipped to and purchased from. Then I can request register receipts for a time stamp of the purchase, and look at corresponding surveillance videos to see if I can track his path visually when he leaves the store. Maybe get a look at what he's driving or anyone he speaks with."

Carly grinned. "Remind me to never try to hide from you."

Opaline chewed her lip. "You might give me a run for my money, but I'm going to find this guy soon. I've widened the scope of my search, and his photo is all over the news. Someone out there knows this guy, so if the PD phone lines are blowing up, that means folks are already trying to help out."

Axel shifted forward, resting his forearms on the table.

"I'm hoping to have a warrant to get inside O'Lear's apartment this afternoon. We've got enough direct links from the bombs to this guy to make the request and get a quick signature from the judge. Chief Drees will keep me posted. The minute it comes in, I want a team over there."

"We can go," Carly offered, motioning to Aria and Selena on either side of her.

Axel cast a look in Max's direction, waiting for his feedback. Axel was the supervisory agent, but Max had taken lead on this case, and he'd saved a lot of lives today. If he said he wanted to be there, he would. Carly hoped he'd take some time to breathe first.

Max nodded. "Yeah. Sounds good. Keep me looped in."

Carly smiled. "Absolutely."

"All right." Axel turned his eyes back to the screen, where Opaline frowned furiously at something out of view. "Can you put together a list of possible targets from the information you have now?"

"Soon," she said, typing wildly on her keyboard, expression deadly serious. "I'll be in touch again the minute I have anything to share."

And with that, she was gone.

Chapter Thirteen

Opaline ordered her favorite Tex-Mex takeout on the way home and changed immediately into her pajamas once the food arrived. Her cats, Snape and Dobby, met her at the door, meowing and attempting to lead her to their food bowls.

She gave them pats, filled their bowls and scratched behind their ears, thankful for the safety and comfort of her apartment, a space where she could freak out, break down and take off her smile as needed. She'd forced the cheer and positivity today until she thought she'd lose it on-screen. She'd basically hung up on the group at the end of their last video conference. The smile was for them. They were in the thick of things, risking their lives, and the least she could do was to be a constant and reliable source of positivity.

Except she was fresh out of happy, and moving fast into rage and despair. If she didn't get her team some information they could actually work with soon, there would be another bombing, and more people would die.

Her chest tightened at the thought. Tonight was a work night. *A fight night.*

And Fritz O'Lear was her weaselly, no-good opponent. She wore her favorite maroon-and-gold-striped cot-

ton sleep pants and oversize T-shirt proclaiming Life's
a Struggle When You're a Muggle. Though tonight she
needed to be a wizard, at the keyboard at least. She
whipped her hair into a messy bun, donned her fuzzy
black socks, then carried her takeout to her workspace.

Dobby and Snape followed, having lost interest in
the kibble once she'd opened the disposable container to
steal a loaded nacho and inhale the cheesy, salty, spicy
scents of her favorite chicken enchiladas. "You each get
one bite," she said, pinching off a shred of chicken and
offering the kitties a tiny little morsel. "I have to work.
You have to go be adorable somewhere else until I take
a break. No distractions. And you can't have any more
of my dinner, so don't get any ideas." The cats stared,
and Opaline caved. "Okay. One more bite, but that's it."
She gave them each another taste before digging into
her work.

"All right, O'Lear. It's time to stop this nonsense and
show yourself." She forked a bite of enchilada, sipped
the steamy coffee and got busy.

Opaline had been up against a lot of criminals in the
past, but none with less of a digital footprint than this
guy. Some of the younger nuts she'd chased through cy-
berspace had even bragged about their crimes. Gang
members were the worst, or maybe the dumbest. Definitely the most prideful, posting images of themselves
with rolls of cash, guns, drugs and everything else to
their social-media accounts. They boasted. Called out
enemies by name, and their latest hookups, too, often
adding location tags. Those criminals were so easy to
locate that they practically invited her to hang out. Fritz
O'Lear, on the other hand, was giving her fits.

She crossed her legs on the office chair, then powered up her laptop. Four independent screens flickered to life on her desk. She selected her favorite, work-all-night playlist, popped her phone onto the speaker dock, then snagged another nacho.

"Who are you, Fritz O'Lear?" she asked for what felt like the thousandth time in a few days. Serial bombers and psychotic killers didn't live in a vacuum. Someone knew this guy. And someone had gotten a bad vibe from him along the line. She needed to find one of those people. O'Lear or the person who knew where to find him. She wasn't picky.

Fritz O'Lear was just old enough to have missed spending his youth online, and apparently he'd never picked up the lifestyle. If he had an email address for personal use, it was registered under an alias, because she couldn't find it. He didn't have a LinkedIn profile, nor a Twitter account. His Facebook page hadn't been updated in years, and even then he'd barely bothered to use it. He claimed to like country music and a handful of old sitcoms in his barely completed profile. Grand Rapids was listed as his hometown, and the local high school as his alma mater. He only had a handful of friends and no family listed.

Not exactly a treasure trove of information.

Opaline opened each of his friends' profiles in new windows and scrutinized their lives, looking at how and where they'd intersected with O'Lear through the years. She scanned his personal photos and images where others had tagged him. Noted places in town where he'd spent time, then followed each of his friends around the world wide web. Jumping platform to platform, attempting to understand O'Lear by getting to know his friends. The more she understood who he was, the easier it would be to find him.

One pal stood out, and his name was Mark Waters. According to a photo Mark had tagged him in, the two were "lifelong friends." Unfortunately, that lead, like all the others, came to a dead end, literally, when Mark's obituary surfaced. He'd been in an accident ten months ago. But Opaline wasn't letting go of a lead that easily. Instead, she used the online memorial page to track down Mark's parents, who conveniently still lived in town. A lifelong friend of their son's might be someone his family remembered, maybe even someone they'd known personally.

She thought of messaging some of Fritz's other social-media friends, using an alias, to ask if they knew where Fritz was because she had to get in touch with him about some money he'd inherited. But that could accidentally alert him to her search, so she held off. She'd use that tactic if necessary, but first she'd try tracking down this Mark fellow's family.

Snape climbed onto Opaline's lap after midnight, purring and sniffing the nearly empty take-out containers. She stroked his fur, thankful for the kitty comfort, but wholly dissatisfied with her progress on the case. She needed a smoking gun. But all she'd managed to find was smoke. Nothing tangible. Nothing concrete.

"What do you think, Snape?" she asked, a yawn opening her mouth wide. "We need more than the names of an old friend's family members to offer the team tomorrow. We need the name and location of someone who's actually talked to this guy in the past year. Preferably on a personal level, not the employees at Ramsey Realty."

Snape stretched on her lap and bumped his head

against her chin, nuzzling and purring more loudly. He kneaded his paws against her middle, then curled into a fluffy black ball on her lap.

OPALINE'S HEAD FELL suddenly forward at two thirty in the morning. She let out a yelp, and Snape screeched away. "Sorry," she whispered, pushing onto her feet for a stretch.

She went to the kitchen and tucked her food containers into the fridge. Then she bumbled into the bathroom to splash cold water on her face. From there, she put on a pot of coffee.

Images of Max's expression as he'd walked out of that building, half stunned, half horrified, burned in her mind. Opaline had waited with the masses, holding her breath and sending up silent prayers that he would return at all. She tried to imagine what kind of person it took to go into a building and look for a bomb. Then to find a device counting down, with only three minutes left before detonation, and not turn away and run. How did anyone do that? Especially someone who'd nearly died doing the exact same thing once before.

A brewing tear-storm stung her eyes and nose. Mental and emotional fatigue weighted her limbs. Her throat clogged, and a sudden sob broke in her chest.

Lives were at stake. Lots of lives. Including the lives of her teammates. And her sister.

Tears spilled, hot and fast, over her cheeks.

Fritz O'Lear had been prepared to murder forty people today. He had to be stopped. The TCD was ready. But they couldn't stop him if they couldn't find him, and that was on her.

And she was failing.

She thought again of the images she'd seen on television. All those pets and people O'Lear had been ready to blow up so he could feel powerful for one second. So he could punish someone who'd made him feel weak. And she thought of the funerals that were coming tomorrow and the next day, as his recent victims were laid to rest. The families they left behind, forever changed because O'Lear had been rejected, because he'd been teased.

Opaline scrubbed heavy hands across her face and against her eyes as determination overtook despair. She wiped tears and shook away the feelings of failure and fatigue. She had the rest of her life to question her skills and beat herself up, right after she got back in her chair and helped her team.

She poured a bowl-sized mug of black coffee and marched back to her desk. She couldn't physically defend her teammates on the front line, but she could have their backs on her turf. Online. She could and would get them the information they needed to stay safe and protect others. And she wouldn't stop trying until she succeeded.

She didn't lower her head again until the sun began to rise.

Chapter Fourteen

Max arrived on Allie's doorstep with a bouquet of flowers and a tiramisu from the local baker, hoping she'd still let him in after the way they'd left things today. He'd replayed the earlier exchange a million times in his head, and it looked worse to him with every review. Hindsight helped him recognize the subtle change in her tone and slight rigidity of her posture, in ways he hadn't been able to comprehend in the moment. He'd known he'd come off as abrupt but hadn't fully understood that he'd hurt her until she was gone.

Now he could only hope the flowers and dessert were enough to get him through the door. From there, he had a lot of explaining to do. He knocked lightly, a few minutes early. If she hadn't changed her mind about making him dinner, maybe she'd let him help with the work.

The door swept open, and Allie stared out, a surprised expression on her face and Max Jr. on one hip. "You came," she said, hazel eyes widening. "I was sure you'd be working all night." She pressed her lips into a pale, thin line, and he realized she was being polite.

She'd assumed he'd blow her off again. Choose work over her, the way he had when they were married.

He stepped inside as she made room for him to pass. "I've been looking forward to this," he said. "Nothing was going to keep me away. Here, I'll trade you," he suggested. "Flowers and dessert for one pint-size little man?"

"Is that tiramisu?" she asked, a hint of delight dancing in her eyes.

"Yes, ma'am." Max smiled, making the trade for his sweet baby boy. He took in Allie's appearance as they made the swap. The familiar tilt of her head and set of her jaw. That soft green sweater and those perfectly fitting black pants. Allie had always been in great shape when they were married, a result of long morning jogs. She was thin and willowy, but she was different now, stronger-looking, with obvious definition in her limbs and shoulders. And try as he might to be a gentleman, he couldn't help imagining what those changes would look like under the clothes.

"Tiramisu is my favorite," she said. "Thank you."

"You're welcome, and it's the least I can do after you offered to make dinner again." Max buried his nose in Max Jr.'s fluffy curls and inhaled deeply, savoring the perfect scent of his son. "Man, I've missed you, little guy."

"I can't believe you remembered," Allie said, still apparently baffled by the simple dessert. "The bouquet is lovely, too. I should put it in water."

The shock in her tone was a kick to Max's gut. She really hadn't thought he'd remember the things she loved? Or show up tonight? How far wrong had he gone in their marriage that she didn't think he knew her at least this well? *Far enough that she divorced me*, he reminded himself. So, *way* too far.

"How are you?" she asked, heading for the kitchen.

"I've been better," he admitted. "A lot of things went wrong today. I'm hoping to see improvement moving forward."

Allie set the tiramisu in her refrigerator, then turned a curious look on Max. "You stopped a bomb. Saved dozens of people. I'd say at least a few things went right."

He followed her to the kitchen, bouncing his son gently in his arms and debating how to begin all the things he wanted to say.

"I made a pot roast," she said, retrieving a vase from the cabinet below the sink, then filling it with water for the bouquet. "Carrots and potatoes with rosemary as a side. And I have French bread."

"Everything smells amazing." Max set his son in his high chair, then kissed his forehead and turned to Allie, rubbing eager palms together. "How can I help?"

She smiled, dutifully arranging the flowers in the vase. "Set the table?"

Max put out the plates and silverware while Allie pulled the bread from the oven and set it on a rack to cool. "I was surprised to see you today," he said. "I'm sorry I pulled back like I did."

Allie glanced over her shoulder at him, her smile strikingly more distant than it had seemed before. "You were working. I was out of line."

"No. You weren't. I was, and I want to explain." He shook the tension from his hands, struggling for words. Talking about his feelings wasn't easy. His instincts for the preservation of his pride demanded he change the subject. But Max had chosen his comfort over Allie's needs too many times, and it was his turn to start making real sacrifices for her. Pride be damned.

She turned away to remove the pan of roast and vegetables from her oven, then set it on the stovetop. "I saw
what was happening on the news, and I panicked," she
said, apology thick in her tone. "You were in a building
with a possible bomb, and I couldn't just sit here, watching the screen for updates like everyone else. I'm not everyone else."

"You're not," he said softly. "I'm glad you were there.
I mean that, and I need you to hear me."

Her shoulders slumped, and she deflated, resting her
backside against the counter. She stripped off her oven
mitts and stared. "I've never been that scared in my life."

"I'm sorry," he said, meaning it to his marrow.

"I wasn't trying to intrude. I acted without thinking.
It was an emotional response to my fear." She lifted and
dropped her palms in defeat.

Max took a step closer. "When I was trying to shut
that bomb down, all I could think of was you and Max
Jr. I was terrified I'd never see you again, and I hadn't
made things right between us. Then I walked outside,
you were there, and I thought, *This is my chance. I can
do the right thing.*"

She crossed her arms and chewed her lip.

He recognized the defensive posture and pressed on
before she shut him down. "I pulled away from you today
because I realized that if the bomber sent that text, then
he knew I was there, and that I'd stopped his attack.
Whether he was in the crowd, or watching from another
location, I couldn't be sure, but if he had eyes on the
scene and saw you with me…" Max trailed off, unable
to voice the unthinkable truth.

Allie's expression softened, and her arms fell loose at
her sides. "He might've seen you holding me."

"I didn't want him to see you anywhere near me." Max groaned. He leaned a hip against the counter and scrubbed a heavy hand over his face, the scruff of his beard grinding against his palm. "The realization that my feelings for you could put you in danger—" he swallowed hard, forcing the words through a tightening jaw "—was a hell of a lot scarier than any bomb."

A fresh blush washed over Allie's cheeks, and she turned away to slice the bread. "You were protecting me," she said shyly. "I'm not sure how I misinterpreted that. I guess it's what you do."

Max moved into the space behind her and set a tentative hand on her lower back. "I also have a bad habit of hurting you, and I wish I could take that pain back. I gave you the impression my work was more important than my family, and it's just not true."

Allie stilled her knife against the bread. Her body tensed.

"Dada!" Max Jr. called. He smacked his high-chair tray and squealed. "Dada! Dada!" He released a long round of raspberries with his tongue, and Allie laughed.

Max moved away from Allie. "I've got this." He opened the cupboard and collected one of Max Jr.'s plastic plates, then a baby spoon and fork from the rack. "I think he's trying to tell us how delicious this meal smells, and how much he'd like some. Right now."

Allie smoothly moved a few baby carrots and tiny potatoes onto the little plate beside some bits of roast.

Max sliced the food for their son, then followed Allie to the table. She set the pan with her roast and vegetables on a wooden trivet, then took a seat beside Max Jr.'s high chair.

"We still make a good team," Max said, enjoying the familiar ease of working at her side.

"Teamwork was never one of our problems," she said, serving roast and potatoes to Max, then portioning some for herself. "You and I were always good together."

Something in her tone sent heat through Max's core, and a surge of unbidden, deeply intimate memories of their early days together flooded into mind.

"Do you really think I could be in danger?" she asked.

The thought doused Max in ice.

Allie's gaze flickered to Max Jr., then back. "Could *we* be in danger?"

"I don't know," he admitted, tension returning to his muscles, gripping his back, neck and shoulders painfully. "I can't be sure what the bomber saw today."

"Maybe you should go back to your hotel tonight," she said softly. "It's not that I don't want you to be here. I just don't want to take the risk. What if he follows you?"

Max turned his attention to the meal before him, hoping to hide his horror at the possibility. He'd been careful, but what if he'd missed something? "I understand why you'd say that, and it makes sense on the surface," he said.

Eventually he wiped his mouth on his napkin and refocused on the gorgeous blonde across from him.

"But," she guessed.

His lips twitched, and he fought a small smirk. She knew him so well. Unfortunately, he'd taken a risk by coming for dinner, even if the extremely overdue apology he owed Allie seemed paramount at the time. Now that he was there, it was too late to turn back. "I'm already here," he said. "I can't be sure O'Lear doesn't know that. Leaving you alone could be the opposite of helpful, if he knows this is where I came after work."

Her shoulders sagged before squaring once more. Her expression was unreadable.

"I won't let anything happen to you or Max Jr.," he vowed.

"I know." Allie pushed the food around her plate, clearly thinking, but not saying a word. Max could only imagine where her thoughts had gone. His job might've put her in danger. Exactly what he'd tried to avoid throughout their relationship.

"You were a real help, going to the station and working with the sketch artist," he said, changing the subject. "I don't think I thanked you properly for that. Knowing you saw him watch the Burger Mania blast goes a long way toward building our profile. Combined with the text he sent today, I can confidently say this guy likes to watch the explosions. He enjoys the destruction and seeing the chaos unfold. We think he takes a day between bombings to bask in the power rush."

Allie paled. Her chewing slowed, and she turned her eyes on their baby. "Do you think there's any chance he recognized me? From that night in the car? Then again at the scene today?"

The food turned to sawdust on Max's tongue as the remote possibility took hold. How could he stay another minute with Allie if being there could put a target on her? And how could he leave if Fritz O'Lear already had her in his sights?

How could Max know if either was true?

ALLIE CLEANED THE kitchen after dinner, watching and listening as Max played with and cared for their son. The moments were bittersweet and nostalgic, and she didn't want Max to go. She missed hearing his voice and laugh-

ter. She missed his comforting and protective presence.
She missed his touch.

She scrubbed the table a little harder, attempting to
distract herself from the growing sense of loss, knowing he had to leave again soon. She'd spent the months
after her divorce the same way, trying to distract herself
from the pain. She'd joined a gym, thrown herself into her
work and concentrated on being the very best mother she
could. But one look at Max, lying on his back on her liv-
ing-room floor, with their son held above him like a tiny
superhero, was ripping apart any progress she'd made.

She put on a kettle for tea and arranged a pair of mugs
beside the stove. Max used to tease her for her preference for tea over coffee, but he'd learned to appreciate the
drink. Like she'd learned to appreciate draft beer. He'd
begun to go on morning runs with her. She'd started joining him in the weight room at his gym. She and Max had
always been a perfect team of give-and-take. Teacher and
student. Partners in every sense of the word. Until the
TCD called, and his real team took him away for days,
even weeks on end. Usually at the drop of a dime. Always to rescue or protect another family.

Until today, all those missions had been abstract.
They'd felt false. Distant. Not worth letting him go at
every turn. But being there today with the crowds and the
team had changed that. She'd felt the suffocating tension
and fear in the air, and she'd seen the faces of all those
residents as they were moved to a safe location. The helpless pets loaded into crates. The elderly. The children. It
had nearly torn her heart in two.

And knowing Max had saved all those people by putting their lives and safety ahead of his own had given
Allie a brand-new perspective on absolutely everything.

Including what she needed from Max, if he was willing to consider it.

She dried her hands on a towel and moved to the island that separated her kitchen and living room, greedy for a closer look at the two most amazing men in her life.

They were seated now, a book between them. Max Jr. yawned and rubbed his eyes.

"Aw. Hey, now," Max said, steadying their wobbly son. "Looks like someone's getting tired." He set the book aside, then cuddled Max Jr. to his chest before rising gracefully to his feet.

Allie admired the long, lean muscles of Max's body, and the fluidity with which he moved. It was so easy to forget a prosthetic limb replaced his lower left leg and foot. He'd nearly died before they met. It was unbelievable how close she'd come to never meeting him. If everything that happened after that blast hadn't happened exactly as it did, Allie's life would have been completely different, as well. But she chose to believe that fate had saved him for her, because from the moment they'd met, Max had been her everything. He was the reason she believed in soul mates.

"I think I might've worn him out," Max said, cradling Max Jr. in his arms. "Do you mind if I do the routine tonight? Is it still a diaper, a song and a kiss?"

Her heart swelled. Max remembered that, too? She'd never thought he'd paid much attention to her bedtime routine with the baby. "Yeah," she said. "It hasn't changed." It was too bad so many other things had.

Max smiled. "Then I'll be back in a few minutes."

Allie tiptoed to the baby monitor and powered it on, listening as Max spoke softly to their son. He whispered a story as he changed his diaper. Then he began to sing.

Max Jr. cooed and gurgled, fighting sleep without crying, a definite improvement over the last few miserable nights of teething.

She drifted back to the kitchen and turned off the kettle, no longer interested in tea. Then she slipped into the bathroom to check her hair and face in the mirror. Her cheeks were flushed and her eyes were wild. Pretty much what she'd expected. She took a moment to settle her thoughts, then headed back into the hallway to wait for her ex-husband.

He'd told her he was leaving tonight, but she had something she needed to do before she let him go.

Max crept from the nursery several minutes later and pulled the door shut behind him. He narrowed his eyes when he saw her, though she doubted he hadn't known she was there. He'd always seemed to know where she was. How she was feeling. And what was on her mind. "Can we talk before I go?"

Allie stepped forward, wetting her lips and pushing away from the wall. "We don't have to talk," she said. "I know your time is limited, and I don't want to keep you, if you're sure that leaving is for the best."

Max stilled, his brows coming together in confusion. "What?"

"I understand how much you're needed on this case," she said, feeling the confession begin to flow. "I realize how selfish I was before. I couldn't see it then, but I do now. And I'm sorry."

Max moved closer, his eyes locked with hers. "I'm the one who owes you an apology. You and Max Jr. have always been my priority, but I didn't act like it."

Allie's attempts to keep herself from falling apart

ended with his words. She closed the remaining gap between them and rose onto her toes to kiss him.

Max tensed, momentarily, as her lips grazed his, then quickly came to life under her touch. His arms curled around her back as she sank against him. His mouth met hers, press for press, and she moaned as he deepened the kiss.

Heat licked over her neck and chest, then pooled low in her core. She stepped back, fuzzy-headed and infinitely lighter, lips full from the urgency of their kiss.

Max looked equally dazed, a small smile on his slack, handsome face.

"Sorry. You said you wanted to talk?" she asked, trailing her fingertips down the hard planes of his chest. "I interrupted."

He rubbed a palm over his face, then pierced her with a pointed stare. "I wanted to tell you I was scared today," he said. "I had flashbacks, and the PTSD hit so hard I didn't think I could get past it. Somehow, I pushed through. Then I found that bomb, and I had clarity about what's important and how badly I screwed up. I knew what I'd done wrong. I understood why you left me. And I know I need to say so."

Allie let her hands fall away, shocked and utterly unnerved at the unexpected change of subject and sudden tension between them.

Max caught her hands and pressed them against his heart, covering her fingers with his. "I thought that keeping you separate from my job would keep you safe, but not letting you in was a mistake. You deserved answers to your questions, then and now. You asked me how I was feeling when I got here, and I skipped around it. The truth is that I was nervous to see you. I was terrified that

I'd ruined things for good when I pulled away without explanation this afternoon. I was hopeful that I didn't, and I'm still finding my way through the residual panic of the bomb. The one I disarmed today, and the one that nearly killed me all those years ago. I never talk about my feelings, because I don't like to, and I don't talk about losing my leg because it's hard to manage the memories. I don't want you to think of me as weak. Because I can't protect you if I'm weak."

Allie started to respond, but Max took a deep breath, and she knew he hadn't finished.

"It's no excuse for pushing you away before," he said, looking more guilty and ashamed than anyone she'd ever seen, "but once I found out you were pregnant, I went from being overjoyed to being terrified. I let the PTSD take ahold of me, and I spent every day knowing that if something happened to you, I'd lose the both of you, and it was more than I could stand. So I pulled away, cowardly. I was angry with myself for not being stronger, for keeping you upset, for failing you. I became consumed by the negatives. I hid behind my job, and I lost sight of what was right here in front of me. I am deeply sorry." He pulled her close and swept the backs of his fingers across her cheek, tucking hair behind her ears and looking at her as if she was the only thing that had ever mattered. "I'm able to say all that now, because I took your advice after the divorce. It was too late to save us, but I talked to someone at the VA who helped me figure out my mess."

Allie's breath caught, and hope curled through her heart. All she'd ever wanted was to be a part of Max's life. *His whole life.* She wanted him to trust her with his feelings and talk to her like she was his best friend, because he had always been hers. She'd told him those things a thousand times, but she'd never thought he heard her. His unexpected confession meant more to her than anything else he could possibly have done. She turned her hands in his and squeezed. "It doesn't have to be too late."

She cupped his cheek, caressing the sweet stubble and rising back onto her toes. "You are all I've ever wanted. But I need all of you, not just the pieces you think are best. You have to trust me with everything. Like our marriage vows said, for better and for worse. I need more than a protector, Max. I need a partner. And so do you." She locked her stubborn gaze with his remorseful one. "Even fancy explosives experts and war heroes need someone to take care of them once in a while."

A slow smile spread over Max's handsome face. "Are you offering?"

Allie pressed her lips to his, then curled her fingertips in the material of his shirt. She stepped backward, tugging him toward her bedroom. "I am."

He followed easily, still smiling. "You think I'm fancy?"

Allie laughed as she closed her door behind them and pressed him against it. "I do. Now shut up and kiss me."

Chapter Fifteen

Max woke to the sounds and scents of breakfast. Running water, the gentle clang of pans and soft sizzle of bacon floated to his ears in the small one-story home. Allie's sweet voice rose above it all as she sang a silly song, presumably to their little boy. A smile broke across Max's face as he let the moment settle in.

He was glad Allie had agreed to let him stay last night. Honestly, he wasn't sure he could have brought himself to leave. If she'd insisted, he'd probably have slept in his car outside her front door. He wasn't completely sure how he could leave her today. Or ever again, but that was something he'd have to work out later. They'd have plenty to talk about, and some complicated things to figure out, once his case was closed and it was time for him to return to Traverse City. Like, did she mean it when she'd said there was still a chance for them? For more than a few nights?

Max swung himself out of bed and reached for his prosthesis. He arranged the heavy liner at the bottom of his residual limb, then rolled it slowly up his leg, careful not to leave any air against his skin inside the liner. He bent his knee to pull on the device, then rolled the sleeve up his thigh. He dressed slowly, taking time to wake up

and enjoying the moment. The scent of Allie's cooking
in the air, and the scent of her on his skin.

Max Jr.'s laugh trickled down the hall, pulling Max to
the kitchen. The toddler shoved chubby fistfuls of dry cereal and strawberries into his mouth while Allie flipped
bacon in a frying pan. She sang a song Max didn't recognize, full of animal names and rhymes. Then she turned
to bow for their son.

Both men clapped.

"Hey!" Allie pointed her spatula at Max. "No creeping."

"I was admiring," he said. "Can you blame me?"

She grinned, cheeks pink and wearing his white V-
neck T-shirt like a nightgown. "When the person you're
admiring doesn't know she's being watched, it's called
creeping," she said. "I should call the FBI about you." She
turned back to a pan of scrambled eggs beside the bacon.

"Please do," he said. "I know a guy who'd love to
get your call anytime." Max kissed his son's head, then
poured a mug of coffee, taking his time before he reached
his ex-wife. "I've missed this," he said, setting a hand on
her back and leaning in to kiss her cheek. "I've missed
you."

"Back at ya," she said, shooting him an impish look.
"How'd you sleep?"

Max laughed. "Deeply. I haven't slept for six hours
straight in months."

"Have you ever?" she asked. "I remember you sneak-
ing out of bed most nights when we were married. Into
your office to work."

Max sipped his coffee, remorseful for all the time he
could've spent with her, but he'd willingly stayed away.
He probably hadn't slept a full night since he'd joined

the military. Definitely not since joining the TCD, but he could've spent those sleepless hours in her arms instead of buried in his work. "I'm not sure how you got away this morning without me noticing."

Allie turned the fire off under each pan, then offered Max a sad smile. "Maybe the fact you haven't slept in the better part of a decade had something to do with it."

"Maybe," he said, admiring her body as she ferried a plate of eggs to their son. Her legs were long and lean, visible nearly to her perfect backside in that shirt, and he ached to take her back to bed.

"Hungry?" she asked.

"Ravenous."

She blushed again, and he had to remind himself there was a toddler in the room.

Determined to behave himself, and enjoy another family breakfast before he had to go, he fixed two plates of eggs and bacon, then carried them to the table.

"Thanks," Allie said, taking a seat.

Max lowered onto the chair across from her, then dug into his meal. It didn't take long before a sliver of guilt wiggled into his bliss. The rest of his team had likely lost sleep last night, chasing leads and trying to find the bomber. Max had essentially taken a vacation.

"You're frowning," Allie said. "What's wrong?"

He forced a smile and nearly told her it was nothing, then remembered that move had cost him everything once before. "I'm wondering how things went with the search of O'Lear's apartment, and if there were any more bomb threats or news since I fell asleep."

Allie considered him. "You haven't checked your phone?"

Max fished his phone from his pocket, shocked that it hadn't been the first thing he'd done when he woke.

"I can also say with complete certainty that if your team had needed you, they'd have shown up at my door and knocked it down if necessary."

He laughed at the imagery. She wasn't wrong about them coming for him, if they'd truly needed him.

"Don't feel bad for getting some sleep," she said. "You can't be at your best when you're running on empty. It's as if you did them all a favor. You'll be sharper from the rest."

Max scrolled through his missed texts and emails. Chief Drees had come through with a warrant to search O'Lear's apartment just before Max stopped back at the hotel to shower and change for dinner with Allie. The team had sent regular updates with photos and appeared to have carefully overturned every object in a show of extreme due diligence. A footlocker in the back of his closet held enough evidence to link O'Lear to both blasts and to the bomb in Teske's office. Packaging and receipts for four pressure cookers. Multiple Tannerite containers, and a mother lode of empty labeled containers meant for nails, bolts and BBs.

And a journal.

Max smiled. If the bomb-making materials alone could have possibly been argued in court as circumstantial, the detailed personal account of O'Lear's perceived wrongs, his plans for action and the step-by-step guide to building and detonating his bombs would put him away for life. All that was missing were the names of his targets. O'Lear had only used pronouns.

Simultaneous relief and anxiety flushed through Max as he processed the news. The TCD had everything they needed to put O'Lear away, but they still hadn't found him, and they didn't know when or where he'd attack again.

And to make matters worse, O'Lear had probably seen his apartment being searched, which meant he knew they had him. With nothing left to lose, someone as unhinged as the Grand Rapids bomber would become more dangerous than ever.

"Meeting at eight," he said, tucking the phone back into his pocket.

The team had been busy, but they'd gotten along just fine while he'd rested.

He went back to his meal, itching to hear more about O'Lear's apartment search straight from his colleagues' mouths. He'd also like to stop by and take a look for himself. If he hurried, he could get to the station early enough to spend some time with the emails he'd just flipped through and familiarize himself with all the information he'd missed last night, before the meeting began.

Allie wiped her pretty mouth with a napkin, her plate nearly empty. "I can see your mental wheels turning. You're eager to get out there and chase the bad guy."

"I am," he admitted, drawn back to the moment, to the good things in his life, and away from the darker pieces. "Can I see you again tonight?"

"Yes, please," Allie said, smiling sweetly across the small table.

It took more willpower than he thought he had, but Max removed himself from the table, showered and dressed for work. He kissed Allie and their baby goodbye at the door. The moment felt a lot like old times, except better. There was a new peace and understanding between him and Allie now, one he wished he'd been able to facilitate a year ago, before the divorce papers had arrived.

"Be safe, okay?" she said, a hint of fear in her warm hazel eyes. "And come back to me."

He wasn't sure if she'd simply meant for him to come back for the evening, or if there'd been a bigger request in the words. Either way, he'd absolutely return to her. And he'd stay, gratefully, for as long as she'd allow him. "I promise."

FRITZ O'LEAR HAD watched as nervous cops and anxious reporters gathered around his apartment building. As the infuriating bomb squad and some FBI goons stopped his third bomb.

He'd watched as the interfering lawmen passed his text message among themselves, trading cautious looks and scanning the crowd for signs of the sender.

He'd watched as they later returned to rummage through his things. To steal from him, and to try to stop him, which they couldn't.

Fritz saw everything. He'd even cased the ritzy hotel on the edge of town where the team was staying. He'd seen their matching SUVs there last night when he'd headed to a dingy motel outside the city limits, where he could pay with cash and no identification was required.

He hated everything about the feds' hotel. Too tall. Too showy. Too self-important. Just like all of them. He'd parked across the street, considering.

Should he add one more location to his list of targets? Wouldn't blowing up the team who'd come to stop him make the perfect finale to his show?

Hiding a bomb in a hotel would be easy. People came and went all the time. And no one paid any attention.

He'd slipped out of his car and walked the perimeter of the hotel, getting a feel for the job. He could take his time exploring the building's interior tomorrow, when the agents left for work. He couldn't be sure when they might return tonight. Likely on high alert, and all wound up from their little victory.

The agents probably assumed their win earlier in the day meant they were better than him, but they were wrong, and he'd make sure they knew. The FBI had interfered. Broken into his home. Taken his things. And it was time they were put in their places. Reminded who was in charge.

Then, in a perfect twist of fate, as Fritz had made his way back around the building, the big glass doors to the hotel's lobby parted, and the agent who'd stopped his bomb walked out. Alone. Fritz had hated him since the moment he'd seen him on television. With his flawless brown skin and that peculiar, cocky strut. This one was all superiority, muscles and attitude. Probably trained to disarm bombs in some high-tech federal facility. A man who'd never known real problems in his life but had made a career out of causing others, like Fritz, trouble. And that just wasn't okay.

Fritz had waited while the man climbed into an obnoxious government vehicle in the hotel parking lot, and then Fritz had made a run for his car. His old-model Toyota wasn't new or expensive like the SUV he followed through town, stopping at a bakery and another little shop, but it was too old for GPS tracking and still registered to the previous owner, a friend who'd died in a motorcycle accident. Which made Fritz untraceable. A ghost.

Chapter Sixteen

Max arrived at the station early, as planned. He greeted the officers he passed on his way to the conference room, already beginning to recognize many of the morning crew and a few of those finishing the night shift.

He carried his quickly cooling cup of drive-through coffee toward the TCD's temporary headquarters, then slowed as the door came into view. Light spilled unexpectedly through the small rectangular window, suggesting he wasn't the first to arrive, despite the time. Most of his team had been awake through the night, sending emails and correspondence as he'd slept. Those agents should have slept until the last minute and be arriving as the meeting began. At least, that had been the norm for the past seven years.

Max reached the door, still guessing who might be inside. Grand Rapids PD had been directed to stay out when a member of the TCD wasn't present, and the cleaning crew had the same orders. Maybe Rihanna, the only teammate he hadn't received any overnight messages from, had gotten a jump on her day. Or maybe one of the others simply couldn't sleep. Sometimes insomnia trumped fatigue when investigators got this close to catching a killer. Adrenaline-laced anticipation could be impossible to ignore.

He swung the door open and stepped inside, unable to make a guess. Regardless, he would have been wrong.

Director Suzuki sat at the front of the table, signing a stack of papers and saying her goodbyes to a vanishing face on the screen where Opaline would soon appear. "Good morning, Max," she said, barely looking up.

"Director." He went to the front of the room and set his coffee on the conference table across from her. "I didn't know you were coming into town. Is everything okay?" He could only hope she wasn't there to drop a massive figurative bomb in his lap. Something about Fritz O'Lear. A game changer that would set the team back to square one.

"Yes," she said. "All is well." She signed another paper, then set her pen aside. Poised and graceful as always, and not a hair out of place, she folded her hands in her lap. Her tailored navy suit was unwrinkled. Her legs crossed. "I'm here to meet with Chief Drees and the commissioner about the progress we've made so far. They're pleased with Rihanna's work, but you know I like to leave my mark whenever I can." Her smile was small, warm and mildly defensive.

Max suspected she was there to make sure her team was being treated well and had everything they needed, no holdups, red tape or resistance of any kind.

"How are you, Max?"

"Good. Thanks."

"You're early. The morning meeting won't begin for another forty minutes," she said, evaluating gaze roaming over his face. "Were you able to sleep?"

"I did," he said, struck once more with guilt for that

truth. "I thought I'd come in a little early and review the information we have so far. Maybe ferret out a potential next move or find a new lead. Something I could offer at the meeting."

Alana watched him, assessing, he assumed. She'd no doubt seen the footage of him at the bomb site like everyone else in Michigan, via local news and the internet. And Max was sure she'd spoken with Axel, the supervisory agent, about Max's state of mind after the fact.

It wasn't uncommon for Alana to meet with the local officials in a case like this one, but she always did that by phone or video conference. "You don't normally visit field sites. Is there anything of particular concern here?"

Her lips tipped up at the sides. "Yes. You."

"Me?" He felt his brows furrow.

"This is a big case for you," she said.

Max's muscles tightened. He didn't like where this was going. "Yes, ma'am."

"We've chased bombers before," Alana said. "But this case is different. We aren't here to assist in a manhunt after a major attack. This is the TCD's first active bomber case. And you haven't had to face off with an explosive device like you did yesterday since before we met."

Max dipped his chin, once, in agreement. Tension rolled down his spine, and the phantom pain he sometimes felt, where his leg no longer existed, plucked at him, begging him to reach for it. But he refused. Lacing his fingers on the table where his hands were folded instead.

"You did a miraculous thing," she said. "Brave. Professional. Effective." She paused until his eyes met hers. "Heroic."

"Necessary," he countered.

Her smile faded and her sharp brown eyes narrowed. "You did a good job out there, Max. I came here to say so, in case you missed the memo."

He frowned. "You came to Grand Rapids to check up on me?" Max wasn't sure if that was heartwarming or a sign she thought he needed babysitting.

"Impressive feats of bravery aside," she said, tilting her head slightly over one shoulder. "You were the one who requested we pursue this case. Allie and Max Jr. are here now. And I know that's on your mind, as well. Which means you're under a lot of pressure all around. Not to mention, as the TCD explosives expert, you've been taking lead on this. So let me ask again. All pretenses aside, and please be frank. We've known one another long enough for you to know I don't need or like my answers sugarcoated. Tell me friend to friend. How are you really doing?"

Max worked his jaw, deciding what and how much to say. Alana was a friend, but she was still his boss. The one who'd recruited him. The one who had his back, but also the one who handed him his backside as needed. "All right," he said, stretching his legs beneath the table. "Facing the bomb was tough. Tougher than I'd expected. A good example of theory versus reality. In theory, I knew what to do and was ready to do it. In reality, I nearly froze. I felt the panic rising before I'd even entered the building. And I wasn't convinced I could do the job once I was inside. Then I found the bomb, and part of me wanted to leave. The people were out. Their pets had been moved to safety. The only thing left in danger was an old, poorly maintained building."

Alana waited while he struggled to find words for his racing thoughts.

He kneaded his hands on the table, working to hold her eye contact, though his gaze darted away on its own more than once. "I couldn't let him damage the building. The apartments are people's homes. The residents were forced to leave everything behind when they evacuated. Their necessities, personal things, photos, mementos. Not to mention their security and peace of mind. Many of them likely had nowhere else to go." He paused to wet his lips, feeling another fact fall to his tongue. "And I wanted Fritz O'Lear to know who he was dealing with. I didn't want him to think he'd won. Or that he could win. Not by any measure."

She shifted, uncrossing and recrossing her legs. "And now?" she asked.

"Now I'm concerned he saw my interference as a challenge, and that instead of intimidating him, I provoked him. I'm worried something else will explode at any minute, this time taking lives in the process."

"Well, I'm not worried," she said, confidently. "I knew you were the best when I asked you to join my team, and I'm more sure of that today than ever. You've never let me down before. So there is no precedent to expect any differently in the future."

Warmed by her words, he felt his cheeks twitch as he fought a smile. "No precedent, huh?"

"None."

He released his grip on his hands and let them fall to his sides, shaking them out at the wrists.

"Have you been able to talk with Allie since your arrival?" Alana asked. "Better yet, tell me you've had a chance to kiss that chubby-cheeked son of yours."

"I have," he said, answering both her questions at once. "Allie and Max Jr. are both doing well."

"Excellent." Alana nodded in approval. "Well, I can see you're just fine, as expected. I suppose I'd better go and meet with the who's who and get back to Traverse City before that snake, Jenkins, makes another play for my job while I'm not there to keep a heel on him."

Max chuckled. "You'd think he'd be smarter than to mess with you."

She stretched to her feet and collected her things, a small smile on her lips. "You'd think." She offered her hand in a gentle shake as she passed.

Max held on to her a beat longer than necessary and gave her fingers a soft squeeze before releasing them. "Thank you for coming here, Alana. Your confidence means a lot."

A bloom of pride colored her cheeks. "You've got this, Max. I have no doubt Grand Rapids is in excellent hands. If you need anything, let me know."

ON LESS THAN two hours of sleep and far too much caffeine, Opaline donned her favorite eyelashes, then loaded up on lavender eye shadow and matching lip gloss in preparation for the morning meeting. She'd risen with the sun and gone to the office early, eager to share her new leads.

"Good morning!" she trilled at the sight of her teammates. "Hope you all got a little sleep last night."

A collective grumble rolled through the conference room on-screen. They'd clearly had as little rest as Opaline, but also not as much coffee.

Surprisingly, the teammate who normally looked the most fatigued seemed the most awake. She smiled at Max, wondering if his fresh-faced look had anything to do with his ex-wife arriving at the site of yesterday's bomb scare.

"Why don't we get started," Axel said, lifting a hand toward the camera. He'd worn his usual dark dress pants, white dress shirt and tie. His hair was mussed and damp, likely from a recent shower, and when he raised his hand to run his fingers through the fair locks, his biceps were quite impressive. Axel Morrow was sexy and single, but the heavy dose of brotherly chemistry between him and Opaline stopped her thoughts on the matter right there.

But what was this? Opaline felt her brows rise. Her sister's gaze was fixed on their supervisor, too. Selena's eyes were dark, her lips parted, and there was something about the color in her cheeks. Dear sis had noticed the bod on their supervisory agent for this assignment, as well, and there was nothing sisterly about the way she was staring.

"We sent updates as they came available," Axel went on.

Selena turned her eyes back to the screen, completely in the zone.

Opaline reconsidered what she'd seen. Maybe she'd misread her sister's previous expression. It wouldn't be the first time or a surprise. She and Selena had been at odds so long she barely felt connected to her these days, beyond the thread of mutual frustration.

"A number of details and photos were sent from our search of O'Lear's apartment," Axel said. "We need to compile the data into one quick-view document for ease and convenience of access."

"I can do that," Opaline said. "I'm also running scans on bar codes I pulled from the images of the discarded pressure-cooker boxes. I'm hoping to use those numbers to determine where they were purchased. Same with the Tannerite. Maybe someone at one of those stores will remember something useful about our bomber. I'm still trying to track down info on his burner phone, but that's been slow."

Axel nodded. "Excellent. We've officially moved into manhunt mode. There's no question in my mind that Fritz O'Lear is our guy. The goal now is to find him before he strikes again." Axel's expression was hopeful as he looked into the camera. "Tell me you've got something we can run with today."

"I do," she said proudly. "I'm sending the overview now." She sat taller and launched the group email she'd set up before the call began.

The team reached for their phones.

"From the top," Opaline began. "I found a man named Mark Waters, who called himself O'Lear's lifelong friend. Bad news—the guy was in a fatal motorcycle accident about ten months ago. Good news—Waters's parents still live in Grand Rapids. I sent you their address and contact information. If O'Lear was truly a lifelong friend of their son, chances are they will remember him."

"Nice," Axel said. "Who's got this interview?"

Carly lifted her pen. "I'll go."

Axel nodded. "Take Aria."

The two women exchanged nods.

"Also," Opaline continued, "when I ran Mark Waters through the system, I found a car title in his name. Since he's not driving it, and was on a motorcycle when he passed, I'm guessing the car is either in storage or the new owner hasn't taken the time to transfer the title." She pursed her lips and waited.

"Maybe O'Lear is using it," Aria said. "We'll ask the family."

"Good work," Axel told Opaline. "Anything else?"

"I pulled up the names and contact information for three families who purchased homes from O'Lear when he worked for Ramsey Realty," she said.

"Who is Pamela Berry?" Max asked, obviously skipping ahead on the file Opaline sent.

Opaline grinned. That was her biggest news. "Pamela is Fritz O'Lear's high school sweetheart, and according to her Facebook account, he's someone she still sees from time to time."

A slick smile spread over Max's face. "I've got the girlfriend."

Selena's eyes widened and locked on Max. "I want in on that interview."

"Done," he agreed.

Opaline beamed. "The most recent selfies of Pamela with O'Lear were taken at pool halls or bowling alleys in town, which fits well with the hobbies list I gave you yesterday."

"We're on it," Max said.

Opaline smiled back. "Keep me in the loop. I'll try to locate the suspect while you all go on interviews."

"Do we have a description on that car?" Carly asked.

"Yes." Opaline switched screens, seeking and finding the details. "Beige, 1999, Toyota Camry. I can send a photo of Mark Waters with the vehicle about three years ago. It's not the clearest image of the car, but it's not the worst."

"Thanks," Carly said.

"Plate number?" Aria asked.

Opaline scanned the screen, then rattled off the information.

Max set his phone aside and turned to Rihanna, dutifully tapping away at her phone while the team made plans for the day's investigation.

She looked up and caught his eye. "Yes?"

"Can you get that vehicle description and plate number to the local PD?" Max asked. "Request officers and traffic cams begin looking for it. If Fritz is behind the wheel, we can track and capture him."

Rihanna wiggled her phone in one hand. "Already on it."

"Nice." He gave an approving nod.

Opaline felt her ever hopeful heart grow impossibly lighter. She'd provided leads that got the team energized. She'd boosted her friends' spirits, and the positive vibes flowing through her screen were her drug of choice.

"Anything else?" Max asked.

"That's all for now," she answered. "I'll be in touch as new information comes available."

"Thanks, Opaline," Max said, stretching upright. He pocketed his phone and threaded his arms into a black wool coat. "I think it's time I get to know Pamela Berry."

"Yes." Selena rose and collected her jacket, as well. She looked into the camera with a small, begrudging smile. Proud, but frustrated. "Good job, Opaline."

"Thanks." Opaline held her breath as she disconnected, and went out on the high note.

Chapter Seventeen

Max moved around the table to Selena as the others broke into groups, plotting their next steps.

Rihanna slipped out of the room immediately. Back to coordinating TCD efforts with local PD and media.

Selena tracked Max with her gaze, brows furrowed. "I hope you got some sleep last night. Some of us were concerned when we didn't hear from you."

"I did," he said, guilt tugging at him once more. "I came in a little early to review the information sent during the night. I think I've got a good handle on everything."

"Okay," she said. "For what it's worth, I'm glad you took the night for yourself. We need you sharp, so stop feeling guilty." She smiled. "It's written all over your face. Knock it off, McRay."

Max groaned. She'd known exactly how he'd been feeling. And if Selena had noticed, so had everyone else on the team. *Hazard of working with a group of federal agents*, he thought.

"Do you have any questions about the images and information we sent from O'Lear's apartment?" Selena asked.

"No, but I wouldn't mind taking a look at the place

later. Being in his space might help me get a feel for who this guy is," Max said. "I'd like to see the evidence you brought in, too. Photos are fine. In person is better."

"Sounds good." Selena swept sleek dark hair off her shoulders, then shrugged into her coat. "We can hit the evidence room on our way out."

Max moved toward the door with his partner for the day, eager to get a look at everything taken out of O'Lear's apartment. "The pictures made it look like there weren't many materials left in the footlocker."

"There weren't," Selena agreed, pausing to tie the belt on her coat. "Lots of empty boxes."

"Makes me think the next bomb has already been made," Max said. "I'd kind of hoped you'd turn up the next device and bring it in, or all the materials to make it. Then we'd know he was stopped, at least temporarily. We could've kept watch at local stores, assuming he'd be on the hunt to purchase more."

"That would have been better."

Max frowned. "Yeah. Now we can't be sure if he's already made another device or not."

"So we'd better get moving," she said.

Axel reached the door first, phone in hand. He glanced at Max and Selena as he dialed. "I'm calling the local Department of Transportation to see if I can get someone to review traffic-cam footage from a three-block radius around the known bomb sites. Rihanna requested cops and cams watch for the Toyota moving forward, but I think it's worth looking backward, as well. Excuse me." He slipped into the hallway and out of sight.

Carly palmed her keys and caught the closing door. "Aria and I will go see what Mark Waters's family knows about O'Lear and their son's car. If we can confirm who has the vehicle, we'll let you know."

"Sounds good," Max said. "Stay in touch. I've got a bad feeling about the text O'Lear sent yesterday. We've pushed him, and he'll be out to punish us."

The team traded weary looks.

Carly circled a finger in a roundup motion. "Well, let's move out."

Max held the door for Selena, following Aria and Carly into the hallway. He and Selena took a look at the evidence confiscated from O'Lear's apartment before heading out in search of Pamela Berry.

Selena strode ahead of him into the lot. "Care if I drive?"

Max lifted his hands. "Nah, but I'm starting to feel like Miss Daisy. Axel drove me around all day when we went out together."

"Yeah, well, Aria drove me," Selena said, looking a little pale with the words.

Max chuckled. The rookie agent's driving had frightened more than one of his teammates so far, but Max, thankfully, hadn't had the pleasure.

"She is a terror behind the wheel. I'm not kidding. She took some turns that had me clutching my pearls."

Max climbed into the passenger seat, secretly thankful for Selena's offer to drive. He needed a few more minutes to think before jumping mentally into the day. His mind was still on Allie and how much he'd hated to leave her this morning. He hoped she wouldn't spend the day getting in her own head about what had happened between them last night, because it wasn't a mistake. Not for him. In fact, he hoped it was the first step on their path to finding their way back together. Permanently.

He'd kept himself from telling her he loved her, last night and again when he left this morning, but he already regretted the missed opportunities. She didn't want him to keep things like that from her again, and he understood the importance of being open with one another about what they were feeling, but this was different. When he'd held back on personal transparency during their marriage, it had been because he didn't want to think about how he felt or why he behaved the way he did. This time, he simply hadn't wanted to scare her off, and something told him that taking it slow right now would help rebuild her trust. He needed her to believe he was taking this seriously. Not rushing in.

Selena cast a number of curious looks in his direction as she drove, but it was several minutes before she finally spoke. "Have you dug into this woman's social-media profile? Opaline didn't give us a lot of personal details to go on. We could use the information to decide our best approach for this interview."

Max nodded, then kicked himself for not having done that already. A couple of feds showing up on Pamela's doorstep at breakfast could put her off. "Good call. I'll check that out."

He used his phone to search for Pamela Berry, then navigated to the only profile by that name in Grand Rapids. "Her bio says she has an associate's degree from Grand Rapids Community College. Looks like she just celebrated her thirty-sixth birthday," he said, describing everything that caught his attention as he scrolled. "She's platinum blonde with dark roots. Thin in the extreme. Extremely tan in the Christmas photos taken last month. Long hair." He flipped through several more shots before commenting again. "She's either dressing a little young for her age or trying to look high-fashion on a serious budget. She's got a couple candid photos of her with a birthday cake in a medical office setting. Plain clothes, not scrubs. I'm guessing she has an administrative position."

"So there's nothing in there to indicate she's unreasonable or has a bias against law enforcement?" Selena asked.

"No." Max breathed a little easier for that. Interviewing individuals with a grudge against the police made it more difficult to get straight answers. Everyone in America today seemed to have a strong opinion on law enforcement, one way or the other. Hopefully, Pamela was on the side that trusted and respected what he and his team were doing. Or at least preferred them to her ex. Otherwise, their best link to O'Lear would become another dead end.

Selena hit her turn signal and cruised into a gas station. "We're getting low on fuel, and I don't want to have to stop later if we get into something good." She pulled up to a pump, then settled the engine. "Be right back."

Max knew better than to offer to pump for her, despite the ridiculous temperature and snow on everything in sight. Selena and Aria had both shut him down for acts of chivalry in the past, making their preference for equality on the job crystal clear. Though the minute the workday ended, neither of them would've passed up the opportunity to stay warm in the SUV while he froze his other leg off in the cold. Carly, on the other hand, welcomed any act or offer of kindness by anyone at any time.

Thinking of kindness sent Max's mind back to Allie, and he dialed her number. He'd forgotten to ask her to stay home from the mall again today. Part of him said that staying home should be assumed, but the rest of him remembered what his mama used to say about assuming things. Plus, he wanted to hear Allie's voice and know she was okay. A gnawing feeling that trouble was coming hit him hard as he pressed Call.

"Max?" Allie answered on the first ring, a thread of fear in her voice. "Everything okay?"

"Yeah." He smiled, glad her fear was only born of concern for him and nothing more. "I'm calling for a favor," he said. "I need you to do something for me. I wouldn't ask if it wasn't important."

"I'm only going into the mall for five minutes today," she said, in her all-knowing way. "My parents are taking Max Jr. out for a day on the town, and I'm going to see how many online orders I can fill with no distractions. I'm hoping it will keep my mind off worrying about you."

"Only five minutes at the mall?" he clarified.

"Yep. I'm running in to grab a few things I left in the kiosk. Then I'll be working from home the rest of the day."

"Thank you." A wave of relief swept over him. "We're close to getting this guy now, I promise. You won't have to stay away from the mall much longer."

"Good, because I can't," she said. "The lease on that kiosk requires more sales than I make online."

"I know," Max admitted, "and I'll help you out however you need as soon as this is over. Until then, knowing you and Max Jr. are safe will help me concentrate so I can get this done."

"Fine."

He could practically hear her smile in the response.

"I appreciate you for doing this for me," he said.

"And I appreciate being given a choice instead of an order," she replied dryly. "So we're both having a good day."

Max laughed. "I guess we are."

"Now hurry up and catch the bad guy. Then come home to me."

His chest puffed with pride over the progress they were making. And her confidence filled him with everything he didn't know he needed. "Baby, there is nowhere else I'd rather be."

He said goodbye and disconnected with Allie as Selena returned to the driver's side.

She set a disposable cup of coffee in each of the two cupholders, then placed a white paper bag on the console between them while she buckled up. "They sold Krispy Kremes in there," she said, her expression caught somewhere between guilt and excitement. "I bought two. Be the partner I need right now and eat one so I don't eat them both."

Max grinned. "A doughnut and coffee on the job. I've never felt like more of a lawman than I do right now." He opened the bag and offered it to her first.

Selena tapped her doughnut to his before taking a bite. She moaned with satisfaction, then finished half before starting the SUV's engine. "Okay, now I'm ready."

Max smiled. "Let's start with the medical office where Pamela works instead of her home. We're closer to the office, and we can always head to her house from there if she has the day off."

"Agreed." Selena sipped her coffee, before shifting into gear. "Address?"

Max entered the name of the small family practice

from Pamela's photo into a search engine, then tapped the address into the dashboard GPS.

It was time to catch the bad guy so Max could get home to his family.

Chapter Eighteen

Carly parked the SUV on a curving asphalt driveway outside a stately brick home in an upscale gated community. Two large stone pillars stood on either side of the property's entrance. A house number was carved into one pillar. The name Waters was carved into the other.

"Wow," Aria said, unfastening her safety belt and turning to stare through her window. "I think my entire extended family could live in that house, and there are thirty-five of us in Traverse City alone."

"I don't know. That's a lot of Italians," Carly said, enjoying the look on Aria's face. Not awe, exactly—more like she might actually be calculating the available square feet per family member. Before she got too caught up in that, Carly delivered the bad news. "There's probably only one kitchen."

Aria laughed, spell broken. "You got me there. My aunts and grandma would kill each other." She climbed out and buttoned her coat to the top.

"Not your mom?" Carly asked, locking up and meeting Aria at the front of the vehicle.

"Nah. My mom would be cleaning something and protesting the arguments. Bless her, but she wants to be the voice of reason in a family who'd debate the sky was blue if you challenged them."

Carly laughed. It was hard to imagine growing up surrounded by family the way Aria had been. But it would've been interesting. "Well, the sky is definitely not blue today," she said, rolling her gaze heavenward. The dreary January day was gray from top to bottom. Gray clouds overhead. Dirty gray snow everywhere else.

The agents moved onto the massive front porch of the sprawling colonial home and stood beneath a giant wrought iron lantern. Carly rang the bell.

Aria leaned back, craning her neck for a scan along the snow-covered landscaping. "You think this looks like the kind of house where a kid who'd grow up with Fritz O'Lear lived? I pegged O'Lear for a broken-home, blue-collar family. How would he ever cross paths with a kid from this neighborhood?"

Carly pulled her lips to the side. It was an excellent question. Opaline hadn't been able to find O'Lear's parents yet, but the process wasn't always cut-and-dried. Maybe Fritz had a different last name than his parents. He could've run away and changed his, or maybe their names were never the same. Anything was possible, and despite her online sleuthing skills, Opaline was still working to locate his birth certificate, which would have made the task much easier. If they'd had any money, odds were that he wouldn't have lived in that run-down apartment building. "Hopefully we'll soon find out."

The door opened, and a petite woman in black dress slacks, a red blouse and diamond earrings looked out. She had fire-red hair and heels, nails and lips. Her eyes were green, like the cat who lived outside Carly's condo. Hopefully, the lady was nicer.

"Hello." She smiled politely, curiosity tugging her tightly Botoxed brow. Opaline had included an image of Mark Waters's parents, and this was definitely his mom.

Aria lifted her badge. "Hello, Mrs. Waters. I'm FBI special agent Calletti. This is Special Agent Welsh. We'd like to ask you a few questions about someone you might know. May we come in?"

The woman's artificially inflated lips opened and closed. "Well, yes. I suppose." She shuffled back a few steps, allowing room for them to enter.

"Thank you," Carly said softly, taking over where Aria had begun. "We won't keep you long. We're just looking for information on a man named Fritz O'Lear. We believe he was a friend of your son Mark's."

The older woman's eyes misted and her face flushed. She stood taller, likely attempting to remain in control of the unexpected emotion.

Carly knew grief when she saw it, and her heart broke immediately for the mother before her.

"Mark's been gone almost a year now."

"We know," Carly said, a little softer. "We're deeply sorry for your loss. We wouldn't bring up such a tender subject if it wasn't absolutely necessary. Would you like to sit down while we talk?"

Mrs. Waters fished a tissue from the box on a side table, then ushered them down a marble-floored hallway. One side of the space was lined in windows overlooking a snow-covered patio and garden, complete with stone statues and a large empty fountain. Carly assumed it was an extraordinary view in better weather. The opposite side of the hallway had wainscoting and a chair rail, above which hung a row of floral paintings in ornate, gilded frames. The hallway spilled into a vast gourmet kitchen.

More windows. More fancy everything. Granite counters, an elaborate tile backsplash, cherry cabinets, top-of-the-line appliances and about two miles of kitchen island.

A balding man in a polo shirt and Dockers pulled a set of half-glasses down the bridge of his nose as Carly and Aria followed Mrs. Waters into the room. "Annie?"

Mrs. Waters went to the man's side. "Darling, these women are with the FBI, and they want to talk to us about Mark."

The man paled but extended an arm across the island. "Anthony Waters. What's this about?"

Aria took his hand first. "Special Agent Calletti. This is Special Agent Welsh."

"You can call me Carly," Carly said, accepting the man's hand for a shake. "We'd like to see if you remember a man named Fritz O'Lear. We believe he was connected to your son, Mark, and we'd like to know more about him. We're running thin on ways to do that."

The Waterses exchanged a troubled look.

Aria leaned against the island, separating the agents from the homeowners. "An older entry on your son's Facebook page referred to O'Lear as a lifelong friend. We hoped you might know him."

The couple shook their heads.

"Marky had a lot of friends," Mrs. Waters said. "Can I get you something to drink?" She switched her attention from Carly to Aria, then back. "I can make tea? Or coffee? I have bottled waters and juices."

"No, thank you, Mrs. Waters," Carly said. She brought up the images of O'Lear on her phone and passed the device to Mr. Waters. "Does he look familiar to you at all?"

Mr. Waters pushed the glasses back up the bridge of his nose. "Not this guy," he said, poking the more recent photo. The image changed, and the man's gaze jumped to Carly. "Sorry. I did something to it."

"No, it's fine." She pointed back to the screen. "This is another image we wanted you to see. Do you recognize him?" The image of O'Lear all shined up for Ramsey Realty centered the screen.

"Hmm." Mr. Waters took a longer look. "Maybe this man. Annie?" He handed the device to his wife, who'd already put on her glasses.

She drew the phone close and frowned. "I think I might. He looks incredibly familiar. I don't recall his name."

"Fritz O'Lear," Aria supplied. "Your son called him a lifelong friend."

Mrs. Waters returned the phone to Carly, biting her round bottom lip. "Maybe." She looked to her husband. "It's been years, but could that have been the name of Doris's little boy?"

"Who?" he asked, looking genuinely confused.

"Doris," she repeated. "She cleaned for me for several years after we moved here. Marky was young and still attending St. Joan of Arc school."

Her husband looked to the ceiling a moment, then back to his wife. "I don't remember Doris. How would I know her little boy?"

"He came with her sometimes," Mrs. Waters pressed, sounding more sure of herself by the moment. "When we had parties, she'd come on the weekends to clean up afterward, and she had to bring her son because she wasn't married. No family in town. No school on the weekend."

Mr. Waters listened, considered, looked to Carly, then shrugged. "She would know. I barely remember those days. I worked eighty hours a week back then. I was lucky to attend my own parties."

Carly forced a tight smile. "I understand." She moved her gaze to Mrs. Waters. "What happened to Doris? Any chance you have contact information for her now?"

"Or before," Aria said. "We're glad to work with anything you can offer. The matter is time-sensitive."

Mrs. Waters's expression fell. "I'm sorry, but no." She stepped closer, pressing her middle against the island between them. "Doris stopped cleaning for me when she got sick. I heard later from some of my friends who'd used her, too, that she didn't make it. Cancer." She whispered the final word.

"Did Doris work for a cleaning agency?" Aria asked.

Mrs. Waters shook her head. "She walked door-to-door one spring. She had her son with her. He had a little bike with training wheels. She put paper flyers in the mailboxes, offering spring cleaning. She did such a nice job that a lot of us hired her to come back regularly."

Aria's shoulders slumped.

Carly kept her warm smile in place. Hoping this wasn't another dead end. "Do you remember anything about her little boy? It sounded as if your son kept in touch with him after the loss of his mother."

Mrs. Waters shifted, and her gaze darted away briefly. "No. We never saw the boy outside the times he came with Doris to clean," she said, "but it's possible he and Mark saw each other again. The truth is that Mark had some troubles in high school, and we didn't get to meet a lot of his friends."

"Got kicked out of St. Joan of Arc for using pot," Mr. Waters said, his voice going hard and gravelly. "Don't let her sugarcoat it for you just because he's gone. Mark was caught drinking here more times than we could count, and that was before he was old enough to drive. He was busted with pot at his overpriced private school. He blew off college. Moved out at eighteen and didn't look back. He showed up here from time to time, mostly when he needed money. The next thing we know, there are highway patrolmen on our doorstep at three a.m. telling us he crashed a motorcycle going a hundred miles an hour in the rain." He tore his glasses off and tossed them onto the countertop. "That's what I know about my son. I don't know anything about who he did or didn't call a friend. What do you want this guy, O'Lear, for anyway?"

"Serial bombing," Aria said.

Mr. and Mrs. Waters's eyes widened a moment before Mr. Waters cursed. "I'm going to the study. Good luck, Detectives." He headed for an ornately carved archway on the other side of the kitchen, then vanished through it.

Carly shot a look at Aria, whose mouth had pulled into a frown. They were special agents, not detectives, and the lack of success they'd been having on this case made that fact abundantly clear.

"Mrs. Waters," Aria said, turning a compassionate look on their hostess, who was still staring after her husband. "Just one more question, if you don't mind. Did you know your son owned a Toyota Camry when he passed?"

She stilled, turning her attention back to the agents. "We bought Mark a Camry when he turned eighteen. Before he moved out. We wanted him to have a way to come home and visit after he left."

"Any idea where that car is now?" Aria asked.

"No." Mrs. Waters sucked in a ragged breath. "It was the last thing we bought him. We assumed he sold it for drugs or cash a long time ago. Maybe even that he traded it for the motorcycle he was on when he…" She pressed the tissue to her nose again. "I'm sorry. I just can't believe he's gone. There's so much I would do differently if I could."

Carly pulled a business card from her pocket and set it on the countertop. "We'll get out of your hair now. Please apologize to your husband for us, if we upset him. We're truly sorry to have put you through this today. If you think of anything later that you want to tell us, just give me a call."

"We can see ourselves out," Aria said.

Carly followed Aria back down the hall to the front door, then into the freezing winter day. They didn't speak again until they climbed into the SUV and cranked up the heat.

"Well, that was a bust," Aria said. "We upset those poor people for nothing."

"Yeah." Carly admired the big house another moment before backing down the drive and pulling away. "Hopefully Max and Selena are having better luck."

Aria sighed. "I can't see how they could be doing worse."

Carly's phone rang, and she recognized the number on-screen. She answered using the speaker option. "Hey, Axel," she said. "You've got me and Aria."

"Hey. How'd it go with the Waters family?" he asked. "Were you able to catch them at home?"

"Yep," Aria said. "Nice people. Total dead end."

"Their son was estranged at the time of his death," Carly explained. "They weren't familiar with his friends, and his mom didn't even realize he still had the Toyota. It was a gift from her and Mark's father when Mark was eighteen."

"So O'Lear could potentially be driving that car?" Axel asked.

"It's possible," Carly said. "Mrs. Waters thinks O'Lear might be the son of her former cleaning lady, Doris. Unfortunately, Doris passed away years ago, and according to Mrs. Waters, she didn't have any family other than her son."

Axel made a disgruntled sound. "So we know this guy's had it rough. Single mom. Potential feelings of abandonment by Dad. No father figure. Mom cleans for rich people in town, which could've led to being teased. Then Mom gets sick. Income stops. Medical bills pile up. She dies, and his anchor goes with her. Do we know how old he was when she passed?"

Carly shook her head. "No."

"So he was potentially orphaned," Axel continued. "That's a lot of weight for one kid. He's probably felt like an underdog his whole life. I'll see if Opaline can find any record of him in the foster system."

"Good call," Aria said. "Have you spoken with Max and Selena?"

"No. Not yet," Axel answered. "I'm going to reach out to them when I finish here. I've got O'Lear's face on a flyer, and I'm canvassing the neighborhood around his building. I have about a half dozen more apartments to go before I call it quits on this area and move to the block with Burger Mania."

"Learning anything?" Aria asked.

Axel gave a humorless laugh. "Most people don't answer their doors. The ones who do are a split. Some don't want to talk to me. The rest say they don't recognize O'Lear's picture. A couple of men on the sidewalk said they thought they knew him from some bar downtown. They had no idea he lived on this block."

Carly glanced at the phone on her outstretched palm. "Opaline said he and his ex-girlfriend liked to bowl and play pool. You can shoot pool at a lot of bars, and a lot of bowling alleys have bars and billiards."

"I guess I'll head downtown next instead," Axel said. "It'll be nice to get inside and warm up. I'll give Max a call when I'm finished at Shaky's Bar. You can tell by the name it's going to be a good one."

Aria laughed. "Sounds like someplace I'd find my brothers. Bad music. Dim lighting to hide decades of wear and tear, an awesome burger and about ninety beers on tap."

"I could go for a good burger right now," Axel said, wind whipping through his cell phone's speaker.

"You need any help over at Shaky's?" Carly asked. "Maybe we should rendezvous there for lunch."

"Yes," Aria answered. "Greasy burgers. Salty fries. I'm in. Tell Selena and Max."

"How's Max doing?" Carly asked. "Yesterday had to be a tough one for him. Then he didn't respond to any of our messages last night."

"I think he's just fine," Axel said, a peculiar lilt to the words.

"You think?" Carly rolled the words and tone around in her mind. "Oh," she said. "So he wasn't at the hotel when you got back, then?"

"Nope."

"And he wasn't there when you got up for work this morning either?" she asked, trading grins with Aria as the facts set in.

"Nope."

Carly felt her smile widen. Max had gone to see his ex-wife and son for dinner, and he'd stayed the night. "I guess you're right. He's doing just fine."

Chapter Nineteen

Grand Rapids Family Practice was housed in a squat one-story brick building near downtown. Max held the door for Selena as they entered the small medical office. According to the website, GRFP had four full-time doctors and a handful of regular staff. Currently, they also had a mostly empty parking lot and a completely empty waiting room.

Mauve-and-green padded chairs lined the waiting-area walls, interspersed with small rectangular tables. A hodgepodge of picture books and popular magazines topped the tables, and there was an indestructible-looking, topless toy box against one wall.

They crossed the silent space to the check-in desk and smiled politely at the woman on the other side.

"Hello," Selena greeted the platinum blonde behind the desk. The woman's name badge identified her as Pamela, but Max didn't need that to recognize her. She looked exactly like all her photos on Facebook.

"Good morning," she answered. "How can I help you?"

Selena raised her badge, giving Pamela a serious look before tucking the identification away. "We're hoping to have a word with you. Is there somewhere we can talk privately?"

A second woman stalled as she passed by, apparently noting the distinct and sudden tension. "Is everything okay, Pamela?" she asked, coming to stand beside the seated woman.

"Yes. Fine," Pamela said. "Thank you."

The second woman wore pink scrubs, orthopedic shoes and had at least twenty years on the rest of them. She put her hands on her hips. "Then maybe I can help you," she suggested, fixing a warning look on Selena and Max.

"No." Pamela stood woodenly, then forced a bright smile. "I've got this. But can you cover for me? I'll only be a minute."

The older woman narrowed her eyes at Selena and then Max. "Okay." She unhooked the stethoscope from around her neck and lowered herself into Pamela's vacant seat. "Let me know if you need anything."

"Thank you." Pamela lifted a hand in goodbye, then went around to open the door separating the waiting area from the offices and exam rooms. "We can talk in the kitchen."

The area beyond the waiting room was like every other doctor's office Max had ever seen. Watered-down paint colors. A tall scale and height device pressed against a wall with coat hooks. Open exam-room doors with empty tables covered in paper. A handful of men and women in colorful scrubs looking at open files as they buzzed around.

The office's kitchen was as simple as the rest of the place. A countertop and sink on one wall. A lunch table down the middle with plastic folding chairs around it.

Zero bells and whistles. A laminated evacuation map taped above the sink.

Pamela shut the door once they were all inside. She moved around to the kitchenette and leaned against the small counter, knocking into a collection of assorted coffee mugs. Her khaki pants and white sweater were snug on her lean frame, and she wore trendy on-brand sneakers instead of the plain, comfort-first footwear worn by the other staff they'd passed in the hallway. "Is someone hurt?" she asked, pushing a swath of platinum hair off her shoulder.

"No." Max offered her his hand. "I'm Special Agent Max McRay. This is Special Agent Selena Lopez. We'd like to ask you a few questions about a man we think you know. His name is Fritz O'Lear."

"Fritz?" Pamela asked, swinging her gaze from Max to Selena, then back. "And he isn't hurt?"

"No," Selena answered. "He's not hurt."

Max and Selena waited then, allowing Pamela time to ask herself what the FBI wanted with her ex, before moving forward. Max evaluated her expressions as she worked through the situation. Surprise. Confusion. Concern.

"What do you want with Fritz?" she asked, crossing her arms and leaning away. Not a great pair of body signals. She was putting up a barrier, then adding additional space, though she could only manage an extra few inches from her position at the counter.

"We need to get in contact with him," Selena said, her silky voice adding a measure of calm to Pamela's visible tension. "Do you have any idea where he might be?"

Pamela shook her head. "I haven't seen Fritz since Christmas."

"Tell us about that," Max said, doing his best imitation of a tough guy. He hadn't gotten a good read on her yet and didn't want to give her the time to decide against being helpful. If the surprise of their appearance at Pamela's office was all they had going for him right now, he needed to make the most of it.

She released a nervous breath. "I ran into Fritz at the bowling alley's holiday party a few days before Christmas." She ran her hand up and down one bicep, but didn't uncross her arms. "We played a couple games of pool. Had some drinks." She smiled. "There was a lot of mistletoe and nostalgia, so I invited him back to my place for the night." Her cheeks pinkened at the admission. "The holidays are a confusing time. It's easy to feel lonely. And I've known him for years."

"How did he seem that night?" Selena asked. "Was he upset about anything in particular?"

Pamela's brows arched. "A little." She chewed her lips, choosing her words. "Before he left, he told me he's always regretted we didn't end up together, and he thought maybe we could have a second chance."

"And?" Selena asked.

Pamela wrinkled her nose. She looked at her shoes, then her pale blue fingernail polish. "I laughed at him." She raised her eyes again, looking the way Max might if he'd accidentally kicked a small puppy. "I told him what we had was great for high school, but it ended for a reason, and that our one-night stand was only that. We remind each other of when we were young and fearless. Then got carried away. Nothing more."

Selena gave an understanding nod. "How'd he take that?"

"Not great. I tried to explain, but I think I made things worse the more I talked. I said he was romanticizing what had happened between us. It was a onetime adult hookup, and I barely remembered our monthlong high school romance. I told him those things aren't meant to last. Then I remembered he didn't date back then. In hindsight, I think those dates when we were teens, and the night after the bar, all meant more to him than me. I feel terrible for hurting him. Fritz has had it rough." She tucked a fingernail between her teeth and began to gnaw.

Max traded a pointed look with Selena. He hadn't known what to expect from Pamela before they spoke, but this wasn't it. She'd just described a third recent rejection for O'Lear. For someone already teetering on the edge of a mental break, and with little left to lose, it could've been enough to push him over the edge, especially after the Burger Mania employee's rejection and this one from Pamela. "Do you have any idea where Fritz could be now?" Max asked. "If you wanted to get ahold of him, where would you start?"

Pamela shrugged. "Have you checked his apartment? He doesn't go out much, and he's not working right now, or he wasn't at Christmas anyway, so you might catch him there. I have the address. I can write it down for you." She turned to collect a pen from the top of a small microwave, then froze. She turned back, looking a little greener. "You were at his place yesterday. I remember now." She pointed to Max. "You were the guy in the bomb suit. I watched you talking to the local police after you left the building. I was worried because I recognized Fritz's building."

Selena took the chair opposite Pamela. "Breathe."

Pamela made a small strangled sound.

Max crossed his arms and widened his stance behind

Selena, running mentally through the possibility Pamela was next on O'Lear's hit list.

She looked from agent to agent. "Do you really think Fritz is the Grand Rapids bomber?"

"We know he is," Selena said gently. "And he knows we know."

Pamela gasped.

"He's hiding, and probably unhappy we stopped his attack yesterday," Selena said. "So it is imperative that we find and stop him before anyone else gets hurt."

Max stepped forward, then crouched before the table. "You said you see Fritz around sometimes. But you haven't seen him since Christmas." Since she'd rejected him. "Is that common?"

She frowned. "I'm not sure. It's barely been a month, and there were holidays in between, but he wasn't at Shaky's for New Year's Eve." She wet her lips. "He hasn't missed that party in a decade, but I figured he was avoiding me. I knew I'd hurt his feelings, and I was hoping to apologize. I didn't get to."

"You don't have a phone number for him?" Selena pressed. They had one for the text he'd sent, but maybe he used another phone.

She nodded, then gave them the number they already knew.

Max cast a look in Selena's direction. "I can make some calls and get a safe house set up for her."

"What?" Pamela said, voice cracking with panic. "For me? You think he'd try to kill me? Because I didn't want to rekindle a high school relationship?"

Maybe, Max thought. *O'Lear has certainly killed for less.* He stretched onto his feet and liberated the phone from his pocket while Selena spoke with Pamela.

"We think he's been targeting people who've recently rejected him," Selena explained, as Max sent a series of update texts to Axel, Rihanna and the team.

"That doesn't make any sense," Pamela complained. "Fritz and I are friends."

"Is there anyone else he might have a beef with?" Selena asked. "We know he has at least one more attack planned, and we think that could happen at any time."

Pamela cried.

Axel and Rihanna both responded almost instantly to Max's text. Axel would have a safe house arranged through Grand Rapids PD. Rihanna had a cruiser on its way to collect Pamela and take her to the new destination.

"Pamela," Selena said. "I know this is upsetting, but can you think of anyone else Fritz was upset with? Did he mention someone specific the last time you saw him?"

"No." She batted confused, tear-filled eyes. "Maybe. I don't know. I can't think."

"Look," Selena said. "I know we've given you a lot to process, and you're probably feeling scared, betrayed and a little ambushed right now, but there are lives at stake, so I need you to be sure."

Max forwarded Axel's and Rihanna's texts to Selena, then went to join the women at the table.

Pamela stilled, brows furrowing. "There was someone. A guy from his old neighborhood works at Coffee Coven now."

Max lifted his phone once more. "What's his name? I'll get Grand Rapids PD to pick him up and protect him while we check out the lead."

"I don't know." Pamela shook her head. "Fritz thought the guy spit in his drink, and when he demanded to speak to the manager, the guy tapped his badge and laughed at him. I guess he was the manager. The whole exchange got the other workers laughing together behind the counter. There's a bunch of teens and college kids that work there these days. They're all obnoxious. I only go there because it's the best place for a latte in the entire mall."

Chapter Twenty

Allie turned off her blow-dryer and rubbed a towel over the steamy bathroom mirror, clearing the fog. She'd made a quick trip to the mall and set up a workstation in the kitchen before indulging in some long-overdue self-care. It wasn't often that her parents took Max Jr. for more than a couple of hours, mostly because Allie hated to be away from him, but today, she was eager for the time alone. Before she got to work, she wanted to bask in the afterglow of a perfect night with Max and dream about where that renewed connection might take them. Hopefully back to her bed. Maybe even back to the altar.

She'd stood beneath a stream of piping hot water, the volume on her radio cranked up to support her one-woman shower concert, and she'd stayed there until she'd shaved, shampooed and exfoliated every inch of herself. She stepped out feeling shiny, fresh and about five years younger.

Her hair had dried and swelled to twice its usual size under the heat and pressure of her dryer, a device she rarely had time for these days. The wild blond curls Max loved to run his fingers through were softly scented with her favorite apricot deep conditioner.

Allie opened the bathroom door to release the steam

and better admire her work in the foggy mirror, then went into her adjoining bedroom to dress. She slid into her softest jeans and an olive-colored sweater that brought out the green in her hazel eyes.

She'd made a decision in the shower.

When Max came for dinner tonight, she would tell him exactly how she felt. Whatever had gone wrong in their marriage, she still loved him. She'd never stopped. And in hindsight, she was a contributing factor in their breakup. She'd played the victim at the time, wanting more from him than he could give, then tucking her tail and turning away when he didn't comply. In truth, she was no more a victim than Max. She was his wife, and she should have fought for him. She should have stayed and demanded he get the help he needed to ease his PTSD and stop burying himself in his work. The love he and Allie shared was bigger and stronger than any trauma, and she should've been beside him every time he entered and exited that counselor's office. Max had told her the other night that he'd abandoned her when she was his teammate, but she'd abandoned him, too. And she was ready to do what it took to make that up to him.

A soft creak caught her ear, somewhere outside her room, followed by the sound of footfalls on her hardwood floor.

She smiled with the realization her parents had stopped home for something. It wasn't unusual. They often popped in and out when they had Max Jr., grabbing an extra change of clothes, another blanket or toy. If they'd been shopping, they occasionally stopped in to show off their bounty before heading out again.

"Talk about perfect timing," she called, pressing small diamond stud earrings into her pierced lobes. "Tell me what you think of this sweater." She hurried out to catch her mom, but the home was silent as she padded down the hall.

The kitchen and living room were empty.

Allie turned in a small circle, gooseflesh crawling over her toasty warm skin. She scanned the rooms for signs her mom had dropped something off, or maybe picked something up, then left. Nothing seemed out of place.

Had she been wrong about the footfalls?

An icy chill swirled through the kitchen, forcing the back door open wide. The gust hit Allie in the face and chest, complete with flurries from the world outside.

She rushed toward the door, sliding in melted clumps of snow on her kitchen floor. Footprints, she realized, but her mother never used the back door.

No one did.

Fear-laced adrenaline shot through her limbs, and she lunged for the door, slamming it shut and twisting the lock. Then she ran for her bedroom. Allie grabbed her phone from the nightstand and stared in disbelief at the notification of seven missed calls from Max.

She'd been in the shower, been drying her hair.

She locked her bedroom door, creating a barrier against the intruder, then stifled a whimper as she fumbled to unlock the device with suddenly shaking hands. Either someone had been in her house, or they were still there now. She could only pray it wasn't the latter. Her thumbs moved woodenly over the screen as she mentally processed the possibility someone had been inside her home. Someone could still be inside her home. And wherever Max was, it was too far away to help.

A flash of blinding pain shot through her head without warning, pitching her forward and knocking the phone from her grip. Her palms and knees slammed against the floor. Her cell phone skittered into the doorjamb with a crack!

A sob broke on her lips, and a scream built in her chest. Confusion faded into pinpoint clarity, and Allie knew it was too late for anyone to help. A feral yell ripped from her core, leaving her throat burning and raw. She couldn't dial 911, but she could fight. Max had taught her how.

Allie rocked onto the balls of her feet, prepared to deflect her intruder, then make a run for help.

Instead, angry fingers curled deep into the back of her hair, hard fingernails scraping the skin of her scalp. With one thrust from her assailant's arm, Allie's forehead beat against the carpet, effectively stopping her flight.

Blood pooled in her mouth. Her tongue and lip throbbed, one bitten, the other busted as her face connected with the floor.

"Shhh," her assailant whispered into her ear. His heavy knee pressed against her spine, crushing her stomach into the rug beside her bed. "You don't want to do that," he warned. Hot tears fell from her eyes. His dank breath clung to her cheek as he spoke. "No fighting. No running. I have your family."

Allie sucked in a shallow, ragged breath. Her sobs instantly silenced. She waited, biting back the cries, desperate to know what he would say next, and prepared to comply.

"Attagirl," he said, easing his weight off her. "I've attached a bomb to your parents' little station wagon. They're taking your boy out for ice cream. You wouldn't want to see them all go boom, now, would you?"

Allie pressed her lips against the building sob. She shook her head. She would do as he said. Anything he said.

"Give me any trouble at all, and I'll dial the number that detonates that bomb," he promised. "Their safety depends on you. Understand?"

She nodded hard and fast, tears blurring her vision and the taste of blood turning her stomach.

He yanked her up by her hair, and she cried out unintentionally, shocked by the fresh jolt of pain and struggling to get her feet beneath her. "Move," he growled. "Now."

She stumbled forward as he shoved her into the hall, through the kitchen, then out into the snow.

He didn't have to tell her who he was. Allie already knew.

This was Fritz O'Lear. The Grand Rapids bomber. And he was going to kill her.

Chapter Twenty-One

Max breathed easier when he and the TCD arrived at Great Lakes Mall, the shopping center where Allie leased a kiosk, and found she wasn't there. It had only taken a few minutes of speaking with Emilio West, the Coffee Coven manager, to erase any doubt from Max's mind that he was the bomber's fourth target. Emilio had answered the phone when Max called, then ranted, complained and guffawed through a half dozen stories about how much he hated Fritz O'Lear.

According to Emilio, O'Lear had been a loner in school and a stalker of Pamela, before they dated and afterward. He claimed that O'Lear lurked on the outside of groups, often lingering near attractive women, attempting to flirt, but always failing. And allegedly visited the mall several times a week.

Emilio said O'Lear had a bad habit of coming into Coffee Coven to bother the young girls behind the counter. He made the baristas uncomfortable and held up the lines, so Emilio had told him to leave, loudly and often. And the last time O'Lear had been in for coffee, Emilio had incited the workers to laugh at him. He hadn't been back since.

Max dialed Allie once more as he walked the still

escalator, back to the food court for a rendezvous with Axel. The squeak of gym shoes on tile floors told him another wave of exiting employees and shoppers was on the way out. Local PD had coordinated with mall security to evacuate the building. Meanwhile, Sergeant Sims was rounding up the bomb squad to help Max search.

Max's call, like all the others before it, went to voice mail.

Axel met him at the base of the unmoving steps, brows furrowed in concern. "Any luck?"

"No, but at least she isn't here."

"True." Axel bobbed his head, looking a bit relieved, as well. "The place is nearly emptied," Axel said. "We'll get started soon and be done before you know it. Then you can swing by and check on Allie yourself."

"It's a big mall," Max said, pulling his attention back to the job at hand. He liked the idea of checking on Allie in person, but it would take time to do a thorough job in a building this size. "It's a lot of ground to cover."

Fire and Rescue was on the way, along with multiple ambulances, in preparation for a worst-case scenario.

Max could only pray they were as lucky as the last time.

"Good news," Axel said. "When I expressed the same concern to Chief Drees, he suggested we reach out to a local training center for search-and-rescue dogs. Grand Rapids PD has used their services to find missing people and locate bodies. There's also a team trained to find accelerants."

Max felt his mood lighten. "Nice." He'd worked with bomb-sniffing canines overseas, and their abilities were astounding. Nearly unbelievable.

"Rihanna gave the training center a call, and they're rallying a set of handlers and canines as we speak."

"That's good. The dogs will make short work of the search." Max pressed his fists to his hips and scanned the strangely off-putting scene. The bright neon signs and colorful food-court decor seemed unnatural in their silence. The tables and counters were empty. The individual eateries dark. Only the faint, peppy notes of music on a mall-wide sound system remained. Forgotten by whoever had been in charge. Leaving an eerie abandoned-carnival vibe to rival any childhood nightmare.

Axel's phone screen lit, and he turned it over to check the message. "We've got about twenty minutes on the canines," Axel said. "Looks like they're on their way. We can brief the handlers while they suit up before heading in."

"That works. Emilio said this was his afternoon to do payroll in the office instead of helping at the counter. My best guess is that O'Lear would try to hit him then, when he would be predictably immobile for a long period. Stuck at his desk pushing papers." Max angled away from Axel, discreetly checking his phone for messages.

"Have you tried Allie's parents?" Axel asked, knowing exactly what Max was up to. "They live right next door. If she isn't with them, they can at least run over and check on her to put your mind at ease. They can probably get it done while you're on the phone."

Max had considered the idea already but hadn't followed through with making the call. Allie would say he was overreacting, which she hated.

"Hey," Carly called, moving toward Max and Axel in long, determined strides.

Aria and Selena were on her heels.

"Media has arrived," Aria announced. "Local PD created a perimeter and are pushing evacuees to leave the lot. Most are dragging their feet. Wanting answers. Everyone's making calls. The whole city probably knows what's happening by now."

"City Planning delivered the most recent set of blueprints," Carly said. "We spread them out in the surveillance transport that Chief Drees arrived in. His men are taking a look now. I told him you'd be there soon to mark the search route."

"Thank you," Max said. "Let's take a look."

Axel lifted a finger on one hand, then pulled the cell phone from his pocket and frowned. "It's Chief Drees now." He swiped the screen. "Morrow."

Selena moved to Max's side, crossing her arms as she looked across the cavernous space. "Any ideas how you're going to tackle a place this size?"

"Some." He widened his stance and waited as Aria and Carly moved closer. "We'll break it into quadrants for efficiency and clear them one by one. Starting at Coffee Coven, then spreading out in an arch. We'll use two teams. One on each floor, both covering the same quadrant, then sweeping out. We want to make sure O'Lear didn't plant the device above his target, with the intent of collapsing a section of the building onto the shop."

"And we won't have to search the entire place," Aria said, casting a look at Max for an affirmative nod. "There wouldn't be a reason to plant a bomb in a maternity store or nail salon."

"True," Max said. "Knowing Emilio is the target and Coffee Coven is the scene of the perceived offense, we have a place to start. If we don't find the device there, we'll move to other key locations in Emilio's typical workday. Places O'Lear might have expected him to be at a specific time. Where he took breaks. Ate meals. Used the restroom. Shopped." Max would add those locations to the search plan when they went out to review the blueprints. "Same protocol for each area, searching both floors as we go. Honestly, I'll be surprised if O'Lear hadn't planned to go for him at the Coffee Coven office. So far, he's been very direct in his attacks."

"How big a blast are we talking?" Aria asked.

Max rolled his shoulders, attempting to relieve the building tension. "The devices O'Lear builds will create a fireball twenty feet wide. The projectiles packed inside with the Tannerite will move like shrapnel, through walls, through flesh and bone, traveling faster than the speed of sound and for more than a hundred yards. If you're nearby when the device detonates, you'll be injured before you've even heard the explosion, and the resulting shock wave will reach the buildings across the road, potentially to the end of the next block." He glanced back and forth as if he could find O'Lear lurking in a corner. "We have to move fast. If he's tipped off by news reports, he might pull the trigger sooner rather than later."

Aria rocked back on her heels, appropriately speechless.

"We've got a problem." Axel's projected voice turned the foursome around once more. His expression stole the oxygen from Max's lungs.

"What is it?" Carly asked.

Axel gripped the phone in one lowered hand, his knuckles nearly as white as his cheeks.

"The woman you spoke to earlier, Pamela Berry, is a leak," Axel said. "The team had her call Fritz and leave a voice mail, asking for him to call her back. We started tracking her cell-phone activity this morning after Opaline provided her information as a potential contact. Chief Drees says she didn't wait for O'Lear to call her back, but phoned him again and tipped him off."

Max cursed. "How the hell did that happen? Didn't they take her phone after she left the voice mail?"

"Apparently not fast enough," Aria said.

Selena frowned. "Why would she do that, tip him off?"

Axel rubbed his tired eyes, looking more agitated by the moment. "I don't know, but she apparently asked him point-blank if he was the Grand Rapids bomber. When he didn't answer, she started crying and begging him not to hurt anyone else. She mentioned you and Max by name. Also the mall, Coffee Coven and Emilio West. Then she begged O'Lear's forgiveness for whatever happened between them and told him not to bother trying to hurt her, because the FBI was sending her to a safe house. I guess she went on and on, telling him everything we absolutely didn't want him to know, until he hung up. Then he called her parents. Her sister. Her friends." Axel stopped to draw in a long, aggravated breath before releasing it with a fresh scowl.

"Well, that explains how the media got here before the building was even empty," Aria said.

Axel groaned. "She's either a truly emotional wreck, too far gone to realize the damage she's doing, or she's a drama junkie seeking a spotlight. Either way, she's blown the whistle."

Max scrubbed a hand over his face. "I did not see that coming." He laced his fingers on top of his head and paced. O'Lear had a heads-up. So what was his next move? "The bomb is either already here, or it isn't. If it isn't, he's not getting in here now."

Aria inched toward the massive two-story windows along the front entrance. "He's going to be mad we've interfered again. If the bomb's here, he could detonate early, like you said. Wait until he thinks you're near, then press the button. Is it even safe to search now?"

Selena joined Aria at the glass. "What if we reach out to one of the news channels?" she suggested. "We could ask them to quietly pan the crowds for him or the Toyota. Maybe he's here, and we can get him into custody before the search."

Max considered the option. "That could help. Without O'Lear, our chances of a safe search and seizure increase. I don't like the thought of him out there, waiting. Luring us close enough for maximum damage."

"On it," Carly said. "I'll call Rihanna to place the request."

Selena nodded. "Thanks."

Max let the plan settle in. They'd already decided O'Lear liked to watch, so it was reasonable to think he might be nearby. "Until Pamela called him, he probably assumed he still had some measure of invincibility. He knew we had his name, image and address, but not his whereabouts. It probably seemed to him like he still had the upper hand. After Pamela called, things changed. He knew he'd been caught and we were closing in."

"Which is an emotional rush in itself," Carly said. "There's a freedom in being this close to arrested. He'll feel as if he can do anything because the worst has already happened. He's been found out, and he will go to jail. He's got nothing left to lose."

Axel's phone lit, and he lifted it to check the new notification. "Opaline."

Max checked his watch while Axel read the text. With a little luck, the canines and handlers would be ready to work soon. Max was eager to get over to Allie's place.

"Max." The word was hard on Axel's tongue.

"What?" Max froze, certain something terrible had happened.

Had another bomb gone off? Was Max wrong about the final target?

"Traffic cams got a hit on that Camry," Axel said. "And a clear shot of O'Lear behind the wheel."

Max's gaze snapped back to the windows. "Is he here?"

"The footage is from last night," Axel warned. "Outside our hotel."

Max narrowed his eyes. "Damn it!" They'd evacuated the wrong building. "Call Rihanna. We need a team over there to get those people out. Can we redirect the canines and handlers?"

There were hundreds of rooms at the hotel. A wedding party had checked in last night as Max had headed out. Families. Children. The potential casualties were at least double that of the apartment building.

"Max," Axel warned. "The Camry followed you to a bakery, then a shop on Main Street. We lost track of both vehicles when you reached the residential area east of downtown."

Max's vision tunneled and his ears rang. O'Lear hadn't targeted the hotel. "He followed me to Allie's."

"Give her another call," Axel suggested, lifting his phone to his ear. "He followed you last night, but you've spoken with Allie a few times today, and she's been fine.

I'm going to send a cruiser to check on things. I'll ask the officer to report back, then stay out front until we can wrap this up and get over there."

Max nodded, torn between leaving the mall to check on Allie immediately and beginning the search on his own, to save some time, so he could get to Allie's as soon as possible. He was leaning toward the former when his phone rang. "It's Allie's mom."

"Hello? Mrs. Fedder?" he asked. "Is everything okay?"

"No," his former mother-in-law cried. "She's gone. I called the police. They said someone is on the way, but I don't know what to do."

"What do you mean she's gone?" Max demanded. "When? How?"

Axel pried Max's hand and phone away from his ear, then tapped the speaker option on the screen. "You're now with the TCD, Mrs. Fedder. What details can you give us about the situation?"

Panic raced in Max's heart and limbs. "Max Jr.?" he asked, suddenly realizing he wasn't sure when his ex-wife went missing or if their son was with her.

"He's with us," she answered, regaining herself slightly. "We took him out so Allie could work. The back door was open when we brought him home. There's snow in the kitchen. There's blood on the bedroom carpet."

The team's phones buzzed and dinged around Max as rage and remorse circled in his gut. His worst nightmare had come true. He'd brought danger into Allie's life. O'Lear wanted to hurt him, and he'd known exactly how to get the job done.

"Max," Axel said, turning his phone to show the message just received.

You took something important to me. Now I'm taking something important from you.

Beneath the horrific words was a photo of Allie. With a bomb around her neck.

Chapter Twenty-Two

Allie opened her eyes slowly, fighting the pain in her head and the blur of her vision. Her muddled thoughts scrambled to process an unusual scent. The hard, cold slab beneath her and the unfamiliar touch against her throat.

Slowly, the strange smell registered. Disinfectant. And her eyes, open as far as she could manage, came into focus, along with the memories of her predicament. She was on the floor, not her bed, in what seemed to be a janitor's closet. A large yellow wheeled bucket stood across from her in the small space, a mop handle sprouting from within.

Allie moaned, and her eyelids fluttered open once more, though she hadn't recalled closing them. And Fritz O'Lear came into view.

She gasped at the rush of memories, now plowing through her like a freight train.

She'd been abducted by the Grand Rapids bomber. He'd taken her from her home. She'd gone willingly to protect her family from a bomb he'd somehow left with them. Then he'd hit her from behind as she slid onto the back seat of his car. "Where are we?" she croaked, her throat dry and tight. "What are you doing?"

O'Lear moved closer, lowering to her side, then setting cold hands on her neck. "Be still," he warned coldly. "You'll blow us both up."

Allie's heart spluttered as the full realization of her situation took shape. Her attacker had fastened something large and heavy around her neck. Cold and hard like metal, the device forced her chin into an uncomfortable angle at the front.

He'd fitted her with a bomb collar.

Allie's chest tightened and her stomach rolled. She'd learned all about bombs like these while married to Max. Had read about the victims but couldn't recall any survivors. "Why are you doing this?" she whispered. "Please, just let me go."

"Shut. Up," he snarled. "Open your mouth again, and I'll detonate the bomb I left with your baby."

Allie's mouth snapped shut. Her parched tongue seemed to swell behind her teeth. And her limbs began to shake.

O'Lear leaned away and smiled. The dim light of a caged overhead bulb cast long shadows over his maniacal expression. "Now sit up." He grabbed her shoulder before she could obey and hoisted her roughly into a seated position. He jammed her back against a row of boxes along the wall. The tile where she'd been lying was stained with blood from her swollen lip, and probably her head where he'd knocked her unconscious.

She scanned the room with squinted eyes, fighting nausea as he fumbled for his phone. He was likely planning to taunt Max and the team with a text or photo. To flaunt his insanity. His deranged idea of superiority.

But a picture isn't a bad thing, she realized, shreds of hope floating in her battered, aching head. A photo was her chance to send the team a message. Opaline would find the clue, if Allie could leave one.

O'Lear tapped his phone screen, presumably writing his message.

Allie had seconds at the most to come up with a plan.

Think, she willed herself. It wasn't time to give in to the pain. Right now, she needed clarity. A way to alert the TCD to her location.

There were rows of cleaning materials on the shelves across from her, but nothing to suggest where she was. A pile of boxes pressed against her back, but she didn't dare attempt a look. She couldn't move. Couldn't risk drawing O'Lear's attention or somehow detonating the bomb.

O'Lear stepped back with a snarl, glaring at his phone. His heel crushed a small empty box, and he kicked it aside. The logo on the address label sent a jolt through her core.

Great Lakes Mall.

If the boxes behind her had the same label, there was still hope for Allie.

She pulled her arms in front of her, curving her shoulders and making herself as small as possible. Attempting to give the best view possible of the boxes at her back.

When O'Lear raised the phone in front of him, eager to snap a photo of his battered, bomb-clad hostage, she wilted forward and to the side. She did her best to appear as injured as she felt, as if she couldn't possibly remain upright any longer, even while seated on the floor. A flash of light drew her haggard gaze up to meet his.

"Now he'll see," O'Lear said, tapping the screen with a sinister grin and palpable energy. "Now he'll know.

I'm in charge here. And he's going to regret he ever provoked me."

And Allie hoped he was right on the first point. She hoped Max would see.

MAX PACED THE sidewalk outside the mall. Anger replaced the fear he'd felt all day while worrying for Allie's safety. Now he knew. He'd been right to worry. His initial bout of self-loathing had morphed quickly into primal rage as he'd waited, helpless, unable to save her. Not knowing where to begin.

He imagined the scene on repeat in his mind. Saw O'Lear breaking into Allie's home and overpowering her. Hitting her until she bled on her bedroom carpet. Had she been napping? Changing clothes? Had she heard him enter, then run to her room to hide?

Now she could be anywhere.

She could be dead.

Max pressed the heels of his hands against his eyes, forcing the thought away. If Allie was gone. If Max was too late. There would be hell to pay for Fritz O'Lear, all consequences be damned. Because when Max got his hands on O'Lear—*when*, not *if*—he was going to tear him apart.

Thankfully, Allie's parents and Max Jr. had been taken into protective custody. He didn't have to worry for his son or in-laws. He could concentrate on O'Lear and Allie, as soon as he had something to work with. Until then, he was in a holding pattern. Simmering with fear and rage. Biding his time until someone told him where to find the criminal who'd dared lay a hand on Max's ex-wife.

Around him, his teammates made phone calls and chattered among themselves. Carly called Opaline to check her progress on finding O'Lear. Rihanna spoke privately with local news channels, requesting they scan the crowd and nearby area for signs of the bomber or his Toyota. Axel contacted Pamela, determined to get an idea of where the psychopath might've taken a hostage. He also asked the officer looking after her to use her phone to text Fritz, asking for a callback, but he didn't hold out much hope they'd get an answer, now that the man knew her phone was compromised.

Aria and Selena were meeting with the Grand Rapids bomb squad and a team of handlers and bomb-sniffing dogs on Max's behalf. Reviewing mall blueprints and relaying the plan Max had outlined for their search. Whatever was happening with Allie, the mall still needed to be searched. If there was a ticking bomb meant for Emilio West, the device still needed to be disarmed and recovered.

Max had removed himself from the mission. He couldn't do the job with his heart and head so inextricably tied to thoughts of Allie's abduction.

A sharp whistle turned him toward the group of hard-working TCD teammates, and he broke into a jog to reach them. It was the first they'd called for him since he'd walked away to pull himself together several minutes before, and he knew they wouldn't have intruded without a substantial lead.

"You have something?" he called, as his friend waved him close.

"Opaline was able to manipulate the photo of Allie." Axel passed his phone to Max. "We have confirmation on her location at the time the photograph was taken."

Max stared at the enhanced image on Axel's phone screen and felt the snap of purpose in his limbs.

The barely visible address label on a box against the wall behind her bore a familiar logo.

Great Lakes Mall.

ALLIE DRIFTED IN and out of consciousness, nauseated and dizzy with pain. She'd tipped back over, sliding down the collection of boxes to press her burning cheek and body against the cool tile floor. Her head spun and her stomach churned. Bile pooled in her mouth and sweat broke across her forehead. Her thoughts wound over sweet, distant memories and through the more recent hell she'd lived today.

A round of footsteps tugged at her mind, piercing the hazy thoughts and bringing her back to the moment once more. She pressed her eyelids closed and her lips together tightly, praying Fritz O'Lear would just leave her alone. She couldn't run. Couldn't hide. Couldn't fight. What was left for him to do to her?

Besides press the button and blow her up.

Curiosity peeled her dry, itchy eyelids open to half-mast, and she was surprised by the darkness of the room. The overhead light had been extinguished, leaving only a faint red glow across the floor before her. A countdown, she presumed, from the bomb fixed around her neck.

Tears welled and slid over Allie's cheeks. She was both desperately thankful her parents had agreed to take Max Jr. for the day, and hopeful that O'Lear had kept his word not to hurt them.

At least this way, Max Jr. hadn't been home when O'Lear had broken in. Her baby hadn't been injured by the lunatic, or worse. He wasn't in jeopardy, and he hadn't witnessed his mother's abduction. All things she couldn't have protected him from.

She'd likely be dead soon, but at least her cooperation had saved her son.

Her breath caught, mid hazy thought. Whoever had been approaching stopped outside the closed door across from her. There was a strange snuffling. A heavy, breathy huffing. She blinked gritty eyes, sure it was a hallucination. The sound wasn't human. It was animalistic and wild. The noises scratched at her consciousness, but her eyes fell shut again. The nausea was back, and pulling her under once more.

THE BOMB-SNIFFING canines and their handlers stopped before a brown metal door in a long corridor beneath the mall. The dogs sat, and the men turned to Max, tipping their heads and first two fingers toward the barrier.

Max motioned the men and canines back, then reached carefully for the doorknob, twisting the cool metal with his left hand and a silent prayer. He raised his sidearm in his right hand, ready to fire as needed, and hoping it wouldn't come to that in proximity with a bomb.

He swung the door open slowly, on high alert, as a wedge of light spread across the closet floor. A familiar form appeared on the ground across from him.

"Allie!" Max rushed to his ex-wife's side and fell to his knees on the tile. She was pale and bleeding, sweating and shaking. The collar bomb around her throat gave him only twelve minutes to set her free, and time was ticking.

A team of men and women, along with three canines, waited in the hall, lingering at the doorway. Dog handlers, bomb-squad members and Axel. Max had grabbed them all as he'd torn into the mall with one thing on his mind. Finding Allie.

Now here she was, with small red numbers counting

down beneath her chin, and none of them were safe if Max screwed up.

"Get back!" Max yelled. "Retreat. I've got her. Everyone out!"

He didn't turn to watch them leave. The sounds of jogging feet and the rhythmic click of canine toenails told the story as they faded into the distance.

Max held Allie's cold tear-and-blood-streaked face between his palms. "I've got you," he whispered, taking a closer look at the device beneath her chin.

A small digital clock had been attached to a galvanized pipe. The steel was bent into a circle around her neck. An imperfect device, and an obvious rush job in comparison to the precision designs of O'Lear's pressure cookers. He'd created this bomb in anger instead of reverence. And the haste had likely made the device far less stable.

Allie's eyes opened by small slits. Her swollen lip quivered, but her body remained eerily still.

"What can I do?" Axel asked, his voice booming in the dim, silent space.

Max started, twisting for a look over his shoulder at the man who'd been with him through every manner of danger and challenge. A man clearly too stupid to leave so he wouldn't be blown up. "What are you doing here?" Max scolded. "This bomb is unstable. Get back. Go with the others."

"Not a chance," Axel said. "I'm not leaving, and you don't have time to argue, so you might as well tell me what I can do."

Max wavered, torn between saving Axel's life and improving the odds of saving Allie. It was dark, and Max couldn't hold a light and work on the bomb. Plus, Axel was right. Every second spent arguing was a moment lost to the countdown. "Hold a flashlight over here."

Max didn't dare touch the switch on the wall. He couldn't trust it or anything else in this room not to blow them up. At less than ten minutes to go now, he'd have to make do with the tools on the utility vest he'd strapped on. Axel had insisted he wear a bomb vest beneath the tools, but they both knew the added protection was more of a talisman than protection. Nothing could save their lives at this range. Max was doubly thankful he hadn't taken the time to dress in a proper EOD suit before entering the facility. Time would have run out before he geared up, then slogged through the mall, down maintenance stairs and along the subterranean corridor to Allie.

A beam of light hit her pale face and she whimpered. Axel swore.

Max knew the feeling. Allie's blood was visible everywhere beneath the light. On the floor and smeared across boxes, saturating the hair at the back of her head. She wasn't opening her eyes or speaking, probably because she couldn't. These kinds of injuries. This much blood. She was likely concussed. Probably weak, dizzy and nauseated. It was a miracle she was conscious. "I'm going to sit you up slowly," he explained. "I want to get a look at the entire device."

Max tilted her upright, then slightly forward, pushing hanks of sweaty and blood-soaked hair away from her back and shoulders. The sweet blond curls he loved were stuck to her skin and shirt. Max's eyes blurred with emotion. Seeing her like this was enough to undo him. "Okay," he said, satisfied there was nothing else to see. "I'm going to lay you down now."

"Go," she whimpered, tears falling from her eyes as

Max lowered her to the floor. "Protect our baby. There's a bomb with him and my parents."

Max stilled. He glanced at Axel for confirmation. Axel shook his head. Negative.

"There's no bomb," Max told her. "Max Jr. and your parents are with the police. They're safe."

Allie's chest quaked, and a cry broke free. "I didn't fight because he told me…" She trailed off, sobs replacing words, and Max felt bile rise in his throat. O'Lear had threatened her family, and Allie had bent to his will.

Max settled her on her back, then caressed her cheeks with the pads of his thumbs. "You're going to be okay, too, baby. I will never leave you. And neither of us are dying here today."

He tipped her head against the tile, using extreme care. "Axel."

His partner moved into position beside him, crouching to focus the light so Max could work.

Allie's hand dragged across the floor, seeking and finding Max's knee. "I'm so sorry I believed him."

"This isn't your fault," Max assured her. "You couldn't take the risk. I would've done the same thing if I thought you or Max Jr. was in danger." He pulled a small screwdriver from his vest and removed the bottom panel from the clock.

"That can't be good," Axel whispered.

"Nope." Max stared at the tangle of wires and liberal use of putty. There were visible gaps between the metal and the clock from this viewpoint. Sloppy. Amateur. Reckless work. A visual representation of O'Lear's limited time and skills.

"What's the verdict?" Axel asked.

"Not good." The collar bomb was clearly as unstable

as its maker. "There's no pressure. The blast will barely escape this room if it detonates. But it would destroy all the lives in it."

Axel nodded. "Then you'd better stop it before it goes off."

Max turned back to the wires, sorting and logging them quickly and mentally. "He doesn't want to kill me right now. He wants to punish me. Make me fail in my attempt to save her. But there's a flaw in his plan. I will never let that happen."

"No?" an unfamiliar voice asked.

Max and Axel jerked around, hands on guns. Stalling at the sight of Fritz O'Lear with a makeshift detonation device in his grip.

"You didn't think I'd leave again, did you?" O'Lear asked. "The last time I set a bomb and left, you went rushing in and took it away."

"I'm not going anywhere without her," Max said. "So your plan is cracked. And you aren't leaving this building without handcuffs or being in an ambulance."

O'Lear smiled. He wasn't much to look at up close. Five foot ten, 180 pounds of dough. Unkempt beard, disheveled hair. He looked wild and childish, a grown man throwing a fit. Demanding respect instead of earning it.

What he needed was a time-out. Preferably in a federal prison with a lifetime of therapy. But that would come later. After Allie was safe.

Max turned his attention back to the bomb. Done wasting precious seconds on a psychopath.

"Stop!" O'Lear growled. "Get away from her."

Max ignored him. There were six minutes on the bomb. Six minutes left in Allie's life. He had to work fast.

"You should be grateful," O'Lear said, inching into

the room. "You think you're doing the right thing. Being the hero. But she dumped you. She vowed to be with you forever. Richer and poorer. Good times and bad. But she left. She broke her promise." His voice grew louder with each new phrase, the words shaking from his tongue, as if he could barely contain the anger. "She humiliated you," he continued. "Tossed you aside, made you feel weak and pathetic, like you were an embarrassment. Like you were nothing. And she deserves payback."

"That was you," Max said. "Not me. None of this is about me. Or Allie." He ran his fingers along a set of thin wires connecting the clock and pipe. The space was small, his fingers broad, making it difficult to see and to work. "I love this woman," he said firmly. "I don't want to punish her. I want to save her." He patted his vest in search of the needle-nose pliers. If he could wiggle the wires out a bit, create some leeway in the tension, he might be able to disrupt the connection between the bomb and the detonator. Effectively removing O'Lear's power.

"Stop!" O'Lear screamed. "Stop touching her! She deserves punishment for what she did to you. And you deserve punishment for what you've done to me. You watch her die. Then I watch you die. You get the same thing they all get. Because I'm the one in control. Not you!"

"In five minutes, we all die," Max said. "Maybe you should start running."

"Hey, now," Axel said sharply, throwing his hands wide like an umpire. "I don't want to die. I'm just here on assignment. Someone told me to help this agent because a woman was in trouble." He turned his back to Max and Allie, leaving his light on the floor, pointed toward the bomb.

"What are you doing?" O'Lear asked.

"Pleading for my life," Axel said, lifting his palms and engaging the killer. "Please don't do this. I can understand why you want to. Women are spiteful and mean. But I want to live."

"This isn't about you," O'Lear sneered. "Shut. Up!"

"My girl broke my heart once," Axel continued. "She cheated. With my brother. And my best friend, Sarah."

O'Lear growled. "Women." He spit the word. "They make you feel good before they stab you in the heart. Men aren't any better. They all want to puff themselves up. Feel powerful, but they aren't."

"You are," Axel said. "You literally have power over our lives right now."

Max worked the tip of his small pliers under a pair of parallel wires, buried among the rest. Then he tugged slow and steady. Four minutes on the clock.

"What if you and I run?" Axel said. "There's still time. We can avoid the blast. Police will rush in, assume we're all dead, and we can get away."

"We won't get away," O'Lear said. "Not really, and not for long. There's no life for me out there now. That's why I've stayed. I'm finishing what I started."

Max's ears rang with that truth. It was a suicide mission all around. O'Lear had never intended to leave alive. He'd only wanted to spend his last few breaths knowing he was in control.

"I can't get Emilio. His bomb is still in the car. But I can get an FBI agent, and that's a good trade."

Max took a steadying breath and focused. Three minutes. He'd separated the most likely two wires to break the connection, but he didn't know which to cut. One wrong snip and they were dead.

"I came here with the police," Axel said, pressing on,

apparently willing to distract O'Lear to his dying breath.
"They pulled me off my shift for this. I can show you how
to get out without being seen. You can start over. Maybe
once things settle, you can come back and finish your
work," he suggested. "Kill Pat and Emery."

"Pam and Emilio," O'Lear said. "And I'm not stupid.
I know who you are. I've seen you on television with the
others. You're FBI, he's FBI, and I'm in charge here."

Silence gonged through the room as O'Lear went still.

And Max understood. The timer had another two and
a half minutes, but he was out of time. O'Lear never intended to let the timer reach zero. He had a detonator because he would decide when they died. He was in control.
And control was all that mattered to him.

"Do it," Allie whispered, the sound calling him back
to the wires at hand. Her pretty hazel eyes bored into
him, tired and wary, but unafraid. She gripped his knee,
squeezing where her fingers had rested through it all, a
constant connection to him as he worked. "I trust you."

Max cut the yellow wire, following his gut as the familiar click of a detonator registered in the stillness behind him.

The red numbers on the clock disappeared.

And Axel lunged at the bomber.

Max ripped the clock and wires away from the device, separating the explosives from a potential spark. He
worked the metal pipe off Allie's neck with trained and
certain hands, then swept her into his arms and headed
for the hallway.

Axel and O'Lear stumbled and fought as Max slipped
past them. It would only take seconds for Axel to bring
the assailant into submission. No one was better at hand-
to-hand combat than Axel.

"Max," Allie whispered. Her eyes rolled back, and she began to convulse.

"Allie?" Terror shrieked through him as his wife shook violently in his arms before going completely limp. "No! Allie! Stay with me," he pleaded.

The earsplitting boom of a discharged firearm ricocheted through the corridor a moment before Axel screamed, "Gun!"

Max dropped on instinct, squatting immediately and setting Allie on the floor. He twisted at the waist, gun drawn inside the next breath, and took aim at the scene behind him.

O'Lear raised his gun, and a second blast ran through the narrow space.

The bomber's gun toppled from his hand. He howled in pain as blood erupted from his thigh.

Max never missed a target. He scooped Allie's lifeless body back into his arms as Axel rolled the bomber onto his chest and cuffed him.

Then Max began to run.

Epilogue

Max led Allie into the elevator at TCD headquarters in Traverse City. It was a team tradition to celebrate with dinner after a job well done. It was also the first of these dinners that Allie had attended with Max since their original engagement, in the days before he'd begun to pull away. And he was humbled every moment by her willingness to join him tonight. Despite all he'd done wrong, Allie trusted him to change.

He wouldn't let her down.

She leaned into him and pressed a kiss against his lips as the elevator soared upward. "Have I thanked you for saving my life?" she asked sweetly, her small hands pressed to his chest.

"Once or twice," he said, gently kissing her back. "You know that without your quick thinking to make the mall's logo visible in O'Lear's photo, I wouldn't have found you in time." In Max's book, it was really Allie who'd saved her life. Her level head had made all the difference. And during questioning at the hospital, O'Lear had admitted to his plan of letting the clock reach zero if Max hadn't shown up. In that scenario, O'Lear would have beaten Max and left town victorious. But once Max had found her, and all the lawmen outside knew where they were,

O'Lear had decided to use his backup plan. The detonator would allow him to maintain control. He'd die in the process, but it would be on his terms.

"How are you feeling?" Max asked, watching her expression for signs of bravado. "Your doctors said not to overdo it for a couple of weeks. It's only been one."

"I'm alive," she whispered, her gorgeous hazel eyes twinkling under the elevator's fluorescence. "I want to live. I can rest when we get home."

"One hour, tops," he said, skimming his fingers over the warm exposed skin along her collarbone. "Then I'm taking you home and getting you into bed."

She smiled. "If only that meant what I wish it meant."

"It means you need your rest," he said, pressing a kiss to her forehead.

Clingy black velvet covered her from wrists to waistline, hugging her perfect curves in delicious ways. A black-and-white floral pattern fell loosely over her hips and stopped at her knees. She was business casual, office chic, and as beautiful as any model or actress on the red carpet. Twice as smart and infinitely more desirable. In fact, there was no one else Max ever wanted on his arm again.

Too soon, the elevator stopped, and the doors parted.

Allie turned on simple flats, twining her fingers with his as they stepped onto the seventh-floor lobby.

The voices of Max's teammates and their guests rose above the din of clinking glasses, soft music and laughter.

"There they are," Alana called, crossing the space immediately to greet them with a warm smile. "You look stunning. Both of you," she said, dropping air-kisses near Allie's cheeks before squeezing Max's hand. "I'm so glad you're here. Come. Eat. Drink. Share."

"Thank you for putting the dinner off a few days," Max said. "This was the first night Allie has felt like herself." And he wouldn't have left her side if she hadn't been up to the trip.

"Yes, thank you," Allie agreed. "I really didn't want to miss it."

Alana smiled kindly in response. "We would've put this off as long as you needed. You're our guests of honor, after all."

The twinkle in the director's eye told Max she hadn't missed the presence of an engagement ring on Allie's finger. Or the reemergence of one, to be more accurate. To Max's complete delight, Allie had agreed to be his wife once more. They would be married in the spring, with their closest friends and family members at their sides. Afterward, Max had promised to take her anywhere she wanted to go, and Allie had requested a beach, someplace warm, without interruption. Her parents had cheerfully volunteered their babysitting services.

Aria and her fiancé, Grayson, were the next to approach. Each carrying a drink in both hands. Aria passed a glass of wine to Allie. Grayson handed Max a beer. "You made it," Aria said, attention fixed on Allie. "I guess the rumors are true. You are one tough cookie."

Allie laughed. "I try, but I probably shouldn't stay long." She accepted the drink, then offered Grayson her hand. "I'm Allie McRay. I had the pleasure of meeting your fiancée last week when she and this team saved my life."

"Grayson," he said, accepting the shake. "This team has saved me, too. In more ways than one," he said, shooting a tender look at his date.

Max wound a protective arm around Allie's waist,

fighting the flash of memory that always accompanied the subject of Fritz O'Lear. Allie had been lucky to escape with her life.

Allie rested her head against his shoulder, sensing his unease, or maybe feeling the same residual emotions herself. "I was lucky," she said. "Despite a homicidal serial bomber's best attempt, I made it home from the hospital with only a few stitches. No concussion, though Max and an EEG say I had a seizure. I don't remember that. The rest, I wish I could forget. But as long as I don't do too much at one time, I'm feeling remarkably well. I'm expecting a complete recovery."

"We're all very glad," Aria said.

Allie gazed up at Max. "I'm not ashamed to admit this is the first time I've worn anything but pajamas in a week. Though I can't say I've had cause to wear a dress in about two years. Being the mother of a toddler isn't as glamorous as you might think."

"You are preaching to the choir," Aria said, her smile going wide at the mention of her newest family member. "Our son, Danny, barely lets me brush my teeth these days." She hooked her arm through Grayson's. "But I wouldn't change a thing."

Max sipped his beer, enjoying the moment. He'd been given a second chance with Allie that he never thought he'd have, and he didn't want to miss a single one of her smiles.

"It gets easier." Allie laughed. "Eventually they sleep through the night, or so I'm told."

"What does?" Carly asked, sliding between Aria and Allie, with her fiancé, Noah, on her arm.

"Babies," Allie said.

Carly smiled, and Noah pulled her close. "Well, I'm

glad you all found a sitter," she said. Her gaze trailed curiously over Max and Allie, then stopped at Allie's diamond ring. "What is this?" She lifted Allie's left hand in both of hers. "It's back!"

Allie laughed. "It is." She passed her wine to Max, so she could hug Carly with both arms.

He set the glass on a nearby table, happily enjoying the view. Allie was beautiful, fierce and so incredibly kind. He'd been a complete idiot for ever letting her go.

Opaline's laugh carried through the room, and Max turned to catch her eye. "Max!" She started in his direction, then adjusted her path slightly when she noticed Allie at his side. "Allie!" The women hugged, and Allie's eyes misted.

"I missed you," Allie confessed. "You look amazing. As always."

Opaline did a weird curtsy, then spun in her vintage pinup dress and heels. "Back at ya. I didn't expect to see you here. What are you? Superwoman?"

Allie sniffled and batted back tears. "I think that title already belongs to you."

A wolf whistle turned the group around, and Axel strode into view. His gaze jumped to Selena, still across the room, before pulling back to Allie. "Ms. McRay." He lifted her left hand to inspect the ring when he arrived. "You know it's not too late for us, right? I've got a car waiting outside."

"In your dreams," Max said, clapping his buddy warmly on the shoulder. He owed Axel everything. He couldn't have saved Allie on his own.

"How are you?" Axel asked, looking more serious as his gaze trailed over Allie's face, lingering on the barely masked split of her lip.

"I'm okay," she said. "All things considered. It's my first outing since we left the mall, unless you count leaving the hospital."

"I don't," he said. "But I'm glad you're here." Axel's gaze jumped to Selena as she made her way toward the group, and the muscle in his jaw ticked.

"Hello," Selena said, widening their circle by another half foot. She bit into her lip and looked away from Axel. "How's everyone doing?"

Max looked from Selena to Axel, wondering what he'd missed and hoping they hadn't slept together. Things would be inevitably awkward after that.

Allie studied the pair, as well, brows furrowed as she considered them. "Axel, I've been meaning to ask you. When you were distracting O'Lear from killing me, you told him women were the worst."

"Boo," Carly said. Aria scoffed, and Selena wrinkled her nose.

Axel raised his palms. "I was only trying to keep him busy. You all know I love women."

"Boo," Carly repeated. Aria laughed, but Selena still wrinkled her nose.

"You said you'd had your heart broken," Allie went on. "Was that true?"

Axel shrugged. "Sure. Everyone's had a heartbreak. Right?"

"I suppose," she agreed. "Are you seeing anyone now?"

"Hey," he said softly, "I was serious about that car waiting outside."

Max chuckled. "Watch it, Morrow."

"All right," Allie said. "At least tell me Fritz O'Lear is going to be punished for the lives he took."

Axel nodded. "That I can confirm. Alana and I worked

with the Grand Rapids PD and the TCD to create an iron-clad case against him. O'Lear will be held fully account-able for every crime he committed. His victims and their families will have justice."

Allie wrapped her arms around Max's middle and rested her head against his side. "Thank you. All of you," she said, dragging her attention to each member of Max's team.

Pride swelled in Max's chest, and he saw it reflected in his teammates' eyes.

Opaline raised her brows at Selena, and Selena looked away.

Hopefully, the sisters would work out their differences sooner rather than later. They were lucky to have one an-other, and the members of his team knew firsthand that no one was promised another day.

"Let's eat," Axel said, waving an arm toward the ca-tered buffet behind them. "I'm starving."

The group slowly folded in on itself, breaking up slightly as they made their way toward the food.

Time to eat, drink and celebrate what they had. A large and growing family. One that Max was proud to see Allie become a real part of.

He pulled out a chair for her at the table, and she turned to kiss his cheek.

Her hands grazed his chest, looping lazily around the back of his neck and pulling him down to meet her. "I love you," she whispered. "Thank you for bringing me here tonight. And for finally letting me be part of your team."

Max released the chair in favor of circling her with his arms. "You are my team," he said and brushed a kiss against her ear.

* * * * *

HOMICIDE AT
WHISKEY GULCH

ELLE JAMES

I started this book around the time my mother was diagnosed with pancreatic cancer. I finished it in a fog after she passed away. Losing a parent is never easy. I still find myself reaching for the phone to call her and talk about something, anything and sometimes nothing much at all.

I just want to hear her voice one more time. This book is for her. If not for her love, support and encouragement, I might never have become an author. She was my first proofreader and cheerleader. She loved reading and always had a book in her hand. When I was a teenager, she worked at the library in our small town and came home with sacks of books to read. I got my love of stories and my artistic f lair from her. I also got my love of the color orange from my dear mother.

Though I miss her, she will live on in my heart. Dear Mom, I'm wishing you bright colors and sunshine, and all the paint your brush can hold.

Chapter One

Master Sergeant Wade "Trace" Travis moved into position a block from the designated alley where they were to collect the dead drop. Darkness had long since descended on the Afghan city of Jalalabad.

They'd arrived inside the city near dusk, driving a nondescript van. They'd worn the traditional loose clothing of the Afghan male over their operational uniforms. On their heads, they'd chosen to wear the triangular *karakul* hats.

Trace had driven the small team into the city. Staff Sergeant Levette "Levi" Warren had ridden shotgun. Staff Sergeant Joseph "Irish" Monahan had been dressed similarly but relegated to the back seat.

Dressed as locals, they hadn't drawn attention and had found a quiet alley to park the van not far from their dead-drop location. They'd waited until nightfall to shed their outer garments, don their helmets and communications devices, and take up their arms. Levi was the only man on their team who remained dressed in the traditional Afghan garb.

Trace turned to Irish. "You ready to perform your last mission with Delta Force?"

Irish snorted. "Couldn't let me sit this one out, could they?"

"Are you kidding? Special Operations Joint Task Force

wouldn't let you out of the theater without one last hurrah." Trace grinned.

"I couldn't believe your name came up when they tagged us with this dead drop," Levi said. "It's pushing your luck. You're bugging out. Why tempt fate?"

Irish shrugged. "It's just an intelligence gathering mission, not an assault operation. We'll be in and out. No big deal."

Trace prayed that would be the case. If he had some wood to knock on, he would have. Because Irish was forty-eight hours away from a flight back to the States. His luck could be bad and jeopardize this short mission.

Trace rubbed the lucky Susan B. Anthony coin he kept in his pocket. It was the one his dad had given him to ward off danger. He'd never considered himself superstitious until he'd joined Delta Force ten years ago and witnessed luck in action. Training was key to performance, but luck, fate and faith had played a part in seeing him through many missions. He'd watched more than one man on the cusp of redeployment back to the States get assigned to a mission and not make it out alive to return home to his family.

"Tell me again why you're getting out of the army?" Levi asked.

Irish laughed. "I've been deployed more times in my career than I care to count. Each mission seems to get more and more dangerous. Hell, we never know for certain who is friend and who is foe."

Levi nodded. "True. But you knew that before volunteering for Delta Force."

"I know." Irish adjusted the strap beneath his chin. "I'm just ready to live life out of the line of fire. Look at us." He pointed to Trace and Levi. "What do we have to show for all we've done in Delta Force? A couple of medals for missions we can't talk about. When was the last time you kissed a girl?"

"I kissed one last time I was at Fort Bragg," Levi said.

Irish crossed his arms over his chest. "Yeah? What was her name?"

Levi shrugged. "I don't remember."

"Exactly," Irish said. "We don't have wives for a reason. We're never home to nurture a relationship."

"Some of us don't want wives," Trace said. The only woman he'd ever loved had sent him into the military having cheated on him. He hadn't found another woman he cared about or trusted enough to make her part of his life.

"Yeah." Irish's lips firmed. "But some of us want a wife, children and the house with a picket fence."

"What are you going to do for a job when you get out?" Levi asked.

Trace already knew. He and Irish were from the same part of the country.

Texas.

"I'm going to work with animals," Irish said.

Levi's bark of laughter filled the van, grating on Trace's nerves. "How's that going to help you get a woman?"

"I have to figure out life after the military before I bring a female into the mix. I've had enough of fighting people. Animals aren't as difficult to figure out. Besides, I need the time to unwind and decompress. I'm no good to any woman the way I am now." He hefted the submachine gun in his hands. "All I've known for the past ten years is killing. What skills do I bring to civilian life? None."

"What kind of animals are you planning on working with? Dogs, cats, guinea pigs?" Levi snickered. "Going to work in a pet store?"

Irish shook his head. "Horses and livestock. I'm going to find a ranch to work on. Good, honest work."

"How does that kind of work pay?" Levi asked.

"Not worth a darn," Trace said. "Not as a ranch hand."

"I'm not going into ranching to make money," Irish said. "I want the quiet time and to lower the stress level."

Levi snorted. "You'll be bored after a week."

"I could use a little boredom. Beats being shot at." Irish nodded toward Trace. "How long are you planning on staying with this gig?"

Trace shrugged. "I haven't thought about it."

"You grew up on a ranch. Don't you ever want to go back?" Irish asked.

"Someday." Trace looked away. He'd wanted to go home the day he left. He missed the life, he missed his mother. And since he'd left, he'd come to grips with his feelings for his father. The man had wanted the best for his only son. That hadn't included being involved with Lily Davidson, daughter of one of the worst families in the county. Hell, though she'd cheated on him, he missed Lily.

"Don't you miss working with livestock?" Irish gave Trace a chin lift. "I know you used to ride horses. Don't you want to ride like the wind and not worry about taking a bullet because you're out in the open?"

Too many times to remember, Trace had dreamed of riding Knight Rider, the black stallion he'd raised from a colt and trained as a cutting horse. As far as he knew, the stallion was still alive and well. His mother kept him abreast of what was happening on the ranch through her long, handwritten letters, delivered once a month, like clockwork. "I miss it," he admitted. "But not enough to quit the army." Quitting the army would mean he'd have to go back to Texas. Back home. His father might construe his quitting as a sign of weakness or failure.

Trace had joined the army to prove to his father he didn't need the family fortune, and that he could make his own decisions and be successful in his own right.

Granted, he would never be as rich as his father, not working for the army. But he was rich in friendship, honor and integrity. He was part of something even bigger than Whiskey Gulch Ranch. He was in the business of protecting an entire country. How much bigger could his contribution get?

Too bad his father hadn't thought much of his decision to join the army. It didn't matter. That had been eleven years ago. He'd barely spoken to his father since, other than the few times he'd been home on holiday.

Over the years, James Travis had mellowed and actually expressed his version of pride in his son's achievements. But he'd expected Trace to return home once he'd "gotten the need to prove himself" out of his system.

As an only child, Trace was expected to take up the reins when his father chose to retire from actively running the large cattle operation and his other investments.

Trace knew how to run the ranch and the other businesses in which the Travis family were involved. Hell, he'd been groomed from birth to handle the family fortune. That wasn't the issue. His father would never turn over the reins. He'd be involved with the daily operations until the day he died.

Pulling his head out of the past, Trace focused on the task ahead. "It's getting dark. Time to get this party started. In and out. No drama."

"That's right," Irish agreed. "All we need to do is retrieve the dead drop and get back to the base."

Levi grabbed his sniper rifle and tucked it beneath the long folds of his disguise. "I'll be in touch." He slipped from the passenger seat and out into the alley. Moments later, he'd disappeared to find his way to the top of a building overlooking the dead-drop location.

Trace gave Levi ten minutes to get into place. When he didn't report in, Trace spoke softly into his radio microphone, "Levi, report."

"In position on top of the building opposite the dead drop," Levi said through Trace's headset. "All clear."

"Moving in." Trace motioned for Irish to leapfrog to the corner of the alley they'd been directed to by Military Intelligence.

They were supposed to gather the information from a metal box left in the alley. Military Intelligence had indicated the message had been left by a Taliban insider who was intent on revealing the depth of traitorous activities.

They'd performed this type of mission on numerous occasions. Only half had gone without a hitch. Trace prayed this one was in the boring, no-hitch category. Irish deserved a nonevent for his send-off.

Once Irish was at the corner of the alley, Trace moved up to his position and started past Irish into the dark passageway between the buildings.

"Oh, no, you don't." Irish's hand shot out, grabbing Trace's arm. "Let me go first."

"I'm going in," Trace said and tried to shake off Irish's hand.

"That's not how it works, and you know it." Irish pushed past him. His weapon at the ready, he eased into the darkness.

"The box is ten feet in front of you," Levi said from his position above them.

Trace had Irish's back, as did Levi. But they couldn't account for what the man might find in the box. For a long minute, Trace held his breath, a heavy sensation settling in the pit of his belly.

Something wasn't right about the mission. No one had attempted to stop them. In fact, the streets had been deserted. No guards had fallen asleep at their posts, no children cried in the night. Nothing.

"It doesn't feel right," Trace murmured into his mic.

Irish paused. "I'm almost there."

"Hold up," Trace said.

"I've got nothing up here," Levi reported.

"That's just it," Trace said. "It's too easy. It's too quiet."

"Yeah. I've got a chill running the length of my spine," Levi admitted. "What do you want to do?"

"Abort," Trace said. "Pull back, Irish."

"Man, I'm within reaching distance of the box," Irish said. "What if that message is important?"

"It's not worth losing your life over," Trace said. "Abort."

For another long moment, Irish hesitated. Then he sighed. "You're the lead on this mission." He turned and took several steps toward Trace. He hadn't gone more than a couple yards when a loud explosion shook the ground beneath Trace's feet.

Trace was thrown backward, landing hard on his back, the wind knocked from his chest. He fought to drag air into his lungs. Though he could tell someone was talking to him, he couldn't make out the words over the loud ringing in his ears. He sat up and shook his head. His weapon lay on the ground beside him.

What the hell had happened?

Then he noticed Irish lying facedown, sprawled in the alley.

Trace's heart raced as he pushed to his feet, grabbed his weapon and lurched toward his friend. He staggered a few steps, tripped over his own feet and fell hard on his knees, his head spinning.

"Irish!" he called out, his voice sounding as if it were coming from down a very long tunnel. He got to his feet again and forced his legs to carry him to where his teammate lay on the ground.

"Trace? Irish?" Levi's voice sounded in Trace's ear.

"I'm okay," Trace responded. "Irish is down." He felt for a pulse and breathed a brief sigh. "He's alive."

"Then get him up and out of there," Levi said, his tone urgent. "We've got company."

Trace shook Irish gently. "Hey, buddy, nap's over. Gotta get you outta here. There's a chopper with your name on it taking you to Bagram Airfield to catch your flight home."

"You don't have time to talk him into leaving on his own two feet. Get up and out of there. Two trucks full of heavily armed militants less than a block away," Levi reported. "Damn. They're climbing out of the trucks, headed our way."

Trace shook back the dizziness. He propped his and Irish's weapons against a wall, grabbed one of Irish's arms and rolled him up over his shoulder in a fireman's carry. With Irish's full weight bearing down on him, he reached for their weapons, turned and half walked, half ran to the end of the alley.

Levi met them at the corner, slung the two weapons over his shoulder and held his out in front of himself. "Go. I've got your back."

Trace had no way of protecting himself or Irish. All he could do was get his friend out of there as quickly as possible. Levi had to do the job of fending off a dozen militants.

Praying Levi would be all right, Trace headed for the extraction point outside the village.

By the time he reached the edge of the stone, mud and stick buildings, he was breathing hard and his shoulders ached with the weight of his teammate's inert body. But he couldn't stop. Not yet. He had to get to the helicopter.

Five Delta Force operators ran toward him. One split off and came to help Trace.

"Don't worry about us," Trace grunted. "I'll get Irish to the chopper. Help Levi. He's knee-deep in bad guys."

The five men ran past him. Moments later, gunfire lit up the night.

Trace remained focused on getting his friend to the

chopper. The others would follow, once they had the situation contained.

His legs shaking, his lungs burning, Trace staggered up to the helicopter. The copilot jumped down to help the medic take Irish from Trace and lay him out on the floor of the Black Hawk.

"Give me a weapon," Trace shouted.

The medic tossed him his M4A1 rifle and went back to work on Irish.

Trace turned and ran back toward the little town and the continued sharp report of gunfire. Before he reached the village walls, three members of his team who had passed him minutes before came running from the village.

"Where's Levi?" Trace shouted.

"Beck and Jimmy are covering for him." Sergeant Parker Shaw slowed to a stop beside Trace. "We've called in an airstrike. They told us to get out."

"Not without Levi, Beck and Jimmy."

"They were the ones who told us to get out," Parker said. "Levi nearly took a shot at me."

"Not leaving without them," Trace said and ran toward the village.

Parker fell in step beside him.

More gunfire sounded as they neared the village.

Then the night erupted in a fiery explosion, knocking Trace backward. He staggered but regained his footing and resumed his forward movement.

Parker rolled to his feet and kept pace beside Trace.

"I see movement ahead," Trace said.

What looked like a clump of moving parts emerged from the village into the open.

Trace could make out two men holding up a third between them, running while twisting around to fire rounds to their rear. Several bogeys popped up over the tops of the walls.

"They need help." Within two hundred yards of the compound, Trace dropped to his knee, aimed his rifle and fired at one of the men perched at the top of a wall. The man slumped and fell from the wall to the ground.

Another explosion rocked the landscape as a round from an unmanned aerial vehicle, driven by a young air force lieutenant back at a base in Nevada, slammed into the village.

The three Delta Force soldiers running toward him staggered but remained upright, pushing forward to their destination.

Parker dropped down beside Trace.

Soon, the other two Delta Force members set up a line of fire to either side of Trace and Parker.

Jimmy, Beck and Levi made it past them and onto the helicopter waiting to extract them.

Another round smacked into the wall of the village. The enemy element who'd been firing at them lay dead or had scattered.

"I'll cover," Trace said. "The rest of you get to the chopper."

"Not going without you," Parker said. "The rest of you... move!"

"We'll go together, or not at all," Jimmy's voice rang in Trace's ears.

Overruled by his team, Trace rose and ran backward toward the waiting Black Hawk. The last man to climb aboard, he hovered close to the door, his weapon aimed at the village and any possible bad guys who might decide to take a shot at the chopper as it lifted off the ground.

The helicopter rose into the air, but not nearly fast enough for Trace. Not until they were well away from the village did Trace let go of the breath he'd been holding and turn toward his friends.

The medic worked over Irish. He had Parker applying pressure to a wound while he established an IV of fluids.

As soon as he had Irish stabilized, he turned toward Levi.

"Don't worry about me," Levi said. "Just a flesh wound."

Beck was wrapping Levi's leg in gauze. "Yeah. Right. The man bleeds like a stuck pig."

"I'll live," Levi said. "Thanks to you guys." He winced as Beck tied a knot over the wound.

The medic had the pilot call ahead to have the medical staff ready to receive the wounded.

They were met by a military ambulance, and Levi and Irish were loaded into the back.

"I want to go with them," Trace said to the driver.

"Not enough room," the driver said, closing the back of the van.

Trace looked around for transportation to get him to the hospital. A captain dressed in a clean uniform hurried toward him. "Are you Master Sergeant Wade Travis?"

With a frown, Trace nodded. "I am."

"I'm Captain Williamson. Your CO heard you would be here and wanted me to personally contact you."

"Should I know you?"

"No, sir. I'm a chaplain."

Trace stiffened. "Our guys are going to be okay. The medics are taking care of them."

"I'm not here about your teammates," Captain Williamson said.

He might not have been there about Levi and Irish, but the rest of Trace's team gathered around him. When a chaplain singled you out, it was never good news.

Parker, Beck, Jimmy and the others stood beside him.

"Could we talk in private?" the chaplain asked.

Trace's heart squeezed hard in his chest. He squared

his shoulders and lifted his chin. "You can say anything in front of my team."

The chaplain stared from Trace to the men surrounding him. "Are you sure?"

With a nod, Trace braced himself. "What's on your mind, Captain Williamson?"

Glancing down at a paper in his hand, the chaplain took a deep breath and faced Trace. "Your father was murdered two days ago. You've been recalled home."

Chapter Two

"There's a truck coming up the drive." Lily entered through the back door of the ranch house into the kitchen.

Rosalynn Travis worked over the stove, tossing ingredients for a beef stew into a stockpot. "Cross your fingers this applicant knows which is the business end of a cow." She turned off the stove, wiped her hands on a dish towel and hurried toward the front of the house.

Lily grabbed the shotgun from the corner of the kitchen and followed her boss.

The older woman was out the door before Lily could catch up.

A man with scraggly, oily hair and dirty jeans dropped down out of a beat-up pickup and walked toward the porch.

Lily pushed through the screen door and called out, "That's far enough."

The man ambled to a stop.

Rosalynn crossed her arms over her chest. "What's your purpose?"

"I'm Randy Sweeney, and I'm here about the job I saw advertised at the feed store," the man said and smiled through crooked, blackened teeth. "This is the Whiskey Gulch Ranch, isn't it? And you *are* advertising for a ranch hand, aren't you?"

Rosalynn nodded.

He hooked his thumbs through his belt loops and rocked back on his heels. "I'm here to apply for the job."

Rosalynn shot a quick glance toward Lily, before returning her attention to their applicant.

"When was the last time you worked on a ranch?"

"Well, now, ma'am, I ain't actually worked on a ranch, but how hard can it be? You poke cows, ride horses and get fed by pretty girls." His gaze slid to Lily, who'd moved up to stand beside Rosalynn.

Rosalynn shook her head. "Sorry, mister. The advertisement specifically asked for experienced ranch hands. We don't have time or the inclination to train anyone."

Instead of turning to leave, Randy took a step forward. "I understand you ladies need a man around the ranch. I'm pretty handy in a fight."

"We're not planning on having a fight," Lily said.

"Ain't you Brandy Jean and Marcus Davidson's little girl?" The man's smile turned into a sinister smirk.

"I am." Lily's jaw firmed, and her hands tightened on the shotgun. "Not that it's any of your business."

"Heard you'd come to work for the Travises." The stranger scratched his chin. "Didn't expect you'd still be working here after old man Travis's death." His gaze slid from Lily back to Rosalynn. "Thought for sure his old lady would have sent you packing by now."

Lily raised the shotgun in her arms, her eyes narrowing.

Rosalynn snorted. "I'm not old, and Lily isn't leaving. She's been more help to me than any of the worthless ranch hands who've deserted us since my husband's death."

"You'd better leave now before I put a load of buckshot into you." Lily raised the shotgun up to her shoulder and aimed it at the man on the ground in front of her.

Randy shook his head. "You ain't gonna pull the trigger on a gun that'll knock you back on your pretty little bottom."

Lily aimed the shotgun a little to the man's left and

pulled the trigger. The blast jerked her shoulder back, but she remained standing. "As you can see, I can pull the trigger and still remain upright. What's more important… I *will* pull the trigger." She aimed the gun at Randy. "Leave… now."

His brows dipped low. "Just because you have a gun doesn't make you all that."

"No?" She raised an eyebrow. "And just because you're a man and I'm a woman, you think you're smarter and stronger than I am?"

Randy snorted. "You're not like your mama, are you?"

"Not in the least," Lily responded.

"Damn shame." Randy hitched up his jeans. "Two women… Alone on a ranch… You're asking for trouble."

"We aren't asking for anything but a ranch hand who knows ranching. Whether male or female. And you're not the one." Lily jerked her head to the side. "I'll give you three seconds to get in your truck."

Randy took another step forward. "Or what?"

Lily fired off another round, pulled shells out of her pocket and reloaded in seconds. "The next one will be aimed at your body." She raised the shotgun to her shoulder and pointed it at his midsection, then lowered it slightly. "Want to test me? Think I won't do it?"

Randy stood his ground for a moment, his eyes narrowing even more. "You'll regret this."

"I regret that I've wasted two shells," Lily said. "I won't waste another."

"I'll leave, but you're setting yourselves up as targets. Two women running a ranch as big as Whiskey Gulch won't cut it. You'll fail."

"At least we'll fail at what we know how to do, without supporting someone who knows nothing about ranching," Rosalynn said. "Go home, Mr. Sweeney. We're looking for experienced help."

He snorted and turned toward his truck.

Another truck headed toward them, kicking up a tail of dirt on the road leading up to the ranch house.

"Great," Lily muttered. "Another loser come to apply for the job."

Randy hesitated with his hand on the door handle of his pickup.

"My finger's getting itchy," Lily said.

"I'm going." Randy yanked open the door and stepped behind it without getting in. His gaze followed the truck headed toward him.

Lily would rather have had Randy off the property before she had to deal with another *applicant*, but the man wasn't making a move to leave and now had the truck door between him and her buckshot.

A shiny black pickup pulled to a stop beside the beat-up one. The sun glinted on the windshield, keeping Lily from seeing the face of the driver.

"Whoever it is will get one warning." Lily held the rifle against her shoulder and aimed at the newcomer.

The driver stepped out of the truck and rounded the door, his dark hair and blue eyes instantly recognizable.

All of the air left Lily's lungs and her heart stopped beating for a full three seconds. Then it slammed against her ribs and raced, pushing blood and adrenaline through her veins.

The last person she'd expected and the one she least wanted to see strode toward the ranch house. "That's a helluva homecoming for a man who's been away for more than a year."

"Lily," Rosalynn said. "Put down the gun. My boy is home." The older woman ran down the stairs and enveloped her only son in a hug so tight, it had to be cutting off the air to his lungs.

Meanwhile, Lily had forgotten how to breathe and that she was aiming a shotgun at the man and his mother.

"What's *she* doing here?" Trace asked, his chin lifting toward Lily.

His mother glanced back, tears trickling down her face. "Lily works for me."

"Since when?"

The sound of his voice brought back a flood of memories and emotions as Lily lowered the shotgun. "Since the last time you were here, over a year ago," Lily said, finding her voice, infusing judgment into her words. Since then, things had changed.

"She started as my housekeeper," his mother said, "and now she's my one and only ranch hand."

"What happened to the rest of them?" he asked, his gaze shifting from his mother to Lily, his eyes narrowing.

"The men spooked when your father was murdered." Lily snorted, her lip curling back. "They left, thinking the murderer would be after them next."

"Bastards," Trace said. He tilted his head toward the man standing by the old truck. "Who's he?"

"Nobody." Lily glared at the man in question. "He was just leaving."

Randy pushed away from the door of his pickup. "Did I hear right? Are you James Travis's son?"

Trace nodded. "I am."

The man stepped forward, his arm outstretched. "Randy Sweeney. I'm here answering an ad for help. Maybe you're the one I need to talk to."

Trace ignored the man's hand. "The ranch belongs to my mother. What she says goes."

Randy dropped his hand to his side.

"She said to go," Lily said between clenched teeth, her hand tightening on the shotgun.

Randy raised a finger. "Not really." Then he pointed the finger at Lily. "*You* told me to leave."

"Is that what's holding you back?" Rosalynn Travis gave Randy a tight smile. "Then let me make myself clear… You are trespassing on private property. Leave now, or I'll call the sheriff."

The man looked from Rosalynn to Trace as if he didn't quite trust her word.

"You heard my mother," Trace said. "Leave—and don't come back. The Travis family doesn't suffer fools."

Randy bristled. "You calling me a fool?"

"If the shoe fits…" Trace left the statement open.

When Randy refused to move, Trace took a step forward, his fists clenched.

Randy backed away. "Some say Mr. Travis was killed by someone he knew." He shot a glance at Rosalynn. "Most violent crimes are committed by people close to the victims. Usually family members."

"Not in this case," Lily said through clenched teeth. "We'll find whoever murdered Mr. Travis." She lowered her voice and stared at Randy with narrowed eyes. "And make him pay."

Randy raised his hands. "Don't look at me. I didn't do it. I was just looking for a job. Those can be hard to come by in these parts."

"Not for folks who know how to work hard," Rosalynn said.

"You sayin' I don't know how to work hard?" Randy asked, his lip curling on one corner.

"She's saying get off her property," Trace said. "Now, get in your truck, or I'll help you get there." He took a step toward the other man.

"I'm going." Randy hopped into the driver's seat of his old pickup, slammed his door and revved the engine. A moment later, he'd reversed, spun around and headed down the gravel road, spitting up a cloud of dust in his wake.

Lily relaxed her hold on the shotgun but retained the tension in her body as she faced the man she'd loved from the day they'd met in grade school. The one man she couldn't have. The man she'd lied to in order to get him to leave.

By the look on that beloved familiar face, he hadn't forgotten what she'd done to him all those years ago.

She squared her shoulders. Trace needed to hate her. What they had ignored as children and teens couldn't be ignored as adults. They didn't come from the same backgrounds. No amount of wishing could change that. She would never fit into his world. Not with her parents' criminal backgrounds.

Not that he'd ever want her back in his life.

Lily sighed and turned toward the ranch house. "I'll pack my bags."

"The heck you will." Rosalynn moved to stand in front of her, blocking her way into the house where she'd taken up residence since she'd come to work for the Travis family. "I can't afford to lose you, Lily. Please, stay." The older woman turned her attention to Trace. "And you." She poked a finger at her son. "This young woman has been a godsend to us over the past year. I don't know what I would have done without her."

Trace held up his hands. "I'm not telling her to leave. She's a grown woman, she can make up her own mind. Although, I don't know why she's living here when she has a husband to go home to."

Lily stiffened.

Before she could say anything, Rosalynn jumped in. "Husband? What husband?" Rosalynn turned a crooked smile toward Lily. "Does he know something I don't?"

Lily shook her head. She'd always been straightforward with Trace's mother, never wanting to hurt the mother of the man she loved. But she hadn't told her the lies she'd used to drive Trace away from Whiskey Gulch Ranch. "I don't know what he's talking about. I'm not married. Never have been." She met his gaze dead-on, daring him to repeat the lies she'd told him all those years ago.

TRACE'S ANGER BUBBLED up in his chest and threatened to spew from his mouth. He clamped his lips together and ground his teeth. He refused to blast Lily in front of his mother, who apparently thought the younger woman was an angel incarnate.

He'd wait until he could get Lily alone to get answers from her. Not married? Part of him rejoiced at the news. The other part boiled with anger. She'd told him she was in love with Matt Hennessey, and Trace was too straitlaced for her. That had been eleven years ago. They'd been teenagers. Why couldn't he let it go?

Lily lifted her chin, gave Trace one last glance and turned toward his mother. "We need to get moving if you want to get to the funeral home before they close."

Rosalynn nodded. "You're right." She reached out and patted Trace's cheek. "I'm sorry you had to come home to this. Your father was so proud of what you'd accomplished in the military. He didn't say it to you, but he bragged about you to anyone who'd listen." Tears welled in his mother's eyes. "I'm glad you made it home for his funeral."

The knot in his gut hardened. "I'm sorry I wasn't here. If I had been, maybe this wouldn't have happened."

His mother's eyes widened. "Or you could have been the target along with your father." She shook her head. "You can't second-guess the past. It's done. All we can do now is move on." She closed her eyes, drew in a deep breath and let it out. When her eyes opened, she was the mother he remembered, who shouldered burdens during hard times and marched forward. "I have to meet with the funeral director. You can come with me, or not. It's up to you. I won't judge."

His chest tightened. They couldn't bring his father back, but he could be there for his mother. "I'm coming."

"I'll drive," Lily said.

"The hel—" Trace started.

"Trace," his mother said with that stern expression she'd used on him when he'd been a recalcitrant child. "Lily's been driving me since your father's death. I feel comfortable with her behind the wheel. Let her."

His fists clenched, but he didn't argue. His mother had been through enough. "Very well."

"Besides, it will give us a chance to talk."

"What vehicle are you taking?"

"Your mother's SUV," Lily said.

His mother hurried to explain. "I couldn't bring myself to get into the truck. It was so much a part of who he was."

Trace shook his head. "All I knew coming home was that Dad was murdered. I got here as soon as I could. I haven't heard all the details."

Lily followed Rosalynn into the house, calling out over her shoulder, "I'll fill you in on the way. We really need to get moving."

Rosalynn patted Lily's arm. "Thank you, dear. I admit to being a little disoriented lately."

"That's to be understood." Lily pulled Rosalynn in for a quick hug. "You've been dealt a huge blow. Losing someone you love is never easy." She herded Trace's mother through the house, pausing in the kitchen to cover the pot of beef stew. It could wait, uncooked.

Rosalynn walked to a hook on the wall where a man's suit hung, complete with a white shirt and a navy blue tie. She lifted the suit and held it against her chest. She chuckled, the sound catching on a sob. "He hated wearing suits.

But he was a stickler for tradition and would have insisted on being buried in one."

Trace's gut clenched. Seeing his mother's grief brought it home like nothing else. His parents had been married for almost forty years. More than half their lives. He held out his hand. "Want me to take the suit?"

She shook her head. "No. I've got it."

On their way through the house, Lily grabbed Rosalynn's purse, looping it over her shoulder. She snagged her own and headed back out the door, brushing past Trace as she went.

The scent of honeysuckle wafted beneath his nose. Seriously? She still used the same honeysuckle-scented shampoo as she had all those years ago?

With the scent came a myriad of emotions and images crowding into his memories.

Images of Lily lying with her head across his lap, staring up at the endless stars in the Texas sky all those years ago, her voice soft as she named the constellations and the planets. When a meteor streaked past, she'd close her eyes and make a wish.

Trace would bend over and kiss her lips and she'd chuckle.

"I got my wish," she'd say.

"What did you wish for?" he'd ask.

Every time, she'd respond, "For a kiss from the guy I love."

That was just one of the memories pushing to the forefront of his recollections. There were so many more he'd shoved to the back of his mind to keep from going off the deep end. He'd loved Lily Davidson more than life itself. When she'd dumped him for the town bad boy, Matt Hennessey, she'd shattered his heart into a million pieces. Her announcement had been the final straw that had pushed him into leaving home and joining the army.

His father had started him down that path by trying to dictate his life as soon as he'd graduated high school. He was supposed to stay on Whiskey Gulch Ranch and assume more responsibilities of ownership without any actual authority. His father could never release the reins enough to let his son make decisions.

After they'd butted heads too many times to remember, Trace and his father had had a massive argument. His father didn't think him worthy of running the ranch. He hadn't liked Trace's choice of a girlfriend. James Travis was a man who followed rules and laws. Lily came from a family of lawbreakers. She'd drag Trace down and hold him back in whatever he decided to do with his life. If he didn't drop her and start towing the line on the ranch, he would have to move out and find another way to make a living.

That was when Trace had finally realized he needed the freedom to grow into the man his father never believed he could become. He'd never be that if his father ran the show. Having had enough, he knew he would never earn his father's respect until he'd been successful on his own. That day he'd visited an army recruiter, signed the documents and sworn into the army.

With a week to go before he shipped out, he'd gone to Lily and asked her to wait for him. He'd explained that his next step was to go to the Military Entrance Processing Station, where he'd start the paperwork for a security clearance and go through mental and physical evaluations before he shipped out to basic combat training.

The people performing the background checks for the security clearance might come to his hometown and ask questions of the people who knew him to gauge whether or not he could be entrusted with protecting the nation.

That was when Lily had hit him with the news that had ripped his heart out. She'd been seeing Matt Hennessey and had fallen in love with him. She wasn't planning on wait-

ing for Trace to return. She wanted to get married immediately and it was to Matt she'd given her heart.

Trace had felt like she'd punched him in the gut so hard,
he couldn't catch his breath. The woman he loved didn't
love him like he'd thought she did. When he left Whiskey
Gulch, he'd have nothing to bring him back but the occasional visit with his mother.

He'd gone into the army with a desire to prove to dear
old Dad that he didn't need his money to survive. Trace
Travis could make it on his own. As far as making it on his
own, he didn't need a woman in his life to cause him more
pain. Lily had crushed the life out of his heart. For the next
eleven years, he would hold up her example to any woman
he met and judge them based on what they had never done,
but what they might do in the future.

Trace couldn't take another beating like he'd taken that
day. He didn't need the constant reminder with Lily living
and working at Whiskey Gulch.

He helped his mother into the front passenger seat and
then climbed into the back seat of his mother's SUV on the
opposite side from Lily. His position gave him a good vantage point from which to study Lily without her knowing.

She hadn't changed much since they were teenagers. The
soft curves of her cheeks had become more defined. Her
face had slimmed, and she wore her hair in a French braid
instead of the ponytail he used to love pulling. She'd inherited her beauty from her mother. Thankfully, she hadn't
followed in her mother's footsteps.

Brandy Jean Davidson had married Marcus Davidson
when she was sixteen and got pregnant with Lily. Her parents had kicked her out of the house, convinced their oldest
daughter would be a bad influence on their three younger
children. Brandy Jean and Marcus's marriage lasted only
until Lily was born. Marcus wasn't ready to settle down
and take on the responsibility of raising a child. He joined

a motorcycle gang and left the town of Whiskey Gulch, Texas, for California.

Without a high school diploma and no work experience, Brandy Jean went to work at a strip club. She barely made enough money to support herself and Lily, living in a run-down trailer on the edge of town. She found she could make more money off the dance floor. Lily might not have had the best home life, but her mother had tried to insulate her from her business. She wasn't always successful.

Lily pulled out of the yard and headed onto the gravel road leading to the highway. Once they were on the paved road, Trace's mother filled Trace in on what had happened. "Your father was shot while out riding fences." Her voice broke.

Lily reached across the console and squeezed his mother's hand. "Want me to finish?"

His mother nodded and swiped at a tear slipping down her cheek. "Please."

"Your father was hit several times. He fell from his saddle." Lily took a deep breath. "His foot caught in the stirrup and he was dragged all the way back to the barn. The sheriff said at least three rounds hit him. It wasn't an accidental shooting. Someone was aiming at your father."

"When he made it home, he was conscious for only a few seconds before he passed. His foot was still caught." His mother's voice hitched. She stared out the front window. "I couldn't get him down. It wasn't until Roy returned from town that I got his foot out of the stirrup. By then the ambulance had arrived." She swiped away a tear. "Too late for James."

Roy Gibson was the foreman who'd come to work for his father after Trace had joined the army.

His mother shook her head and turned in her seat so that she could see Trace. "Your father didn't have a chance. Someone murdered him."

Rage burned inside him. Though he'd had his differences with his father, he'd never stopped loving him. Unclenching his fist, he reached over the back of the seat and touched his mother's shoulder. "I'll find the bastard who killed him," Trace vowed.

"We'll find him," Lily corrected.

Too angry to argue, Trace let her comment pass.

His mother laid her hand over his. "It won't bring him back."

"No, but the killer can't get away with what he's done," Lily said.

"He has to be caught," Trace said. "He's killed once. If he's not held accountable for what he's done, what's to keep him from killing again?"

Chapter Three

What was to keep the killer from killing again? The thought roiled around in Lily's mind along with the fact Trace was sitting behind her in the same vehicle. She'd never expected to be this close to the man again. After she'd dumped him so brutally all those years ago, she didn't think he'd want to be in the same breathing space with her.

His father's death had taken precedence over any revenge or avoidance dance concerning her. For all she knew, he might not be giving her a second thought. Eleven years was a long time to forgive and forget.

Lily hadn't forgotten one thing about Trace. He was still the man she'd fallen in love with. She hadn't met another who could take his place. From what she could get out of his mother without asking point-blank, Trace hadn't married, nor had he brought a significant other home to meet the parents.

"What happened to all the ranch hands who worked for Dad?" Trace asked. "And where's Roy, your foreman?"

"Since your father was murdered," Lily said, "rumors have gone around the community that Whiskey Gulch Ranch has been targeted, and anyone having anything to do with the ranch could be murdered as well."

"Roy had an accident a few days ago," Trace's mother said. "His brakes failed. He blew through a stop sign in town and smashed into a tree to avoid hitting a family in a minivan. He suffered a damaged foot. He wanted to come back to work right away, but I told him to wait at least a week to keep it up and give himself time to start healing."

Lily picked up from there. "After Roy's accident happened, the ranch hands quit outright or called in sick, indefinitely. Some said their families had been threatened."

"Who's been taking care of the animals?" Trace asked.

"You're looking at us," his mother said. "If not for Lily, I don't know how I would have managed."

"So far, we've only been able to care for the horses, cattle and smaller livestock near the house and barn," Lily said. "We don't know what's going on farther out. If someone is threatening the ranch hands, what else are they doing that we haven't seen?"

"As soon as we're back from the funeral home, I'll ride the fences," Trace said.

"You can't go alone," his mother said. "You need someone to watch your back."

"I don't need help," Trace insisted. "I work better when I don't have to worry about others."

His mother shook her head. "You're taking one of us or you're not going at all."

Lily glanced at Trace in the mirror, a smile tugging her lips.

His mother had used the tone she'd used when she'd been talking to the younger version of Trace so many years ago. She'd always made him go with his father or with a friend, insisting on a buddy system to keep from being stranded out in the middle of the ranch with no way of getting back or sending anyone for help.

"Mom, I can take care of myself," Trace said. "Besides, if one of you goes with me, the other is left exposed to whoever is trying to sabotage the ranch."

"Going out on the ranch alone got your father killed,"

his mother said. "I don't know what I'd do if you were targeted next. You can't go out alone."

"I'm going to pick up Roy from the hospital tomorrow," Lily said. "He can stay with your mother at the house while you and I check the fences and start the search for your father's killer. Your mother will be safer at home."

"I don't need anyone to ride shotgun with me," he said.

"If you don't take Lily, I'll send her out after you anyway," his mother said. "Now, quit arguing. You're making my head hurt."

"And we're here," Lily pointed out as they rolled through town and came to a stop in front of the funeral home. She parked in the lot at the side of the building and climbed down.

Trace got out and opened his mother's door.

Rosalynn sat for a long moment staring straight ahead, clutching the suit, without moving.

Trace touched her arm. "I can meet with the funeral director. You can stay in the car."

She shook her head and turned. "No. I have to face this sooner or later." With a deep breath, she accepted Trace's arm and let him help her out of the vehicle.

Lily's heart hitched in her chest. James Travis had made it clear from the moment Trace brought Lily home to meet his parents that he didn't approve of Trace dating her. Though Trace hadn't mentioned it, she knew from the grapevine that he'd had a major argument with his father over her. Shortly afterward, he'd announced he was thinking about joining the army to get the hell out of Whiskey Gulch and away from his father.

Lily had never wanted to come between Trace and his father. That their argument had escalated to the point Trace felt it necessary to leave Whiskey Gulch Ranch meant his father had given him an ultimatum.

She understood the senior Travis's reservations about

Trace dating her. Everyone in the county knew who she was, and more important, who her mother was. On more than one occasion, Trace had stepped between Lily and someone who thought that because she was Brandy Jean's daughter that her body was for sale as well.

Trace had a couple of scars to show for his interference. Lily had been grateful he'd been there to help, but she'd gotten good at defending herself. As soon as she could navigate the internet, she'd studied Krav Maga. When she was old enough to drive, she'd taken lessons in the art of self-defense from a retired Delta Force soldier. Trace had found out and insisted on taking her to and from her lessons. Lily hadn't been surprised to learn Trace had gone into Delta Force. He'd been impressed by retired Sergeant Major Ketchum, or Ketch, as his students were allowed to address him.

Mrs. Travis led the way into the funeral home, holding her son's arm.

The funeral director met them in the lobby. "Mrs. Travis, thank you for coming today. And thank you for bringing Mr. Travis's clothing." He took the suit and held out a hand, taking hers into his grasp for a long moment. Then he released her hand and turned to Trace. "Trace, it's good to see you back in town."

"Thank you, Mr. Miller," Trace said and shook the man's hand.

"I'm so sorry for your loss and grateful that you were able to get here so quickly to be with your mother in your time of loss." The funeral director released his hand and stood taller. "Thank you for your service to our country. Your father must have been so proud of you."

Trace's jaw tightened. "Thank you for seeing to our family's needs. What more do you need from us?"

He led the way into a conference room and waited for them to be seated before settling into a chair at the end of the table. "I need to know your preferences on the casket and music. Your burial plot has been located and is being prepared. Do you have any photos you'd like to use in the video?"

The more questions the director asked, the more Rosalynn slid down in her seat.

When Lily could stand it no more, she spoke up. "If you have a list of what you expect from us, we can go through it at home. Mrs. Travis has selected the casket. I believe that was the main reason she had to be here today. So, if you'll excuse us, we have to get back to the ranch." She jotted an email address onto a slip of paper and handed it to the director. "Send us your list or your questions, and I'll compose an email with the answers."

The funeral director smiled briefly. "Of course. The funeral is in two days. I'll need your answers no later than noon tomorrow in order to complete preparations."

"You'll have it," Trace said.

"Viewing is tomorrow evening," the director said. "You'll want to get here early so that the family has time to visit before others arrive."

"We'll be here," Rosalynn said.

Trace helped his mother to her feet and guided her out of the room and to the exit.

Once outside, Rosalynn drew in a deep breath and let it out. "I don't know what came over me. I just suddenly couldn't breathe."

"We're headed home. You can rest when we get there. Trace and I will take care of the chores," Lily assured her.

"I need to help," she said, her hand on the door handle to the SUV.

Trace brushed her hand aside and opened the door. "I'm here now. You need to let Lily and me take charge of the ranch."

"Trace is right," Lily said. "Besides, I'm sure there will

be people who want to know about the funeral arrangements. Someone will need to be in the house to field those calls."

Rosalynn sighed. "You're probably right."

"You've done enough over the past three days," Lily said. "Let us take care of things. You need to rest."

"I'm not an invalid," Trace's mother said.

"No, but you've lost someone dear to you. It's emotionally and physically draining," Lily pointed out. "I don't know how you've held up, other than out of sheer cussedness." She smiled at Rosalynn. On the outside, Rosalynn had been a rock since the sheriff had delivered the news of her husband's death. She had to be coming apart on the inside.

A motorcycle pulled up beside them. The man driving it wore black jeans, a black T-shirt and a leather jacket. He dismounted and pulled off his helmet.

Lily braced herself. Of all the people to show up, why did Matt Hennessey have to come at that exact moment?

Matt strode up to Rosalynn. "Mrs. Travis, I just got back into town and heard about your husband." When he reached for her hands, Trace stepped between them.

"Hennessey," Trace said, his face stone-cold, his jaw tight.

"Travis." Matt's eyes narrowed. "I was speaking to your mother."

The tension in the air was thick enough to cut with a knife.

Lily touched Matt's arm. Matt had been her friend when no one else in the small town of Whiskey Gulch would have anything to do with her. With a background similar to hers, he'd been on the fringe of the social spectrum as well.

The bastard son of a woman who worked as a bartender at the local watering hole, he'd grown up with a rough crowd of hoodlum teens. He'd ridden a motorcycle, worn his hair a little long and sported a five o'clock shadow all day long. Sexy and dangerous, he was every girl's secret fantasy. But not Lily's. She'd been in love with Trace since she was in sixth grade.

Matt shook her hand off his arm and met Trace's glare with one of his own.

Rosalynn gripped her son's arm. "Trace, please."

For a moment, Trace stood his ground. Then he stepped back, never losing eye contact with the other man.

Rosalynn smiled at Matt and took his hands. "Thank you, Matthew."

"Let me know if there's anything I can do to help. If you need anything fixed, I can fix anything with an engine and I'm not bad with a hammer."

"That's sweet of you," Rosalynn said. "I might need your help if anything breaks down. With James gone—" she swallowed hard "—and Roy's broken foot, we're short-handed, and although I'm good with the animals, I'm hopeless with mechanics."

"I'm home now. I'll take care of things," Trace said.

Rosalynn nodded but smiled at Matt. "Thank you, Matt. You're so kind to offer."

"Say the word and I'll be there to help," Matt said. His gaze shifted from Rosalynn to Trace, his jaw tightening. "I can be out at the ranch in less than ten minutes." He turned to Lily. "How are you holding up?"

She nodded. Matt was her friend, and she appreciated his concern, but having him in the same breathing space as Trace could be disastrous. "I'm sure you have other things to do."

Rosalynn smiled and turned toward Trace. "Matt has his own repair shop now. He's quite good at fixing things. He can take something other people have given up on and make it come alive again."

Trace gave the hint of a nod, but his expression was tight. "I'm sure he can."

Matt frowned. "I get the feeling you don't like me. What did I ever do to you?"

Lily's heart leaped into her throat. Now was not the time for her lies to surface. She stepped around the two men and hooked Rosalynn's arm. "We'd love to share in this little reunion between you two men, but we need to get Mrs. Travis home before it gets dark. It's been a difficult day."

"Thank you, dear." Rosalynn patted Lily's hand. "I am tired and there are animals to be fed and laundry to be done. Thank you for stopping by, Matt. The funeral is the day after tomorrow." She climbed into the back seat of the SUV.

Lily didn't have the time or energy to deal with the two men. "When you're done puffing out your chests and posturing for dominance, we can get going."

Finally, Trace shifted his glare from Matt to Lily.

"Oh, good," she said, her voice tight. "I've got your attention. Can we go now?"

Trace gave Matt a narrow-eyed stare and said in a low tone, "Stay away from my family."

Matt snorted. "Your mother can speak for herself and Lily isn't yours. You gave her up when you ran off to play soldier."

Trace's hands clenched into fists and he stepped toward Matt.

Lily gave Matt a slight shake of her head.

"I'm not the one who ran out on her," Trace said. "You are."

Matt frowned. "Don't know what you're talking about."

Her heart hammering, Lily did the only thing she could. She threw up her hands and made a scene. "Fine. You two can stand around and be all stubborn, hardheaded and male. I'm taking Rosalynn home. She doesn't need whatever bull you two are throwing at each other. Trace, if you don't want to walk back to the ranch..." She shrugged and marched around the SUV to the driver's side, praying he wouldn't continue the argument or throw a punch at Matt. She climbed in, started the engine and pressed hard on the accelerator without putting it into gear. The engine revved loudly.

For another long moment, the two men stared at each other.

Then Trace turned and climbed into the SUV.

Lily shifted into gear and drove away from the funeral home.

"What was all of that about?" Rosalynn asked. "Am I missing something I should know? Did you and Matt have a falling-out I don't know about?"

"No, Mom," Trace said, his voice tight as if he were talking through gritted teeth.

Lily bit her tongue. Now wasn't the time to fill her boss in on the lie she'd told her son. She wasn't sure she'd ever let her know. Rosalynn had enough trouble on her plate with her husband's death and the threats they'd had to the ranch. And she didn't need to be reminded that Lily had once loved her son.

Hell, seeing Trace again...stubborn and cranky as he was...

She shot a glance at the man in the seat beside her.

He stared straight ahead, his arm resting on the window ledge, his fists clenched. Trace liked to be in control of the driving. He always had.

Lily's lips twitched.

He had to be gnashing his teeth with her behind the wheel.

She drove out of Whiskey Gulch, the town that had been named after the Whiskey Gulch Ranch.

For the first few minutes, silence reigned.

Deep in her thoughts and memories of better times with

Trace, Lily was jolted back to the present when Trace asked, "What else needs to be done on the ranch besides checking the fences?"

"Plenty of things, I'm sure," Rosalynn said. "James had mentioned the hay would be ready soon. It will need to be mowed, raked, baled and stored before it rains."

"Trace and I can manage the mowing, raking and baling, but we'll need help storing the rectangular bales in the barn. Otherwise, it will take days to accomplish."

"I'll see what I can do to muster up some ranch hands," Trace said.

"Good luck." Lily snorted. "I've never seen such a bunch of scaredy-cats in my life."

They were turning into the ranch before Lily knew it. The sun had dipped to hover above the horizon, heralding the end of the day in a startling display of color.

Lily shielded her eyes as she drove the length of the gravel drive to the ranch house. Her pulse quickened as she was reminded that she'd be sleeping under the same roof as Trace. In the room next to his.

Sweet heaven, her heart pounded against her ribs. Why was she so worked up? It wasn't as if they were a couple anymore. That was ancient history. He hadn't shown any sign of attraction or desire for her. He was over her.

The problem was, she wasn't over him.

As soon as Lily parked the SUV beside the house, Trace was out and helping his mother from the vehicle.

"I really can do this on my own," she said.

"I know, Mom, but humor me." Trace smiled down at his mother and walked with her into the house.

As soon as she'd set her purse down, she headed for the kitchen. "I'll rustle up something for dinner while you two take care of the animals."

"Are you going to be all right?" Trace asked.

She gave him a watery smile. "What choice do I have? We have a ranch to run. I don't have time to fall apart."

"And it's not like you to lose it." Trace leaned down and kissed his mother's forehead. "We'll be back in less than an hour."

"Take your time. I started a beef stew, but I'd like to make some corn bread to go with it." She waved him toward the door. "Go on. Lily's likely out there mucking stalls already. That woman is a dynamo. I didn't know what a gem she was until I hired her to take care of the household chores."

Trace paused with his hand on the back doorknob. "Why did you hire her, Mom?"

She shrugged. "I needed help cleaning, since I was doing all the cooking for the hands."

Trace frowned. "What happened to Cookie?"

His mother smiled. "He was getting old, so he retired. He and his wife moved to Florida to be closer to their daughter."

His heart squeezed hard in his chest. Cookie had been with them since Trace could remember. Cookie's daughter, Teresa, had gone to school with Trace. She'd married straight out of high school and moved from Texas to Florida with her husband. He remembered how sad Cookie had been when she'd left.

"I'm glad he was able to retire and move close to his daughter," Trace said. "If you need us, yell. We won't be far."

"I'll be okay. Hurry before Lily does all the heavy lifting. She's a hard worker and stubborn." His mother smiled. "I don't know what happened between you two, but you let a good one get away."

"We were kids. And that was a long time ago."

"Just saying," his mother said.

Trace exited the house and hurried toward the barn.

There was no reason he couldn't work with Lily. What they'd had was long ago and better left forgotten. Since there were no ranch hands, he'd have to make do with Lily.

As he entered the barn, his pulse quickened.

The brushing sound of a rake scooping through muck led him to a stall where Lily was up to her gum boots in soiled straw.

She didn't hear him at first. When she looked up, her eyes widened briefly.

"Where did you start?" Trace asked.

"I worked the first two stalls yesterday." She pointed to the other side of the barn. "The six stalls on the other side need cleaning and the rest of the stalls on this side haven't been mucked for a week, from what I can tell. I turned the horses loose in the paddock behind the barn until we can finish the job. The other rake is hanging on the wall by the door. The second wheelbarrow is out back of the barn." Lily dug into the straw and flipped a pile of dirty straw into her wheelbarrow, her eyes on her work.

For a moment longer, Trace watched Lily, admiring the strength in her arms and her determination to get the job done. She'd always been willing to work, no matter how hard the task. It was one of the reasons he'd fallen so hard for her. Most women he'd known since wouldn't do what Lily was doing for fear of getting dirt beneath their fingernails or, Lord forbid, breaking one.

Trace grabbed the wheelbarrow from outside and went to work cleaning the six stalls on the opposite side of the barn. Every once in a while, he'd catch a glimpse of Lily. Once, he'd found her staring back at him.

Since she hadn't married Matt Hennessey, did she still have good memories about the time they'd spent together as teens? Did it matter? Did he care?

Unfortunately, he found himself caring too much. Over the years they'd been apart, he hadn't been able to move on. Perhaps working side by side, he'd finally be able to let go of the woman who'd haunted his thoughts. He hoped it wouldn't take long for him to get over her. At that moment, his desire was nearly as strong as it had been eleven years ago. He didn't have time to work through his feelings. He had a ranch to run and his father's murderer to locate and neutralize. If he wanted help, he needed men who had skills similar to his. If they had ranching experience, that was a bonus.

As soon as he got back to the ranch, he got to work, making phone calls to the men he knew or had known in the past. He was banking on the strength of brotherhood. He needed his team now.

Chapter Four

Over the next couple of days, Lily kept busy between James Travis's viewing and funeral, taking care of the house, and helping out with the animals. To the best of her abilities, she avoided Trace as much as possible. With her bedroom next to his, she couldn't elude him completely. Knowing he was on the other side of the wall left her sleepless and on edge. Only a few feet separated them physically. But the emotional chasm between them might as well have been as wide as the Grand Canyon.

He barely talked to her, although he worked alongside her in the barn and as they took care of the animals. Gone were the times they would run laughing into the stalls, stopping to kiss and hold each other. They'd been young, in love, happy to be alive and with each other.

James Travis had never liked her. He'd met her in the barn one day when she'd been waiting for Trace to join her for horseback riding. He'd told her she wasn't good enough for his son and that he would never make anything of himself as long as she was around.

He'd known his son was considering joining the military. He'd blamed her for Trace's interest in leaving Whiskey Gulch. If she insisted on staying with him, her background would keep him from getting his security clearance. She'd ruin his career in the army before it started.

When Trace walked in on his father telling her these

things, Trace had blown up. He'd told his father to stay out of his life and he'd stay out of his.

That day Trace had loaded Lily into his truck, taken her home, and then driven to the nearest US Army recruiting station and enlisted. The staff sergeant who'd taken Trace's information informed him that he'd have to complete clearance forms and a background check.

Still shaking from that encounter with James Travis, Lily let the patriarch's words sink in. If she stayed with Trace, she would hold him back. She'd never been in trouble with the law, but her mother had been arrested on multiple occasions for prostitution. Her biological father was in prison for armed robbery. She'd been so afraid her parents' legacy would taint her and thus him in his background check. Once again, the sins of her parents were impacting her.

Lily had known for a long time that Trace had a need to get out on his own. He'd been talking about joining the military since he started high school. As soon as he graduated, he wanted to leave Whiskey Gulch Ranch and make it on his own. His father kept such tight reins on the ranch that, if he stayed, Trace would never be allowed to make decisions for himself.

From Trace's first mention of joining the military, James Travis had discouraged his son's decision. He'd assumed Trace would stay and eventually run the ranch, his inheritance.

Trace knew better. He would never run the Whiskey Gulch Ranch until his father died.

As Lily listened to James Travis that day, she'd come to the realization that Trace needed to get away from his father. If he didn't, he would grow to hate the man even more, and possibly hate himself.

The only way he'd make it past the background check was if she wasn't in the picture with her family's checkered past. He'd said he'd get in, go through bootcamp and advanced training, then he'd send for her. As close as they'd become, if she'd tried to break up with him, he'd still try to convince her to wait for him.

She stopped seeing Trace and quit calling him over the next few days. It was the only thing she could think to do. Lily paid a visit to Matt, hanging out with him, watching baseball with him and taking a selfie photo with him. They'd been friends for a long time. He hadn't seemed to think anything of it.

When it came time to let go, Lily had hated lying to Trace. But it appeared to be the only way to get him to leave and ensure his background check passed without the hitch of her and her parents. So, she'd waited until he was scheduled to ship out for in-processing and then broken it to him that she wasn't going to wait for him. She wanted to remain in Whiskey Gulch and she'd been having an affair with the sexiest hoodlum in town, Matt Hennessey. She was going to stay and marry him.

At first, he hadn't believed her and blamed the fight with his dad for her sudden change of heart. Then she'd showed him the photo of her and Matt in his trailer, sitting on his leather sofa drinking beer.

To say Trace was angry would have been an understatement. He'd been so mad, his face turned a ruddy red. He'd gathered his duffel bag, turned and climbed aboard the bus that would take him to San Antonio's Military Entrance Processing Station and his future in the army.

Lily had cried all the way back to the run-down shack where she'd lived with her mother.

She didn't see Trace for five years following that fateful day. Then for the next six years she'd only caught glimpses of him from afar when he came back to Whiskey Gulch to visit his mother.

As far as she'd known, he'd never patched his relationship with his father, and he hadn't spoken to her.

That morning, she was out in the barn, cleaning the hooves on one of the registered quarter horse mares James Travis had been so proud of.

Lady was temperamental and impatient with the process, but she'd collected a number of rocks and sticks and needed them cleaned out before she developed sores and went lame.

After the fourth time Lady jerked her hoof out of Lily's hand, she straightened her aching back and shook her head. "I get it. I'm not as good at this as James or Roy, but it has to be done."

"Leave her to me," a voice said from the door to the barn.

Lily stiffened. Though he stood blocking the sunlight, and his face was shadowed, he was unmistakably Trace.

Her heart skipped several beats and then raced ahead. "I can do this. It just takes time."

"Leave it," he said, his tone more direct, unbending and final.

A spark of anger rose up her chest. She marched across the barn. "Look, you can't do everything, but since you think you can, go for it." She held out the handle of the horse hoof pick.

When he took it from her, his fingers brushed against hers, making her pulse beat faster and her knees tremble.

She backed away too fast and stumbled, teetered and flung out her arms as she fell.

Trace reached out, grabbed her hand and yanked her forward, slamming her against his chest. He held her there until she regained her balance, and then a little longer.

Her pulse pounded as she glanced up into his familiar yet unfamiliar face. Trace had been the boy with whom she'd fallen in love in grade school. He was still the same person, only he wasn't a boy anymore. His shoulders had broadened, the soft curves of youth had hardened in the planes of his face and his arms were steel bands wrapped around her waist.

Lily found it hard to catch her breath, realizing it had nothing to do with how tightly he held her but how pinched her heart was inside.

How different would her life have been if she'd asked him to stay in Whiskey Gulch and move in with her. They could have found an apartment or a little cottage to rent. He could have gone to work on one of the other ranches, or as a carpenter's assistant. She'd worked as a waitress. Between the two of them, they could have survived.

Looking at him now, she knew she'd done the right thing. He'd needed to get clear away from his father, the ranch and the small town of Whiskey Gulch. As the son of the richest man in the county, he never would have shaken the stigma of being the spoiled rich kid.

She looked at him, really looked at him. He was harder, more confident and a man his father would have been proud of. It was too bad James Travis never got to tell him. He'd expressed his pride to Lily, if not directly to his son, and regretted the distance between them that kept him from telling Trace how he felt to his face.

Trace's hands tightened around her waist, warm, strong and steady. They sent ripples of awareness throughout her body, making everything inside her burn.

"You said you were going to marry Hennessey," Trace said. "Why didn't you?"

Like ice water splashed in her face, he brought her back to reality. She pushed against his chest. "It doesn't matter."

His grip tightened, trapping her. "Did you ditch him because he wasn't good enough?"

She held her chin up and stared into his gaze. "It's really none of your business."

Trace lifted his hands, sliding them up her back to tangle in the hair at the base of her skull. "Did he make you moan when he held you?"

Her breathing came in ragged gasps. Pressed against

him, she couldn't ignore the way her body reacted. She was on fire, her core burning with desire. She had no words. None could move past her frozen vocal cords.

"Did he kiss you until you melted in his arms?" he whispered, his mouth descending to hover over hers.

"No," she murmured, the sound swallowed by the crush of his lips against hers.

At first she remained stiff in his arms.

But as his mouth moved against hers, she melted against him. If he hadn't been holding her, she would have slipped bonelessly to the floor, her knees unable to hold her weight.

His tongue traced the seam of her lips.

She opened to him as naturally as if she were a flower opening its petals to the sun. Greedily, she drank him in, her tongue sweeping against his, caressing, thrusting and tasting this man she'd loved so much she'd pushed him away to explore a better life without her.

After what seemed like an eternity and yet a blink of an eye, he raised his head, abandoning her mouth.

Lily drew in a shaky breath and sagged against him. This couldn't be happening. It shouldn't be happening. Trace didn't love her anymore.

"Bet he didn't kiss you like that," he said, his voice gravelly and sexy as hell.

His words brought her back to earth with a jolt. She pressed her hands against his chest and pushed.

When he still didn't let go, she drew in a deep breath and let it out. "Let go of me."

As if he just realized he was still holding her, he let go suddenly and stepped away from her.

"I don't think it's a good idea for you to work here," he said.

"I don't work for you," she said. "I work for your mother. When she's ready for me to leave, I will. In the meantime, she needs the help, and I like working for her." And if she could find another job that paid as well, she would leave in a heartbeat. Being around Trace was harder than she'd ever imagined. "And I'd appreciate it if you didn't do that again." She wiped the back of her hand over her still tingling lips.

"Do what?" he asked, his blue eyes smoldering as he stared down at her.

"You know damn well what."

"You mean kiss the ranch hand?" The corners of his mouth quirked upward.

"I mean it." She lifted her chin, praying her lip didn't tremble. She'd never felt as unsteady and out of control as she did at that moment. "Don't do it again."

He stared at her for a long time and then dipped his head in the hint of a nod. "Okay. I won't kiss you…unless…"

"No unless."

He held up his hand. "I won't kiss you, unless you ask me to."

She snorted. "Good. I won't be asking."

"Uh-huh."

"I won't."

He gripped her arms and drew her close. "You won't?" he asked, his mouth so close she could feel his warm breath across hers.

Once again, air lodged in her lungs and she waited for him to claim her mouth.

As if of its own accord, her head tilted upward to receive his kiss.

The sound of a horn honking shocked Lily out of the trance Trace seemed to put her in. He glanced toward the barn door, a frown creasing his brow.

Another honk sounded.

Trace cursed. "We're not done with this conversation."

"Yes. We. Are." When Lily pushed away, Trace released her.

Her knees wobbled and her breathing seemed to come in shallow gasps, but she was free of his hold on her.

At least his physical hold. Damn the man to hell. He still had a hold on her heart, and that would never do.

TRACE LEFT LILY and emerged from the barn to find a shiny charcoal-gray truck parked beside his black four-wheel-drive pickup.

A man had dropped down to the ground on the other side of the open driver's door.

When he closed it, he looked around and grinned when he saw Trace.

"Trace, you old son of a gun."

"Irish." Trace hurried toward his friend and former Delta Force teammate. "I thought you'd be recuperating for another couple of weeks."

"Seems I'll live after all. The doctors treated my wounds and scanned my head."

"And?"

"Concussion, a few shrapnel wounds, but nothing life-threatening. I was released once I got the all clear from the docs. Then you said you were in need of help." Irish shrugged and winced. He rolled his shoulder and held on to his middle. "So, here I am."

"I need ranch hands who can work hard. You're not up to that yet."

"But I will be within a few weeks. In the meantime, I can still handle a weapon, and I brought my own." He reached into the back seat of the truck and pulled out a gun case. "I have my own AR-15 military-grade rifle, a 9mm Glock and night vision goggles."

"What kind of help did you hear I needed?"

Irish stood in front of Trace, meeting his gaze straight on. "I heard you needed combat veterans to help with the ranch work and protect your family from whoever killed your father."

Trace hated that he even had to call on old friends to help manage the family ranch. His father had run the operation for so many years without much problem. What had changed so drastically that they'd come to this?

"Well?" Irish raised an eyebrow. "Can you use someone like me? I like to think I'm good with animals and you know my combat skills."

Trace held up a hand. "Stop. You know you're hired. But more than that, it's good to see you're all right." He pulled Irish into a bear hug, squeezing him tightly.

"Hey, not so hard," Irish said through gritted teeth. "Injured man here."

With a chuckle, Trace released his friend and stepped back. "Just what exactly can you do right now? Can you haul hay?"

Irish cringed. "As long as I don't reopen my wounds, I can do just about anything."

Trace frowned. "We'll take it easy the first couple of weeks. I can put you to work driving the truck we'll use to haul the trailer full of bales."

"Let me see what I can do with the bales. I bet I can toss a few, no problem."

"Yeah, I bet you can. Then you'll rip a stitch and bleed everywhere. I've seen enough blood to last a lifetime. You can drive the bailing machine."

"When do you want to start?" Irish asked.

"I'd hoped to start tomorrow."

"Sounds good. Who else do you have helping?" Irish glanced around the barnyard. He nodded toward the barn. "Wow. You didn't tell me about the great scenery you had on the ranch. Please tell me she's your sister."

Trace stiffened and turned to find Lily leading the mare out to the paddock, her blue chambray shirt unbuttoned enough to display a significant amount of her cleavage and the shirttails tied in a knot around her waist, displaying her slim midriff.

He cursed beneath his breath. "I'm an only child."

Irish shot a glance toward Trace. "She with you?"

Trace snorted. "No." Then he saw the smile lighting his friend's face as he turned toward Lily. "But she's off-limits," Trace added.

The smile faded as Irish looked back at Trace. "Is she married?"

"No." His lips firming, Trace continued. "She works for my mother."

"She works for your mother, and she's off-limits." Irish shook his head. "Okay." He smiled. "You sure you're not interested in her?"

His jaw tightened as he forced out the words, "I'm sure."

"Well, it wouldn't hurt to get to know her, since she works on the ranch, too. Are you going to introduce me?"

Trace didn't want to introduce Irish to Lily. Irish had a reputation with the ladies. And he'd been pretty open about why he was getting out of the military. He wanted a real life with a real job and eventually a wife and family.

The thought of Irish flirting with Lily made Trace's gut clench.

Why was he getting wrapped around the axels about Lily? She wasn't his to claim. She'd made that perfectly clear eleven years ago when she'd chosen Matt Hennessey over him. What had happened between the two of them, he didn't know. But he intended to find out.

His best source for information might be the one closest to him.

His mother.

So many people had been to the ranch before, during and after the funeral that Trace had been hard-pressed to keep an eye on her, the ranch and Lily. The people of Whiskey Gulch had come out in force when the richest man in the area had been laid to rest. Women had shown up with food, groceries and their condolences.

His mother had stood stoically at the funeral home, receiving the guests with a warm hug and an occasional smile when someone mentioned an anecdote about his father.

Trace had stood by her, listening to how much the people had admired his father, some of the charitable actions he'd performed to help out a rancher when he was down, or a business owner who needed a loan to keep going until he could get on his feet.

Who was this man they all knew, and he didn't? His father had done things without any fanfare or expectations of undying gratitude. He'd been kind to people.

Trace had been happy to be a man on his own, making his way through life on his own terms. When he was home, he'd helped with the chores and run errands without being asked. Eventually, when they were seated at the dinner table, just the three of them and sometimes the new foreman, Roy, talk had always turned to the business of running Whiskey Gulch Ranch. Trace had refused to get caught up in his father's narrative about how he should quit the military and come home to work the ranch. His father had never accepted that he was happy with his choice to remain in the army. Never once did he say he was proud of the fact Trace had made it into the elite Delta Force. Trace tried to tell himself that he didn't care. But just once, he would have liked some acknowledgment that his father didn't think of him as a complete loser.

His mother stepped out of the house, shaded her eyes and looked their way. When she spotted Trace and Irish, she hurried out to the barnyard to greet their guest.

Lily had released Lady into the pasture and was on her way back to the barn when Trace's mother called out to her, "Lily, do you have a minute?"

Lily picked up her pace and fell into step beside Trace's mother. They spoke quietly as they closed the distance between them and Trace.

When she stopped in front of Trace and Irish, his mother gave Irish a broad grin and held out her hand. "Hi, I'm Rosalynn Travis."

Irish took her hand. "Joseph Monahan, but my friends call me Irish." He squeezed her hand gently. "I'm so sorry for your loss, ma'am."

Trace's mother gave a weak smile. "Thank you." She squared her shoulders and lifted her chin as she always did when she was being brave. "Are you a new ranch hand or a friend of Trace's?"

"Both," Trace said. "Irish is from my unit. He's coming to work for you at Whiskey Gulch Ranch, if you're okay with it."

Rosalynn frowned. "Of course I'm okay with it. You can hire all the ranch hands you want. We need the help. Our foreman should be back soon. Even then, he will be hobbling on his broken foot for a while." She turned to Lily. "Lily and I had been holding down the fort. We're so glad Trace is home and taking up the reins. Have you met Lily?" She smiled.

"No, ma'am, I haven't." Irish held out his hand to Lily.

Lily smiled at him and took his outstretched hand. "Glad to meet you."

Trace's chest tightened. She used to smile at him like that. For years, he'd wondered where he'd gone wrong with Lily. Why had she been so into him one day and then ditched him for the town bad boy?

Irish grinned. "I'd have given up the army a lot sooner if I'd known Texas was hiding some of the prettiest ranch hands in the country."

Lily's cheeks flushed a pretty pink.

His mother laughed and waved a hand at Irish. "If you were my son, I'd ask you what you were up to."

Irish winked at her. "And I'd say I only want the pleasure of your company."

His mother chuckled. "Well played."

Trace groaned. "If we could pull our feet out of the horse manure being spread so thickly on the ground, we might get some work done this afternoon."

His mother patted his cheek. "Don't be such a grouchy bear. I like your choice of a ranch hand. Irish will fit in quite well." She smiled at the man, slipped her arm through his and started toward the barn. "Come on, I'll show you where everything is. And until we get the bunkhouse cleaned up, you can stay at the house."

"Thank you, ma'am," Irish said as he left Trace staring after him, shaking his head.

"Son of a gun," Trace said beneath his breath.

"Did you warn Irish that we've had some threats here at the ranch?" Lily asked, her gaze following Irish and Trace's mother as they entered the barn. "He's holding his side like he is nursing a wound. Is he up to the rigors of the job and the potential of being a target?"

"Irish knows what's happening here. I gave him the details when I asked him to come," Trace said. "He was injured recently, but he's on the mend. He'll be pulling light duty until he's back to one hundred percent."

"Until then, it's still me and you." Lily's lips pressed together.

"His injury isn't going to affect his ability to shoot." Trace met her gaze dead-on. "And I expect one more recruit in the next day or two."

"Your mother thinks we need to cut the hay tomorrow. Are we ready?"

Trace nodded. "Ready or not, we have to get it done. There's a storm across the Baja Peninsula predicted to come this way in less than a week. We have to have that hay cut, baled and stored before it hits."

"I'm not as worried about the round bales, but you and I are going to be hard-pressed to get the square bales packed into the barn in that short a time frame."

"Hopefully, my guy Beck will be here before we start that hay hauling. He had some commitments in San Antonio to wrap up before he could come out to help. I'm not sure he'll stay for long, and he's never worked on a ranch, but he's strong, smart and loyal. And he's prior Delta Force. He'll be a good asset to have in case we have trouble. In the meantime, we'll mow, rake and bale."

Lily nodded. "Good." She started to walk away.

"Lily, about what happened…"

She stopped and held up a hand without turning. "Already forgotten."

"That's not what I was going to say." Trace closed the distance between them. He touched her arm and turned her to face him.

"Don't—" Lily said.

He couldn't help it. He couldn't forget. "When I kissed you…"

She was already shaking her head.

He continued. "When I kissed you, you felt it, too… didn't you?"

"I don't want to talk about it." She looked up at him and then looked away.

"What happened between you and Matt?" he persisted.

"That was so long ago. Why bring it up now?" When she pulled away, he released his hold on her. "I have work to do."

"We're not finished discussing this."

"We're finished. We have nothing left to say."

"We do," he said. "And we will. Sooner or later. I'd prefer sooner. And if you don't tell me what happened between you and Matt, I'll just ask him."

Her head shot up, her eyes wide for a second before she hooded them. "He will say there never was anything between us."

"You said you were going to marry him. How could there be nothing between you two?"

She shrugged. "Maybe I changed my mind. Maybe I read too much into the relationship. Whatever it was, it didn't work out. It wasn't his fault. He wasn't the right guy for me."

Trace pressed his lips together. "Neither was I."

"It was a long time ago." She shook her head. "Let it lie." This time when she turned and walked away, he let her go.

The entire conversation left him with more questions than answers. He felt as if Lily wasn't telling him the whole truth. What was she hiding? Had she been in love with Matt? Had he dumped her? What had happened to drive them apart?

What did it matter? Lily had made it perfectly clear eleven years ago. She didn't want him then and she didn't want him now.

Then what the hell had happened when he'd kissed her? Because, though he might be rusty and maybe a little deluded, she sure as hell had kissed him back.

Chapter Five

Lily spent the rest of the day helping Irish find his way around the ranch. After Rosalynn had left him in her care, she'd shown him where the feed was stored, what and how much to feed the animals, and where the tack was stored.

"If anything is too heavy or awkward for you to lift," Lily said, "just let me know. I can help."

"I can handle this," he assured her.

Lily watched him out of the corner of her eye. He'd clutched his side occasionally when he lifted anything over twenty pounds. They had been scooping feed from the feed bins that afternoon when he clutched his side and grunted.

"Look," Lily said, "I'd rather you take time to heal. If you rip stitches now, it'll take longer for you to mend. I'll handle the hay bales, you can feed the horses, pigs and chickens."

"I can do more than that," Irish insisted and bent to lift a scoop full of sweet feed out of the bin.

She chuckled. "Oh, you will. We need to check the fences around the property. There's always some that need mending. What can you do? What do you have experience with?"

"I was a sniper in the Delta Force."

"Ever worked on a ranch?" she asked, not sure this man who'd been injured would be an asset even after he recovered fully.

"I did, one summer when I was in high school." He gave her a weak smile. "Does that count?"

She carried a bucket full of grain to one of the horse stalls and hung it inside the pen, then turned. "Did you work with the animals?"

Irish carried another bucket over to the adjacent stall and hung it inside. "I was in charge of hooking the horses up to walkers, cleaning hooves, currying, feeding and exercising them. I also helped corral the cattle to administer worm medication. Not to mention hauling hay, mending fences and anything else that came up."

"All in one summer?" she asked.

He nodded. "I wasn't raised on a farm, but I loved working with animals." He looked over the stall door at the horse happily munching on the feed. "When I processed out of the military, I wanted to get back to working with animals."

"Well, Mr. Monahan, you're back. Be ready for some hard, dirty and altogether rewarding work." Lily smiled. "I wasn't raised on a ranch, either. I learned as I went. If you aren't afraid of hard work, you'll do well here."

"I'm ex–Delta Force," he said, puffing out his chest. "I didn't get there by being lazy."

Lily nodded. "I can see why Trace brought you on board."

"That, and I'm good with a variety of weapons." Irish frowned. "Trace gave me a brief synopsis of what's been happening around here. I was sorry to hear about his father. Has the local law enforcement come up with any indication as to who was responsible?"

Lily shook her head. "He was alone when it happened. No witnesses. The other ranch hands were working together on another part of the ranch. They weren't anywhere near Mr. Travis. Our foreman had gone to town for supplies. No one from the Whiskey Gulch Ranch was anywhere near Mr. Travis when he was shot."

"Did they question the neighbors?" he asked.

"They did." Lily nodded. "They all had alibis."

"Figures." Irish returned to the feed bin for another bucket of feed.

"What about you?" Lily asked. "Why did you decide to get out of the military? Or did you have to get out because of your injuries?"

He chuckled. "My team was mystified as well." He tapped his torso. "The injuries weren't life-threatening. Yeah, I had a concussion, but thankfully, it doesn't appear to be a traumatic brain injury. And I've had worse shrapnel wounds." He carried the bucket to another stall. "I've been deployed so many times, I don't remember where I live half the time. I've also watched some of my buddies get married and then get divorced. Their wives couldn't handle them being away so often. I'm in my thirties and, if I want a home and a family, I don't stand a chance of finding anything that would last if I stayed on active duty."

Lily chuckled. "So basically what you're telling me is that your biological clock is ticking, and you didn't want it to run out before you had a chance at having a wife and children." She touched his arm. "I don't mean to laugh. I just think it's ironic."

"What about you?" Irish raised an eyebrow. "I don't see a ring on your finger. Does that mean you aren't married? Or that you don't like to wear jewelry when you're up to your elbows in horse manure?"

Lily laughed. "Both. I'm not married. And I wouldn't wear jewelry to muck out stalls."

"How did a beautiful woman like you manage to escape the matrimonial ring?"

She shrugged. "I guess I just haven't found the right person. Or he hasn't found me." She hung her bucket in a stall and wiped her hands on her jeans. "We're done in here. We should go wash up. Mrs. Travis should have dinner on the table soon."

She led the way out of the barn and closed the door behind her.

"I've known Trace four years, and I didn't know that he was the heir to all of this." Irish waved a hand at the barn, the pastures and the massive ranch house. "He never mentioned that his family was loaded."

Lily smiled. "He never considered himself rich. It was his father's ranch, his father's money and his father's life. Trace wanted to make it on his own."

"Sounds like Trace," Irish said. "He was always so focused and driven. I guess that's why."

She nodded. "They butted heads often."

Irish shook his head. "He was just one of the guys. He never expected special favors, and he always had our backs. We could count on him."

Lily's heart pinched hard in her chest. She'd known he'd make it on his own. He was so much like his father, he couldn't have failed. They both worked hard and smart to make things happen.

"If you don't mind my asking," Irish started, "what's up between you and Trace? I sense an undercurrent and I can't quite put my finger on it."

With a shrug, Lily picked up the pace. "There's nothing up between me and Trace. Nothing." Out of the corner of her eye, she could see Irish studying her, his eyes slightly narrowed. Lily held her breath, praying Irish didn't continue along his current line of questioning.

"I was just asking. You know…pretty, single girl on a ranch. I might want to ask you out." He winked. "But if you're spoken for, I don't want to step on anyone's toes."

"I'm single. You're not going to step on anyone's toes, but I'm not interested in dating at this time."

"Okay, then. Maybe we can just be friends?"

She smiled. "I'd like that."

He held out his hand. "Deal?"

She shook his hand. "Deal."

As she climbed the steps up to the back porch, Lily smiled.

The door to the kitchen opened and Trace came out, carrying a tray of raw steaks. He frowned when he saw her and Irish.

"You need a hand with those?" Irish asked. "I've been known to grill a mean medium rare steak."

Trace shook his head. "I've got this. You can grab a beer and keep me company, though."

Irish grinned. "Now you're speaking my language. Point me in the right direction."

Without making eye contact with Trace, Lily touched Irish's arm. "I'll show you where they keep the beer after we wash up."

"Great." Irish grinned at Trace. "Lily's been a big help clueing me in on what has to be done around here."

Trace grunted and walked by, his gaze capturing Lily's. "I'll get these on the fire. You might check with my mother to see if there's anything else she wants to cook out here." His tone was clipped, his frown seemingly carved into his forehead.

"Got it. I'll be out in a sec." Lily dived into the house to escape Trace's piercing glance that seared straight through to her soul. Her face heated and her palms were sweating by the time she reached the downstairs bathroom.

"Are you all right?" Irish asked as she passed him to enter the washroom first.

"I'm fine. I'll be right out." She shut the door between them and stood staring at her flushed face in the mirror. Why did Trace have such a huge effect on her after all these years?

The answer was the kiss.

She should have stood her ground, turned her face, done anything rather than let him kiss her.

The truth was…she'd wanted that kiss as much as she'd wanted to take her next breath. Hell, she was in so much trouble where Trace was concerned. She wasn't over him by any stretch. The only thing she could do was stay away from him and get on with her life. The kiss had meant nothing to him but a way to prove a point. That he could still turn her willpower to mush.

After washing her hands and splashing water on her face, she felt more like herself. She exited the bathroom with a smile pinned to her face. "All yours. Think you can find your way to the kitchen when you're finished?"

"I've got a keen sense of direction," Irish said. "Which way do I go?"

She gave him directions.

He gave her a mock salute. "Got it." Irish entered the bathroom and closed the door.

Rather than go out to the porch and relax in one of the rocking chairs, Lily went straight to the kitchen. "Anything I can do to help?" she asked.

"Actually, yes." Rosalynn shot a smile over her shoulder. "You can set the table and put ice in the glasses."

Lily pulled cutlery out of the drawer and plates from one of the cabinets, enough for four people.

"We'll need an extra setting," Rosalynn said.

"Oh?"

"Yes. I've hired another man to help haul hay. He's supposed to be here any moment."

"Anyone I know?"

"I think so." Rosalynn pulled the Dutch oven full of baked beans from the oven, set it on a trivet on the table and wiped her hands on a dish towel. "I'll be right back."

Curious, Lily quickly set the table with the silverware and plates. Then she put ice in the glasses and placed a pitcher of tea in the center of the table. It felt weird and sad that Mr. Travis wasn't at the table. Before he'd passed, he'd insisted on having dinner at the formal dining table. Since his death, his widow had gone to having dinner at the large table in the kitchen.

Still, his powerful presence was missed.

Having Trace home helped. At least, it helped his mother. She'd seemed so lost without her husband. Sure, she'd taken up the reins of running the ranch even though she'd been devastated, but when she'd learned that the foreman had run off the road and crushed his foot the same day, Lily thought Rosalynn would fall the rest of the way apart.

But she hadn't. Not even when the ranch hands had each called to say they couldn't work there anymore because their families had been threatened. Rosalynn had squared her shoulders, visited Roy in the hospital briefly and gone back to take care of the ranch her husband had loved so much.

Lily had gone from being household staff to a ranch hand, doing the best she could to keep the animals fed, the barn clean and Mrs. Travis from working herself into an early grave with her husband.

She hadn't wanted to notify the Red Cross of her husband's death to bring Trace home to help.

Frankly, neither had Lily, but the situation had become impossible to handle. Either they got someone there to help, or Rosalynn would be forced to sell the ranch or at least all the animals on it. She couldn't keep up with the amount of work it took to keep it going. Not by herself. Lily had made the call to the Red Cross. She'd waited until it was too late to recall the notice to tell her. Rosalynn had been relieved. Despite her protests to the contrary, she needed to have her only son there for the funeral and to help her decide what to do next. After all, if she wanted to keep the ranch, it would eventually go to Trace.

Lily sliced lemons for the iced tea and set out the fresh salad Rosalynn had cut up, steak sauce and napkins. By the time she was finished, Irish appeared in the doorway, carrying a tray of baked potatoes wrapped in foil. A moment later, Trace appeared, carrying another tray filled with juicy steaks. The aroma filled the air, making Lily's mouth water and her tummy rumble. She hadn't realized just how hungry she was until that moment.

When her gaze met Trace's, all thoughts of hunger jumped from food to desire. She physically ached for this man, and they could never be together.

Lily took the tray of potatoes from Irish with a smile that hurt her face. "Thank you." She plucked a potato from the tray and nearly dropped it, her fingers on fire. "Ouch."

"Careful." Irish frowned. "They're fresh from the grill and hot."

Lily shook her hand, wincing in pain. "I know that... now."

Trace set his tray on the table and crossed to her. He took the platter of potatoes from her grip and set it beside the steaks. Then he gripped her wrist and studied the red mark on her fingertips. "Come on." He led her to the sink and ran her hand beneath cool water.

With Trace holding her hand and standing so close to her that his hip bumped against hers, Lily could barely breathe, much less think.

After a couple of minutes, he turned off the water and stared down at her hand again. "That might blister."

"I'll be okay," she said, her voice kind of breathy. Hardly the strong voice of a confident woman who could handle anything.

Anything but Trace.

"Oh, good, I'm glad everyone is ready to eat," Rosalynn said from the entrance to the kitchen. "I want you all to welcome our guest."

Lily turned a split second after Trace did.

His fingers tightened around her wrist.

Lily felt the blood drain from her face when she spied the man following Rosalynn.

"Most of you know Matt Hennessey," Rosalynn started, "am I right?"

"Yes. The question is, what the hell is he doing here?" Trace demanded.

Mrs. Travis frowned at Trace and smiled up at Matt. "He's agreed to help us bring in the hay and whatever else needs to be done. At least until we can hire full-time staff to do the work."

"We don't need help," Trace bit out. "Especially from him."

"Now, Trace, Matt is our guest," Rosalynn said.

"He doesn't belong here," Trace said.

His mother lifted her chin and met his stare with one of her own. "You said it yourself, it's my home and I will decide who stays and who goes."

Lily could almost hear the sound of Trace's teeth grinding together. The tension in the air was so tightly strung, Lily could easily feel it plucking at her nerves.

Matt stood with a half smile tugging at one corner of his mouth. "Told you it wasn't a good idea." He turned. "I'll just be leaving."

Mrs. Travis grabbed his arm, her chin lifting, her mouth pressing into a thin line. "This is still my house, and I'll invite whoever I want to the dinner table. *And* I'll hire whoever I want to help bring in the hay. Matt has so graciously offered to take time away from his own business to help us get the hay in before it rains. I don't expect you to smile, but you *will* say thank you. No one else in town has offered to help. The animals depend on us to provide feed throughout the winter. Now, if you'll excuse me, I have a pasta salad in the refrigerator." She jerked her head toward the table. "Please, Matt, have a seat. Dinner is served."

His half smile became a grin. "Thank you, ma'am. I haven't had a home-cooked meal in a while."

"Well, you'll have one tonight. My son grilled the steaks and potatoes. You know Trace and Lily." She reached into the refrigerator for a large bowl and straightened. "Irish is the new ranch hand. He's a friend of Trace's from the military."

Irish held out his hand. "Joseph Monahan, but you can call me Irish. I'm fresh off active duty."

Matt shook Irish's hand. "Army?"

Irish nodded. "Ten years."

Matt tipped his head. "I did seven years in the Marine Corps."

"Deploy?"

Matt's lips thinned. "A number of times. Would have stayed, but a bullet ruined my knee. Uncle Sam kindly asked me to retire."

"Matt owns an engine repair shop in town." Mrs. Travis set a pasta salad on the table. "We'll only have him until the hay is harvested and stored."

"Thank you, Matt," Lily said softly, her pulse hammering so hard in her veins she could hear it thumping in her ears. She couldn't think of a worse situation.

How was she going to endure sitting at the table with the man she loved and the one he thought she'd ditched him for?

She supposed karma had a large part in the circumstances. Some lies seemed to have a life of their own.

Chapter Six

Trace sat at the opposite end of the table from his mother with a clear view of the man he'd hated for eleven years sitting as pretty as he pleased across the table from the woman he'd loved all those years ago.

He guessed he deserved it for holding on to those feelings for so long, letting them define his life and relationships. If he'd let go long ago, he might have found someone else to love even more than his high school sweetheart. Instead, his love hadn't faded but morphed into a wound that festered and fed darkness into his soul.

"I ran into Matt today at the grocery store. When he offered to help me in any way he could, I don't think he expected me to take him up on his offer." Trace's mother smiled as she scooped pasta salad onto her plate and passed the bowl to the left.

Trace stabbed a steak with his fork and dropped it onto his plate. What he didn't understand was how easily Lily sat across from Matt without glaring at him or kicking him beneath the table. He would have expected her to be a little less generous toward the man who'd promised to marry her and then dumped her. Was the man insane? Trace would have held on to her with everything in his power.

Then why hadn't he tried to change her mind?

He had been so hurt, he'd buried himself in his new life in the army, working harder than anyone. The more he pushed, the less time he had to mourn the loss of Lily's love. He'd pushed so hard and so fast, he'd caught the attention of his drill sergeant, who recommended him for further training that eventually led him to the army rangers and selection into the elite Delta Force.

Irish took a steak off the platter and passed it to Lily.

"I'd heard the rumors around town that you were having trouble keeping help after Mr. Travis's death." Matt peeled the foil off a baked potato and cut it down the middle. "He was a good man. He helped me get a start with my shop when the banks wouldn't loan me the money to buy the building."

Trace had been at loggerheads with his father for so many years, he hadn't known his father had helped other people in the community from time to time. But Hennessey? What a cruel trick of fate that his father had helped the one man who'd taken the only woman his son had ever loved away from him.

Now his mother was fawning over the guy in front of him. Yeah, fate was cruel.

"I still owe half of what he loaned to me a year ago," Matt said. "I promise to pay it off as soon as I can."

"I'm not worried about the money," his mother said. "I know you're good for it."

Trace would have to pull his mother aside and warn her about being too nice. People would take advantage of her, thinking she was a pushover.

"We need to start cutting hay tomorrow afternoon," his mother said with a smile.

"Why not in the morning first thing?" Trace asked.

His mother looked down at her plate, her smile fading. "We have a meeting at the attorney's office to go over your father's will." She glanced up, her gaze going to Lily and Matt. "The attorney asked that Lily and Matt be present for the reading."

Trace felt anger rise up inside him. "Why? I thought Dad would leave everything to you."

His mother set her fork beside her plate and folded her hands in her lap. "Don't worry. He took care of me. But he wanted to be certain others were taken care of as well, if he should pass before I did."

"I don't understand," Trace said. "You were his wife. You have every right to all of his estate."

"Just so you all know, I was with him when he put the provisions into the will. I signed it as well. I'm aware of everything the lawyer is going to say tomorrow."

"Then why don't you tell us now?" Trace demanded.

"I think you need to hear what the attorney has to say first, then I'll tell you why your father and I did what we did." She lifted her fork.

When Trace opened his mouth, his mother gave him *that look* that meant the discussion was over.

He bit down hard on his tongue to keep from shouting.

Not only had the man stolen his girl, but Matt had also wormed his way into his father's good graces and somehow stolen money from his family. Trace didn't want his father's money, but he sure as hell didn't want Matt Hennessey to have a single dime.

Lily reached out to touch Trace's mother's hand.

His mother glanced up at her and gave her a watery smile.

That exchange of silent communication reminded Trace that his mother had just lost the man she'd centered her life around. They'd been married for more than thirty-five years. Most of their lives had been spent together.

His anger was uncalled for in the wake of her loss.

Despite his differences with his father, he'd loved the man. His father had been the one who'd taught him the important things in life. Like how to ride a horse, how to throw a baseball and football, and how to love a woman.

James Travis had been a force to be reckoned with. His concern for his son came from the heart. He'd wanted the best for his son. That didn't include marrying a woman whose parents were a prostitute and a thief. He'd probably thought he was giving Trace good advice. What he didn't know was that Trace wasn't a kid anymore. He could make his own decisions, and he resented his father's interference in making those decisions. His father hadn't understood that Trace needed to be the master of his own destiny, to make his own mistakes and follow his heart where it led.

Based on the way things had turned out, his father might have been half right. Trace had decided he wanted Lily. Lily had made the decision for him that he wouldn't have her. His father might have seen that coming and tried to spare him the heartache.

That wouldn't have changed Trace's mind about joining the army. He'd have done it anyway. He was glad he had. For the first time in his life, he was his own person. Not the son of the richest man in the county. And he'd done well for himself. If not financially, then for his own state of mind.

Irish broke the silence with "What's in this pasta salad, Mrs. Travis? It's really good."

Trace's mother smiled, the lines of tension easing from her face. Soon, Irish had the others laughing over stories about his antics as a young recruit going through basic training.

Before long, the meal was over. The steak Trace had eaten sat like a rock in the pit of his belly. What had his father left in his will for Matt and Lily? And why them? Did he know they were once a couple? That they were responsible for breaking his son's heart?

Trace carried his plate to the sink.

"I'll pull KP," Irish said.

"No, I've got this," his mother said.

"Seriously, you've been working as hard as anyone,"

Irish said. "You need to relax and go watch that sunset I can see through the window."

Trace's mother filled the sink with soapy water. "If we all pitch in, we can get it done faster and then we can all see that sunset." She handed Irish a dry dish towel. "I'll wash, you dry, Lily and Trace can put the dishes away, and Matt can open a bottle of wine and pour me a glass."

With tasks assigned, they worked together to get the dishes done in record time.

Once they had everything put away, they adjourned to the porch to watch the brilliant orange-and-mauve-painted sky as the sun sank below the horizon.

Matt leaned against the porch rail, staring out at the last rays as they disappeared. "This place is amazing. Don't let anyone take it away from you."

"We have no intention of letting that happen," his mother said. "It's been in the Travis family for more than a hundred years. But it's not the life everyone would choose."

Trace tensed. He knew she was talking about him. Before he left for the army, one of his last arguments with his father had been over the ranch and who would inherit it. He'd told his father that he didn't care who he left the ranch to. But, good Lord, not Matt Hennessey.

LILY SAT ON the porch swing beside Irish, talking quietly about life in the little Texas town of Whiskey Gulch. Irish asked questions and she answered but didn't go into the details of how she'd been ostracized by most of her peers growing up because of who her parents were. She didn't tell him that she'd been bullied and picked on by the mean girls and propositioned by just about every male in the county who thought she was like her mother.

Trace had been one of a handful of people who hadn't been mean to her. He'd seen her for who she was, not who her parents were.

When Irish excused himself and went inside, Trace gathered the empty beer bottles and carried them into the house.

Lily stood and stretched. "I'm going to check on the barn cat. I think she's expecting to drop a litter of kittens soon. I want to make sure she's okay. I might need to relocate the kittens if she's had them up in the loft, since we'll be filling that space soon."

"I'll go with you," Rosalynn said.

"No need," Lily said. "I'll only be a minute. I'm sure she's fine."

"We'll need to catch her and get her and all the kittens spayed or neutered before we end up with a couple dozen cats around here. But that'll be after the kittens are weaned." Rosalynn settled back in her rocking chair. "If you're sure you don't need me, I'll just sit here and listen to the cicadas sing. James loved the sound. I always thought they were loud." She smiled. "I miss him."

Lily touched her shoulder. "I miss him, too."

Rosalynn covered her hand on her shoulder. "Thank you for being here for me, Lily. I don't know what I'd have done without you."

"I haven't done anything anyone else wouldn't have. I'm glad I was here for you." She leaned down and pressed a kiss to the top of Rosalynn's head. "I'll be back in a minute."

Lily left the porch and strolled out to the barn. After the tension of dinner and being in the same space as Trace and Matt for an extended period of time, she needed to get away from the house, from Trace and from her own thoughts.

The mama cat would do fine birthing her kittens. She didn't need Lily to help her along, but it had been a good excuse for her to step away for a few minutes by herself.

Lily entered the barn and flipped the switch on the wall. The lights blinked on, giving the interior a soft yellow glow.

Several soft whinnies greeted her.

Lily chuckled. "You've already been fed."

Lady stomped her foot impatiently.

She reached over the stall door and rubbed the mare's nose. "Your hooves must be feeling better if you're doing that."

A sound near the back of the barn caught her attention. She squinted, trying to see into the shadows. "Patches, is that you, girl?" Lily stepped toward the sound.

Lady stomped louder, her hoof hitting the wooden wall, making a loud banging sound.

"It's okay," Lily said and reached back to pat the horse.

A shiver rippled across Lily's skin. The day had been hot, but with the setting of the sun, the warmth disappeared, and the night had cooled at least fifteen degrees.

Rubbing her arms, Lily searched the corners and shadows for the mama cat.

The animal wasn't behind the feed bins or nestled in the stacks of empty feed sacks. The tack room door was kept closed to keep her out. Had someone inadvertently locked her inside?

Lily pushed the door to the tack room open and peered inside. "Patches?" she called out. When she started to turn around, she caught movement in her peripheral vision. Before she could duck or move out of the way, something dark swung toward her and hit her on the side of her head, knocking her to the ground.

She lay stunned, her vision blurred, her head spinning and pain knifing through her temple. How long she lay there, she didn't know until someone stepped into the doorway. With the yellow lighting behind him, he appeared a dark, shadowy figure.

Lily whimpered and tried to scramble away from him. "Don't," she said and raised her hand to shield her face.

"Lily?" a voice said as if from a distance. Then the figure squatted down beside her and she could see his familiar face.

Trace.

When he reached for her, she fell into his arms.

"It's okay," he murmured. "It's okay." He smoothed his hand over her hair.

For a moment, she let him hold her. "No." She pushed away from him, frantically trying to get around him to see what was on the other side of his hulking body.

"What?" Trace asked.

"He might get you." Lily shook her head, trying to clear the fog. It hurt, but she couldn't be deterred.

"Who might?" Trace rose and helped her to her feet. "What are you talking about?"

"He might hit you." She pushed him to the side and stood in front of him.

"He who?" Trace gripped her arm. "Lily, why were you lying on the floor?"

"Someone hit me," she said.

Immediately, Trace shoved her into the tack room. "Stay here and don't unlock the door until I tell you to. Promise?"

Fear gripped her. Not for herself, but for Trace. "What are you going to do?"

"I'm going to find whoever is in the barn." He closed the door. "Lock it," he said from the other side.

"What about you?" she asked, her voice shaking.

"I'll be all right." He paused as if waiting for her to comply. When she didn't, he said, "Lily, lock the damn door."

Lily turned the lock and waited on the other side, her ear pressed to the wood, listening and praying Trace would be okay.

For what felt like an eternity, she held her breath.

"You can unlock the door," Trace's voice said from the other side. "Whoever was here is gone."

Lily twisted the lock, ripped open the door and flung herself into his arms. "Thank God… I was afraid…"

He held her until she stopped shaking, smoothing the hair at the back of her neck. After a while, he leaned back and stared into her face. "Where did he hit you?"

She touched her fingertips to her temple and winced. "Here."

He tipped her head to the side to allow the light to shine down on her face. "You have a small cut that will likely boast a bruise by morning. Let's get you into the house and put something on it."

Lily stepped out of the tack room, shaking her head. "Who was in here?"

Trace's jaw was tight, and his eyes narrowed. "I don't know. I don't like it. From now on, no one ventures out at night or any other time alone. We have to have a buddy system." He cupped her elbow and guided her toward the barn door.

Lily dug her heels in, bringing them to a halt. "Patches."

Trace frowned. "Patches?"

"The mama cat who lives in the barn. She's due to have kittens anytime. I came out here to check on her."

"She'll know what to do when the time comes. Let's get you inside and take care of your wound." Again, he tried to guide her to the door.

She pulled free of his grip. "You can go ahead. I'm not going until I know where she is. If she's hidden in the loft, we could trap her in when we stack the hay." Lily strode toward the stairs leading up into the loft.

"Wait." Trace caught her around the waist as she started up the stairs and swung her back to the ground. "If anyone is going up, it's me."

She tipped her head. "If you go up, that leaves me alone on the ground."

His lips twisted. "You've got a point. Okay. I'll go up

first in case your attacker is hiding up there. You come right after me."

Lily didn't like the idea that the attacker might still be in the barn, waiting for one of them to climb up into the loft. Nor did she like the idea that Trace was going up first and could be coldcocked like she'd been. However, he was bigger, better trained in combat skills and pretty darn intimidating.

"Okay," she said.

Trace grabbed a riding whip from a hook on the wall and started up the stairs.

The bulb hanging from the ceiling gave just enough light for them to see the loft, except in the far corners where several stacks of last year's hay stood, three bales high.

Trace edged his way across the wooden floor to a stack of hay, holding the riding whip in front of him. "Remind me to start carrying my Glock."

"Start carrying your Glock," Lily whispered.

He snorted. "Remind me when I'm still in the house." Slowly, he circled the short stack of hay until he stood to the side and could see behind it. The shadow hid anything below the top bale.

Lily pulled her cell phone out of her back pocket, turned on the flashlight feature and shined it down the back of the bales.

The light reflected off a pair of red orbs.

"Patches!" Lily brushed past Trace and knelt beside the gray-and-white cat.

The mama cat had given birth to five kittens in varying shades of gray, white and wheat gold.

"Look at you," Lily cooed. "Five pretty babies and you found a nice warm and dry place to have them." She studied the kittens, all tiny creatures, their eyes closed, struggling to find purchase at one of their mother's teats.

"We need to move her before we stack the hay in here," Lily said.

"If we move her, she could move them back," Trace argued. "She probably had them here because she felt safe."

"True." Lily touched a finger to her chin and looked around the loft and over the railing to the barn below. "Where would she be safe and not feel like she had to move them again?"

"I don't know. But let's leave them here for now. We probably won't stack hay for a couple of days. We'll cut tomorrow, let it dry and then rake and bale. When we get close to hauling the hay, we can relocate her to the tack room until we're finished."

Lily nodded. "That would be best." She smiled down at the tiny kittens crawling across Patches's belly instinctively looking for something to eat.

When she pushed to her feet, she swayed a little.

Trace reached out and pulled her into his arms. "I shouldn't have let you come up here when you've had a head injury." He brushed her hair away from her temple and stared at the wound. "Let's get you back to the house."

"Yes. I'm worried about your mother. She was sitting alone on the porch."

"She was going in for the night when I stepped out of the house." He walked her to the stairs leading downward. "Need help getting down?"

Lily shook her head. "No. I got up on my own. I can get down on my own."

His lips quirked. "Always were independent."

She tipped her chin upward. "You used to like that about me."

His gaze shifted from her eyes to her lips. "There were a lot of things I liked about you."

Lily's heart beat a rapid tattoo against her ribs.

Trace stood so close, she could reach out and touch him.

If she stood on her toes, she could press her lips to his and kiss him. Lily swayed toward him, caught herself up before she lost her mind and lurched toward the stairs.

Trace took her wrist and pulled her back. "Me first."

Lily held back, letting him descend to the ground, giving her a little more time to pull herself together. Had he felt that tug of desire, that longing for more than just words? He'd kissed her earlier that day. Had it meant anything to him?

It meant something to her. It meant all those years of trying to forget him had been a waste of time. Trace had been and always would be the only man she would ever love. When the time came, she'd have to leave. She couldn't stay around to see him fall in love and marry another woman. That would wreck her, shatter her into a million pieces.

She couldn't let that happen. If it meant leaving Whiskey Gulch Ranch and her hometown, so be it.

Chapter Seven

After the sheriff's deputy had come to investigate the attack in the barn, looked around and taken Lily's statement, Trace went around the house, checking windows and doors to make sure all had been securely locked.

His mother had doctored the wound on Lily's face.

Irish, having been trained as one of the medics on the Delta Force team, had checked Lily's pupils for possibility of concussion.

When he'd suggested she see a doctor, Lily had promptly refused, claiming she hadn't been knocked unconscious and she was feeling much better. Irish then offered to check on her throughout the night to make sure she didn't show any signs of complications. Again, Lily had thanked him but politely refused.

Trace spent the night tossing and turning. Sleep eluded him. Worried about Lily, he'd listened for sounds through the wall between their rooms. At one point, he'd left his bed, tiptoed out into the hallway and tried the door to her room.

It had been unlocked. Feeling a little guilty, he'd stepped inside and checked to make sure she was breathing. For a few long moments, he'd stood beside her bed until he saw the reassuring rise and fall of her chest beneath the sheets. Relieved, he'd wanted more than anything to kiss Lily and hold her like he had when they were younger.

Unfortunately, they were no longer hormonal teens.

They had matured into adults and gone their separate ways. Only now those ways had converged.

When he'd left his unit, he hadn't thought far enough ahead of getting home to know where his future would lead. Now that he was back on the Whiskey Gulch Ranch, he couldn't imagine going back to his unit and leaving his mother with only the help of their foreman and Lily to manage the ranch on their own.

If his mother planned to stay, he'd have to stay as well. If she wanted to sell the ranch, he couldn't stop her. As far as he knew, she would inherit his father's ranch and had the authority to do whatever she wanted with it.

As he worked in the barn, in the fields and around the house, he remembered growing up with the world at his feet. His father had demanded that he work hard, but he always had chances to play hard as well.

Many summer afternoons, he'd ridden horses with his friends across the pastures to the creek, where they would swim and lie in the sun until dusk.

Lily had been with him on many of those occasions. That was how he'd started to fall in love with her in the first place. She'd been his friend before she'd been his lover. She'd been his first love. They'd picnicked by the creek, chased squirrels and lain in the back of his truck to witness the shooting stars in a heaven full of diamonds. The most beautiful stars were those reflected in Lily's eyes.

He'd been so in love with her that when she'd broken up with him, it had hit him like a physical blow. He had not seen it coming.

Now that he was back, and she was underfoot, he couldn't avoid her or the feelings that had resurfaced after all these years.

Rather than disturb her sleep, he'd left her room, returned to his and lain on top of the covers, willing sleep to take him.

It hadn't.

Unwilling to wait for morning to dawn, he'd left his bed, dressed and gone out to the barn as the sun edged up over the horizon.

"You're up early," a voice called out to him from the open door of the barn. Irish stood in the sunshine, wearing a clean gray T-shirt and jeans. "Couldn't sleep?"

"No." He stacked a saddle on a saddle tree, adjusting the stirrups to hang free on either side.

He'd spent the morning cleaning and rearranging the tack room. With Roy out of commission for the time being, he could get in, assess and decide what needed to stay and what could go. Roy had a tendency to hoard everything, even long after its expiration date or usefulness. Trace made a list of supplies he needed, from horse feed to wormer, fence nails to new curry combs and brushes.

"Worried about your father's will?" Irish grabbed a broom and swept dust and straw out of the far corner of the tack room.

Trace hadn't really thought about his father's will. He'd been too busy thinking about Lily and how much he'd wanted to kiss her. Now that Irish had reminded him of the will, he might actually shift his obsession from her to whatever his father had done with his holdings. "My father owned the ranch. He and my mother have every right to do with it whatever they want."

Irish's brow rose. "You don't want a part of it?"

"Not if they don't want me to have it," Trace said.

"Would be a shame for it to go out of the family."

"Ranching is hard work," Trace said. "My father and his father before him built this place to what it is today with their own sweat and blood."

Irish snorted. "And you didn't help them in their efforts?"

"Not as much as my father would have liked." His father had always found fault with his work, no matter how much effort he put into it.

"He wanted you to stay and run it, didn't he?" Irish guessed.

Trace didn't respond.

"This place is amazing." Irish waved a hand around the interior of the barn. "Why would you want to join the army and barely make a living when you had all this?"

Anger bubbled up inside Trace. "Because it wasn't mine, and I had no say in how it should be run. If I'd stayed, my father would have continued to run Whiskey Gulch Ranch the way he saw fit. He didn't trust me to make any of the decisions. And why should he? I'd never had to be responsible for anything as long as he was in charge."

Irish nodded. "I get that."

Trace looped a bridle over a peg on the wall and faced Irish. "Yeah, well, he didn't. You ready for breakfast?" He headed out of the barn and strode toward the house. The scent of bacon made his stomach rumble. Although he was hungry, his gut was knotted in anticipation of the contents of the will. He really did care what happened to Whiskey Gulch Ranch. Like his father and his father's father before him, they were rooted in the place. Trace had left to prove to himself he could be himself, not the son of James Travis. In the back of his mind, he knew he'd eventually come home. He hadn't thought it would be for his father's funeral.

Irish fell in step beside him. "Just so you know, I don't expect to be fed and housed by you and your family."

"No worries. The ranch employs ranch hands who live here and those who don't. Most of those who don't have families and live in town. The single guys have a choice of living here or in town. We have a bunkhouse my father converted into small apartments to give the guys more personal space. It's up to you. When we have a cook, he—" Trace paused, thinking about Lily "—or she will provide a hot breakfast and dinner and the means to make a sack lunch if you want it."

"I appreciate everything you've done for me. I'd like to stay on the ranch at least until I figure out the area. I can help get the bunkhouse ready, so that I don't take up room in the big house."

"No hurry. Our main focus, after hearing what is in the will, is to get the hay in before it rains." Trace glanced up at the clear blue sky. "It is Texas, and the rain may or may not happen, but we have to be prepared."

"Got it." Irish squared his shoulders. "I'll do the best I can."

Trace clapped a hand on his friend's shoulder. "I know you will. That's why I asked you to come. I just hope you stick around. Ranching life isn't for everyone. Especially guys like us who've been where we've been. It can be boring here. There's not always that adrenaline rush of going into battle."

"I'm looking forward to that," Irish said. "I could use a little downtime."

"Especially to give yourself time to heal." Trace gave Irish a pointed glance. "We need your help, but only as much as you can do without reinjuring yourself." Trace frowned. "Will you be all right here alone while the rest of us are in town at the lawyer's office?"

Irish nodded. "Someone has to stay here and guard the homestead. I'll be sure to keep an eye out for danger. You don't have to worry about me."

Trace climbed the porch to the big house. "Be sure to keep your weapons where you can use them."

"I'll pack my pistol when I step outside and keep my rifle handy." Irish opened the back door to the house and held it for Trace.

"Whoever is causing trouble is getting cocky and dangerously close. I don't want you having just come back from a war zone to be injured or killed stateside."

Irish gave a crooked smile. "That would be the ultimate irony."

"Yeah. Don't let it happen. Stay close to the house and be careful, my friend." He clasped Irish's hand in a firm grasp and pulled him in for a hug. "Don't make me regret asking you to come."

"Wouldn't dream of it. I owe you one for saving my butt back in Afghanistan."

"You don't owe me a thing. You've saved me more times than I can remember."

"Any idea who might be targeting the ranch?" Irish asked.

"None." Trace clenched his fists. "Whoever hit Lily in the barn got away clean. He must have come in on foot and left in a hurry."

Irish shook his head. "Why do you think he was in the barn? He couldn't have known Lily would go out after the chores were complete."

"I don't know." Trace led the way to the kitchen and the smell of bacon cooking. "We'll just have to be more vigilant."

"Who will have to be more vigilant?" his mother asked from her position at the coffee maker.

"We all will." Lily stood at the stove, pushing fluffy yellow scrambled eggs around in the pan. "Y'all ready for breakfast?" When she turned, the bruise at her temple and the cut were evident.

Trace's blood boiled all over again. If he'd caught the guy who'd hit her, he'd have pummeled him to near death.

"I'm starving," Irish said. "What can I do to help?"

"Tell me what you want to drink and have a seat," Trace's mother said. "Everything is ready and on the table except for the eggs, and Lily has that under control."

"Done." Lily scooped eggs into a large bowl and carried it to the table.

Trace couldn't help but watch her as she moved across the floor in jeans, a powder blue blouse and her cowboy boots. She had her long blond hair pulled back and secured in a ponytail at the nape of her neck. Several tendrils had worked their way loose and curled around her cheeks.

A deep, physical ache pinched his chest.

Irish held a chair for Trace's mother. "Ma'am."

She smiled at him. "Please, don't call me ma'am. It makes me feel old."

"Yes, Mrs. Travis."

Her eyes filled. "No." She drew in a deep breath and forced a bit of a smile. "Call me Rosalynn."

Trace had been so focused on Lily and his lingering feelings for her that he hadn't been nearly as attentive to his mother. He waited for her to take her seat, then sat at the opposite end of the table from her. "You all right?" he asked softly.

She met his gaze, a tear slipping down her cheek. "You look just like your father when he was in his thirties. Seeing you sometimes hurts."

"I'm sorry," he said.

She laughed, the sound catching in her throat. "You have nothing to be sorry about. I like to think he's still here, in you. You two were so much alike."

Growing up, Trace had wanted to get away from his father as fast as he could. They never saw eye to eye, and they were constantly butting heads. Back then, he'd never considered that they had similar personalities.

Now he could see what his mother had observed back then. They were both stubborn, driven, and they liked to be in control of a situation. He'd come to grips with this when he'd been in the army and performing operations with his Delta Force team. Until he'd gained enough experience, he'd had to give control to those who'd been at it longer and knew the tricks and techniques that would keep them alive.

In retrospect, his father had been like the senior member of his Delta Force team, weathered, knowledgeable and full of understanding only experience could give.

"I checked with the sheriff this morning," his mother said. "They don't have anything more on the attack last night. No others have reported anything similar, and they had a rather quiet night otherwise."

"I didn't figure they'd find anything, if we couldn't." Trace shook his head. "I'd like to get my hands on the bastard." He looked from his mother to Lily and back. "Take this threat seriously. No one is to go out after dark to take care of the animals without a backup. You must have a buddy."

"We're pretty shorthanded to have to wait for a buddy every time we need to run out to the barn," his mother said.

"I don't care," Trace said. "If it keeps you safe, that's all that matters."

His mother smiled. "That's what your father would have said."

Too many reminders of his father's absence made Trace wish he'd been home before his father died. Now he would never have the opportunity to fix the rift between them. His father wouldn't know that his son finally understood him.

Breakfast was finished in a few short minutes. Cleanup went just as quickly with all four of them helping to set the kitchen straight.

"Matt is meeting us at the attorney's office in thirty minutes." Trace's mother hung the damp dish towel to dry. "We need to get a move on."

"I'm driving," Trace said. "I need to pick up supplies on the way back. We'll go in my truck."

"That would be nice, since Lily was injured last night."

His mother slipped the strap of her purse over her arm and started for the door.

Lily opened her mouth and closed it again without arguing.

Trace was glad she hadn't insisted on driving. If they encountered any more threats, he wanted to be in control of the vehicle. He wasn't certain how the reading would go or how he would feel afterward. His mother was being far too secretive for his liking. Which probably meant he wasn't going to like what she and his father had decided would happen with the Whiskey Gulch Ranch. Though he'd told Irish he didn't care what his parents had decided, he cared about what happened to the family home and land. He didn't like the idea of it being split up and sold to the highest bidder.

"Be careful while we're gone," he said to Irish. "We'll get started harvesting hay as soon as we get back this afternoon."

Irish popped a salute. "I'll keep a close watch on the place and be ready to go when you return."

Dread sank like a lead weight to the pit of his belly. He knew he shouldn't let the contents of the will worry him so much, but it did.

Trace helped his mother into the passenger seat and closed the door.

Lily climbed into the back seat and buckled her seat belt.

By the time Trace slid into the driver's seat, the breakfast he'd consumed was roiling.

He had to tell himself that whatever happened, it was meant to be. He couldn't change it now. Frankly, he'd rather have his father back than have his father's ranch.

LILY SAT BEHIND Trace for the drive into town to the attorney's office. She made use of the time sitting in the back seat to study the man from behind.

Maybe it was an illusion, but he seemed taller than he had when he left to join the army. His shoulders were much broader and thickly muscled. His hair was cut in a crisp military style with the back and sides shaved short and the top a little longer, but not much. He carried himself straight and unbending, proud and sexy as hell. Her mouth tingled all over again at the memory of his lips on hers. Her body burned where his had touched hers the night before.

As she studied him, she caught Trace staring at her in the rearview mirror.

Heat rushed up her neck and suffused her cheeks. Leaning toward the side window, she moved out of range of his mirror and focused instead on the fields they passed on their way into town.

Why couldn't she focus on the coming meeting with Mr. Travis's attorney? Instead, she was mooning over a man she could never have. What would it get her? Absolutely nothing. The man was so far out of her league, he might as well be from another planet.

Sure, she was good enough to be a ranch hand or a housekeeper. But Trace deserved better than what she brought to the table. Besides, he'd never forgiven her for dumping him before he left for basic combat training. Telling him she'd been seeing Matt Hennessey had killed anything Trace might have had for her. As far as he was concerned, she'd been cheating on him. He'd cut her from his life and never once tried to contact her in the past eleven years.

She'd done it for him. If she'd stayed with him, he might have given up on going into the army. He would have stayed with her and lived in the run-down trailer park where she lived just to spite his father. He'd have been miserable, and she would have felt guilty for not letting him go to join the army and get away from the ranch and his father.

No, she'd done the right thing for Trace. Losing him had broken her heart. She'd stayed in Whiskey Gulch, foolishly hoping that one day he would return and forgive her for the lie she'd told. After eleven years, she'd given up and resigned herself to life without Trace in it.

They pulled to a stop in front of the attorney's office beside an older truck with a smashed front fender.

"Roy's here." Rosalynn frowned. "I told him he didn't have to come. We could have called him with the outcome. Hopefully, he's up to this." She smiled and waved at the foreman.

Before anyone could get out of their vehicles, Matt rolled in beside them on his motorcycle.

Immediately, Trace tensed, and his hands tightened on the steering wheel until his knuckles turned white.

"Oh, good. Matt's here, too," his mother said.

Lily leaned to the right to catch a glimpse of Trace's face in the rearview mirror.

His lips had thinned, and his jaw was set in stone.

How truly unfortunate she had used Matt as the man she'd left Trace for.

Trace stepped out of the truck and helped his mother alight.

Roy exited his truck, sliding gingerly to the ground, wincing as his foot hit the pavement. "Mrs. Travis," he said with a nod. "You're looking good."

She nodded. "Thank you, Roy. I'm glad to see you're getting around, though you should be at home with your foot up."

His lips slid into a smile. "Just like you to worry about everyone else. I'll be all right."

Rosalynn waved her hand toward the building. "Shall we?"

Matt reached the office door first and held it open. Mrs. Travis led the way inside, stopping at the reception desk. "Could you tell Mr. Phillips that Mrs. Travis and her party are here to see him?"

The woman behind the desk nodded and lifted her desk phone, announcing their guests. A moment later, she rose and led them into a conference room with a long table and a dozen chairs grouped around it.

"This really won't take long," Mrs. Travis said.

A man in a gray pin-striped suit entered the conference room with a folio tucked beneath his arm. He went straight to Mrs. Travis and hugged her. "I'm sorry you've had to come to me under these circumstances. You, James and I didn't expect we'd have to invoke the provisions of this will quite this soon."

She gave the attorney a watery smile. "Thankfully, we had the opportunity to put things in place before my husband passed. If you don't mind, we need to get right to it. We have hay to cut today."

"Perfect," Mr. Phillips said. He pulled out a chair, dropped his folio on the smooth dark wood of the conference table and took his seat.

With careful deliberation, Mr. Phillips opened the folio, extracted a document and laid it on the table. "I'm required to read this to you all. Please have a seat and bear with me."

Matt held Mrs. Travis's chair until she was seated and then took the chair beside her.

Trace sat on her other side, angry that Hennessey was even at the table.

Roy sat across the table from Trace.

Lily sat next to Roy with her hands in her lap.

"James and Rosalynn met with me a couple of months ago to iron out details and to record James's wishes in the following document." The attorney turned the cover over to the first page. "James was adamant the wording be such that anyone and everyone would understand what he wished to happen in the occurrence of his death."

Lily twisted her hands in her lap and wondered for the thousandth time why Mr. Travis had included her in the reading. They weren't related. She shared a glance across the table with Matt, also unrelated to the deceased. Why were they there with the family?

Her stomach twisted into a tight knot as her gaze shifted to Trace.

He turned to stare at his mother.

His mother met his gaze and held it while the attorney presented the will.

"Let me start by stating that, as his widow, Mrs. Travis is entitled to all of James Travis's estate. However, the couple wanted people close to them to receive certain holdings should one die before the other. They felt it important to make this happen sooner than later."

Mrs. Travis nodded silently.

The attorney drew in a deep breath and announced, "James Travis and Rosalynn Travis have set up a trust fund for Miss Lily Davidson to be paid out in monthly installments for the rest of her life."

Lily gasped. "What? I don't understand. I just work for the Travises. I'm not a blood relative." Her gaze shot to Trace.

He glanced at her briefly and then returned his gaze to his mother, his brow wrinkling slightly.

His mother nodded with a hint of a smile, as if saying it was okay.

"Mr. Travis wanted Lily to know he wasn't always fair when it came to his treatment of her." The attorney smiled toward Lily. "He wanted to make amends by ensuring you never had to worry about supporting yourself again."

Lily's eyes filled. "But I don't want his money. It belongs to his wife."

"What you do with it is now your business," the attorney said. "Let's continue."

Trace's mother reached out and covered Lily's hand with her own. "He wanted to do this. Please, let him."

The attorney went on. "To Roy Gibson, he left the ranch truck, knowing that if he passed and the ranch was sold, Roy would need a new truck to move on to his next place of employment if the new owners didn't employ him. If the ranch is sold, he's also to receive six months' pay, to tide him over until he can secure alternate employment."

Roy's eyes narrowed. "Mr. Travis didn't owe me anything. He gave me a job when I needed one."

"He knew how much you needed a better truck and wanted you to have the one you used on the ranch." Trace's mother smiled softly. "He cared about his employees."

"Those were the minor assignments," the attorney said. "The will leaves the rest of the estate to James Travis's children to be held in a trust. If one chooses to sell his interest, the entire estate must be sold, the proceeds to be divided in equal shares."

Trace's brow dipped. "What do you mean, children?"

His mother leaned forward, her gaze pinning her son's. "Trace, your father and I wanted to tell you about this but didn't want to do it while you were deployed. It's something that needed to be done in person. You have a brother. Or rather, a half brother."

"What?" He shook his head, his gaze going from his mother to Lily and finally to Matt Hennessey, sitting at the same table with them. He looked as if he'd been punched in the gut. "You?"

Matt nodded slowly. "It was as much of a shock to me when I found out."

Trace turned back to his mother. "You've got to be kidding."

She shook her head. "No, sweetheart, I'm not. Your father didn't even know he had another child until Matt's mother was murdered, God rest her soul."

"How can a man not know he has another child?" His frown deepened. "Was he cheating on you?"

Mrs. Travis raised her hands. "No. No. It wasn't like that. Matt is two years older than you. James had been dating his mother when she got pregnant. Shortly after they stopped dating, she left Whiskey Gulch for a couple years. When she returned, she had a toddler with her. James never did the math. It wasn't until she passed a year ago that her lawyer sent a letter to James, informing him that he had a son by her. James felt awful that he hadn't known about Matt and that he'd missed knowing his son for all those years. This was his way of making it up to Matt."

Trace leaned back in his seat, shaking his head. "By giving him the ranch?"

"By giving you *both* the ranch. He wanted to leave it to his sons." She looked from Trace to Matt and back to Trace again. "But he didn't want it split up."

"Then why the hell did he leave it to the two of us?" Trace pushed back from the table. "How do you even know he's really my father's son?"

"Matt was as concerned about it as you." Mrs. Travis nodded toward Matt. "When he learned the truth, he offered to have a DNA test conducted. The results were 99.9 percent conclusive. He's your father's son."

Lily sat in stunned silence, trying to take it all in.

Not only had Trace's father left her money, which would only make Trace madder that his inheritance was going to the woman who'd cheated on him, but now he was locked into dual ownership of the Whiskey Gulch Ranch with a man he barely knew. A man who, it turns out, was his brother.

If she thought there was even the slightest chance at a reconciliation between the two of them, there was no way it would happen now.

Chapter Eight

Trace leaned back in his chair, his head spinning, anger burning in his belly. At that moment, he wished he was back in Afghanistan fighting bad guys. That was easier than dealing with his father's last wishes. Even from his grave, his father was dictating his life for him.

"There's more legalese in the document, but that's what it all boils down to," the attorney said. "I suggest you take time to think about it. If either of you decide to sell your portion, the entire ranch will have to be sold. Your mother would have to give up her home and find another place to live. It was James's hope that his two sons would come to an agreement on how to manage the ranch holdings and keep it in the family for another one hundred years. He also understood these are changing times and owning land might not be as appealing to the younger generation. He didn't want the ranch to be a burden. Mrs. Travis will retain a portion of the assets to see her through the end of her life. James left her a small cottage in town she can choose to move into or sell."

"Mom." Trace stared at his mother. "You let him do this?"

She nodded. "I knew I wouldn't want to run the ranch without your father. He was what made it so successful. Not me. It was his to give. Not mine. I didn't mind taking care of it until you two came on board, but I'm not the one

to do this. I want to cook, crochet and help raise grandba-
bies." She gave him a gentle smile. "And if you decide to
sell, I don't need the money. I have plenty of my own. I can
start over wherever I decide to go."

"It's your home," Trace said. "You should be able to live
there the rest of your life."

"Without your father, it's not the same." She shrugged.
"I knew that's how it would be. I told him I didn't want
the ranch if he passed before me. It belongs to his children
and their children's children…if that's the route you two
choose to go."

Her comment brought him back to the table and the man
seated so near. Trace jerked a thumb toward him. "He's
never worked a day on the ranch. Why leave it to him?"

"Your father regrets that he didn't get to know Matt
while he was growing up. He couldn't undo the past, but
he was determined to make it right for the future. Both you
and Matt are his children. By leaving the ranch in a trust for
both of you, he'd hoped to bring you together as brothers."

"He could never be a brother to me," Trace said. "My
brothers are Irish, Levi and Beck—men from my team.
They've had my back since I joined the force."

"Goes both ways. The only brothers I've known are
the ones I met in the Marine Corps," Matt said. "And like
Trace said, I know nothing about ranching." He glanced
at Trace's mother. "I'm sorry. I offered to help you, and I
will. But long-term…it just won't work."

"And I'm scheduled to go back on active duty when
things settle down here," Trace said.

For a brief second, his mother winced, then a mask settled over her expression. "This has all been a shock to you
two. All I ask is that you think about it for a few days. Even
if you end up selling the ranch, you need to keep it running, take care of the animals and prepare for winter by
stockpiling hay. And that doesn't even take into account the

threat that's hanging over everything. Someone is causing problems that could impact the sale of the land and cattle."

Trace clenched his teeth. He didn't want to have to work with Hennessey, but they had to do something to bring closure to the danger. "You're right, we have to neutralize the threat. Until then, no one is safe on the ranch. I'll table the discussion until I've had more time to resolve issues and come to a decision."

Hennessey nodded. "Agreed. And I'll still help haul hay. I might not know much about ranching, but I'm not afraid of hard work."

Trace's mother smiled at Matt and then at Trace. "A little time and help is all I ask. Thank you."

The attorney gave them copies of the will and his condolences and escorted them out of the building.

Matt mounted his motorcycle and pulled on his helmet. "I'll see you at the ranch." He started his engine and roared away.

Roy limped out behind them, took Trace's mother's hands and squeezed them. "I'm really sorry about your loss. Mr. Travis was a decent man and a good boss."

"Thank you, Roy," she said, ducking her head. "He was a good man."

"I'll be back at the ranch soon. I think I can get back to work at least at some of the light duty."

"Take your time," Rosalynn said. "Now that Trace is home, Lily and I have help."

Roy nodded. "Nevertheless, I need to get back to work. I don't like the idea of you being out there on your own, in case someone turns on you." He gave her an awkward hug and stepped back.

She smiled. "I'm okay for now." She turned her smile toward Trace. "I have my son to protect me."

Roy slid into his truck, rolled down the window and

tipped his head, first toward Trace and then Rosalynn. "Take good care of her. Your mother is special."

"I know."

Trace helped his mother into the truck while Lily slipped quietly into the back seat. When he started to turn left and head toward the ranch, his mother reminded him, "Don't we need some supplies at the feed store?"

He altered his direction and drove to the store, his thoughts still on what the attorney had said and the fact his mother had known about Matt being his half brother but hadn't told him.

At the feed store, Lily and his mother got out along with him and went inside.

Forcing himself to focus on what he needed, he mentally checked off his list one item at a time.

"Mrs. Travis, sorry to hear about your husband," a voice said one aisle over from him.

"Good morning, Chad," his mother said. "Thank you for your concern."

Trace grabbed a new brush and curry comb from the shelf and walked to the end of the aisle to see the face of the man who was talking to her.

He was a tall, lean man, wearing jeans, a denim shirt and worn cowboy boots. It had been years since Trace had seen him, but he recognized the man as Chad Meyers, the owner of the Rafter M Ranch adjacent to the Whiskey Gulch Ranch.

"How's Alice?" his mother asked.

"She's doing better since she had that back operation. Not getting around as fast as she'd hoped, but better."

"Tell her I'm thinking of her." His mother smiled up at Mr. Meyers. "I'll try to get by this week to check on her."

"We were shocked to hear about what happened to James." The man shook his head. "We had our differences, but I didn't wish ill will on the man."

His mother patted Mr. Meyers's arm. "I'm sure you both meant well. Tell Alice hello for me."

Mr. Meyers thanked her and moved away.

"You all right?" Trace asked.

His mother gave him a tight smile, her eyes glassy with unshed tears. "It'll take time." She left him and walked over to say hello to another neighbor.

"Talk about disagreements, Meyers and your father had a bit of an argument right here in the feed store last week," a voice said behind him.

Trace turned to face a man with white-blond hair and gray eyes. "Do I know you?"

The man held out his hand. "Oswald Young. I own the property north of the Whiskey Gulch Ranch."

Trace frowned as he shook the man's hand. The only ranch he knew of to the north was the Rocking J, owned by the Johnsons. "Which property?"

"The Rocking J," Oswald said. "Purchased most of it from Ken and Minnie Johnson six months ago. They couldn't keep up with it anymore and they didn't have family to leave it to."

"I didn't know that." He'd known the Johnsons all his life. "I went to school with their son."

"Apparently, he didn't want the ranch. They were ready to sell and…right place, right time. Now I'm the owner of thirty-two hundred acres of the Rocking J Ranch."

"Congratulations," Trace said, though he couldn't care less about the man's purchase.

"We're setting up an outfitting service for game hunters. The land is full of wild hogs, turkey, white-tailed and axis deer. We hope to introduce buffalo and elk as well." The man puffed out his chest and grinned broadly. "We have big plans."

"Interesting," Trace said, searching for his mother…or

anyone who could extricate him from his new neighbor's conversation.

Lily appeared at Trace's side. "Your mother is ready to go."

"Nice to meet you, neighbor," Oswald said. "See ya around."

Trace carried his items to the counter, ordered several bags of feed and paid. His mother stood beside him, greeting townspeople who stepped up to pay their respects and condolences for her loss.

Oswald approached her, his smile gone, his brow furrowed. "Mrs. Travis, I'm so sorry for your loss. Please accept my sincere condolences. If there's anything we can do at the Rocking J, just let us know." He reached for her hand and held it in both of his.

"Thank you, Mr. Young."

"Please, call me Oswald."

"Oswald," Trace's mother said.

"And, Mrs. Travis… If for any reason you decide to sell the Whiskey Gulch Ranch, please, let me know. We're looking to expand the Rocking J even more."

Trace's mother winced.

If Trace hadn't been watching her, he wouldn't have seen her pain. He wanted to punch Oswald Young square in the face but knew it would only upset his mother further. Instead, he stepped between his mother and Mr. Young. "Let's go, Mom." He hooked his mother's elbow in his grip and led her toward the door. By the time they left the store, his mother's face was pale, and she looked more fragile than Trace had ever seen her.

He helped her into the truck and closed the door.

Lily stood beside him. "It's been too much. She's been holding up for too long, bottling it in. I don't know how she hasn't broken down."

"We need to get her home." Trace thought about the word

home. His mother and father had just given their home to him and a stranger. The shock had yet to wear off. Why would his mother do that? The ranch was just as much hers as it was his father's. She'd put every bit of her love and hard work into making it a profitable business and home for her family. He couldn't let her just move out and take up residence in a cottage in town, or God forbid, Florida.

Anger burned in Trace's gut. Even from his grave, his father was still calling the shots.

Trace couldn't wrap his mind around what was happening or what the future might hold, but he had to keep his mother safe and help her find happiness after the death of the only man she'd ever loved.

He climbed into the truck and turned to his mother. "Think you can stand to be in town for a little longer? I want to stop by the sheriff's office for a minute."

She nodded. "I'm all right. I'm more concerned about you."

Trace shook his head. "Don't be. You worry about you."

Her smile was crooked, but gentle. "I'm your mother. No matter how old you get, I'll always worry about you."

Trace drove to the sheriff's office. "Do you want to come in with me?" he asked.

His mother shook her head. "I'll wait here."

He didn't like leaving her in the truck but understood her reluctance to meet with the sheriff and dredge up all the pain of what had happened to his father. "I won't be long."

LILY OPENED THE back door of the pickup. "I'm coming." She slipped out of the truck and paused. Then she opened the passenger seat door and looked up at the woman who'd taken her in and treated her like family. "Will you be all right on your own?"

Rosalynn nodded. "I'm fine, just a little tired."

Lily lifted Trace's mother's hand and pressed it to her

cheek. "Hang in there. You're surrounded by the people who love you."

Rosalynn curled her fingers around Lily's cheek. "I know. Now go. See if the sheriff has learned anything new. You can tell me all about it on the way home."

Lily closed the door and met Trace on the sidewalk in front of the truck. He opened the sheriff's office door for her and held it as she entered.

Her heartbeat fluttered as she brushed past him. She could smell the outdoorsy scent that was solely Trace, and her knees wobbled just a little.

Inside, the sheriff stood at the counter, talking to one of his deputies. When he spotted Lily and Trace, he turned and held out his hand to Lily first. "Lily, I'm glad you came."

"Sheriff Owens, you remember Trace Travis?" Lily said.

The sheriff nodded and offered his hand to Trace. "I do. I was still just a deputy the day he hopped on the bus to join the army. I remember his mother seeing him off." He shook Trace's hand. "Good to see you back. I'm sorry for the circumstances."

Trace dipped his head. "Good to see you, Sheriff Owens. Congratulations on moving up in the department."

"Don't know what possessed me to run for sheriff, but the town voted me in. Guess I better do right by them." He winked. "What can I do for you?"

"What's happening with the investigation on my father's murder?" Trace asked.

The sheriff waved them toward a hallway. "Come to the conference room. We have the investigation laid out in there."

Lily followed the sheriff into the conference room, fully aware of Trace right behind her. Her body was tuned into his nearness, her nerves hopping at every chance brush of his skin against hers.

The room had a long table in the middle with chairs all

around and a long whiteboard stretched across one entire wall. Names were written in black. Lily recognized many of the names, including some of the people who'd worked on Whiskey Gulch Ranch—Roy Gibson, their foreman, and Marty Bains and Alan Holden, the ranch hands who'd bailed as soon as things got hot on the ranch. Beside their names were those of the neighbors whose land bordered the Travises' ranch—Oswald Young of the Rocking J, Chad and Alice Meyers of the Rafter M Ranch. Matt Hennessey's name was listed alongside Lily's and some random townsfolk. There were other names Lily didn't recognize. The name on the board that surprised her most was Rosalynn Travis.

Lily frowned. "Are all of these people suspects in Mr. Travis's murder?"

The sheriff shook his head. "Not necessarily. We list all those close to the victim in proximity, people who owed James money and family ties who were present when the murder occurred." He nodded toward Trace. "You're not on the board because you were deployed at the time."

Trace's eyes narrowed. "You don't think my mother or Lily killed my father, do you?"

"No, we don't," Sheriff Owens said. "But we have to talk to everyone who might have seen something or might know of someone with a motive to kill your father." He pointed to the board. "We've questioned every one of the people listed on the board so far."

"And?"

The sheriff shook his head. "So far, we haven't identified anyone with a motive." He pointed to Marty and Alan's names. "The ranch hands weren't even close to Mr. Travis when he was shot. They had just left for town with Miss Lily to get more supplies for the barnyard gate they'd been working on when Mr. Travis's horse brought him home."

"Roy had gone to town that morning," Lily murmured,

remembering that horrible day. The images flashing through her mind made her stomach roil.

The sheriff nodded. "That's the day he crashed his truck into a tree and hurt his foot. He hobbled the rest of the way into town after the wreck."

"What about the neighbors?" Trace asked. "We've known the Meyerses all my life. I can't imagine they'd have a motive for killing my father."

"They are in dire financial straits," the sheriff said. "But Mr. Meyers claims he was home with his wife all day. She's recovering from back surgery and requires someone to be with her at all times."

"The new owners of the Rocking J?" Lily asked. "Mr. Young asked Rosalynn if she wanted to sell the ranch."

The sheriff nodded. "We did ask him where he was at the time of the murder. He was with a group of hunters at the new lodge he had built on the property. They can all vouch for his and everyone else's whereabouts."

"Which leaves us back at ground zero," Trace said.

"It would help if we could find where he was actually shot. He could have been anywhere on his spread. We sent out twenty deputies and volunteers to look. With over twelve hundred acres to search, we didn't know where to begin. We did our best, but it wasn't good enough. Finding a bullet casing or tracks was nearly impossible. And the ground was hard and dry, not conducive to making tracks if someone had been on foot, on horseback or in a vehicle." The sheriff sighed. "I'm sorry I can't tell you more. We're running background checks on Oswald, since he's new in town. Other than that, all we can think is some random poacher might not have been watching where he was shooting and hit your father by accident. It's been known to happen."

Trace nodded. "Thanks for trying." He shook the sheriff's hand. "You'll keep us informed if you hear anything else?"

"You bet," said Sheriff Owens.

Trace led Lily out of the office. "I'd like to talk to the ranch hands sometime soon."

"They had been working on a gate in the barnyard. They didn't do it. I was there all day."

"Yeah, but they might know something about what was going on around the place."

Lily's lips firmed. "They're just a bunch of cowards, more interested in where they could get their next beer."

"Agreed. Any man who'd leave two women unprotected after something like that isn't worthy of working on this ranch," Trace murmured. He opened the back door of the pickup and waited for Lily to climb in. Once she was settled, he stared up at her. "Thank you for being here for Mom," he whispered.

"I heard that," his mother said from the front passenger seat. "She's been a blessing. I couldn't have done it without her."

Lily's cheeks heated. "I did only what a decent person would have done." She nodded at Trace. "I love your mother. I'd do it all again."

Trace's gaze met hers for a moment longer, sending a ripple of a different kind of heat through her body.

Then he shut the door and slid in behind the steering wheel. The moment was gone, but the feeling lingered all the way back to the ranch.

Irish and Matt were waiting in the barnyard when Trace parked the truck.

Lily braced for his anger at seeing Matt again.

Trace didn't say a word. He might not like the result of the will, but he couldn't turn away help when they had so much work to do.

Lily hooked Rosalynn's arm and escorted her into the house. She made her a cup of iced tea and had her sit in the air-conditioned living room. "With Trace, Matt and Irish out there cutting hay, they won't need me. I'll take care of the animals and dinner. You rest. It's been a hard day. You stay here, I'll get some things together for the guys."

Lily hurried to the kitchen, filled an insulated jug full of ice and water, and made six sandwiches out of the leftover ham a neighbor had brought over the night before. After she wrapped the sandwiches and stored them in a sturdy basket, she carried them out to the barn, where the men were unloading the supplies from Trace's pickup.

Lily handed the jug and the basket to Irish. "You'll need this out there."

He smiled and thanked her.

Before Trace and Matt emerged from the barn, she was back at the house, glad to have avoided the awkwardness of being in the presence of the two men together. At one point in the near future, she would own up to the fact she'd lied about being in love with Matt. At the very least, it might ease the tension between the brothers.

Lily returned to the living room to find Rosalynn where she'd left her.

The older woman smiled. "Thank you, Lily. I don't know what I would have done without you the past few days."

She hugged Rosalynn. "I'm glad I was here to help. You've done so much for me."

The older woman shook her head. "Sweetie, you've done more for me and James."

"You two gave me a job and a place to live. That's pretty big." Lily stared down at the woman who'd come to mean so much to her. "I don't know why you and James did what you did."

"James wanted to gift you with security. He felt so badly about how he treated you when you were dating Trace. He didn't know you and judged you unfairly."

Lily shrugged. "He didn't have to do what he did to make up for it. We'd come to a pretty good understanding of each other over the past year. I loved him like the father I wished I'd had growing up."

Rosalynn took her hand. "He felt like you were the daughter he never had. He only wished he'd figured that out sooner." She squeezed Lily's fingers. "Let us do this for you."

Lily frowned. "It's too much. I don't need that kind of money."

"He wasn't sure how things would turn out on the ranch if he passed and the boys inherited." Trace's mother looked toward the window that overlooked the barn and the men gathering around a tractor.

"Do you think they'll work it out?" Lily stared out at the same view, her gaze seeking Trace.

"I don't know," Rosalynn said. "Trace loves being a part of the Delta Force. He'd have to give it up to come home. I'm not sure ranching life would be enough to keep him happy."

"He always loved the animals and the wide-open spaces," Lily offered, knowing Trace's mother was right. The man had been fighting wars. Ranching would mean slowing down. On the selfish side, she'd love if he was back for good, even if he wasn't back for her.

"I only need a few minutes of rest," Rosalynn said. "No need for you to handle everything by yourself. I'll help with dinner and with feeding the animals. I don't want you out there on your own while the men are away in the field."

"I'll be all right. Now that I know there might be someone lurking in the shadows of the barn, I'll be hyperaware and keep my eyes open for danger."

The older woman shook her head. "I can't risk it. You know Trace will insist on the buddy system."

Lily settled in the seat beside Rosalynn's. "Then I'll wait with you until you're ready to go out. We've had an eventful morning and could use the rest." No sooner had she settled on the seat, she popped up. "Let me get us both a fresh glass of iced tea." She gathered Rosalynn's glass, hurried to the kitchen to refill it and poured one for herself. Lily laid the glasses on a tray, added a small plate full of cookies from the cookie jar and returned to the living room.

"Thank you, Lily." Rosalynn took the glass of tea and a cookie and waited for Lily to settle beside her.

"You've been working here for over a year, but you never talked about what happened between you and Trace." Rosalynn took a bite of the cookie and pinned Lily with a curious stare.

Lily took a sip of her tea and swallowed hard before she met Trace's mother's gaze. "It didn't work out."

"Was it because of the big argument he had with his father? You knew about it, didn't you?" Rosalynn sighed. "James wanted the best for his son."

"And I wasn't the best," Lily added.

"It wasn't until you came to work for us that James got to know you. He regretted what he'd said to our son. On more than one occasion, he told me he wished Trace had married you. You would have been good for him."

"Your husband was right. Trace was going into the military. If I'd stayed with him, his association with me and my family could have hindered him getting the security clearance he needed."

"So you let him go without you," Rosalynn said.

Lily bent her head for a moment and then looked up again, her chest tight. "I told him I was in love with someone else. When he asked who, the only person I could think of was the guy with the worst reputation in the community at that time."

"Oh, dear Lord." Rosalynn's eyes widened. "Was that someone else Matt Hennessey?"

Lily nodded.

"Matt Hennessey, the man who stole you from him and

now has stolen half his legacy." Rosalynn smacked her hand to her forehead. "No wonder he was so angry at the law office."

"Trace never forgave me for telling him that I was in love with another man," Lily said. "I can't blame him. I'm sure my announcement came to him out of left field. I had to do something to make sure he left and there wasn't a reason for the people who performed the background checks to come looking for me or my family. He didn't need to have any strikes against him when he entered the military. I'm not certain how closely they would have checked into his friends and acquaintances, but having a girlfriend from my background wouldn't have helped him in the least."

"You're not responsible for your family's actions."

"I know that, but no one else seems to take that into account." Lily shrugged. "Guilt by association. I don't have to tell you. Everyone in the county knows that my father is in jail. My mother has a questionable occupation and has been in and out of jail herself."

"You're a good person, Lily. Anyone who gets close to you knows that," Rosalynn said. "Trace knows that, deep down. He'll figure it out."

Lily shook her head. "It's okay. After eleven years, I've gotten over him. We were young and stupid. Trace has his life now and I have mine."

"But you two were meant for each other," Trace's mother said.

"Don't," Lily said. "We're over each other. That was a long time ago. We have more important things to worry about right now. I'd appreciate if you didn't talk with Trace about our past. We're on different paths now."

"You're living under the same roof," Rosalynn pointed out.

Lily gave her a tight smile. "That's just logistics, not love."

"Oh, but life is too short," Rosalynn said, her eyes filling with tears. "You have to grab for the joy and hold on to it for as long as you can."

"I'll keep that in mind. In the meantime, I'm going to see what we can thaw out for dinner." Lily hurried out of the living room before Rosalynn noticed the tears in her own eyes. There had been a time when she'd been filled with the joy of love and laughter. When she and Trace had been young and head over heels in love.

Eleven years was long enough to forget how good they'd had it, wasn't it?

Chapter Nine

When Trace drove the first tractor out of the shed he noticed a wet black spot in the dirt where the vehicle had been parked.

"Something's leaking," he said as he dropped down from the enclosed cab.

"I'm pretty good with engines," Matt said. "Let me take a look."

Trace stiffened. He'd worked on tractor engines from the time he was tall enough to reach the hood. Granted, the tractor he was looking at was a newer model than what he'd worked on in his youth, and it had been eleven years since he'd tinkered with engines. But he just wasn't ready to let Matt into his world. If he ever would be ready. "I'll check it."

After a few minutes and banging his knuckles a couple times, he realized it would take him a lot longer to figure out the engine and all its components. Because he didn't have time to call in a mechanic, and they really needed to get that hay cut, Trace knew he had to step aside and let Matt take over. It grated on his nerves and he ground his teeth. Short of waiting a day or two for a mechanic, he had to let go of this one thing.

He straightened and turned to Matt, who leaned against the barn, his arms crossed over his chest, his eyebrow cocked.

"I don't have time for this. If you think you can fix it, have at it." He stepped aside.

Matt didn't move from his relaxed position. "Say please."

It took every bit of his limited restraint to keep from punching the bastard in his smug face. "Please," Trace gritted out.

With the hint of a cocky grin, Matt pushed away from the side of the barn. Within minutes, he had parts pulled loose or pushed aside.

Trace hoped the man wasn't making it worse.

"Give me a radio, computer or weapons, and I can disassemble and reassemble in a heartbeat," Irish said. "Vehicle engines? Not so much. I left those to the mechanics in the motor pool."

Matt worked silently, retrieved a small tool kit from the storage compartment on his bike, twisted something, tapped something and reassembled the parts. After returning his tools to his bike, he faced Irish and Trace. "Should be good to go."

Trace climbed aboard the tractor and fired up the engine. One explosive backfire and the engine hummed to life. He pulled forward a few feet, stopped, set the brake and climbed down. Nothing dripped to the earth below.

He didn't want to feel anything toward the half brother who'd stolen his girl and half his legacy. But Trace's sense of fairness overruled his desire to strike out at the man. "Thanks."

"I'll get the other tractor out while you attach whatever implement you need," Matt said.

Trace's inclination was to tell Matt he didn't need the help, but he did, and refusing it would only be petty and childish. Instead, he nodded.

"The sooner we get the hay cut, the sooner it will dry and we can bale." He attached the mower to the three-point hitch of the first tractor.

Matt entered the shed and a few minutes later had the second, smaller tractor out. This one didn't have the air-conditioned cab like the first. He checked the oil, hoses and tires. Trace helped Matt attach another mower to the second tractor. After they filled the tanks, they parked the tractors near the gate to the field that needed to be cut.

Trace returned to Irish, who waited in front of the barn. "Got another tractor?" he asked.

"No. I have a more important job for you while we're mowing." Trace entered the shed one more time. His father kept two four-wheelers inside. He found only one. Had his father gotten rid of the other? As soon as the thought surfaced, Trace shook his head. The man never threw away anything. He'd keep it for spare parts before he let it go. He'd ask Roy about it when the man came back to work. In the meantime, he started the remaining four-wheeler and drove it out of the shed. "Get your rifle," Trace said to Irish. "We need you to cover us while we're mowing."

Irish grinned. "Finally, something I can do until my stitches heal." He hurried back to his vehicle and laid out a case. Inside the case was an AR-15, much like the M4 Carbine rifle they'd used in Afghanistan. He loaded it with a thirty-round magazine of bullets and shoved a couple more magazines into the pockets of a vest. He strapped on a shoulder holster, tucked a Glock into the holster and slipped the vest over it. When he turned, he grinned. "Ready."

"I've never been that ammoed up to ride out on the ranch," Trace said, his gut twisting.

Irish frowned. "Too much?"

Trace raised his hand with a grin. "No way. I'm not complaining. I guess it's a sign of the times."

"I don't know what's been going on around here, but I learned in the deserts of Iraq and the mountains of Afghanistan you can never carry too much ammo." Irish climbed aboard the ATV, revved the engine and followed the two men through the gate, closing it behind them.

The field to be mowed was thirty acres of tall grass the cattle and horses had not been allowed to graze.

Trace and Matt started at the same end of the field, Trace making the first row and Matt holding back long enough to start the second row. They worked closely together that afternoon to make it easier to provide protection for both of them.

Irish rode the four-wheeler around the perimeter of the field and then set up a position where he could keep an eye on both men driving the tractors, while watching the wooded area bordering the southern end of the field.

Mowing was hot and dusty. Trace tied a bandanna over his mouth and nose and forged ahead. Even inside the cab of the larger tractor, he was inundated with fine particles of dirt. The time Trace spent on the tractor gave him plenty of opportunity to ruminate on what the attorney and his mother had said about Matt being his half brother and the stipulations of their combined inheritance. The angry man inside of him made him want to sell the ranch to keep Matt from getting any portion of the Travis lands. Hadn't the man taken enough from him?

First he'd taken Lily, now his family's legacy.

But was it Matt's fault their father felt so guilty that he wanted to make amends for never having spent time with his first son? Hell, James Travis could have decided to leave it all to Matt. Even if he didn't raise him, he was his firstborn.

Dust rose as they cut the hay, making the Texas sunshine hazy and hard to see through. When they'd made it halfway through the mowing, Trace parked his tractor at one end of the field and waited for Matt to catch up.

After turning off his tractor, Matt asked, "Is there a problem?"

"Thought we'd let the engines cool while we get a drink and have lunch."

"I don't need a break, if you want to push through and get it done," Matt said.

"We're making good progress," Trace said. "It won't hurt to break for fifteen minutes and give the tractors time to cool off and us a chance to recharge."

Matt dropped down off his machine and stretched.

Irish rode up on the four-wheeler. "Is it lunchtime?"

Trace frowned. "Takes too much time to go back to the house. I thought we'd just take a break and get back to it."

"We don't have to go back to the house." Irish grinned. "I have lunch in the storage container."

"When did you get that?" Trace asked.

"Lily handed me a basket before we left. I'm not sure what she packed in here." He opened the plastic container and extracted the basket. One at a time, he pulled out neatly wrapped sandwiches.

Trace's heart swelled. Even when she wasn't with them, she was thinking of the men working on the ranch.

Matt bit into one of the sandwiches, chewed and swallowed. "I need to marry that girl. She's a keeper."

Trace's hand froze halfway to his mouth. His blood boiled. He tried but failed to keep his anger under control. "Are you kidding me? You had your chance and blew it."

Matt jerked back as if Trace had hit him. "What the heck are you talking about?"

"You know damn well what I'm talking about." Trace advanced on Matt. "You were supposed to marry Lily, and you dumped her."

"Back off, Travis. You don't know what you're talking about." Matt's eyes narrowed. "You're just mad because *our* father didn't leave you his entire estate."

"I couldn't care less if my father gave you all of this ranch. You still did Lily wrong, and I won't let you break her heart a second time."

"I don't know why you think I broke her heart. I don't love Lily like that."

"Well, she sure as hell was in love with you."

"You're insane," Matt said.

"Uh, Trace," Irish interrupted, "this argument isn't getting the work done."

Trace ignored his friend and stood toe to toe with Matt Hennessey. "You're my father's bastard son bent on stealing from me and my family." Trace punched Matt in the gut.

Matt swung for Trace's face, his knuckles connecting with Trace's jaw.

Trace staggered backward, regained his balance and charged toward Matt.

The crack of gunfire split the air and a puff of dust exploded at Trace's feet. Immediately, Trace, Matt and Irish dropped to the ground.

Irish came up in a prone shooting position and aimed into the woods.

Trace rolled beneath the tractor, pulled his Glock from the holster on his hip and studied the woods.

An engine rumbled somewhere in the trees and underbrush. An ATV took off through the shadows, headed away from where the men lay in the dirt.

Trace leaped to his feet and ran for the four-wheeler, hopped aboard and raced after the departing rider. He lurched across the field and into the woods, dodging trees and underbrush.

For a moment, he thought he'd lost the ATV in front of him. Then a flash in the shadows caught his attention. He yanked the handlebars to the left and hit the accelerator, careening through the woods. In an effort to cut off the guy in front of him, he swerved to the right, then dived into a ditch and back up the other side, veering in front of the other ATV.

The driver jerked his handlebars to the right, on a collision course to slam into Trace.

With little time to react, Trace pulled hard to the right, narrowly missed a tree, dipped down into a ditch and slammed the four-wheeler into a fallen log.

When the ATV stopped so suddenly, Trace flew over the handlebars, flipped in midair and landed hard on his back. With the wind knocked from his lungs, he lay still, unable to move for the next several seconds.

The roar of the ATV engine waned and then roared as the rider circled around and came full tilt at Trace.

Trace was just getting to his knees when the ATV stopped just short of him. The driver leveled a sawed-off shotgun, aiming at Trace's chest.

A shot rang out.

Too late to move, Trace held his breath and braced for the hit and the pain.

When nothing happened, he looked down at his chest, fully expecting to see blood.

Nothing.

He dropped low to the ground, his gaze shifting back to the shooter.

The man on the ATV jerked backward, dropping the sawed-off shotgun across his legs. Clutching his shoulder with one hand, he turned the ATV and drove into the woods, disappearing into the shadows.

"What the—" Trace spun and looked back the way he'd come.

A silhouette of a man stood in the woods, a rifle pressed to his shoulder. When the man lowered it, Trace could see that it was Matt.

The man who'd stolen his girl and half of his inheritance had just saved his life.

LATE THAT AFTERNOON, Lily stood on the back porch, shading her eyes as she peered into the setting sun.

The men had yet to return from the hayfield, which shouldn't have taken them all afternoon to cut. What was keeping them?

"Think one of the tractors broke down?" Rosalynn asked from behind her.

"I don't know," Lily said. Her heart squeezed hard in her chest. She didn't want to say it, but she was afraid for the men. Someone had it out for the people of Whiskey Gulch Ranch. "If they don't come home in the next five minutes, we'll take the truck and go check on them."

Rosalynn stepped up beside Lily and raised her hand to shade her eyes as she stared out across the pasture. "I'm ready whenever you are. I've already lost one member of my family. I don't want to lose another."

"You're not going to." Lily patted Mrs. Travis's arm. "Trace has all that combat training. He knows how to take care of himself and others. He's fine."

"I hope so."

"He is."

A tractor appeared on the horizon, a dark shape growing larger as it moved closer, stirring up dust as it rolled across the land. That was one.

Lily held her breath until the other tractor appeared behind it. "There they are."

"Good," Rosalynn said. "I'll put the dinner rolls in the oven." The older woman turned and entered the house.

Lily remained on the porch until the tractors got closer. Then she hurried out to the gate.

As they neared, she noticed the tractor in the rear of the procession had the four-wheeler following too close to be safe. Only it didn't have a rider.

Lily frowned and shaded her eyes. Someone stood behind the driver of the second tractor, holding onto the back of his seat. The second tractor didn't have the mower behind it. Instead, a heavy-duty strap was attached to the rear of the farm machinery and the front of the mangled four-wheeler.

Matt drove the first tractor through the gate. Trace, with Irish perched behind him, entered with the other.

Her gaze on the second driver, Lily's eyes widened, and her pulse raced.

Trace's face had a gash and a bruise on one cheekbone and his shirt appeared to be torn and dirty. Nothing like what she would have expected for a day seated on a tractor.

As soon as they stopped the tractors, she converged on him. "What happened to you?"

Trace shot a glance toward Matt. "I fell."

Matt rubbed his belly. "The hell he did. He got the bruise on his face when he punched me in the gut. He might not have realized I punch back."

With a shrug, Trace nodded. "He got that right. I did punch him first and fully deserved the punch he returned."

"Damn right he did." Matt stepped down from his tractor.

Lily frowned. "Did he knock you down and roll you around in the dirt as well?"

Matt snorted.

Trace waited for Irish to dismount from behind his seat before he stood and brushed some of the dust from his shirt.

"No," Trace said. "The rest was from when I fell off the ATV."

"You fell off the ATV?" Lily glanced at the four-wheeler they had towed behind the tractor. The front rack was bent, the handlebar was crooked, and there was dirt and leaves jammed in places that shouldn't have dirt and leaves. "What happened?"

Trace climbed down and stretched, wincing. "I hit a fallen log."

Irish stepped around him and unhooked the strap they'd used to haul the four-wheeler back to the barn. "He hit the fallen log after he was nearly run over."

"Run over?" Lily shook her head. "By one of the tractors?"

"No," Matt said. "By the shooter."

Lily's heartbeat stuttered. "Wait. What shooter?" She turned to Trace. "Someone shot at you?"

"Yeah. And I went after him." He glanced toward the house. "It's not a big deal. I wouldn't mention it in front of my mother. The shooter must have been a really bad shot."

"No big deal?" Lily threw her hands in the air. "Are you kidding me?"

His lips quirked. "Are you worried someone shot at me, or that you can't tell my mother?"

"This isn't some kind of joke. Your father was killed by a shooter. You've been shot at. Someone hit me in the barn. The Whiskey Gulch Ranch is under attack and you're afraid to tell your mother?" Her pulse still hammering through her veins, Lily marched toward the house. "I'm calling the sheriff. You can go back out and play Russian roulette with your shooter. I'm going to make sure your mother is taken care of when they drag your body back to the house."

Lily's chest hurt. Trace could have been shot and killed today. Her eyes stung and she wanted to vomit. How could he be so flippant?

A hand caught her arm and spun her around. "I'm sorry. I didn't know you cared so much."

She stared at the hand on her arm, wanting to fling herself into his embrace. She clenched her fists and held on to her control by a thread. He could have been killed. For a long moment, she fought the urge to throw herself into his arms, pound his chest, then kiss him until he loved her, too.

Instead, she drew herself up and lifted her chin. "I'm

calling the sheriff. This cannot continue. Your mother would be devastated if she lost you, too."

He didn't let go of her arm. "And you? Would you be devastated?"

She stared into his eyes, wanting to tell him just how broken her heart would be. "I'd hate to see your mother go through that kind of loss again." Then she shook her arm free of his grip and ran for the house.

She didn't look back but burst through the door into the house and let the screen slam shut behind her.

Rosalynn hurried out of the kitchen, carrying a wooden spoon. "What's wrong?"

"Ask your son," she said and went straight to the phone in the hallway. "I have a phone call to make." She dialed 911. When the dispatcher answered, Lily said, "I'd like to report a shooting."

Rosalynn gasped behind her and ran out the back door.

After she finished her call to the sheriff's office, Lily felt a twinge of guilt. Mrs. Travis didn't need the stress of hearing about a shooting after losing her husband the same way. But, damn it, Trace couldn't die. It would kill his mother.

Lily clasped her hands together and pressed them to her chest. "And it would kill me, too."

Chapter Ten

"Wade Richard Travis, you are not going back out in that hayfield. Not if I have anything to say about it." Rosalynn Travis stood with her hands fisted on her hips, a frown denting her brow.

Trace wanted to shake Lily for telling his mother about the shooting. But Lily was right to report it to the sheriff. At the very least, they could be asking around and on the lookout for anyone who showed up at any of the nearby clinics or hospitals with a gunshot wound.

It still stung that Matt had hit his mark and saved Trace's life. That made him beholden to the man. He couldn't be mad that it had happened. Not when it meant he might be dead now if Matt hadn't followed and fired when he had. Who knew his half brother was such a good shot? Hell, he didn't know a whole lot about the man who was his father's firstborn son. If only he hadn't been the man Lily had fallen in love with. Trace wasn't sure he could ever be cordial to him, knowing he was the one Lily had chosen over him.

And it burned him up that Matt had disavowed loving Lily. How could he make her fall in love with him and then leave her when she thought he would marry her? All these years, Trace had thought Lily had married the love of her life. He'd tried to be content with the thought that she was happy and well taken care of. Even if he wasn't the love of her life, he'd wanted her to be safe. All this time, she'd been alone.

And she hadn't let him know.

Still…she'd responded to his kiss. There was something there.

Was it enough?

Did she care enough about him to want to give them a second chance?

Trace wrapped his mother in his arms and squeezed her until she quit shaking. "Mom, I'm all right." He held her at arm's length and smiled. "See? I'm perfectly fine."

She looked up at him and frowned. "No, you aren't. Did the bullet graze your cheek? Do I need to take you to the hospital?"

Someone snorted somewhere behind him.

Trace glanced over his shoulder to see Matt checking the fuel level on one of the tractors. He didn't care if Matt thought he was a mama's boy. His mother meant a lot to him, and she'd suffered a huge shock with the death of her husband. "I'm okay, Mom. It's just a scratch I got out in the field."

"I punched him, Mrs. Travis," Matt said. "The cut on his cheek has nothing to do with the shooter." He glanced down at his bruised knuckles. "I'm sorry if that distresses you. I'll understand if you don't want me to stay."

Trace's mother's frown deepened as she glanced from Matt to Trace and back. "No. No. I'm sure there was a good reason for you two to argue. I'm sure it has to do with the woman calling the sheriff as we speak."

Trace's eyes narrowed as he stared down at his mother. "What do you know about it?"

She patted his chest. "That you better not get yourself shot." His mother hugged him close and then stepped free of his arms. "I have dinner ready whenever you're done here. Lily and I fed the animals, so all you need to do is wash up and come inside. Now, if you'll excuse me, I have rolls in the oven." She turned and rushed back into the house.

"Your mother has spunk," Irish said. "And something smells good. I could eat a horse."

On cue, a horse whinnied from the barn.

Irish's eyes widened.

"Watch what you say around the livestock," Trace warned. "We only raise the most intelligent horses on Whiskey Gulch Ranch." He said it with a straight face.

Irish chuckled and then frowned. "You're kidding, right?"

Trace raised his eyebrow in response. Then he turned away. "Mom's a good cook. Better hurry if you want to eat." Trace headed for the house and the two women who meant the most to him. Over his shoulder, he said, "That includes you, Hennessey."

The two men followed him into the house and washed their hands in the downstairs bathroom. The table was set with five place settings. In the center lay a platter of crispy fried chicken and another of roasted potatoes.

Lily entered the room and took a seat next to Matt. "The sheriff will be here in ten minutes."

"I'll set a plate for him." Trace's mother jumped up from the table and brought another place setting.

They settled in, passing the platters around the table.

Once they all had food on their plates, his mother said, "Okay, fill me in on what happened."

Trace gave her an abbreviated version of what had happened, leaving out the fight with Matt. He ended with "We finished the mowing. As hot as it's been, the hay should be dry enough to bale tomorrow."

"I don't want you all going out tomorrow. It's too dangerous," his mother said.

"We've got this, Mom," Trace said. "We were a little distracted today, but it won't happen again."

"If you insist on going, we're all going," his mother said.

Trace stiffened. "You need to stay home, where it's safe."

"I'm not staying locked in the house because someone is attacking my family," his mother said. "I know how to use a gun. Besides, we need all the help we can get to bale and store the hay before that storm system gets here sometime over the next couple of days. Roy called and said he'd be back tomorrow to help. He can drive the truck and also provide some backup, even if he can't do much in the way of heavy lifting."

Trace didn't like it, but his mother was still in charge, as far as he was concerned, even if his father had left him and Matt with the ranch. "Okay, but you're staying inside a vehicle."

"Deal," she said with a smirk. "I'll stay inside the cab of the tractor while I'm running the baling machine."

"I'll run the baling machine," Trace said.

His mother snorted. "Not if you want to get those bales loaded and stored. Unless you want me to toss eighty-pound bales up onto the back of the trailer." She raised her eyebrows and waited for his response.

"No. I'll toss bales. You can drive the baler, since you know how to run it."

She wouldn't be inside the house, but being in the enclosed cab of the tractor was better than nothing. Irish would have to be on his toes while the rest of them were busy loading the bales onto the trailer.

They were halfway through the meal when the sheriff showed up to take their statements. He accepted Mrs. Travis's invitation to join them, eating only a little before he got to work.

Trace, Irish and Matt took him out to where they'd been mowing so that he could see the tracks in the dirt, not that it would help much. The ground was dry, the wind had lifted some of the dust and deposited it into the grooves left by the four-wheeler's tires.

By the time they returned, dusk had settled over the land, making it difficult to distinguish anything in the shadows.

The sheriff promised to ask around for anyone who showed up at the clinics or hospitals nearby with a gunshot wound. He'd also check with the neighbors to see if any of them showed signs of wounds. Other than that, they had no other leads.

Once the sheriff left, Trace entered the house. He didn't want to admit to himself he was looking for Lily…but he was.

He didn't find her in the living room or the kitchen, so he climbed the stairs and hovered outside her door. With no real need to talk to her, he reasoned he could fill her in on their visit with the sheriff. With that excuse in mind, he knocked on her door.

No answer. He knocked again.

"She's out in the barn, checking on the animals," his mother said from behind him.

He forced a casual shrug. "I thought I'd fill her in on what the sheriff had to say."

His mother's lips quirked in an almost smile. "You can fill me in."

He told her the information in a few short sentences.

His mother frowned. "Is that all he can do?"

"We don't know who was after us, only that he rode an ATV and wore a helmet," Trace concluded.

His mother nodded. "Thank you. Now, go find Lily. I don't like the idea of her out in the barn alone." The older woman held up her hand. "I told her not to go out without a buddy."

"And she listened?" Trace shook his head. "She never listened to me, either."

"What happened between you and Lily?" his mother asked, her tone soft and whispered.

"I don't know. Ask her," he said and moved past his mother. If he knew, he might have fixed it way back when whatever it was happened in the first place. Now it was too late.

Or was it?

LILY WAS ON her way out to the barn when a voice called out. "Lily?"

Lily turned to find Matt leaning against his motorcycle, his gaze on her. She altered her direction, aiming directly for him, anger spiking. "What the heck did you say to Trace to make him mad enough to hit you?"

"I only told him the truth," Matt said. "I told him that I never loved you like that. And for that I got slugged in the face." He rubbed at the bruise on his cheek. His eyes narrowed. "Trace was under the impression that you and I were getting married. Where did he get an idea like that?"

The anger drained out of her and Lily's shoulders sagged. "It's a long story."

"I have a few minutes. I'd like to hear it." Matt crossed his arms over his chest.

Lily glanced out at the horses grazing peacefully in the pasture and wished she could be as calm as they were. "I couldn't ruin his military career before it even began." She glanced back at Matt. "I was afraid that if he was associated with me, he wouldn't have passed the background check."

Matt frowned. "So what did that have to do with me?"

Lily looked again at the horses. "I had to do something that would make him leave me and not look back. Something that would break our connection so finally, no one would think we were ever together or had a chance of getting back together."

"So you used me," Matt stated.

Lily's chin dipped. "Yes. And I'm sorry. I told him that I was dumping him because I'd fallen in love with you."

A smile quirked the corners of his lips. "And that's such a bad thing?"

She glanced up into his face. "Of course not. But to anyone else in town, it might have appeared to be. Not that this is news to you, but you were the biggest badass in Whiskey Gulch. Everyone would expect someone like me to be with someone like you. Not Trace."

Again, Matt rubbed his cheek. "So, you told him you were busting up with him to marry me." He shook his head. "No wonder he was mad. You must have meant a lot to him if he's still mad after all these years. And that would explain why you came over to my house out of the blue to watch television and why you took a photo of the two of us sitting on my couch."

Lily grimaced. "Yeah, about that…"

Matt held up a hand. "Don't worry about it."

"I'm sorry I used you," Lily said.

"What I don't understand is why you haven't set the record straight."

Lily stared down at her feet. "I guess in the back of my mind, I'd hoped he would come back and fight for me. When he didn't, I listened to his mother's accounts of how well he was doing in the army, going from a soldier to Delta Force in such a short amount of time. He was a hero. He was much better off without me. I couldn't regret my decision to let go."

"You underestimate yourself," Matt said. "You aren't your parents."

She gave him a weak smile. "No. But…"

Matt nodded. "I get it. Reputations are hard to overcome, whether they are earned or inherited."

Lily frowned up at Matt. "You won't tell him any of this, will you?"

"Of course not," Matt said. "But you should. Seriously. Tell him."

Lily shook her head. "It's too late for us. Eleven years is a long time. Enough time to get over someone."

Matt tipped her chin up. "Are you over him?"

Lily's bottom lip trembled, and a single tear rolled down her cheek. She wanted to kick herself for letting her emotions show. Especially to this man.

Matt snorted softly and brushed the tear away with his thumb. "I guess that answers my question."

Lily's eyes widened. "Please, don't tell him."

"Hey." Matt stared down into her eyes. "Your secret is safe with me. My lips are sealed."

Lily flung her arms around his neck and hugged him tightly. "Thank you. Thank you, Matt."

"Don't mention it," Matt said. "Promise me that the next time you embroil me in one of your lies, at least clue me in. I don't mind getting punched in the face as long as I know the reason why."

Lily reached up and brushed her finger across the bruise. "I'm really sorry about that. I promise I won't do that again."

Matt looked over her shoulder and grimaced. "Well, we might have inadvertently done it again."

Lily's heart skipped several beats as she turned to find Trace standing behind her as she stood in Matt's arms.

With a sly grin, Matt leaned down and pressed a kiss to Lily's forehead. "This one's for me." Then he left her standing there and walked by Trace, bumping his shoulder accidentally on purpose as he passed.

Trace's face could have been set in stone as hard as his jaw was set. Lily recognized the tic in his cheek indicating just how angry he was. She'd seen it only when he was beyond angry with his father. Now he was mad at her.

Heat filled her cheeks. She refused to give in to her

desire to excuse what he'd just witnessed. He didn't own her and had no right to tell her who she could or could not hug—or kiss, for that matter. Squaring her shoulders, she spun and walked toward the barn without uttering a comment. Maybe he would be mad enough to leave her alone.

That wasn't to be. Footsteps behind her made her very aware that he was following her. The roar of a motorcycle engine reminded her of what Trace had just witnessed between her and Matt.

Good. Let him stew on that image.

"What kind of boyfriend leaves his girlfriend to walk into a barn alone?" Trace said. "Especially into a barn where she'd been attacked before. Recently."

Lily didn't bother to turn around. "He's not my boyfriend."

"At one point, you thought he was. You thought he was close enough that he was going to marry you."

She entered the barn, turning only her head to say over her shoulder, "Apparently, I was wrong."

"So wrong that he never considered marrying you. Or even considered you as his girlfriend."

"Yeah, well," she said, "my bad."

Trace grabbed her arm and spun her around to face him. "Look, I don't like being lied to and I don't like being made to look like a fool."

Anger stung her chest. "If that's all it was to you, my apologies for making you look bad." She yanked her arm free and turned away from him, crossing the barn as quickly as she could, putting distance between them.

"Lily Davidson, we're not done talking," Trace boomed.

"Yes, we are," she said. "We were done talking eleven years ago." She swallowed hard on the lump in her throat, refusing to look at him, afraid that if she did, her love and disappointment would be all too evident in her eyes. She marched toward the steps leading up into the loft.

"What if someone's up there waiting to hit you again?" Trace asked.

"Then I guess I'll get hit." She didn't slow, too angry and sad to slow. Maybe being hit in the head wouldn't hurt as bad as the pain in her heart. Lily didn't care if someone was up there. That someone could put her out of her misery once and for all.

No one was there, but the shadows were deep and dark. She reached for her cell phone, but she'd left it on the counter in the kitchen. Without her cell phone, she didn't have a handy flashlight to find her way around in the dark loft. Too stubborn to go back down and admit to Trace she'd forgotten something as essential as a flashlight, Lily inched her way toward the back of the loft, searching for the stack of hay where Patches had hidden her kittens.

Was that sound someone moving in the darkness? Her gut tightened. She should have brought a flashlight. A heavy one she could use as a weapon.

A click sounded behind her.

Lily jumped and stifled a scream.

Chapter Eleven

"It helps to have a flashlight when you come up into a dark loft," Trace's voice said behind her, and the beam of a flashlight cut through the darkness.

Lily pressed a hand to her chest to calm her wildly beating heart. "I don't need your help," she muttered.

"Maybe not, but you need the light."

Lily didn't want to agree with him, so she didn't say anything at all. She did need the light if she wanted to snag the mama cat and get the kittens moved before they stacked more hay in the barn the next day. She continued on her quest to find the cat and her kittens.

When she reached the stack of hay, Lily pulled from her back pocket an old pillowcase she'd found in a cupboard in the house.

"Is that for the kittens?" Trace asked.

She shook her head. "No. The kittens won't be a problem. Patches was a feral cat that made her home in the barn. Catching her will be the challenge. Holding her will be even more of a task." She held up the pillowcase. "The pillowcase is for her."

"I'll get the cat," Trace said.

"No," Lily said, shaking her head. "She's more used to me than you."

Trace took the pillowcase from Lily. "Do you have to argue about everything?" His lips twitched. "I've got this." He shoved the flashlight at her. "Blind her with the light. Ready?"

No. Lily wasn't ready. She wasn't even sure how this would play out. Before she could utter a protest, he leaned over the top of the haystack. "Shine the light," he commanded.

Lily leaned over the hay and shone the light down into Patches's eyes.

The cat stared up at her, blinking in the sudden glare.

Trace didn't hesitate. He shoved his hand down into the gap, snagged the cat by the back of her neck and pulled her out of her cubby.

Patches screamed, yowled and fought to be free, twisting and cavorting, sinking her claws into Trace's arm and wrist.

He shook out the pillowcase and placed her down into it.

Lily grabbed the top of the case and closed it tightly.

Inside the case, Patches howled, scratched and hissed.

Blood dripped from several wounds on Trace's arm.

"You're hurt," Lily said.

"Doesn't matter," Trace said, his voice clipped. "I've got the cat. You get the kittens. We need to turn this one loose before she hurts herself or her milk dries up from stress."

With the flashlight in hand, Lily eased into the nesting area and gathered kittens one at a time until she had all five tucked into the pockets of her jersey jacket.

All the while they mewed for their mama and she called back.

Trace was halfway down the steps to the loft when Lily slipped over the haystack and started his way. She snagged a section of hay from a broken bale and hurried toward the stairs.

"Tack room?" Trace called out.

"Yes," she said and hurriedly descended to the ground. Lily passed Trace and opened the tack room door, holding it until Trace came through carrying his wriggling sack of angry cat. Once he was in, she shoved the door closed with her foot.

"I'll hold her until you get the kittens situated," he said.

Lily found a corner of the tack room behind the file cabinet that wasn't visible from the door and would be out of the way, where no one would accidentally step on the kittens. She spread the section of hay on the ground, added a saddle blanket and then eased the kittens out of her pockets, laying them one by one on the warm, soft blanket. Their eyes still closed, they scooted around on the blanket, desperately seeking their mama.

Lily straightened and dusted the hay from her jeans. "You can let Patches go."

Holding the pillowcase at arm's length, he chuckled. "Uh, yeah. We'll see how that goes." He gently laid the bag on the floor and let go of the top.

For a moment the bag lay completely still.

Then Patches shot out of the opening like a bullet out of a gun. She raced frenetically around the room, testing every corner for a path to escape. Finally, she hid beneath the back corner of the desk.

"I'm going to duck out for a bowl of water and cat food," Lily said, wishing she'd done it before they'd let Patches loose. "Think you can keep her from getting through the door while it's open?"

Trace raised his eyebrows and snorted. "I'll do the best I can. No guarantees. She's mad and scared." He grabbed the pillowcase from the floor, positioned himself in front of the door and held it up like a red cape in front of a bull. "Go," he said.

Lily darted through the door, quickly closing it behind her. She found the water and food dish where she usually fed the cat, filled them and returned to the tack room. Knocking lightly, she waited for Trace's response.

"Make a run for it," he said through the thick paneling.

Stacking the water bowl on top of the food bowl, she freed one hand to open the door. Lily entered, careful not to slosh water into the food. Once inside, she closed the door with her foot and set the bowls on the ground. "Has she come out yet?"

"No." Trace wadded the pillowcase. "She won't until she's calmed down. Hopefully, it won't take long. The kittens are hungry and telling her about it."

Lily checked on the kittens. They were mewing softly, nudging at the blanket in search of their mother. "The sooner we leave her alone, the better off she is."

Trace nodded and headed for the door. With his hand on the knob, he waited for Lily to join him. "On three," he said. "One…two…" He jerked open the door, shoved her through and closed it quickly as a flash of fur raced toward them.

Lily gasped and ducked out of the way while Trace slammed shut the door.

Collapsing against the door, Lily laughed. "All that for a cat." She laughed until she held on to her sides.

Trace chuckled. The chuckle turned into a laugh and soon he was holding on to his sides.

When they finally slowed, Lily noticed the streaks of blood on his arm. "We need to take care of those scratches. We can't have you getting cat scratch fever."

"I'll be all right. They aren't bad. Just flesh—"

"Wounds," she finished for him. "How many times did you say that when you were on a mission?" Her smile faded and she stood in front of him, her heart hurting. So many times, she wondered where he was on the other side of the world. She'd wondered if he was all right, if someone was shooting at him, if he would live to come back to Whiskey Gulch. Her vision blurred with the tears she'd refused to shed. "Let's get you inside. There's antiseptic ointment in the downstairs medicine cabinet."

He allowed her to lead the way to the house and into the bathroom, where his mother kept a first-aid kit.

Slowly, painstakingly, Lily cleaned and dressed his wounds, smearing soothing ointment over the injury, then covering the larger ones with adhesive bandages.

When she was finished, she couldn't bring herself to look him in the eye. If she did, he'd know just how much touching him had affected her.

Matt's words came back to her.

Tell him.

That she loved him? That she'd lied to get him to leave Whiskey Gulch Ranch and join the military?

No. She couldn't. If he'd loved her as much as he'd said he'd loved her, he would have cared enough to fight for her.

Lily left the bathroom and hurried up the stairs to her room. Lost in her thoughts, she didn't hear footsteps behind her. She'd almost made it to her room, when Trace stopped her.

"Why?" he asked. The one word echoed within her soul.

"This isn't going to work," she whispered.

Trace's brow furrowed. "What isn't going to work?"

"As soon as we get the hay put up, I'm out of here," Lily said.

He tipped her chin up. "Is that really what you want to do?"

As he raised her chin, she lowered her eyelids. "Yes."

"Look at me, Lily," he said.

The warmth of his breath brushed against her cheek. She looked up at him. "What do you want from me?"

His lips turned up at the corners. "A kiss."

She shook her head. "No. I'm not going to ask you to kiss me," Lily stated, lifting her chin slightly.

"Are you sure?" He lowered his head until his lips hovered over hers, only a breath away.

"I'm sure—" Her voice caught in her throat as their breaths mingled.

Kissing Trace would be a huge mistake. But she wanted it more than she wanted to breathe.

"Do you want me to kiss you?" he asked.

Though she shook her head no, her mouth said, "Yes."

"Tell me, Lily," he urged. "Tell me you want me to kiss you."

"I don't—" Finally, her gaze met his and she recognized the desire in his eyes that matched the fire burning deep in her core. "Oh, hell," she muttered. "Who am I kidding?" She rose up on her toes and brushed her lips across his.

Trace leaned back, shaking his head. "Uh-uh," he said. "Not until you say the words."

Anger heated by desire made her words harsh. "All right, damn it. I want you to kiss me."

Trace gathered her close and lowered his head slowly, taking her lips in the most gentle and tender kiss she'd ever experienced.

Anger, need and desire bubbled up inside Lily. She didn't want the kiss to be tender. She wanted it hard, fast and deep, reminding her she was alive, and he was with her. After all these years, their bodies still remembered each other. She melted against him.

He pushed her up against the wall.

Lily wrapped her arms around him and pulled him impossibly closer. A kiss was not enough. She wanted him inside her. Wrapping her calf around his, she rubbed her center against his thigh and whispered against his lips, "I want more."

"Are you certain?"

"Yes," she breathed.

His lips left hers as he bent and scooped her up in his arms. Trace fumbled with the door handle.

Lily brushed his hand aside, twisted the knob and pushed open the door.

Trace carried her across the threshold and kicked the door closed behind them. He crossed the room in three easy strides and lowered her legs to the ground slowly. Then he gathered her close, kissing her hard and deep.

Lily had wanted this for so long. Her pulse hammered against her eardrums as she reached for the buttons on his shirt. She fumbled with one, two, three buttons.

Impatient, Trace yanked the hem from his waistband and pulled open his shirt, popping the remaining buttons free.

Lily laughed, dragging her blouse over her head and tossing it to the corner.

They worked in a frenzy, shedding clothing. He helped her, she helped him. They helped each other until they both stood naked at the foot of the bed.

"Sweet Lily, you're even more beautiful now than I remember," he said, his voice low, resonant and warm on her naked skin.

She smoothed a hand over his broad shoulders. "You got taller…and bigger." Her gaze slipped over his broad chest and down to his narrow waist and lower still to where the evidence of his desire jutted out prominently.

He cupped her cheek and stared down into her eyes. "Are you sure this is what you want? All you have to do is say no, and I'll walk away."

Lily's belly tightened. "No way. I want this." She'd been waiting so long for this moment. Trace had been her first. And he didn't know it, but he'd been her only.

Still, she wasn't a fool. "What about protection?"

He dived for the jeans he'd left crumpled on the floor, pulled his wallet out of his back pocket and unearthed a foil packet. He held it up with a grin.

Lily raised an eyebrow. "Just one?"

"There's more in my room," he said.

She nodded. "Good to know." Lily slid a hand along his cheek and to the back of his neck. She pulled him down to kiss her.

As they kissed, he backed her up until her legs touched the mattress. Then he eased her down until she lay across the bed, her legs dangling over the side. Using his knees, he parted her thighs, stepping between. When he leaned over her, she wrapped her arms around him and pulled him close for a kiss.

His tongue thrust past her teeth to hers, caressing it in a long, sensuous glide. Then he left her lips and trailed his lips across her cheek and down the long column of her neck to where her pulse beat frantically at the base.

Lily trailed her fingers across his shoulders, loving the feel of his hard muscles encased in smooth skin.

Trace's mouth seared a path over her collarbone and down to her right breast. With his tongue he flicked her nipple and then rolled it between his teeth.

Lily arched her back off the mattress, urging him to take more. Take it all.

He sucked that breast into his mouth as deeply as he could, pulling hard.

Gasping, Lily's breath caught in her lungs and her core tightened.

He played that breast until she thought she would come apart in a million pieces. Then he moved to the other and performed the same teasing, flicking nips.

Lily thrashed against the mattress, her desire growing at an exponential rate. She wanted all of him. "Please," she cried.

He chuckled. "Please what?"

"Foreplay…is…overrated."

His chest pressed against her torso. When he chuckled again, the rumble vibrated through her. Abandoning her left breast, he trailed his tongue and lips across her ribs and down her flat abdomen, dipping his tongue into her belly button. As he neared the juncture of her thighs, he slowed, then paused.

Lily held her breath, willing him to take her there. Take her with his fingers, with his tongue, with his staff.

Trace cupped her sex and dipped a finger into her wet channel.

Oh, sweet heaven...take me, she thought.

As if he'd heard her, his fingers parted her folds and he blew a warm stream of air over that heated strip of flesh.

Lily bunched the comforter in her fists.

His finger slid up inside her.

Lily moaned.

"Oh, baby, I've only just begun," Trace said, his breath warm against the inside of her thighs. He touched her there.

An explosion of sensations roiled over her. Her hands flew from the comforter to his hair, weaving through the strands to pull him closer. "Trace!" Lily cried.

"Does that mean you like it?" he asked. "Or do you want me to stop?"

"Don't," she gasped. "Don't stop."

He touched his tongue to her again.

Lily arched off the mattress. "It's good. Oh, so good."

Trace flicked and laved her there until she writhed beneath him, beyond her senses. She couldn't think, couldn't see, couldn't breathe. A ripple of electricity started at her core and spread like wildfire along her nerves, working its way outward to her very fingertips. Wave upon wave of sensations washed over her. She rode the wave all the way to the end. As she drifted back to earth, she collapsed against the mattress, dragging in deep gulps of air. Even after she got her breathing under control, that ache deep down continued. She threaded her hands in his hair and pulled. "I want you. Now."

Trace moved up her body, climbing up between her legs to claim her lips with his. He tasted of her.

Lily moaned against his mouth as Trace touched her entrance with the tip of his shaft.

She gripped his buttocks in an attempt to bring him home.

"Not yet." He leaned up on one arm, grabbed the foil packet, tore it with his teeth.

Lily took it from him, pulled out the protection and rolled it over his engorged staff.

Then Trace kissed her and pressed into her damp channel.

Impatient, Lily grabbed his hips and pulled him all the way into her.

Trace inhaled deeply and let out the air slowly as he gave her time to adjust to his girth. "Lily, you feel so good."

"Mmm," she murmured.

Trace settled into a steady rhythm, pumping in and out of her.

With her hands gripping his hips, she encouraged him to go faster, pump harder.

He moved through her slick center with ease, his thick member stretching her deliciously. His pace increased until finally he slammed into her and he held steady, his shaft pulsing with his release.

Lily's fingers dug into his backside, holding him close.

When at last he relaxed, he fell down on top of her, rolled them both onto their sides and held her there.

Lily pressed her cheek against his chest. Tears slipped from her eyes. She swallowed hard to keep from sobbing aloud. This was what she'd been waiting for. He was who she'd waited for. But making love didn't solve anything. It only complicated matters.

Chapter Twelve

Trace felt the dampness of her tears against his skin. His heart squeezed hard inside his ribs. "Lily."

She shook her head and raised a hand, touching a finger to his lips. "Don't." The one word came out thick with emotion.

"But, Lily, we have to talk," he insisted.

"Not tonight," she said.

"Then tomorrow."

She didn't answer. Lily lay in his arms, her body pressed against his.

He didn't want the night to end. He was afraid that when it did, she would slip from his arms forever. Trace couldn't let that happen. Not again.

Lily draped a leg over his and an arm across his chest. Soon her body relaxed against his, and her breathing deepened. She'd fallen asleep.

Trace lay for a long time, staring up at the ceiling, wanting to wake her and force her to talk to him. He wanted her to tell him why she'd said she was going to marry Matt, when in fact she'd had no intention of doing so. Had she been afraid of leaving her home? Had she not wanted to be a military wife? Had she been afraid of marrying a man who put himself in harm's way?

She lay so peacefully that Trace couldn't bring himself to wake her.

Eventually, he fell into a troubled sleep. He woke in the cool, gray light of predawn and stared around at the walls, trying to get his bearings. He wasn't in his room.

The previous night came back to him in a flood of memories. He rolled over in the full-size bed, already knowing but needing to verify that Lily was already gone.

He threw back the sheets and swung his legs out of the bed.

Damn. How had she left the room without waking him? He was in her room, for Pete's sake. How had she dressed and then opened and closed the door without him hearing a thing?

He gathered his clothes, dressed quickly and pulled on his boots. When he stepped outside the door of her bedroom, he paused and listened. Sounds of people moving about came from downstairs. His mother would already be up, cooking breakfast for everyone. Had Lily gone down to help her?

Trace ducked into his room and changed his shirt for one with long sleeves. Hauling hay was a dirty, itchy task if one didn't cover as much bare skin as possible. The more he covered, the less he'd be poked and stabbed by the strands of hay. He crossed the hallway to the bathroom, splashed water on his face, combed his hair and brushed his teeth. When he was finished, he hurried downstairs to the kitchen.

Irish stood at the counter, buttering toast. Matt was at the coffee maker, pouring fresh brew. Roy hobbled through the back door on his damaged foot and called out, "Good morning."

Trace's mother manned the stove, scrambling eggs.

There was no sign of Lily.

"Good morning, sleepyhead," his mother sang. "Grab a cup of coffee. Breakfast is about ready. If you're looking for Lily, she just stepped out to go to the barn to check on the cat."

"I offered to go with her," Irish said. "But she insisted she would only be a minute."

"She was stepping into the barn when I drove up," Roy said.

His gut clenched. Did she not understand the danger of going out by herself? "I'll go check on her." Trace exited through the back door. He'd made it to the top of the porch steps when he saw her striding toward him from the barn.

She didn't appear to be harmed in any way.

Trace breathed a sigh of relief.

She met his gaze only briefly. "Patches was confined to the tack room all night and will be there all day until we get the hay put up. I fashioned a litter box out of an old, shallow box and filled it with dirt and gravel so that she can relieve herself. Otherwise, there was no telling what she'd do to that tack room."

"Good thinking," Trace said.

When she went to pass him, he snagged her arm. "Lily."

She paused but still didn't look up at him.

"Oh, there you two are," his mother called out from the porch. She turned and reentered the house.

Trace looked down at Lily. "We will talk."

She nodded.

Trace released her arm and Lily ran up into the house.

For a long moment, Trace stared up at the house. What had changed from last night to this morning? Or had nothing changed, and he hadn't recognized a problem remained between the two of them?

Who was he kidding? Sex didn't solve anything. It just made the situation more complicated. By the time Trace entered the house and kitchen, everyone else was seated and talking about the day ahead.

Already they were making assignments of who would do what.

Lily would drive the tractor with the rake, piling the

dried straw into neat rows. His mother would follow on the baler. Roy would drive the truck that would pull the trailer. Trace and Matt would load the rectangular bales onto the trailer while Irish rode around the hayfield protecting them from potential attacks.

"We'll have to move quickly," Roy said.

Lily nodded. "The storm headed our way has picked up some speed and will get here sooner than previously anticipated. It's expected to hit late this afternoon." She picked up her plate of half-eaten food and carried it to the sink. "I'll be out at the barn when you are ready."

"I'm done," Irish said. "I'll go with you."

Lily waited by the back door for Irish to stow his plate and glass in the sink and grab his hat.

They were gone by the time Trace finished his breakfast and cleared his place setting from the table. When he reached the barn, he found Irish and Lily loading fuel into the tractors from the large tank positioned several yards from the outbuildings.

When Lily finished pumping fuel into the large tractor, she climbed aboard and moved it to where implements were lined up against a fence.

Trace followed.

Lily backed the tractor up to the baler, and Trace attached the baler to the three-point hitch. When all the mechanics were working correctly, Lily drove the tractor to the gate and parked. On the other tractor, Roy drove to where Trace stood among the implements. He backed the tractor up to the acreage rake, and Trace attached the tool to the second tractor. Roy parked the tractor behind the baler.

Trace's mother came out of the house dressed in jeans, with her hair pulled back in a braid, a hat shading her face, and carrying a large basket. She looked years younger. Trace could imagine the pretty girl his father met and fell for decades ago, and his heart hurt for the love lost. Rosalynn deposited the basket on the back seat of the pickup and climbed aboard the baling tractor.

Irish and Matt stood by the damaged ATV from the day before.

Matt shook his head. "I don't think this thing is going anywhere. Even if we could get it started, the frame's bent. It'll take a lot of work to get it straight again."

Irish's brow crinkled. "Well, what am I supposed to use to provide protection? Needs to be something that's not fully enclosed. A truck won't do."

Trace's lips twitched. "I don't suppose you ride horses, do you?"

Irish grimaced. "I have ridden, but it's been a long time."

"It's like riding a bicycle. Once you learn how, you never forget." Trace grinned.

Irish frowned. "Tell that to the horses. They seem to have a sixth sense about their riders' experience."

Lily came out of the barn leading a mare, saddled, bridled and ready to go. She approached Irish and patted the horse's neck. "This is Lady, one of our gentlest horses. She won't give you a bit of trouble."

Irish eyed the animal with suspicion and then glanced around at the others. His gaze landed on Roy. "I don't suppose—"

Roy raised his hands. "Don't ask me. I've got a bum foot. Can't keep it in the stirrup."

Irish shrugged and took the reins and handed his rifle to Trace. "Guess it's you and me, Lady." He placed his foot in the stirrup and swung his leg over the animal, landing hard in the saddle. Once he was settled, Trace handed him the rifle. Irish rested it across his thighs and gathered the reins in his hands.

Lady stood patiently without dancing around, like some horses had a habit of doing.

While Trace opened the gate, Lily climbed onto the tractor with the rake. Matt hopped into the bed of the pickup.

Trace's mother drove through first, followed by Lily, then Roy in the truck and Trace on foot. Once through the gate, Trace closed it and climbed up into the passenger seat of the pickup.

When they reached the mown field, Lily led the way, raking the hay into neat rows. Trace's mother followed behind the rake with the baler, making neat, rectangular bales and dropping them in the row.

Roy dragged the trailer behind the baler.

Matt and Trace tossed the bales onto the trailer, forming rows and then stacks as they went.

The day warmed into a sweltering heat. Sweat dripped off the men as they stacked bales.

Irish rode the perimeter of the field, rifle in hand, keeping a close eye on the shadows in the tree line. Knowing him, he wouldn't let the surprise attack of the day before happen again.

At noon, Rosalynn stopped her tractor and waved to Lily, indicating she should stop as well. The group gathered in the shade of the trees with the basket Trace's mother had stowed in the back seat of the pickup. It was full to the brim with fried chicken, sandwiches and potato chips.

Irish remained on guard until Trace finished his food.

When Trace was finished, he relieved Irish of his rifle and stood guard while Irish rested and ate.

Clouds built in the distance, an ominous dark wall moving their direction.

His mother moved to stand beside him, a frown puckering her smooth brow. "We need to get moving if we want to finish this field before that rain hits."

Trace nodded and turned to the others. "Saddle up. We have more work to do before we can call it a day."

"I'll be done raking soon," Lily said. "Then I can help stack bales."

Trace nodded. "We can use all the help we can get to load all those bales."

As soon as Lily finished raking the hay, she drove the tractor up to Trace. "I'm taking the tractor back to the barn."

"I'll go with you," Trace said. He called out to Matt, "I'm going with Lily to the barn. You got this for a few?"

Matt tossed a bale onto the trailer. "Got it."

"I can get to the barn and back by myself," Lily argued.

"I'd rather not risk it," Trace said and crawled up on the back of the tractor, hanging on to the back of her seat.

"Seriously, I'll be fine on my own," she muttered.

"The more you argue, the longer it will take." He waved a hand toward the barn. "Drive."

She shot a glance over her shoulder, her lips twisting. "Bossy much?"

He chuckled. "Only when I need to be." He winked.

"Better hold on, then." Lily's lips twitched into a brief smile before she popped the clutch and the tractor lurched forward.

Thankfully, Trace was holding on tightly, or he'd have been thrown off. "Hey, don't forget I'm back here."

She snorted. "Believe me, I didn't."

He liked when she was sassy. It reminded him of when they'd been teens and racing horses across the fields. Trace wished it could be like this all the time. He suspected they had some rough patches yet to overcome. He hoped they overcame them without ending their relationship. If he had his way, they'd skip over the trials and get right back to making love and teasing each other.

Yeah, and pigs could fly.

LILY HAD GOTTEN up early that morning and slipped out of the bed she'd shared with Trace. No matter how much she wanted to be with him, she realized physical attraction was not enough. She loved Trace more than she needed to breathe. But the fact was, he hadn't come back to fight for her.

After all the years of pining for him, Lily wanted more. She wanted a man who would move heaven and earth to be with her. A man who wasn't afraid to tell her how he felt and who wanted what she wanted, a lasting relationship that would weather any storm.

She stopped at the gate and waited until Trace dismounted from the tractor and opened it. Then she drove through, backed the hay rake into position next to the other tractor implements and waited while Trace unhooked the three-point hitch. Once he had it loose, she parked the tractor in the shed, where Trace's father had stored it.

Trace reached up, fitting his hands around her waist, and lifted her from the tractor seat, letting her slide down his torso until her feet brushed the ground. His hands remained around her waist.

Lily didn't want him to let go. She inhaled the scent of the outdoors, dried sweat and male. She'd missed him so much. Her body swayed toward him, ready to pick up where they'd left off the night before. For a moment she really considered it.

A rumble of distant thunder brought her back to reality. She straightened and stepped out of his grasp. "We'd better get back to the others." Did her voice sound disappointed? She hoped not, even if she felt it.

"Walking back?" he asked.

She shook her head. "You can walk. I'll ride." She entered the barn and strode to the first stall on the right. Dusty, the buckskin gelding, pawed at the stall door and whinnied when she drew near. "Hey, boy. Wanna stretch your legs?" She clipped a lead onto his halter and opened the stall door. The horse pushed through, nudging her shoulder to hurry. "All in due time," she assured him as she tied him to a hook on the wall.

Trace tossed a saddle blanket and her saddle over the animal's back.

"How did you know which one I use?" she asked.

"I remembered," he said, tightening the girth around Dusty's belly. "Things haven't changed much around here."

Other than his father's passing, Trace was right. The saddles they'd used as teens were still functional. What had changed was the people. Lily had grown up and Trace had moved on with his life in the army.

Lily left Trace to complete tightening the girth and eased into the tack room for a bridle.

Patches ducked her head around the corner of the filing cabinet. When she spotted Lily, she walked out, leaving her kittens mewing in protest. The cat weaved her body around Lily's legs and paused long enough for Lily to scratch her beneath the chin.

"How are your babies?" Lily asked.

Patches meowed and walked toward the door.

"I know you want out, but you'll have to wait a little longer." Lily checked the water and food dishes. They were still full and the litter box she'd fashioned out of a cardboard box was still unused. "Sorry, girl. We'll let you out as soon as we have the hay put up."

Grabbing a bridle from a nail on the wall, she squeezed through the door, shutting the cat inside.

"How's Patches and the kittens?" Trace took the bridle from Lily's hands.

"Patches is impatient, but the kittens are fine."

Trace slipped the bit between Dusty's teeth, looping the leather straps over his ears. Unhooking the lead from the animal's halter, he led the horse out of the barn and handed the reins to Lily. Then he bent and cupped his hands.

She could have gone straight for the stirrup. It was a

stretch, but she'd done it many times before. Instead, Lily put her foot in his hands like she had all those years ago and swung her leg over the saddle.

Before she could slip her foot into the stirrup, Trace grabbed the saddle horn, stuck his boot into the stirrup and swung up behind her, landing lightly on the horse's rump, just behind the saddle's seat.

"You could have saddled your own horse," she said.

"Why?" he said, wrapping his arms around her waist. "This is much cozier."

Lily frowned and looked over her shoulder at him. "Back when we were young, you always made me ride in the back."

"I liked it when you wrapped your arms around me," he said. "But I find I like wrapping my arms around you even better."

Another rumble of thunder reminded them of the impending storm.

Trace stared into the distance at the dark clouds building on the horizon. "Much as I enjoy being alone with you, we'd better get back to the others. I'm thinking we have less than an hour before that storm hits."

Lily nudged the horse's flanks and reined him toward the open gate. Once they were through, Trace leaned down and pushed the gate closed.

Free of the barn and out in the open, Dusty took off, galloping across the field, his legs stretching out, eating the distance between the barn and the people working the hay.

Trace held on tightly around Lily's waist.

She loved the strength in his arms and the solid wall of muscles he pressed against her back. If only they didn't have to haul the hay, she'd keep riding, without a care for the future and what might happen next.

All too soon, they reached the others.

Rosalynn was just finishing baling the last row of loose

straw. She parked the tractor at the end of the field and climbed down, walking toward the truck.

Lily aimed Dusty toward the tree line for a place to tie him up where he could be in the shade and still graze while they loaded hay.

After a brief squeeze, Trace slipped off the horse, landing nimbly on the ground. He held up his arms for Lily and helped her from the saddle.

Irish waved at them and nudged his horse toward where they were standing.

Trace took the reins from Lily and tied them to a low-hanging tree branch.

He was just turning back toward Lily when she heard a rustling in the trees.

Lily spun toward the sound and ducked low.

She couldn't see anyone moving in the shadows, but the rustling continued, and a loud snort sounded close by.

Her heart stopped. If that sound was what she thought it was, she had seconds to get the heck out of there.

"Run!" Trace yelled as he pulled the pistol from his holster and aimed it toward the spot where Lily stood.

For a nanosecond, Lily froze. Then she launched herself from the position where she had been standing and ran out into the open. The truck and tractor were too far for her to make it fast enough, so she ran toward a hay bale, wishing it were a heavy round bale instead of an eighty-pound rectangle that wouldn't provide any protection from what was hiding in the woods.

The sound of feet pounding against the ground behind her made Lily run faster.

Out of the corner of her eye, she saw Trace take careful aim.

The blast of a gunfire sounded.

Lily dived behind the hay bale and crouched, pulling her body in on all sides, out of sight of what was chasing her.

Another shot rang out and the sound of something crashing hard against the earth brought her head up and she dared to look over the top of the bale.

Lying in the dust and hay stubble was a gigantic feral hog with wicked tusks. It heaved a last breath and lay still with two gunshot wounds to the heart.

Lily collapsed against the bale, her knees trembling, her pulse still thundering through her system.

Trace hurried toward her, running past the hog to gather her into his arms. He held her for a long moment. "Are you okay?"

She nodded. "Thanks to you."

Irish rode up on Lady, his rifle in one hand, the other managing the reins. "Wow. That was some good shooting. That hog didn't look like he was going to stop for one tiny bullet." Irish slipped from the saddle and walked around the dead animal. "Should be some good eating. Anyone fancy ham for dinner?" He glanced at Lily. "You all right?"

She nodded from the reassuring comfort of Trace's arms. "I am."

"I would have fired the rifle, but you were in direct line of fire from where I stood. Trace had to get him, or…"

"Or the hog would have gotten me," Lily said softly.

"He didn't," Trace said and smoothed a hand over her hair. "And Irish is right. That hog will make good eating."

"That's right," Rosalynn said, joining them. "Better us eating him than him gouging one of us."

Matt trotted toward them from the direction of the truck and trailer. "You guys all right?"

"Yes," Trace assured him.

Irish grinned at Lily. "I've never seen anyone run so fast."

"A good thing she did. That hog wasn't far behind her," Matt said. "I'm glad he didn't catch up with you."

Irish winked. "That's right. We need all the help we can get loading the rest of that hay."

Lily appreciated that they all were rallying around her. But the wall of clouds was nearing, and they still had half a field to load onto the trailer and get to the barn before the skies opened up and dumped rain on them.

Another, louder rumble of thunder caught everyone's attention.

"We'd better get back to work," Rosalynn said. "Lily and I can stack the hay."

"Let's do this. We don't have much time," Trace said. "I can already smell the rain."

Lily sniffed the air. She, too, could smell the earthy dampness of the weather system moving toward them. She and Rosalynn climbed up on the back of the trailer.

Matt and Trace tossed the bales as high as they could, and Lily and Rosalynn moved them into neat rows, layering them carefully so they held in place as the layers grew higher. Trace threw the last bale up onto the trailer and climbed up after it. "We don't have time to tie it down. You two go on back to the barn. I'll ride back here with the hay to make sure nothing starts sliding off."

"We stacked it in crisscrossing layers," Rosalynn said. "It'll hold. Ride up front with Roy and Matt. I'll take the tractor."

"And I'll ride Dusty," Lily said. She didn't offer but left it open for Trace to suggest he ride double.

Trace frowned at the tall stack of hay. "If you're sure it'll hold, I'll go with Lily in case there's another hog hiding out in the underbrush."

Lily let go of the breath she hadn't realized she'd been holding and ducked her head to hide her smile. She was glad he would be riding double with her. Especially after he'd saved her from the charging hog.

Roy drove the truck and trailer to where the hog lay. Matt

tied a rope around the animal's back legs and to the back of the trailer. They would drag it back to the barn, where they could field dress it and process it for the freezer.

Lily shivered as she passed the hog.

"You were smart," Trace said. "You moved fast."

Her lips pressed into a thin line. "I would not have been fast enough to outrun that thing," she said. "You're the reason I wasn't mauled or killed." She turned to him. "Thank you."

Trace pushed a hand through his hair, his gaze searching the undergrowth, as if expecting another feral hog to jump out. "I'm glad I was here, and that I had a gun."

"Me, too." Lily untied Dusty's reins from the tree branch and looped them over the saddle horn.

Trace cupped his hands and bent low.

"You know I can reach the stirrup, don't you?" she asked, her lips twisting in a wry grin.

He looked up at her, his face serious. "Humor me, will you? I almost lost you to a hog today." Not a smile curled the corners of his lips, and there was no twinkle of laughter in his eyes. The man appeared to be years older than he'd looked at the beginning of the day.

Lily nodded. "Okay, then." She placed her foot in his cupped hands and pushed up until she could swing her leg over the saddle.

She moved her leg back, giving him room to place the toe of his boot in the stirrup.

He swung up behind her.

"You could have ridden in the saddle," Lily said. "I don't mind riding behind."

"The stirrups are fitted to the length of your legs. Besides, I'd rather have your back as we return to the barn."

Lily frowned, her mind working through what he'd just said.

He had her back. Meaning, if someone shot at her, he'd get Trace first. Trace would take the bullet, instead of her.

Her hands tightened on the reins and her pulse sped. "Trace, I don't like—"

He leaned into her back, his lips brushing her earlobe. "Don't go getting your panties in a wad. Give the horse his head. He'll get us back to the barn in no time."

"But—"

Trace squeezed his legs against hers and dug his heels into the horse's flanks.

Dusty leaped forward, got the bit between his teeth and took off at a full gallop across the field, headed for the barn and his dinner.

Lily was glad the horse raced across the field. Maybe if he went fast enough, and with Irish bringing up the rear, they wouldn't take a bullet. Now that Trace was back, Lily didn't want anything to happen to him. Heck, the man had fought in the Middle East through several deployments. He couldn't die back in Texas on his own property. That would be all kinds of wrong. And Lily couldn't live knowing he was gone.

Chapter Thirteen

Trace held on to Lily as the horse loped across the field. They caught up with and passed the truck hauling the trailer full of hay and arrived at the barn with enough time to remove the saddle and run a quick brush over Dusty's sweaty coat before the others got back. Trace stepped out of the barn as Lily led the horse into a stall and the truck stopped in front of the barn.

Irish rode into the yard and slipped out of the saddle to stand on his feet. He squatted several times and rubbed his backside. "Those are some muscles I don't use that often," he said, grimacing.

Trace grinned. "I know how you feel. If you don't ride on a regular basis, one day in the saddle will make you sore for a week." He grabbed a bale of hay and carried it into the barn. Between him and Matt, they got started on unloading the trailer.

Lily joined in, carrying the eighty-pound bales a little slower, but she didn't complain or sit it out. She worked hard alongside the men.

Trace's mother entered the barn and started to lift a bale.

Trace took the bale from her hands. "Mom, you'd serve an even greater purpose if you feed us when this is all done."

She nodded and touched a hand to the small of her back. "But that rain is almost here."

"If we have to, we can back the trailer into the barn to keep the hay dry," Trace said. "You've already helped more than you should."

"What you mean is *for an old woman*."

Trace shook his head. "You're anything but old. Still, you need to take a break. We can handle the rest."

"He's right, Rosalynn," Lily said as she grabbed another bale and carried it over to the foot of the stairs leading up to the loft. "We're going to be starving when we're done here."

"You should go help her," Trace said.

Lily snorted, her brow dipping. "And let you two have all the fun? No way." She came back for another bale. "I will, however, let you guys carry these bales up the stairs to the loft."

"Deal," Trace said. "Mom, let Irish walk you into the house. I know for a fact he's great at peeling potatoes."

"Hey, are you volunteering me for KP?" Irish stood in the open doorway to the barn. "I am pretty good at it." He grinned. "Then, at least, I won't have to stand out in the lightning." He tipped his head toward the southwest. "It's almost here. You have about fifteen minutes before the rain starts."

Lily carried bales to the bottom of the stairs while Matt and Trace took turns carrying them up into the loft. Working as a team, they had the trailer unloaded in less than twenty minutes. Lily carried the last bale into the barn as the sky opened up and rain poured down.

She stood at the door and sighed. Any way she looked at it, if she stepped out of the barn, she'd be drenched in the first five steps. Getting to the house would be very wet.

Matt and Trace joined her at the door.

"We could wait until it lets up," Matt said.

Trace shook his head. "It's predicted to last all night. And I'm hungry." He patted his flat abdomen.

"Me, too." Lily rolled her aching shoulders. "We worked hard."

Matt grinned. "Got it done."

Trace glanced at the massive hog lying in the middle of the barn. "We might as well dress this hog. No use getting a shower until that's done."

"You'll need something to put the meat in." Lily grabbed an empty paper feed sack and lifted it over her head. "I'll be right back with containers and freezer paper."

"Grab an extra knife while you're at it," Trace said. "I'll watch until you get to the house." A crack of thunder rattled the rafters of the barn. "On second thought…you stay here. I'll go get what we need."

"I'm not afraid of a little lightning," Lily said, ready to go out into the storm. She didn't stand around arguing. Instead, she dashed out the door before Trace could grab her and insist on her staying in the barn.

"Damn it, Lily," Trace called out.

"I'll be right back," she said over her shoulder, sure he wouldn't hear her anyway. Not with the rain pounding down on the metal roof of the barn.

Considering she had been hot and sweaty by the time she'd finished unloading the trailer, she should be thankful for the drenching rain to cool her off. The only problem was being able to see as she ran through the deluge. When she finally made it to the porch, she stopped long enough to squeeze the water out of her hair. Too wet to enter the house, she poked her head through the back door and spotted Trace's mother at the stove. "Rosalynn."

The older woman spun, a spatula in her hand. "Oh, my goodness," she said. Turning the flame down beneath the pot simmering on the stove, she hurried over to where Lily dripped on the tile. "Come in, dear. You're not going to hurt the floor."

Lily shook her head. "I'd rather not. We're going to process the hog. I need supplies."

Rosalynn nodded. "I know just what you'll use." She hurried around the kitchen gathering items from drawers and the pantry, stuffing them in a large canvas bag. When she was finished, she returned to Lily. "Let me take it out there. You need to come in and get a shower."

With a smile, Lily relieved the woman of the bag. "No use you getting wet, too. We've got this. Between the three of us, we should be able to take care of things quickly." With the straps of the bag looped over her shoulder, Lily headed back the way she'd come, pausing briefly at the edge of the porch as a bright flash lit the darkness and an answering rumble of thunder rattled the eaves.

Taking a deep breath, she ran down the stairs and across the backyard to the barn. She didn't care that lightning struck nearby. She only wanted to be close to Trace.

TRACE AND MATT strung the hog from one of the rafters and started the process of rendering it for consumption.

They worked in silence.

Trace didn't want to like his half brother, but the man worked hard and efficiently, without complaint. And he was prior service. A marine.

"Why did you get off active duty?" Trace asked, curious about this man with whom he'd have to share the Whiskey Gulch Ranch or sell it.

"Injury," Matt said. "Wrecked my knee. I've since been given a new one, but medical boarded off active duty. Your—our father came to my rescue when I returned to Whiskey Gulch. I didn't know what I was going to do with my life without the military. I was good with car engines, but not much else. He set me up with my own shop, loaned me the money to get started and told me I could pay it back in my own time."

"Generous of him," Trace said. "He never wanted me to do anything but ranching. Blew a gasket when I announced I was going into the army."

"Should have gone into the marines," Matt said with a grin. "He might not have been as mad."

"Whatever," Trace muttered. "He liked to have control of his corner of the world."

"And you didn't like being controlled," Matt concluded.

"That about covers it." Trace worked the hide away from the hindquarters.

Matt helped by pulling back while Trace cut. "Was Lily one of James's control issues as well?"

Trace bristled. He didn't want to discuss Lily with this man. "Let's just say he didn't approve." His tone was deep and tinged with anger.

Matt held up his hands. "Sorry, dude. I didn't mean to stir the hornet's nest. But you need to know, there never was anything between me and Lily... We were friends. Only. She hung out with me for a week, came to my house once to watch a game, and once you were gone, she never came back to hang out."

Trace frowned. "Why would she tell me that she was marrying you?"

Matt shrugged. "Did you ask her?"

"No."

The other man chuckled. "Seems like that would be your first stop."

Trace snorted. "Getting a straight answer out of her can be a challenge."

"One worth taking on," Matt said. "She's a smart, hard-working and beautiful woman."

The more Matt talked, the more Trace wanted to punch him. He straightened, his eyes narrowing. "Look, she's—"

"Off-limits?" Matt shook his head. "Have you told her that? You're going to mess up and lose her if you don't do something about it. I think your boy, Irish, has a thing for her."

"Irish is harmless," Trace muttered and went back to work on the hide.

"Maybe he is. Maybe I don't know what I'm talking about." Matt pulled at the hide. "Irish himself said that Lily was just the kind of woman he'd want to marry." Matt lifted his shoulders. "He could have been kidding or just making a statement. Maybe you need to open your eyes to what's right there in front of you."

Trace looked up, his gaze seeking the barn door.

Lily entered, carrying a bag and drenched. Her blouse lay plastered to her body like a second skin and water dripped off her chin, nose and eyelashes.

Even as sodden as she was, she was beautiful in Trace's eyes. And she stood right there in front of him, a smile pulling at her lips. "In case you didn't know, it's still raining out there."

Matt chuckled. "I think we know." He pointed at the roof the rain was hammering against.

"There's a towel in the tack room," Trace said. "You can let Patches out now. I'm sure she's ready." After his conversation with Matt, his words to her seemed…inadequate.

Lily dropped the bag at Trace's feet. "You made good progress in a short amount of time."

"This is the hard part," Matt said. "It won't take long, once we get going."

Lily disappeared into the tack room, leaving the door slightly open to allow Patches to make her escape.

Trace glanced that way every so often. Patches never came out. At least not while he was watching.

Lily came out patting her body with a ragged towel and squeezing her ponytail to get the water out. She studied their progress. Lily had been with Trace after he'd been hunting deer and had helped by wrapping the meat in butcher paper. The hog proved to be a lot more of an effort than a deer. But with three of them working together, they completed their work.

The worst of the lightning had moved past the house, but the rain continued to beat loudly against the roof.

Lily, Trace and Matt stepped out into nature's shower and let the rain wash away the dirt, hay and blood.

"I can't remember when I've been more exhausted or covered in blood," Lily said.

"I can," Matt said, his tone flat, his gaze on the horizon.

Trace knew exactly how Matt felt. He'd been involved in some bloody battles during his time with Delta Force. But this was Texas, not Afghanistan or Iraq. They'd have good meat in the freezer to last through the winter. If he stayed.

"We got a lot done," Trace said. "Now there's hay to see the horses through the winter."

Matt nodded. "And meat for the freezer, enough to feed whoever lives on the ranch."

"We'll have to wait until the other field dries before we can cut the hay for the big round bales needed to get the cattle through the winter. But that effort won't require tossing bales onto a trailer."

Lily raised her hands in the air and stretched, wincing. "Thankfully, all of that can be done by tractors, not human backs."

"It will still require a lot of work and we haven't checked the fences in a while."

"I can help with that tomorrow," Matt said.

"Don't you have engines to fix?" Lily asked.

"I'll work on them tonight." Matt's lips twisted. "That's what shop lights are for. Fencing needs daylight."

Trace wanted to hate the man who was his father's first-born son, but he couldn't. Matt had worked as hard as he had that day. He'd served his country, and he cared about Lily and Trace's mother. Not that Trace had appreciated his advice on how to handle Lily. But the man's words roiled around in his head, refusing to be ignored.

"I bet Mom's got something amazing ready for dinner," Trace said. "We'd better get cleaned up."

Trace took Lily's hand and walked with her to the house, rain dripping down his face and into his eyes. He wanted anyone watching to know that she was important to him. The Irishes and Matts of the world would have to back off or suffer his wrath. If he could convince her, Lily was his and he wouldn't let her go again. Not without a fight.

Chapter Fourteen

Lily was first in the shower, rinsing quickly, knowing there were two others who needed hot water to get clean. When she was finished, she dried off quickly, wrapped a towel around her hair and another around her body, and stepped out into the hallway.

Right into a solid wall of muscles.

"Oh," Lily said, her hand rising to rest on Trace's damp chest.

He was barefoot, wearing only a pair of jeans, and he was clean.

Lily frowned. "You had a shower?"

He tipped his head toward the master bedroom at the end of the hallway. "I used Mom's shower." His gaze swept over her bare shoulders, his pupils dilating. "Feel better?"

She nodded, her cheeks heating. The only thing between her and his hands was the fluffy white towel. She didn't look up into his eyes, afraid he'd see just how excited she was by his nearness. "Much better. What about Matt? Did he want to jump in?"

"He grabbed a plate to go and left."

Lily frowned. "Was it something we said?"

Trace smiled. "No. He had work to do at his shop." He tipped her chin up, forcing her to look at him. "Thank you."

"For what?"

"You were amazing today." He leaned down and

pressed his lips to her forehead. "I'll rub your back for you, after dinner."

She shrugged. "You don't have to do that." Though the thought of him rubbing her back and a lot of other places sent shivers of excitement throughout her body. That little bit of anticipation chased away some of the ache in her back.

"I know I don't have to." He touched his lips to her temple. "But I'd like to."

Lily closed her eyes and sighed. "Mmm. Sounds nice." Then she remembered her resolve to leave as soon as the hay was put up. Unfortunately, or maybe fortunately, the rain had delayed her departure even more. Now she'd have to wait for as long as it took for the grass to dry enough to mow. Then they'd cut, rake and bale the round bales.

Then she'd be on her way. To what, she had no idea. For sure, she'd get out of Whiskey Gulch now that Trace was back. If he chose to stay, he needed to marry someone much better than Lily Davidson.

A hard knot formed in her belly. She couldn't stick around and watch another woman give Trace the family he deserved.

As much as she loved when he kissed her, she couldn't stay and be disappointed all over again. Trace hadn't come after her in eleven years. What happened last night had been a fling. She was convenient and willing. Lily refused to be a distraction. She wanted more out of life than Trace could give. She deserved someone who loved her so much he'd move heaven and earth for her. He'd come after her and woo her. Life was too short to settle for scraps. She wanted the whole meal.

Lily stepped backward and out of Trace's arms.

He frowned as his hands dropped to his sides. "What's wrong?"

"I'm starving and can't go downstairs dressed like this." She gave him a weak smile, ducked around him and dived through the door of the room she'd shared with him the night before.

"Lily," Trace called out.

She didn't stop to see what he wanted. Instead, she closed the door and leaned against it. Her heart wanted her to open the door. Her head made her pull her hand away from the knob. "I can't do this to myself," she whispered. "I can't keep loving him."

After she'd dressed in jeans and a soft white blouse, she took her time brushing the tangles out of her hair. Purposely procrastinating, hoping he'd eat and go to bed, she finally gave in to her rumbling belly. She had to eat. After burning so many calories hauling hay, she needed to refuel her body.

Easing the door open, she looked out into the hallway. Bumping into Trace again would ruin her efforts to get her head on straight. The man sent her thoughts whirling. She had to keep it together for the next few days until she could pack up and leave.

The hallway was empty.

Lily sighed and eased out of her bedroom and down the stairs. She tiptoed past the study and entered the kitchen on silent feet.

Rosalynn turned from the stove, holding a mug with a tea bag string hanging over the side. "Lily, honey, I was just about to make you a tray of food and bring it up."

"That's not necessary," Lily said quietly, glancing over her shoulder, not wanting to run into Trace. Not when her emotions were so overwrought. She wasn't sure how she'd keep from falling into his arms when that was all she wanted to do.

"If you're looking for Trace, he went out to the barn with Irish to check on the animals and that darn cat." Rosalynn set her mug on the counter. "Sit. I'll serve up a bowl of the stew I made for dinner."

"Thank you," Lily said. "But I can help myself."

"Don't be silly. You're bound to be exhausted."

"As are you," Lily protested.

"I didn't do as much as you."

"You did every bit as much."

"Sit." Rosalynn pointed to the kitchen table. In her "mom" voice, she said, "I insist."

Lily grinned. "Yes, ma'am." She pulled out a chair and sat, releasing a sigh. "It really does feel good to sit."

"Uh-huh." Rosalynn scooped a ladle full of steaming stew into a bowl, grabbed a spoon from a drawer and crossed the kitchen to set them in front of Lily. "Tea?"

"Please." Lily inhaled the hearty aroma of stew and nearly fell into it. She was so tired. "I'm hungry, but I don't know if I'll stay awake to eat this." She drew in another breath and closed her eyes. "It smells so good." She dug the spoon in and carried a heaping helping of beef, carrots and potatoes to her mouth.

Rosalynn brought over another mug of tea along with her own and sat across the table from Lily. "Eat before you sleep. You worked hard today."

Lily nodded and consumed half of the bowl of stew before she paused.

Rosalynn smiled. "Feel better?"

"I do." Lily removed the tea bag from the mug, stirred in a spoonful of sugar and sipped the steaming brew. "This is perfect."

"Speaking of perfect..." Rosalynn set her mug on the table. "When are you and Trace going to stop dancing around and realize you two are perfect for each other?"

As if hit by a strong wind, all of Lily's thoughts of sleep flew out the window. "Excuse me?"

"You heard me. I know you love him. Why don't you tell him?" Rosalynn stared across the table at Lily, an eyebrow cocked in challenge.

Lily gulped. "I can't."

"Can't or won't?" Rosalynn sighed and looked down at her mug. "Look, it's none of my business what you two do with your lives, but, damn it, I want grandchildren before I die."

Her words stabbed Lily right in the heart.

She wanted children. Trace's children. Nothing would make her happier. "I don't think Trace loves me as much as I love him."

"Are you kidding me?" Rosalynn looked at her as if she'd lost her mind. "He can't take his eyes off you. He dogs your every step. If that's not love, I don't know what is."

"Lust," Lily suggested. "If he really loved me, he wouldn't have stayed away for eleven years."

"He thought you were married to someone else."

"He didn't bother to find out whether or not I had, or to try to change my mind." Lily gave Trace's mother a weak smile. "I deserve someone who loves me enough to fight for me. A man who won't take *bug off* for an answer."

"You want to marry a stalker." Rosalynn frowned. "You turned Trace away with a lie. You broke his heart. Why not set the record straight and see where you go from there? What's it going to hurt?"

The food in Lily's belly churned. "What if…?"

"If you don't own up to your lie, how will you ever know what he wants?" Rosalynn reached across the table for Lily's hand. "Lily, I don't want to see you two suffer. And I want—"

"Grandchildren." Lily squeezed Mrs. Travis's hand. "I know."

Rosalynn shook her head. "Yes, I want grandchildren, but more than that, I want to see my child happy. He hasn't been happy for the past eleven years." She laughed, the sound less than humorous. "Believe me, a mother knows." Her smile faded. "And you've come to be like the daughter I never had. I want you to be happy, too. I love you, Lily. I don't want you and Trace to waste another day apart if you were meant to be together."

Tears welled in Lily's eyes. "What if we're not meant to be together?" She swallowed hard.

The clump of boots on the porch heralded the return of Trace and Irish from the barn.

Lily brushed tears from her cheeks. "I have to go."

Rosalynn retained her hold on her hand. "Think about it, will ya?"

With a nod, Lily pulled her hand free and raced out of the kitchen, up the stairs and into her bedroom. Once inside, she closed the door, then leaned her back against the panel and slid to the floor, tears coursing down her cheeks.

Lily had loved Trace for what felt like all of her life. She couldn't bear it if she told him she loved him and he didn't love her in return.

TRACE HELD THE door for Irish and followed him into the kitchen. Everything was as it should have been in the barn. No one had jumped out to hurt them. The buddy system seemed to be working.

His mother sat at the table, staring toward the opposite door leading into the rest of the house.

"Everything all right?" Trace asked.

She glanced at him. "You tell me." His mother pushed to her feet. "Your father is dead, someone is attacking the people who live and work on this ranch, and you're an idiot." She stalked out of the kitchen.

Trace followed her into the living room, where she took down the photo on the fireplace mantel of her wedding day almost forty years ago. "Why did you have to leave me?" she cried, tears rolling down her cheeks as she sank onto the sofa, hugging the framed photo to her chest.

Trace sat next to his mother and slipped an arm around her shoulders.

She turned and buried her face against his shirt. For a long moment, she let the tears fall.

His heart aching, Trace held his mother, knowing how much she'd relied on his father to be there, protect her and run the ranch. Now she was on her own and dealing with a much more difficult situation. He plucked a tissue from the box on the end table and handed it to her.

His mother wiped her eyes and blew her nose before she finally said, "I'm sorry I called you an idiot."

"I'm sure you have every right to call me that. I've been an idiot for more than ten years," he offered.

"Yes, you have," she agreed.

His chest tightened. "I should have cleared the air with Dad a long time ago. I hate to think he died believing I didn't love him."

His mother frowned. "He knew. He felt the same. But that wasn't why I was calling you an idiot."

Trace narrowed his eyes and stared down at his mother. "No? Then what else have I been an idiot about?"

She shook her head. "You have regrets that you didn't patch things up with your father before he died, but you're not looking at what you could do while you still can."

"I can't change things between me and Dad."

His mother smiled. "No, but you can change things between you and people who are still among the living."

His eyes narrowed. "Do I need to fix things between me and you?"

His mother rolled her eyes and sighed. "Of course not. You can be just as hardheaded and dense as your father. When it comes to the women in your life, you really don't have a clue." She set the photo on the coffee table, pushed to her feet and turned to face him. "You love her. It's as clear as the nose on your face. Why don't you tell her, before you lose her?"

"Oh… We're not talking about you and Dad." Trace

couldn't try to pretend he didn't know who his mother was talking about. "That's complicated."

"Sweetheart, it's a lot less complicated than you think." She touched his shoulder. "I love you, Trace. I don't want you to lose this chance to be happy." Her jaw firmed. "Don't screw this up. Now, I'm going to bed." With that, she left the living room and climbed the stairs.

Trace stared at the photograph of his mother and father and wished he could have a marriage like theirs. They'd been together for almost forty years, fighting, bickering and loving each other all that time. Yet they always overcame their differences and never went to bed mad.

Trace's heart tugged hard. His mother had lost not only her husband, but also her best friend.

When Lily had told Trace she was going to marry Matt, Trace had lost the woman he'd loved and his best friend. Dating after Lily had been a useless effort. Once burned, he'd been twice shy, unwilling to risk his heart again, only to have some woman wreck his emotions the way Lily had. He'd been so devastated, it had taken him years and a number of dangerous deployments to harden his heart and get over her.

Only seeing her again had brought back everything he'd thought he'd overcome. He couldn't deny how he felt. His chest hurt and his gut clenched every time he thought of her with someone else.

Hell, he still loved her.

His mother was right. He needed to tell her how he felt and ask her if she felt the same. The sooner he did that, the better off he'd be. If she didn't return his feelings, she'd tell him. Then he could get on with his life.

With this plan in mind, he headed for her bedroom, taking the stairs to the upper landing two at a time. Now that he was ready to move forward, he wanted to get it over with, rip the bandage off and see if the wound had healed.

He hurried past the door to his room and paused in front of Lily's. Raising his hand to knock, he froze.

For a man who'd charged into battle and stared death in the eye, Trace was suddenly more afraid than he'd ever been.

He closed his eyes, sucked in a deep breath and let it out slowly. He wouldn't know until he asked. Forcing his hand to move, he tapped softly on the door and waited.

A moment passed…then two…

"Lily?" he called out softly.

Another few seconds later and no response came from inside her room.

Trace's hand dropped to the doorknob and he twisted it. The door opened.

He poked his head inside and whispered, "Lily?"

The lights were off. A shadowy lump in the bed didn't move.

Crossing the room, Trace came to a halt beside her bed and stared down at her in the starlight streaming through the window beside her, glinting off her hair, turning it a gray blue in the night.

She lay curled on her side, a hand tucked beneath her cheek, her breathing deep and steady.

The woman was sound asleep. After hauling hay and helping dress a hog, she had to be beyond exhausted.

Now that he'd decided to open up about his feelings, Trace wanted to shake her awake and tell her. But he couldn't bring himself to wake her. She needed to sleep, to recharge her tired body.

Bending over her, he pressed a featherlight kiss to her forehead. "I love you, Lily Davidson," he whispered. "I always have."

Her brow puckered slightly, but she didn't open her eyes and respond.

Disappointed that he'd have to wait and say it again, Trace straightened and backed out of the room, pausing at the door to look at her one more time. Finally, he pulled the door closed and descended the stairs, too wound up to sleep.

He entered his father's study and sat behind the desk.

They'd been so worried about getting the hay cut and stored, he hadn't thought about the business side of running the ranch. Not that he felt like looking at accounts, but someone had to get a handle on things. His father had always been the one to handle the books.

Unopened mail littered his father's desktop. Trace glanced at the senders and sorted the envelopes into a pile for bills and another for miscellaneous. He'd go through them tomorrow.

One by one, he opened the drawers. In the top right-hand drawer, he found several envelopes addressed to his APO location when he'd been deployed to Afghanistan. His last assignment before coming home for his father's funeral.

Curious, he turned over the first one. It hadn't been sealed, nor did it have a stamp on the front.

Trace pulled out a letter, folded neatly into thirds.

When he unfolded it, his father's bold handwriting filled the paper in thick strokes.

The first words at the top captured his attention and made him drop back in his father's chair.

Dear Trace,
I should have written you as soon as you left to join the army. I should have sent letters while you were going through basic combat training. I should have been there for your graduation. Arrogance has a way of making you a lesser person without even trying. I wish I could take back all the wasted years and start over in my relationship with you.

I'd start with telling you a few truths.

I was wrong.

I should never have assumed that just because you

were my son, that you'd stay and work the ranch and love it as much as I have. Whiskey Gulch Ranch was my grandfather's dream, my father's life and now mine. It didn't have to be yours. I know that now. You have every right to follow your own path.

Sadly, I can't change the past. But I hope that you can forgive this old man for some of the harsh things he said.

I was wrong.

You are a smart, motivated, hardworking man. No matter the career you choose to pursue, you will succeed.

I was wrong about your sweetheart, Lily. She is not the product of her lineage. Or perhaps she is. Because of who her parents are, she's become a strong, independent and caring young woman. I know now I would have been proud to welcome her into our family as your wife. I wish I hadn't been so pigheaded and obstinate when you first showed interest in her. I hope someday to make it up to her, and to you, for ruining things between the two of you.

Above all, I want you to know how very proud I am of all you have accomplished in the army. I can only hope to understand the training, dedication and commitment it takes to live the life of a Delta Force soldier.

Son, I love you and want you to live the life you choose. If that's remaining in Delta Force, I am at peace with it. You should not be saddled with the responsibility of this ranch. If you choose someday to return and run Whiskey Gulch Ranch, you know I will be happy. But only if you are.

Well, enough of my rambling. I wish you good health and happiness from the bottom of my heart. All my love,
Dad

Trace's heart squeezed so hard in his chest, he thought it might explode. His eyes stung and the hand holding the letter shook.

All the years of anger and disappointment fell away in that one letter.

In that moment, Trace wished he could have had one more conversation with his father. One more chance to mend the fences, to make things right between them. His father had redeemed his side through his letter. But he'd died not knowing that Trace had forgiven him and loved him.

Regret ate a hole in his gut and reminded him that he couldn't waste a single moment wallowing in the past. He had to live in the present and ensure the future wasn't lost as well. He had to make it right with Lily before he could get on with his life. He prayed he had time. Living to the next day wasn't guaranteed.

His father had proved that.

Chapter Fifteen

Lily woke early the next morning with a headache like nobody's business. Quietly, she dressed, grabbed her boots, and tiptoed out of her room and down the stairs, well before the sun rose in the eastern sky.

She hoped to get outside and take care of the animals before anyone else got out of bed.

Sounds from the kitchen made her turn in that direction.

Rosalynn stood at the stove, laying strips of bacon into a frying pan.

"You're up extra early." Lily sat in one of the chairs at the kitchen table and slid her right foot into a boot.

Rosalynn looked over her shoulder with a weak smile. "Couldn't sleep. The bed is so big and empty."

Lily's chest tightened. "I'm so sorry." She shoved her left foot into the opposite boot and pushed to her feet. "Is there anything I can do to help?"

Rosalynn snorted. "Since you can't bring James back, I assume you're talking about cooking." She tipped her head toward the refrigerator. "You could get the eggs and butter out."

"I can do that. Just don't ask me to make the eggs over easy, unless you like them lacy and burned." She reached into the fridge and extracted a carton of eggs and a tub of butter. "My mother wasn't much of a cook. I must have gotten my lack of skills from her."

"You're much more comfortable working outside with the animals," Rosalynn said without any kind of judgment. She flipped a piece of bacon over in the pan. "What's your plan for the day?"

"I have a few errands to run in town. Hopefully, by later this afternoon, the fields will be dry enough to cut." In town, she planned to run by the bank, withdraw her savings and close her account, the first task in her plan. Once the last of the hay was cut and properly stored, she would leave Whiskey Gulch Ranch and her hometown. Staying would only cause her more heartache. She loved Trace. If he didn't love her as much as she loved him, she needed to move on.

Her heart heavy, Lily slid bread into the toaster and waited while it cooked.

Rosalynn broke a dozen eggs into a bowl, whipped them with a wire whisk until they were fluffy and poured them into the skillet. Then she turned to Lily. "What's wrong?"

Lily's head jerked up. "Wrong? What do you mean?"

"You've been frowning since you walked through that door."

Guilt rode up her cheeks in a wave of heat. "I'm sorry. I didn't realize I was frowning." Lily concentrated on easing the tension out of her face. "Is that better?" she asked.

Rosalynn shook her head. "It's not the frown that was bothering me. It's the fact that you're frowning. I think of you as the daughter I never had. When you're stressed, I'm stressed. When you're unhappy, I'm unhappy."

Lily abandoned her duties at the toaster and crossed to the older woman, pulling her into a hug. "I don't want you to be any unhappier than you already are because of me."

"Then tell me what's wrong and let me see if I can help make it right." Rosalynn set her at arm's length. "So?"

Lily laughed, though it took effort. She'd miss this

woman who'd given her a job and made her a part of her family. "You can't fix everything."

"I might if I know what the problem is." She cocked an eyebrow. "Does it have to do with my pigheaded son?" She shook her head. "He takes after his father more than he can ever imagine."

Lily laughed for real this time. "I see it." She smiled at Rosalynn. "You're an amazing woman, you know that?"

Mrs. Travis's brows dipped. "I don't think so. I'm just someone who's trying to get through the day."

"That's what I mean." Lily took her hand and stared at her long fingers, the calluses, cuts and nicks marring the skin. "You just lost your husband, yet you're worried about others' happiness."

Rosalynn shrugged. "I need to be needed and to keep busy. If I sit around with nothing to do, or no one to worry about, I have too much time to ruminate about my own problems." She gave Lily a sad smile. "So, if I can help you, I'd love the opportunity."

Lily hugged her, hating the idea of leaving this woman who'd become more of a mother to her than her own. "I love you, Rosalynn Travis. No matter what, remember that."

After a moment, Rosalynn leaned back. "You say that like you're going somewhere."

"I am," Lily said. "I'm going to town to run some errands after I take care of the animals."

"If your problems include my son," Rosalynn started, "just know, he's a man. And some men aren't good at expressing their feelings. Take James, for example…he rarely told me that he loved me."

"Really?" Lily leaned back. "Everyone could tell you hung the moon in his eyes."

The older woman nodded. "Yes, but he didn't say it. Instead, he lived it. Every time he held the door for me, brought me wildflowers from the fields, held my hand when he walked with me and never started eating before I sat at the dinner table. He didn't have to tell me. I knew he loved me by the little things he did.

"Trace is so much like his father, sometimes it scares me. At others, it makes me happy. I can see James in his face and demeanor. My husband isn't completely gone. He lives on in my son and in my heart."

Tears welled in Lily's eyes. "Yes, he does resemble his father." Rosalynn and James Travis had lived the life Lily had always dreamed of. Not the rich rancher life, but the life of a couple who continued to love each other through thick and thin.

"Tell you what, I don't like the idea of you going to town on your own. Want me to ask one of the guys to go with you?" Rosalynn asked.

Lily held up her hands. "No, that's okay. I can manage on my own."

"With all that's been happening lately, I don't feel comfortable having any one of us going off alone. Irish headed out to the barnyard a few minutes before you came downstairs. Help him find his way around while I cook. When I have breakfast ready, I'll go with you to town. I could do a little grocery shopping while you run your errands."

Lily hesitated for a split second. She didn't want anyone knowing her plan to leave. Until she drove away from Whiskey Gulch Ranch, she wouldn't tell anyone that she didn't plan to return. But if Rosalynn wanted to grocery shop, she could do that while Lily headed to the bank across the street to close her account. "Sounds like a good plan. I'll be back as soon as the animals are fed and watered."

Lily left the house and headed for the barn. She'd really wanted to leave for town before Trace woke. But that wasn't an option, unless she wanted to wait in her SUV until the bank opened at nine o'clock.

Waiting patiently was never one of Lily's strengths.

She'd be better off mucking stalls and currying the entire stable full of horses until their coats shone. At least her hands and mind would be too busy to dwell on her impending departure from the ranch.

She found Irish in the barn, bent low, petting Patches.

"You're up early," he said, straightening.

"Couldn't sleep. Thought I'd get an early start cleaning stalls."

"I'm still new to this ranching gig, but I'm willing to learn and working on getting my strength back. Won't be long before I'm tossing eighty-pound bales with the best of them." He winked. "What's on the honey-do list for this morning?"

"You can feed the horses and the chickens. Beware of the rooster. If he feels the need to defend his hens, use the fishnet hanging on the side of the barn to contain him."

Irish frowned. "Contain?"

Lily laughed. "You scoop him up and hang him on the hook on the barn until you've poured the feed in the chicken pen."

He nodded. "Never knew that was what fishnets were for." He chuckled. "Learn something new every day."

Lily snapped a lead on Lady and led her out of her stall. She tied the lead to a hook and went to work on mucking the stall. When Irish returned from feeding the chickens and the other horses, she had him brush Lady.

Ten wheelbarrows full of sludge from the bottom of the first two stalls and Lily needed a shower before she went to town.

Irish ducked his head into the stall she had just finished. "Mrs. Travis called out that breakfast is ready."

She carried her rake out and hung it on the wall, then followed Irish out of the barn to the house.

He held the door for her to enter first.

Thankfully, Trace wasn't in the kitchen when she passed

through. With thoughts of leaving heavy on her mind, she didn't want to run into him, afraid he'd see her face and guess. Or worse, he'd see her and not give a damn.

She made it through the house and into her room without running into him. After grabbing clean clothing, she poked her head out the door. The hallway was clear. Lily ran across to the bathroom and locked herself inside.

She stripped out of her dirty jeans and shirt and hurried through a quick but thorough shower, washing the manure, straw and sweat from her body. When she finished, she dried, dressed and ran a brush through her wet hair. She didn't want to take the time to apply a blow dryer to the wet strands. The hot Texas sun would dry it soon enough.

Squaring her shoulders, she opened the bathroom door and stepped out into the hallway. If she ran into Trace, she told herself that she could handle it.

"I can," she whispered, knowing she might melt into a puddle of goo if he looked at her just right. Eleven years had passed, and she'd never gotten over the man.

Voices rose from the floor below.

Lily's heartbeat sputtered and then raced. She gripped the rail as she descended the stairs to the ground floor.

Rosalynn stood in the foyer with Trace, Irish and Roy. She grimaced when she spotted Lily. "Lily, honey, I won't be able to go with you to town after all." Turning, she waved a hand toward her son. "Trace has graciously offered to accompany you, if that's okay."

No, it wasn't okay. Lily's heart sank into her kneecaps. The last thing she needed was to be cooped up in the same vehicle with Trace, especially when she was going to clear her bank account. He might get nosy and ask why. Then she'd have to lie or tell him the truth. Either way…she didn't want to know how he'd feel.

Lily stiffened her back. What he thought or didn't think

about her didn't matter. She deserved someone who would fight for her. Someone who loved her enough to tell her.

Trace wasn't that guy. He'd stepped away from her without an attempt to change her mind. He'd left Whiskey Gulch and had remained gone for over ten years. Why would he care about her?

"Fine," Lily said. "But I hope you have things to do, because I don't want you hanging around while I conduct my business."

Trace popped a sharp salute in her direction. "Yes, ma'am."

Lily rolled her eyes. "Oh, and you don't have to call me ma'am. It makes me uncomfortable."

"Yes, your highness," he said with a wink. Before she could protest, he turned and addressed his mother. "We'll be back soon. I thought we'd use the rest of the day to check the fences."

"Sounds like a good plan," his mother said. "The fields should be dry enough tomorrow to mow."

"That's what we're banking on." He leaned down and kissed his mother's cheek. Then he glanced at Irish.

Irish nodded. "I've got her covered."

"Thank you."

"Aren't you going to have breakfast first?" Rosalynn asked.

Lily shook her head. "Thanks, but I'm not hungry."

"In that case—" Trace opened the front door and peered out before moving to the side with a flourish of his arm "—your chariot awaits."

Lily rolled her eyes and marched through the door and out to Trace's truck. She stayed a step ahead of him, hurrying so that she would open her own door.

Frustratingly, he kept up and reached around her to open her door, his arm brushing across hers.

A shiver of awareness rippled through her, throwing her

off guard. Damn. Damn. Damn. This little trip to town was going to be harder than she expected.

Once they were both inside, buckled and on their way, Trace turned to her. "What's wrong?"

Lily snapped, "Why does everyone assume something's wrong?"

He blinked and snorted. "It was a simple question. If everything was all right in your world, you would have answered without jumping down my throat."

"I'm not jumping down your throat," she said, toning down her argument, realizing she was overreacting to his question. Folding her hands in her lap, she drew in a deep, calming breath and let it out. "Nothing's wrong."

"Then why are you avoiding me?" he asked.

Heat filled her cheeks and her fingers curled into the denim on her legs. "I'm not avoiding you," she lied.

"Lily, you never were a good liar." He glanced at her hands in her lap. "Your face is red, and your hands are clenching."

Lily straightened her hands on her thighs and willed the heat out of her face. "I'm fine. And I don't want to talk."

"Okay." He drove for another minute without saying a word. The minute stretched into two very long minutes before he broke the silence. "While you're doing your thing, I thought I'd stop by the sheriff's office and see if they've had any leads on my father's murder."

A frown pulled Lily's brow low. "I'd like to be there when you talk to the sheriff."

"Okay." Trace nodded. "I can wait for you."

"Thank you."

"Where do you want to go first?" he asked.

"The bank," she said. "I'm low on cash. I need to make a withdrawal."

"Drive-through?"

Lily shook her head. "I'd prefer to go inside."

Trace drove into town and parked in the bank parking lot.

"I'll only be a short time," Lily said.

He'd started to unbuckle his belt but paused. "I'll wait here."

Lily hurried out of the vehicle and into the bank. She skipped the teller and went to one of the account managers. "I'd like to close my account and withdraw all my money."

Cecilia Menn was someone Lily had gone to high school with. She frowned. "Is everything okay, Lily?"

Lily's eyes stung, but she managed a nod. "Everything's fine. I'm just moving."

"I'm sorry to hear that," Cecilia said as she typed on her keyboard. "Don't you want to leave the account open until you're established in your new home and then transfer the money over?"

Lily shook her head. "No, I want to withdraw all of it and close it. I'm not sure how long it will take me to find a new bank." A new job and a place to live. Hell, she had no idea where she was going. Just away from Whiskey Gulch. Maybe she'd go to San Antonio. She'd always wanted to visit the Alamo. Her chest tightened. This town had been her life. Not always a good life, but it had been her home since the day she was born. Leaving was going to be harder than she thought. Especially because she was leaving behind the only man she'd ever loved. Tears welled in her eyes.

Cecilia reached across the desk. "Are you okay?" She plucked a tissue from the box on the corner of her desk and handed it to Lily.

"I'm fine. Just a little nostalgic." Lily pressed the tissue to the corners of her eyes, refusing to let the tears slip down her cheeks. Trace couldn't know that she was crying. She never cried in front of him. She wouldn't start now.

"Do you want all cash, a check or a mix?" Cecilia asked.

"Cash."

"That's a lot of cash to carry around," Cecilia warned.

Not really, Lily thought. Not considering it was her life savings. She just hoped she didn't have to use it all before she found another job, in another town. Not to mention an apartment, deposits on an apartment, utilities and more. She might last a couple months before she ran out of funds.

She carried a cashier's check to the teller, who counted out the sum of her savings in hundreds and some change. Lily stuffed the wad of bills into her purse and zipped the opening, feeling like a bank robber making a run for it.

Cecilia closed her account and came around her desk to give her a hug. "I wish you well. And know that you'll be missed in Whiskey Gulch."

"I doubt that," she murmured.

Cecilia caught her arms and stared into her eyes. "I'll miss you. You've always been kind to me when others haven't been."

"Thank you, Cecelia, and likewise. I will miss you." Lily hugged the account manager and made a dash for the door, praying she didn't burst into tears in front of Trace.

She climbed up into the truck, averting her gaze.

When Trace didn't move to start the engine, Lily forced herself to look through the windshield at the street leading to the sheriff's office. "Think they will have found any more information?" Out of the corner of her eye, she could see Trace staring at her.

"We can hope," Trace said. Finally, he started the engine and drove out of the parking lot and down Main Street to the sheriff's office.

When he parked, he remained in his seat a moment longer than necessary. "Look, Lily, if I've said anything or done anything to upset you, I wish you'd tell me. I can't read minds."

"Don't worry," she said, grabbing for the door handle. "You haven't done anything. I told you, I'm fine." Lily pushed open the door and slid down from her seat.

Trace joined her at the front of the truck. He hooked her elbow in his hand and guided her into the office.

Sheriff Owens met them with an outstretched hand. "I'm glad you came by. I had a visit from Marty Bains this morning."

"Why did he come in?" Lily asked.

"I told him and Alan that if they remembered anything about that day of James Travis's murder, no matter how insignificant it might be, to bring it to me."

"And?" Trace prompted.

"He said he remembered looking for the four-wheelers in an outbuilding. He found one, but the other was missing." The sheriff frowned. "He was going to ask Mr. Travis about it, but that's about the time Mr. Travis's horse brought him home."

"Why did he think that was important?" Trace asked.

The sheriff's jaw tightened. "He said it was there that morning."

"If he was working around the barn all day, wouldn't he have heard it moved?" Lily asked.

"He said the only time he and Alan weren't near the outbuildings was at lunch," Sheriff Owens said. "Mrs. Travis invited them in for sandwiches."

"What about Roy? Where was he?" Trace asked.

The sheriff nodded. "I asked the same question. Marty said Roy left the ranch earlier that day, claiming he had errands to run in town."

"So, no one saw who took the four-wheeler," Trace said. "And that four-wheeler is still missing. It could be the person who stole the four-wheeler was the same one shooting at us when we were cutting hay two days ago."

Lily's fists bunched. Trace had nearly been shot that day. It was also the day he'd gotten into an altercation with Matt.

"If we could find that four-wheeler, we might lift some latent prints," the sheriff said.

"A big if." Lily sighed. "We'll keep our eyes open for it. Thanks for letting us know."

"One other thing," Sheriff Owens said. "The medical examiner said the bullet that killed your father was fired in an upward trajectory. Since your father was riding a horse, the shooter had to have been on the ground and close by. If we could find the location of the crime, we might find the bullet casings nearby. It wasn't like the shooter was a sniper several hundred yards away." The sheriff's lips pressed into a firm line. "That's if we can find the crime scene."

"When it could have happened anywhere on the twelve hundred acres of Whiskey Gulch Ranch…" Trace started.

"And it's rained since then…" Lily added.

"It's highly unlikely we'll find the exact spot," the sheriff concluded. "But it's good to know, in case we do."

As they left the sheriff's office, a large, black SUV pulled up next to Trace's pickup and Oswald Young leaned out the window. "Trace, you got a minute?"

Trace crossed to where the other man sat in his vehicle. "What's up?"

"One of my guides was out setting up hunting stands today and noticed some cattle ranging on the Rocking J Ranch."

"So?" Trace asked.

"We aren't running cattle on the Rocking J Ranch. We're a game outfitting ranch. We sold off all but a few head of cattle and keep them in a pasture close to the lodge. My foreman checked and the cattle he found are branded with WG."

"The Whiskey Gulch brand," Trace concluded. "We must have a fence down. If we come collect the cattle, will you have hunters out there shooting at us?"

Oswald shook his head. "We're holding off all hunting until the cattle have been rounded up and removed from the premises."

"So, the sooner we get them off, the sooner your hunters can get back to what they pay you for." Trace held out his hand. "On our way now."

"Thank you. Let me know if you need help. My guys aren't cowboys, but they can lend a hand if needed."

"I think we can handle getting the cattle back over on the Whiskey Gulch and fix the break in the fence," Trace said.

"Thanks." Oswald tipped his head toward the sheriff's office. "Did they find the man who shot your father?"

Trace shook his head. "Not yet."

"I hope they do," Oswald said, a frown creasing his brow. "The sooner, the better. I hate to think there's a killer out there. As an outfitter, it's my responsibility to keep my clients safe."

"That's hard to do when we don't know who killed Mr. Travis," Lily said quietly.

"Exactly." Oswald gave a nod. "Let me know if we can help with rounding up cattle or mending fences. I understand you're shorthanded on the Whiskey Gulch Ranch. But now that you're back, hopefully things will get straightened out."

Lily didn't add that Trace wasn't back for good. Whether he stayed or returned to active duty, she wouldn't know. She'd be somewhere else, starting over and moving on. Lily climbed into the passenger seat of Trace's truck and stared straight ahead.

Trace started around the front of the truck, hesitated and glanced toward Matt's auto shop two blocks away. Then he slipped behind the wheel and drove to the shop, parking out front.

Matt came out, wiping his hands on an oily rag. He tipped his head toward Lily, his gaze turning to Trace. "Everything all right?"

Trace leaned out the window. "If you want to be part of

this ranch," he started, "we could use your help rounding up Whiskey Gulch cattle on Rocking J land."

Matt's brow furrowed. "I don't know much about herding cattle, but I'm willing to learn. I'll be out there as soon as I close up the shop."

Trace pulled out of the parking lot onto Main Street, his lips quirking upward. "I wonder if he's ever been on a horse," he muttered.

Lily wondered if Trace was about to test his half brother. "If he hasn't, you might cut him some slack."

Trace's eyes narrowed as he looked across the console at Lily. "He'll have to go on horseback if he's going at all. We don't have four-wheelers to get us there and we don't know if we can get a truck across the terrain. It's hilly and rocky in a lot of areas on the Rocking J."

"I know. Just don't do anything that will get him hurt. After all, you're brothers." She raised an eyebrow and shot a direct glance his way.

"*Half* brothers," Trace corrected.

"No matter how you feel about Matt, you can't give your mother another body to bury," she said, her voice hard, her lips pressed into a thin line. "Matt didn't do anything to you. If you're mad about what happened eleven years ago, blame me."

Trace's hands tightened on the steering wheel until his knuckles turned white. He had driven five miles out of town before he relaxed. He loosened his grip and his fingers turned back to their normal color. "You're right," he said. "My mother doesn't need another body to bury."

A couple of miles passed in a whir of images blurred by unshed tears.

"Why did you lie to me?" Trace asked.

Lily had dreaded that question for the past eleven years. At the same time, she welcomed it. Finally, she could set herself free of the lie. Then she could move on with her life, away from Whiskey Gulch. "You needed to leave."

"I was leaving."

"You were heading into the military. A relationship with me would have dragged you down. Maybe even kept you from getting security clearance. I couldn't let that happen." She drew in a deep breath. "So, I broke up with you in the only way I knew that would keep you from giving up on your decision to join the army."

Trace's foot left the accelerator, the truck slowing almost to a stop on the highway. "That's it? You lied to me about marrying Hennessey so that my clearance would go through?" He shook his head. "That's about the saddest excuse I've ever heard."

"Yeah, well, we were kids. What did you expect? You needed to be free and I needed to grow up and realize what we had would never have lasted." Lily swallowed hard on the sob rising up her throat. "We were from completely different worlds."

"And you didn't give me the opportunity to decide what was good or bad for me. You made up my mind for me." He snorted. "That's a hell of a note." His foot jammed down on the accelerator. "I guess I should say thanks for saving me from a fate worse than death."

The anger in his voice cut through her like a knife. She fought back the tears by urging her own anger to the surface. "You thought everything would be all roses and sunshine. You've never lost a fight just because of who you were associated with. How would you have felt if the army denied your clearance because you were dating a woman whose father was a convicted felon?" She glared at him. "You would have been stuck here in Whiskey Gulch, hating your father and hating me. That's why I lied to you." Tears slipped from her eyes and spilled down her cheeks. "It broke my heart, but I did it for you, damn it."

Trace slowed the truck again, pulled onto the shoulder of the road and shifted into Park.

"What…what are you doing?" Lily blinked back the tears.

"I'm stopping the truck so I can do this." He reached across the seat, unbuckled her seatbelt, gripped her arms, and dragged her over the console and into his lap. Then his lips were crushing hers in a kiss that stole her breath away.

For only a second, she considered fighting him off. Her body and mouth betrayed her. As if of their own accord, her arms snaked around his neck and pressed him closer. When his tongue traced the seam of her lips, she opened to him, meeting him thrust for thrust, loving the way he tasted and felt. He didn't stop kissing her until they were both out of breath and forced to come up for air.

Trace leaned his forehead against hers. "Do you think I cared about what the army decided was good or bad? I would have walked away from the military if they refused to accept me with you."

"Then what? You and your father were butting heads. He didn't like me. I wasn't good enough for his son."

"You were the best thing that ever happened to me, and still are," he said, kissing the tip of her nose.

"What about your military career? Won't they frown on your association with the daughter of a felon?"

He snorted. "If they do, too bad. They'd have to take me as I am, or I walk."

"But you love the army."

"I love you more." He gathered her close and held her against him in a tight hug. "I don't ever want to be without you. The last eleven years made me realize how much I love you."

"You had eleven years to forget me," she whispered.

"And did you forget me?" he asked, staring down into her eyes.

"I tried," she said. Lily shook her head. "I failed. You were my first…and only love."

Chapter Sixteen

Trace couldn't believe she'd just admitted to loving him. All these years, he'd longed to be right where he was, but he thought he'd lost his chance all those years ago. "I should have come back and fought for you."

"You were busy fighting wars," she said. "But, yes, you should have come back and fought for me, too."

"Can you forgive me for failing as a knight in shining armor?"

"Maybe," she said. "If you can forgive me for the lie I told you about Matt." She bit down on her lip, praying he could.

"I get it now. I didn't get it when I was eighteen." He kissed her again, all the world fading away when his lips touched hers.

The whine of an engine nearing them brought him back to the present and the fact they were parked on the side of the highway, making out.

A motorcycle pulled up beside the truck and stopped.

Trace glanced at the rider as he pulled off his helmet.

Matt Hennessey peered into the truck, his eyes narrowing. "You two all right?"

Trace grinned. "Better than all right."

"Good. I thought you might have broken down." His brow crinkled. "You all right, Lily?"

Lily smiled. "I am."

"Then I'll leave you two to whatever it is you're doing." He slipped the helmet over his head and buckled the strap beneath his chin. "I'll be waiting when you get to the ranch." He glanced at the sun that had slipped past its zenith and was heading toward the horizon. "Don't take too long. No telling how long we'll need to round up those cows." With those parting words, he revved his engine and sped off, kicking up gravel behind him.

Trace sighed. "As much as I'd rather hold you forever, we have cattle to round up."

Lily cupped his cheek and brushed her lips across his. Then she moved back over the console and buckled her seat belt. "Let's do this. Then we can pick up where we left off."

Trace nodded and shifted into Drive. "We need to talk about where we go from here."

"Are we going somewhere?" Lily raised her eyebrows, a smile playing at the corners of her lips.

"Maybe," he said.

She patted her purse. "I'm ready when you are."

He laughed. "What if I decide to stay here?"

She shot a glance in his direction. "Will you be satisfied being just a rancher? I mean, you've been a soldier for eleven years. I'm sure it's more exciting than worming steers."

"I've been thinking about it, and I might have come up with a way to make Whiskey Gulch Ranch a place where I want to stay."

"I'm all ears. Especially if it means I get to see you more often than once every eleven years."

They pulled into the drive leading up to the ranch house.

"We can talk about it tonight," Trace said. "Right now, I need to go find some bovine escapees."

Matt stood beside his motorcycle in the barnyard next to Irish, Trace's mother and Roy.

Feeling lighter and happier than he had in a very long

time, Trace climbed out of the truck and hurried around to open the door for Lily. She already had it open, but she waited for him to grip her around the waist and lift her to the ground.

It felt so good to hold her in his hands, Trace didn't want to let go. Alas, others were waiting for him to help.

His mother smiled as he approached them holding Lily's hand. "You two patch things up?"

Trace pulled Lily into the curve of his arm. "I hope so."

Lily laughed and hugged him around the middle. "Me, too."

"If you two think we can get moving, we're burning daylight," Roy said.

"I take it we'll be riding horses out to where the cattle are," Matt said. "I admit, I've only been on a horse maybe a handful of times, many years ago. If you could point me to the horse that knows what to do, maybe he can train me?" He gave a crooked smile.

Lily hurried toward the barn. "I know just the horse. And it's a she, not a he."

Trace nodded. "I believe she means Lady. If you want to help her saddle up, we can get going. Getting the cattle back on this side of the fence won't be hard. Usually, all we need to do is shake a bucket of grain and they'll come running."

"We'll need to mend the fences," Roy said. "I can drive the tractor out to wherever we find the break."

"I can cover, if you have another horse as tame as Lady," Irish said.

Trace turned to his mother.

She held up her hands. "I'm out this time. Roy took a call from the Meyerses. Seems Chad needs help with Alice. I'm going over to see what I can do for them."

Trace shot a glance toward Irish. "I'd prefer you cover for my mother. We can manage on our own." He turned to Matt. "Are you carrying?"

Matt pulled back his leather jacket, displaying a shoulder holster and a handgun tucked inside. "I'm good to go."

"I've got mine. Plus, I'll bring a rifle, just in case." Trace nodded to Irish. "I want you to go with the women to the Meyerses'."

"Women?" Lily paused as she reached the barn and turned back. "I'm going with you to bring the cattle back."

"Please, go with Mom and Irish," Trace said. "The three of us can keep an eye out for trouble. I'd rather have three of you going to the Meyerses'. Irish is a trained Delta Force soldier. He's good at spotting trouble, and he'll take good care of you."

Irish nodded. "That I will."

Lily's lips pressed into a tight line.

Trace wanted her with him, but he was worried about her being out in the open where a skilled sniper could fire off a round from any direction and take her down. He'd never forgive himself if Lily died because he'd been selfish enough to want her along for the ride. "Please, Lily. My mother might need help with Mrs. Meyers."

Lily held his gaze for a long moment and then nodded. "Okay. But I ride better than Matt, and I know how to fix a fence."

"Matt is also a trained marine," Trace pointed out.

Matt nodded. "I've been deployed four times in five years, fought in battles against enemies we couldn't see. Don't worry," he said. "I'll take care of my half brother."

Lily's face reddened. "Okay. I'll help you saddle up," she said. Then she turned to Trace's mother. "I'll be ready in a few minutes."

His mother nodded.

Lily entered the barn, a frown lowering her brow.

Trace turned to his mother. "We should be back before dark."

"Same here." She touched his arm. "I'm glad you and Lily worked things out."

Trace nodded. "So am I." He bent and pressed a kiss to his mother's cheek. "Thanks for believing in us."

"You only had to believe in each other." She winked. "Now go. You need to get out there and get the cattle back on our spread. I hope to be home in time to rustle up some dinner for you."

"We can fend for ourselves," Trace said.

"Yeah, but I like having my family around me." Her smile faded. "I miss your father."

"I miss him, too."

Roy touched Trace's mother's arm. "Be careful, Ros. You don't know who might be out there. I'd hate to see you hurt."

Trace's mother smiled at Roy. "Thank you, Roy. I'll be careful."

Trace hurried into the barn and saddled Rambo, the black gelding his father had been so proud of. The animal had been trained as a cutting horse. His skills might come in handy if the feed bucket didn't do the trick.

Lily, with Matt's help, finished outfitting Lady with a saddle and bridle and adjusted the stirrups to fit Matt's tall frame.

Within minutes, the horses were ready, and Roy had the tractor out of the shed and waiting on the other side of the gate.

Trace stopped beside Lily and pulled her into his arms for a quick kiss. "Hold that thought until I get back."

"I'll be waiting," she murmured. Lily glanced at the pasture, her brow dipping. "Be careful out there."

He kissed her forehead. "You be careful going over to the Meyerses' place."

Trace mounted his horse and rode through the gate, followed by Matt. His half brother sat his horse well and even posted in his stirrups when Lady broke into a trot.

The man might end up being an asset on the ranch, given time.

Trace glanced back at Lily and his mother, anxious to return and get on with their reunion. He couldn't wait to be with the woman he'd loved for what felt like all of his life.

LILY CLIMBED INTO the driver's seat of Rosalynn's SUV.

Rosalynn slipped into the back seat and Irish into the passenger seat.

The drive over to the Meyerses' place wouldn't have taken long if they could have driven as the bird flies. But the roads forced them to take the long way around.

Twenty minutes later, they drove up to the older ranch house with the faded paint and a front porch that clearly needed to be leveled and the rotten boards replaced.

The Meyerses hadn't been fortunate enough to have children of their own. They ran cattle on their place, but not many. Because of hospital bills and the seven-year drought, they had sold two-thirds of their herd several years ago and were living on what was left of the proceeds.

Chad Meyers stepped out onto the porch, shading his eyes as the SUV pulled up to the house.

Rosalynn, Irish and Lily got out of the vehicle and approached the man.

"This is a nice surprise," Mr. Meyers said. He pushed a hand through his shock of white hair that appeared as if he hadn't combed it in several days. "To what do I owe the pleasure?"

Rosalynn frowned. "Roy said you'd called and needed help with Alice. We came over as soon as we could."

Mr. Meyers's fuzzy white brows dipped. "I didn't call your place." He turned toward the screen door. "Alice?"

An older woman using a walker pushed through the door and out onto the porch. She smiled at them. "You didn't tell me we had guests," she said. "Rosalynn, Lily, it's so good to see you." She turned to Irish. "I don't believe we've met."

Irish climbed the steps. "I'm Joseph Monahan, but folks call me Irish."

"Irish, so nice to meet you. Please, come in." Mrs. Meyers held the door for them. "I just made a pitcher of iced tea."

Rosalynn climbed the porch steps but didn't enter. "It's good to see you up and about." She hugged the woman and stepped back, frowning. "But I don't understand. Roy assured me you'd called and needed help."

Alice Meyers smiled. "So nice of you to come, but I didn't call." She turned to her husband.

"I didn't, either," he said. "The missus has been doing so much better, I thought I might take her to the town for supper tonight."

Rosalynn tapped a finger to her chin. "That's strange. Why would Roy tell me you needed help?"

Chad shook his head. "I don't know. It doesn't make sense. We haven't run into him but at the feed store maybe a handful of times since he went to work for the Whiskey Gulch Ranch."

"Was the same when he worked at the T-Bar M Ranch when he worked for the Talbots," Alice said. "Rarely saw him. He spent most of his time on the ranch."

"Heard he was sweet on Mona Talbot after her husband fell off his horse and died," Alice said.

"He kept the ranch running for several months following Mike's death."

"Then Mona's grown children stepped in and talked her into selling the place. The new owners replaced Roy with their own foreman. Roy was brokenhearted about Mona leaving. He had big plans for the ranch. I think he wanted to marry Mona and take over."

Lily's chest tightened. "I didn't know this."

Alice waved a hand. "It's all gossip we talked about at the monthly quilting bee."

"All I knew was Roy applied for the job. Since he had experience, James hired him," Rosalynn said. She looked up at Alice. "You say Mr. Talbot fell off his horse?"

Chad nodded. "They speculate the horse came across a snake and threw him. He lay for several hours before anyone found him."

"Where was Roy when that happened?" Irish asked.

A sinking feeling hit the pit of Lily's belly.

"Said he was on his way into town for supplies," Alice said. "Why?"

Lily's gaze met Irish's and then moved to Rosalynn's.

"We need to go," Rosalynn said. "Now." She smiled at Alice and Chad. "Let us know if you do need help." She hurried down the steps and half ran toward the SUV.

Lily followed.

"Nice to meet you," Irish said behind her and quickly caught up. "I'll drive."

Lily shook her head. "I'd rather you kept your hands free."

He nodded and held the door for Rosalynn as she slid into the back seat.

Once they were all in the vehicle, Lily drove away from the Meyerses' house. As soon as she was out of sight, she pressed her foot to the accelerator and raced out to the highway.

"How could it be?" Rosalynn sat forward in the back seat, her gaze on the road ahead. "He's always been so nice to me."

"He was nice to Mona Talbot," Lily said.

"Do you really think he expected to marry Mona and take over the ranch?" Rosalynn asked, shaking her head.

"We could be grasping at straws here," Irish said.

"What exactly are we saying?" Lily asked, knowing the answer, but wanting to hear it stated aloud.

"Roy could have been the one to steal the four-wheeler," Irish said.

"He could have been the one to kill James," Rosalynn whispered, her face pale, her fingers turning white on the back of the seat.

"If he thought he could murder your husband—" Irish shot a glance back at Rosalynn "—he might also think he has to do away with your husband's two children in order to get to you."

More color drained from Rosalynn's face.

Lily turned in her seat and covered Trace's mother's hand with hers. "If that's what's happening, the guys are trained combatants. They can defend themselves."

"If they see it coming," Rosalynn argued.

"Besides, there are two of them and one of Roy," Irish pointed out.

"We don't know if any of this speculation is even accurate," Lily said, though deep in her gut, she could feel the truth.

Her gaze on the road ahead, Rosalynn said, "Could you go a little faster?"

"Got the pedal to the floor, ma'am," Lily said, only slowing for curves.

The twenty minutes it took to get to the Whiskey Gulch Ranch felt like hours.

Chapter Seventeen

Trace and Matt rode out on horseback, following the fence line bordering the Rocking J Ranch. Trace carried a sack of feed strapped behind his saddle.

Roy was to follow on the tractor as best he could, depending on the terrain, until they found where the fence was down.

After riding for twenty minutes, Trace noticed the barbed wire was loose on the fence beside him.

"Looks like we're getting to the break in the fence," he said to Matt. He turned to his half brother. "How are you holding up?"

Matt adjusted himself in the saddle. "So far so good. Have to admit, the seat on my motorcycle is a lot softer than this saddle."

Trace nodded. "It takes time to build up calluses. It's been a while since I was horseback riding. I'll be sore as well. This is what it's like to be a rancher." He stared at the man he'd have to share his inheritance with. "Are you up for it?"

Matt shrugged. "I've been in more uncomfortable places."

"Same," Trace said.

"Are you ready to take on the responsibility of running a ranch?" Matt asked.

"I know how," Trace said. "I just didn't figure on coming back to this life so soon."

"Civilian life moves at a much slower pace in some cases," Matt said. "You're used to high-paced action and making a difference in the lives of people who desperately need you." He looked into the distance. "Coming off active duty is an adjustment in itself. The combat skills you trained so hard to perfect aren't as marketable."

"Tell me about it." Trace's lips twisted. "Ranching is in my blood. I learned to ride a horse almost before I learned to walk."

"I didn't grow up on a ranch. But I learn quickly. I didn't ask for your inheritance. I don't want it."

"Yeah, but we're stuck with each other. If you sell, we both sell."

"The question is, do you want the ranch to go out of the family?" Matt asked.

"It's not about me," Trace said. "We're in this together, like it or not."

Matt sighed. "If we don't want to sell Whiskey Gulch Ranch, can we work together to manage the ranch without killing each other or going insane with the slower pace and less fulfilling lifestyle?"

"That's the sixty-four-million-dollar question." Could he work with this interloper? To be fair, Matt hadn't asked to be included in the inheritance. And he hadn't had the privilege of choosing his father. He, like Trace, had the DNA he was born with. By accident of birth, Trace and Matt were related.

It could be worse. Matt wasn't all bad. He'd served in the marines and worked hard to make a living. He wasn't into drugs and he appeared to be honorable and respectful of women.

Trace glanced ahead. "Here we are. This is where the cattle made their break for it."

Several yards ahead, the barbed wire lay on the ground in long loose coils. Several of the metal fence posts had been knocked over and the wire had either been cut or had snapped.

"We'll need to clear this out a little more to get the cows through easily," Trace said.

"They found their way through the first time on their own," Matt pointed out.

"Yeah, but they had all day to pick their way through. I don't plan on taking all day getting them back. They're motivated easily by feed. I don't think we'll have a problem getting them back on this side." Trace dismounted and moved a strand of barbed wire to the side. Matt got down, stretched his legs and back, and started in on another strand, looping it back out of the way.

"You know," Trace said as he stood in the small gap they'd created, "we might want to find the cattle and get them started in this direction. While they're working their way back, we can get here ahead of them and clear their path."

"I'm game," Matt said.

The two men remounted, crossed onto the Rocking J Ranch and climbed to the top of a ridge.

From his vantage point, Trace could see down into a valley. "There," he said and pointed.

Several dozen cows grazed in the north corner of the valley.

"How are we going to get them from down there to up here?" Matt asked. "Not to mention coaxing them through the fence."

Trace grinned. "They're used to being fed some grain through the winter. Granted, it's not winter, and they are feasting on green grass, but old habits die hard. All I should have to do is shake this bag of feed and they'll come running." He nudged his horse forward. "We have to get a little closer so they can see and hear us."

When they were within range, Trace whistled sharply and yelled, "Here, cow!"

Matt chuckled. "Really? They come to that?"

Several of the animals lifted their heads and stared in Trace's direction.

Trace untied the bag of feed from behind his saddle and held it up. "Here, cow!" And he shook the bag.

One cow let out a long mooing sound.

Another one answered. Neither moved.

Trace shook the feed bag again. "Here, cow!"

A number of steers looked up and took several steps in Trace's direction.

Again, Trace shook the feed bag. "Come on, don't make me come after you," he muttered.

Once two or three of the animals started in their direction, the others fell in line.

"Well, I'll be damned," Matt said.

"They're motivated by easy and tasty food." Trace ripped open the bag and poured a little on the ground.

Several of the cows mooed loudly and picked up the pace.

"Let's go," Trace said.

"Won't they stop when they find the grain on the ground?" Matt asked.

"I'll leave a trail of bread crumbs for them to follow," Trace said. "Or in this case, feed crumbs." He dribbled a little feed in a line heading up to the top of the ridge. "We need to get ahead of them and move more of the fence debris."

"On it." Matt passed Trace and topped the ridge.

With the cattle on the move, Trace and Matt hurried back to the gap in the fence, dismounted and went to work. The sound of cattle bellowing urged them to go faster.

Trace moved one of the posts back and forth, working the soil around it loose. When he pulled it out of the ground, something shiny glinted in the dirt. He bent to retrieve what appeared to be a silver coin. When he turned it over and saw the image of Susan B. Anthony on the front, his hand and heart froze.

Matt took the post from where Trace had left it and tossed it to the side. "Find something interesting?" He came to stand beside Trace and looked down at the coin. "I have a coin like that. Your—our father gave it to me." He reached into his pocket and pulled out one that looked just like the one in Trace's hand.

Trace reached into his own jeans pocket and pulled out another. "Dad gave me this one when I left to join the army. He said his always gave him good luck." He pointed to the dent on the edge. "It fell out of his pocket one day when he was working on an engine. It lodged in the sprockets and shut down the motor, saving him from losing several fingers." He met Matt's gaze.

"It was his, wasn't it?" Matt said softly.

Trace's eyes stung and his gut knotted. "Yeah. He never went anywhere without it." He glanced around. "This must have been where he was shot. He might have been working this fence when it happened." Trace looked around. "You take the Rocking J side. I'll take the Whiskey Gulch side. Look for a bullet casing."

"We don't know how far away the shooter was," Matt said. "He could have been yards away from here."

"The sheriff said the ME reported the shots were fired in an upward angle. Like someone pointing at him from the ground at close range. My father was in his saddle when he was hit."

For the next few minutes, they searched the area, kicking aside leaves, tufts of grass and barbed wire. They worked their way outward in a twenty-foot radius.

Matt finally straightened. "It's going to be impossible to find one casing—"

At that moment, Trace spied a shiny brass shell. "Found one! And here are two more."

Trace had bent over and was reaching for the first one when Matt called out, "Don't touch it." Matt hurried over to him, pulled a bandanna from his back pocket and bent to collect them, careful to lift the casings with the fabric of the handkerchief. "Sometimes they can collect fingerprints off the spent casings." Matt wrapped the casings in the cloth and handed them to Trace. "Let's get back to the house and call the sheriff."

As Trace mounted his horse, the cattle emerged from the tree line, headed their way, mooing as they came. Soon, Trace, Matt and the horses were surrounded by cows moving through the gap in the fence.

A loud crack sounded above the sound of the bellowing cows and Trace felt something sting the side of his arm.

"Get down!" Matt shouted.

Trace slipped out of his saddle and dropped to the ground among the herd.

Matt did the same, moving with the animals through the fence to the other side.

Another crack sounded and one of the steers let out a frightened bellow and started running.

Sensing the fear, the rest of the herd stampeded through the gap in the fence.

Matt and Trace dived to the side, away from the column of animals pushing through.

Trace pulled his weapon out of his shoulder holster and waited for the herd to move past so he could see to take aim. The shooter had the advantage. He'd seen them and knew generally where they were.

"We need to move toward the tree line before all the cattle get by," Trace yelled to Matt.

Trace crab-crawled backward, hugging the dirt, moving toward the trees. He prayed he and Matt would get there before their cover dispersed. Otherwise, they'd be easy targets for whoever wanted them dead.

"HURRY!" ROSALYNN URGED.

"Going as fast as I can," Lily said.

Irish winced at every rut they hit, since the SUV was going faster than the vehicle was designed to go over open fields with hidden potholes and dangerous rocks.

"Right," Rosalynn said from the back seat. "Go right. They were tracking along the fence bordering the Rocking J. That's to the north."

Lily jerked the steering wheel to the right and floored the accelerator. When they came to a fence, she turned left and drove through a narrow column between the fence and a stand of trees.

Irish tried to lean forward in his seat, but the seat belt was locked in place, keeping him firmly trapped in his seat.

In the distance Lily could see cattle stampeding through a break in the fence. "There!" she shouted. "Where the cows are running through the fence. Trace and Matt must be somewhere nearby." She strained to see the two men. As they drew nearer, she saw a horse running with the cattle. It had a saddle, but no rider.

"There's Lady," Rosalynn said. "Matt was riding her. Where's Matt?"

Lily saw Trace's black gelding race by, heading for the barn. "Where's Trace?" she asked as she stopped short of the herd of cattle.

Lily grabbed the gun from the glove box and shoved open her door.

Rosalynn leaned over the back of the seat and grabbed her arm. "Lily, you can't go out there. You'll be trampled."

Lily shook the hand from her arm. "If Trace and Matt

have fallen off their horses, they'll be trampled. I can't let that happen." She slid out of the driver's seat and ran toward the fence. If Trace and Matt had fallen off their horses, it would have been because they'd been shot. They might not be able to move away from the cattle leaping through the gap in the fence.

Her breath caught on a sob as she raced toward the stampeding animals.

Irish called out behind her, "Lily! Wait! That's suicide!"

Suicide was a hell of a lot better option than to live after finding Trace dead. Now that he was back in her life, Lily didn't want to live without him—couldn't live without him. It would be more painful than being trampled to death by a herd of cattle.

The sound of an engine revving nearby made her turn her head long enough to see a four-wheeler dodging in and out of the stand of trees, heading in her direction.

Lily didn't have time to get out of the way.

The man on the ATV raced toward her, slowing long enough to reach out and grab her arm. He yanked her over the seat in front of him and gunned the accelerator, sending the vehicle leaping forward.

Lily landed hard on her belly across the man's knees, the breath knocked out of her lungs. When she could move again, she struggled to push out of his grip.

The ATV rocked back and forth as the driver struggled to hold on to her and steer at the same time. When he couldn't do both, he released the accelerator, threw her to the ground and dived on top of her. His helmet rolled off, exposing a shock of gray hair.

"I knew it," she cried.

"So now you're finally getting it," he growled as he twisted his hand in her hair. Then he jammed a handgun against her temple and backed up to the fence. "Just in time to be my ticket out of here."

The herd had crossed through the fence and continued toward the barn, leaving the clearing with the damaged fence in relative silence.

Lily scanned the ground, searching for Trace. She breathed a sigh when she didn't see a body trampled in the earth. "Why did you do it?" Lily leaned back, trying to ease the pain of having her hair pulled so hard it made her scalp hurt. "Why did you kill James?"

"Why should he have had it all? Land, money, a loving wife. He didn't deserve it. He didn't deserve her."

"And you did?"

"I worked hard, and for what?" His hand tightened in her hair.

Lily stood on her tiptoes to ease the pain.

"He fired me." Roy pushed the barrel of the pistol into her temple. "All because I was nice to his wife."

"The same way you were nice to Mrs. Talbot?" Lily asked.

"What do you know? She was going to marry me, and we would have run the ranch together." Roy dragged Lily several yards along the fence line, toward the gap. "Her son talked her out of it. Moved her to Florida and sold the ranch I was supposed to own."

"It wasn't yours," Lily said, trying to make conversation to distract him. To keep him from pulling the trigger.

"Whiskey Gulch should have been mine. I would have gotten away with it if the Travis brat hadn't come home. It would have been mine."

"And finding out the ranch wasn't going to Rosalynn put a kink in your plan?" Lily said.

"Who knew old man Travis had two kids? One was bad enough. At least he didn't want to run the ranch." Roy twisted his hand in her hair. "It doesn't matter. Once they're both out of the way, the ranch will revert to the rightful owner."

"To Rosalynn," Lily said. "And you think she will marry you?"

"Yes."

"After you kill her beloved son?" Lily forced a snort. "Face it, Roy. It's over."

"It's over when I say it's over." He pulled the gun away from her head, fired it into the air and pointed it again at her temple. "If you don't want the girl to die, you'll do as I say," Roy called out.

"What are you doing?" Lily searched the underbrush. Where were Trace and Matt?

"Gibson!" a voice called out from the direction Lily had come. Irish held up his hand. "Let her go. She's done nothing to hurt you."

"No, but she's going to get me out of here," he answered. "If her boyfriend isn't too much of a coward."

"Let her go, Roy." Trace stepped out from behind a tree three yards away from where Roy stood with Lily. He pointed his handgun at Roy's head.

"You won't shoot me as long as I have her," Roy said.

"Are you sure about that?" Trace asked.

"I have my finger on the trigger," Roy said. "All I have to do is squeeze and she's dead."

"What do you want, Roy?" Trace asked, his weapon still pointed at the man's head.

Roy shifted Lily, using her as a human shield. "I want it all. The ranch, the money, Rosalynn. Everything James had."

"You'll never have any of that." Rosalynn's voice came from Lily's right. "Not the ranch, not the money and certainly not me."

"But you liked me."

"I like everyone," Rosalynn said. "I loved my husband, and I love my son." She shook her head. "I could never love you, Roy. Ever," she said, her tone hard, her face angry.

"You killed my soul mate. The only man I could ever love. I hope you rot in hell."

"It's over, Gibson," Matt said. "Put the gun down."

"We notified the sheriff," Lily lied. "He's on his way as we speak."

"Then I'll just have to take you with me." Roy tightened his hold on Lily's hair.

Anger surged inside Lily. Her gaze met Trace's.

Trace frowned. "Lily?"

Tired of being a victim, Lily did what she'd been taught in a self-defense class. She went limp in Roy's arms and sank in front of him.

His hand still knotted in her hair, he had to move the gun pressed to her temple in order not to be dragged down with her.

Lily ducked her head, squeezed her eyes shut and prayed.

Shots rang out.

She couldn't tell if it was two or three. She waited for the pain. It didn't come.

Roy's grip on her hair loosened. He swayed and finally he fell, his body landing on top of Lily, crushing the air from her lungs.

Something warm and wet spread across her back. She struggled to move Roy off her, but his dead weight trapped her beneath him.

Then the weight was gone and Trace dropped to his knees beside her. "Lily, sweetheart, are you okay?" His hands roamed over her body. When his fingers swept over the damp spot on her back, he froze. "Dear sweet heaven, you're hurt."

Relieved she could breathe, she pushed to a sitting position.

"Don't move. We need to apply pressure to the wound." He tried to guide her back to a prone position.

Lily shook her head. "I'm okay," she assured him. "I'm not hurt."

"But the blood," Trace said. "There's so much."

"It's not mine." She managed to sit upright, despite Trace's attempts to keep her from doing so. "Really, I'm okay. None of the shots fired hit me." She glanced toward Roy. "Who got him?"

"I did," Trace, Irish and Matt answered as one.

Rosalynn knelt between Lily and Roy. "Are you all right?" she asked Lily.

Lily nodded. "I can't say the same for Roy."

The older woman stared down at the foreman, her eyes sad. "What gave him the idea he could kill my husband and then marry me?"

Matt joined her and slipped an arm around her shoulders. "He was a sick man."

Lily leaned into Trace. "It's over," she whispered.

He nodded and touched his lips to the top of her head. "Yes, it is."

"DOES THIS MEAN you're heading back to active duty?" Lily held her breath, praying he would say no.

"Only for a little while. I need to put in for separation. I was due to reenlist next month." He pushed to his feet and held out his hand to Lily.

She took it and let him pull her up and into his arms. "And now? Do you want to stay in the military for another nine years to get your twenty?"

Trace glanced around at the people surrounding them. "I think not. I'm needed here."

Lily blinked, shocked by his answer, but afraid it was all a joke, or that she was asleep and when she opened her eyes, she'd wake to an alternate outcome.

He held her at arm's length. "I want to stay," he said. "But only if you stay with me."

Lily's eyes widened and a smile tugged at her lips. "Stay with you?" Her grin broadened. "Wild horses couldn't drag me away."

He pulled her close and crushed her lips with his. "I was so afraid I'd miss," Trace said. "I couldn't live without you. Not again."

"*You* were afraid *you'd* miss." Matt laughed, the sound harsh and without humor.

"I'm glad none of us missed," Irish said, clutching a hand to his midsection. "And, please, don't drive back as fast as we drove here. I don't think my insides can take it."

Rosalynn patted Irish's back. "Thank you. I don't know what we would have done without you."

"I caught most of what Roy said to you." Trace shook his head and glanced at his mother. "I can't believe he thought you'd marry him after losing Dad."

"The man was clearly insane." Rosalynn stared at Roy's body. "If I'd had a gun on me, mine would have been the fourth bullet. For my husband and…" She reached for Lily's hand. "For the woman who has become a daughter to me. I love you, Lily."

Lily smiled at Rosalynn through blurred eyes. "I love you, too."

"I'll stay with the body," Matt said, "while the rest of you head back to the ranch house and wait for the sheriff."

Trace shook his head. "I'll take the four-wheeler back to the barn for the supplies and tools we'll need. Despite the circumstances, we need to get the fence patched."

Lily hugged him around the waist. "I know how to work a come-along," Lily offered. "I'll go with you."

Irish offered his arm to Rosalynn. "That leaves the two of us for heading back to the house."

"We'll call the sheriff and start supper," Rosalynn said. "When the sheriff arrives, I'll send Irish out with him to find you."

"Sounds like a good plan." Trace pressed a kiss to his mother's cheek. "Are you all right?"

She nodded. "I will be." Her gaze dropped to Roy's inert form. "I just wish I'd seen the signs."

"He was good at hiding his dark thoughts," Lily said. "I didn't see it, either."

"Come on," Trace said. "The sooner the sheriff comes to collect Roy and we get that fence done, the sooner we get to go back to the house." He hopped onto the four-wheeler Roy had ridden and scooted forward, giving Lily room to ride behind him.

Lily wrapped her arms around Trace's waist and pressed her cheek against his back. She hadn't been this happy in... well, in eleven years. Now that she and Trace were back together, she didn't care where they ended up, as long as they had each other.

Epilogue

"I've been thinking," Trace said as he sat on the porch swing, looking out over the barn and the pastures beyond.

"That's a dangerous pastime for a former Delta Force soldier." Matt leaned against a porch post, chewing on a strand of hay.

"No kidding," Irish said. "Every time Trace started thinking, we ended up knee-deep in enemy territory."

"Seriously, I think Matt was right. Adjusting to civilian life might be harder than we think," Trace said.

Lily frowned beside Trace. "Does that mean you're going to sell and go back on active duty?"

Trace squeezed her hand. "No. But I think we can manage the ranch, keep our combat skills current and help others."

"How do you figure we can do all that?" Irish asked.

"I'd like to form a security service to help people who can't get the justice they deserve for whatever reason."

Matt crossed his arms over his chest. "Are you talking about a vigilante group?" He shook his head. "If you are, count me out."

"No. I'm talking about people the law or the government aren't helping because they don't have the resources or time. Folks who need a private investigator, bodyguard or security detail."

"And you want the three of us to manage that while

managing a ranch?" Irish raised his eyebrows. "Sounds like a lot."

Trace grinned. "No. I think this concept can be a lot bigger than the three of us. I want to bring on others like us, men and women who have special fighting skills. It will help others while helping our military personnel who have separated from service for one reason or another."

Irish leaned forward. "People like me who are good with a gun and not much else?"

Trace laughed. "Mom says you're a budding chef."

"I can cook a pot of chili," Irish said. "I'm not a chef. But I could really get into being a private investigator or bodyguard."

"Same here," Matt said. "The auto repair business doesn't keep me nearly busy enough to maintain my sanity."

Trace clapped his hands together. "Then we're all in?"

Irish and Matt nodded.

"Now all we need is a name for this organization."

"How about Outriders?" Irish said.

Trace shook his head. "We're not all cowboys or mounted heroes, but I like the ring to it."

Rosalynn stepped out on the porch, carrying a tray full of glasses and a pitcher of iced tea. "I like it." She set the tray on the table, poured tea into a glass and handed it to Trace.

He stared at his mother as he took the cup from her hand.

"What?" she said.

"I like it," Trace said. "It doesn't matter that you're not all cowboys. You're ex-soldiers who want to help and protect those in need."

Lily smiled beside him. "I think it's perfect. You might not all be cowboys, but if you hire all former military, they're all heroes. For serving this country."

Trace raised his eyebrows and looked around at Matt and Irish. "Agreed on the name?"

They nodded.

"Done," Trace said. "Now all we need is to hire more resources and get started with our first case."

Matt took the glass Rosalynn handed him. "I think I have the first case, if you want to test our facilities and communication skills."

"What is it?" Trace asked.

Matt stared across at him, their gazes locking. "I want to investigate the murder of Heather Hennessey."

"A relative?" Trace asked.

"My mother," Matt said.

For a long moment, the people sitting or standing on the front porch paused in silence.

Trace nodded. "So be it. We'll start by finding Heather Hennessey's murderer." He stood and held out his hand to Matt. "Welcome to the Outriders."

Matt pushed away from the post and took Trace's hand in a firm grip. "I don't know about cowboys on horseback, but as long as I can ride my motorcycle, I'm in."

"You got it." Trace pulled him close for a quick hug. "I'm still getting used to the fact I have a brother."

"Half," Matt corrected and hugged him back.

Trace turned to Irish. "And my other brother in arms…" He held out a hand.

Irish took it and pulled him straight into a bone-crushing hug. "I've got your back."

With a grin, Trace turned to Lily and held out a hand.

Lily chuckled. "Are you inviting me into this little bromance you're having?"

"Looks like it. Hell, with you by my side, we'll be unstoppable." He drew her to her feet and slipped an arm around her waist.

Lily tipped her head back and raised her eyebrows. "Will you be accepting applications from cowgirls?"

"You know it," Trace answered. "I *know* I like *you*."

"About time you realized it," she murmured.

Trace brushed a strand of her hair back from her forehead. "I've always known it."

"You two should get a room," Irish said.

"Trust Irish to say what's on my mind." Trace bent and pressed a kiss to Lily's lips. "Now, if the rest of you will excuse us…we have eleven years of catching up to do."

His mother grinned as they passed her, headed for the door. "That's right. I want grandchildren before I'm too old to appreciate them."

Trace threw a thumbs-up over his shoulder as he stepped across the threshold. "Working on it."

* * * * *

COMING SOON!

We really hope you enjoyed reading this book.
If you're looking for more romance, be sure to
head to the shops when new books are
available on

Thursday 7th
January

To see which titles are coming soon, please visit

millsandboon.co.uk/nextmonth

MILLS & BOON

MILLS & BOON

THE HEART OF ROMANCE

A ROMANCE FOR EVERY KIND OF READER

MODERN

Prepare to be swept off your feet by sophisticated, sexy and seductive heroes, in some of the world's most glamourous and romantic locations, where power and passion collide.
8 stories per month.

HISTORICAL

Escape with historical heroes from time gone by. Whether your passion is for wicked Regency Rakes, muscled Vikings or rugged Highlanders, awaken the romance of the past.
6 stories per month.

MEDICAL

Set your pulse racing with dedicated, delectable doctors in the high-pressure world of medicine, where emotions run high and passion, comfort and love are the best medicine.
6 stories per month.

True Love

Celebrate true love with tender stories of heartfelt romance, from the rush of falling in love to the joy a new baby can bring, and a focus on the emotional heart of a relationship.
8 stories per month.

Desire

Indulge in secrets and scandal, intense drama and plenty of sizzling hot action with powerful and passionate heroes who have it all: wealth, status, good looks...everything but the right woman.
6 stories per month.

HEROES

Experience all the excitement of a gripping thriller, with an intense romance at its heart. Resourceful, true-to-life women and strong, fearless men face danger and desire - a killer combination!
8 stories per month.

DARE

Sensual love stories featuring smart, sassy heroines you'd want as a best friend, and compelling intense heroes who are worthy of them.
4 stories per month.

To see which titles are coming soon, please visit

millsandboon.co.uk/nextmonth

JOIN US ON SOCIAL MEDIA!

Stay up to date with our latest releases, author
news and gossip, special offers and discounts, and
all the behind-the-scenes action
from Mills & Boon...

 millsandboon

 millsandboonuk

 millsandboon

It might just be true love...

MILLS & BOON

HISTORICAL

Awaken the romance of the past

Escape with historical heroes from time gone by. Whether your passion is for wicked Regency Rakes, muscled Viking warriors or rugged Highlanders, indulge your fantasies and awaken the romance of the past.

MILLS & BOON

MODERN

Power and Passion

Prepare to be swept off your feet by sophisticated, sexy and seductive heroes, in some of the world's most glamourous and romantic locations, where power and passion collide.

Eight Modern stories published every month, find them all at:

millsandboon.co.uk/Modern

MILLS & BOON
True Love
Romance from the Heart

Celebrate true love with tender stories of
heartfelt romance, from the rush of falling
in love to the joy a new baby can bring,
and a focus on the emotional
heart of a relationship.